A MEMORY OF LIGHT

A MEMORY OF LIGHT

UNTIL THE STARS ARE DEAD: BOOK ONE

ALLYSON S. BARKLEY

atmosphere press

For Muffin, who was my Dav.

CHAPTER 1.

An arrow whistled by, then another. *One, two, three.* When the fourth nearly missed her right ear, Ari gave an authoritative pull on the reins and steered her nervous horse off into the woods without slowing their rapid pace. The gangly chestnut gelding let out an anxious snort as a large calfskin sack thumped against his flank, the goods inside making a steady clank-clank-clank to the rhythm of his stride. Ari chided herself for picking this animal for the job. Geldings were never good in a chase. Stallions were brave, mares had attitude, even donkeys and mules had a sort of cantankerous courage that might suffice if only they could run fast enough. If she could just make it to the river, it would be easy to ditch the horse in the next village and go the rest of the way on foot. Another arrow pinged off a tree in front of her and the chestnut started in surprise.

"Shhhh," she soothed, urging him on with a forceful squeeze. It was difficult to continue at a flat gallop now that they were dodging the ever-thicker forest growth. She hoped that her pursuers were having the same problem. At last count there had been six of them, but cutting through the woods always helped to eliminate one or two, especially when they didn't know the land like she did. Ari took a risky glance over her shoulder, turning back around as soon as she caught sight of two men in brown hoods. From the sound of it, there was still one more behind. If their horses weren't so fast, they would not have been so lucky.

She folded into the gelding's neck as he jumped a fallen log, bringing her dangerously close to some low-hanging branches. The rucksack made an extra loud clank as they landed on the other side, spooking the horse into a new burst of speed. Ari smiled to herself.

They were nearing the river now, and this was the difficult part. There was a hidden passage that cut under the water, known only by locals, smugglers, and thieves. As long as she could get this nervous fool of a horse to run through the ivy wall, she was in the clear.

One more arrow shot by, way off-target. The pounding of hooves drilled into Ari's ears, reverberating through the otherwise-still forest. *Please don't stop*, she begged her mount silently. *Trust me, trust me, trust me.*

Still moving at full speed, they followed a short, steep hill down towards what appeared to be a large, ivy-covered rock. Seeing this, the chestnut flicked his ears forward and then back to her, wondering what was happening, asking her what to do next. Ari could feel his muscles tense, ready to freeze even as they continued flying at the wall. She squeezed her legs as hard as she could and leaned forward slightly, giving him a little extra rein to plunge through the hanging vines. Before the confused horse could decide what to do, they had run straight through the leafy curtain, thundering into the dark tunnel and out the other side in seconds.

"Hey!" Ari could hear the men calling on the opposite bank as she rode back into the trees, putting more and more distance between them. "Where'd she go?"

"Don't look at me – I was following you!"

"He'll kill us for losing her!"

Their bickering grew less and less audible as Ari galloped on at the same rapid pace. The gelding was white at the mouth now, flecks of sweat running from his neck and chest down the length of his body. She couldn't risk stopping until they reached Irlanda, the village closest to the river. Even though her pursuers had been deterred, it would not be long before they discovered the tunnel, or some other way to cross and continue their chase.

As she rode, the forest changed around her. The great old trees began to thin out, giving way to smaller shrubs and saplings that were less densely packed. Wildflowers of white and yellow sprung up in their path, only to be trampled by the chestnut's frantic hooves. They were nearing Irlanda, but the seconds seemed to stretch into minutes, the minutes into hours.

Finally, Ari caught sight of the little town, its brown roofs appearing over the top of a small, grassy hill. Here and there she noted blackened shingles and gaping holes, friendly reminders of the latest attacks. She allowed another cautionary glance over her shoulder. If the brown hoods saw her entering here, it would be much harder to escape again. But there were no riders behind her, and no shouts nor hoof beats to disturb her calm. Bringing the trembling horse back to a canter, and then to a brisk trot, she crested the hill and descended into the village.

Many of the small shops and cottages were shuttered closed. Those that were not bore shattered windows and wooden doors banged in, hanging off their hinges. The air smelled of smoke and it felt empty, though Ari knew it was not. She pulled her hood further down over her eyes and urged the tired gelding into a faster clip.

Irlanda was small and growing smaller. It was only minutes before she had passed quickly through the center and came upon a small barn on the western edge of the village. A young boy sat outside the wooden building, playing with a toy boat in the half-full water trough. His eyes widened as she approached.

"Don't go," Ari called, seeing that he was ready to stand and run inside. "Will you take this horse for me? I'll give you a silver piece."

The boy froze where he was, torn between his fear of her and the temptation of the money. "Are you a Zaera soldier?" he asked, his voice high and sweet, vibrating with uncertainty and excitement.

Ari smiled at him. "No, I'm just a traveler that needs someone like you to take care of her tired horse."

"So, are you in the Malavi?" Still perched on the edge of the water trough, he tugged at his worn shirt, adding a new dirt stain as he did so.

"No," she answered again, now checking the gelding into a full halt and swinging her leg over the saddle in a smooth dismount. She slung the rucksack over her shoulder and patted the flap to be sure that it was still securely sealed.

"Daddy says everyone is either with the Zaerans or the Malavi," the little boy told her, his eyes fixed on the large leather bag and the sword hanging at her hip.

Ari pursed her lips, wishing that the child wasn't causing so much trouble. She was running out of time. "I don't like the war," she told him at last, pulling two silver pieces out of her pocket and holding them out along with the horse's reins. "Some people don't like to choose either side. And your daddy shouldn't let you use those names. Not around strangers."

He looked at her for another second and then grabbed both pieces in one hand, the bridle in the other. Ari gave him a nod, prepared to walk away before he could say anything else, but he was already stuffing the money in his pocket and leading the horse into the barn, whispering a child's tune as he went.

"My father's mother told a tale
from her warrior's life...
The skies, they filled with fire and flame
through that week of strife.
The noble hero she rode in fast
and stole the fire away.
Never again to move an inch
from that chamber where it lay..."

The tune fading out of earshot, Ari strode briskly past the last several houses, breaking into a jog as soon as she reached the edge of the village. A lot of other thieves stole horses and left them wherever and whenever they were done, but she liked to find decent homes for her tired steeds when she could. If the horse was safely stowed away in a barn somewhere, there was less chance that her enemies would find it and track her.

Ari was accustomed to running with her sword, and even with small bags and packages, but this large rucksack was heavier and more cumbersome than her usual loot. It bounced uncomfortably against her lower back as she hurried across the flat, yellowing field that marked the end of Irlanda and the beginning of a no-man's land between that village and the next small settlement a few miles into the dense forest ahead. *Leonor better make this worth it*, she thought as the leather strap cut into her shoulder. Shifting it around to relieve the pressure, Ari saw a shadow slink along the edge of the tree line. It ducked around a rock and then stopped by a thick oak, two bright golden eyes staring out at her without blinking. Still moving at a rapid jog, she ran right into the woods, knowing the bobcat would fall into step behind her.

"We made it, Jag," she told him, hearing the steady padding of his paws on the forest floor and feeling the comfort of his loyal presence. "The brown hoods were good, but not good enough."

The bobcat made no reply but continued to follow his girl. Blinking softly at the familiar sound of her voice, he swiveled his tufted ears back and forth, listening for unwanted company as they moved through the trees. Ari ran without thinking about where she was going, the path ingrained into her mind like the face of an old friend. Tall oaks loomed above and dark pines leaned their needles toward the travelers, swinging out of the way and then flying back into place as Ari pushed them aside with her free hand. She hopped over rough grey rocks and fallen logs, placing her feet surely, never once tripping or faltering. The cat stepped behind her, bounding easily over the same obstacles, his short tail flicking against the scattered purple wildflowers that grew along the edge of the path.

He knew these woods too, perhaps better than his girl, in the way that only a territorial animal can learn the ins and outs of every rock and tree in his forest. When Ari was around, Jagger stuck by her side like a shadow, but when she left him behind he was free to roam, to hunt, to monitor his domain. And this abandoned piece of forest between Irlanda and Nyin was his just as it was Ari's, their little haven away from the war-ravaged cities and decaying villages, the distrustful townspeople and brutal soldiers.

They had moved into the forest together six years earlier, when the last of Ari's ties to Nyin had been violently severed. She preferred to be away from human company, away from the questions and suspicions and fighting. Jagger only cared to be with his girl and, as far as Ari could tell, liked living in the woods better than the village. Now they only ventured into the settlement when she had to take care of a job or make a purchase. Her name was slowly being forgotten in Nyin, becoming a distant, foggy memory to all except those in her line of work.

So it was on days like today that Ari had to force herself to leave the peaceful quiet of the dark leaves and make an appearance in the battered little town, staring down the villagers who gaped at the rough-looking young woman with the short, blonde hair and the long sword hanging by her side. Occasionally, she would get a solemn nod from one of the older men: one who remembered her parents, one who remembered Dav. The women would look away – unable to trust a girl who lived a mysterious, solitary life in the woods – while gawking children either hid in fright or followed her curiously.

She cast an intimidating presence, especially with Jagger dogging her footsteps. There weren't many people who had animas, companion animals, nowadays. It was an ancient tradition that had struggled to survive since the war had broken out. Claiming that the royal families were becoming too tightfisted and desiring more power for their own ranks, the military had overthrown the King, renamed themselves the Malavi, and systematically slaughtered the old families with connections to the Palace. The rebel group formed to oppose the military coup called themselves Zaerans, after the people of the first city to be decimated by the war. Despite their allegedly distinct ideals, they had followed the same patterns as the Malavi, untrusting of anyone not immediately and explicitly aligned with their mission.

Between the efforts of the two armies, few old families remained, and anything resembling sorcery was kept hidden, or eliminated. Ari knew of several other animan – a woman and a wolf anima, a boy with a hawk, even an old man and a black bear – but in Nyin there were none, and her anima made her an object of mystery.

The practice had begun several thousand years earlier, founded by the Old King Rinthorn himself. When his first son, Gaven, was born, Rinthorn had taken a wolf pup from its mother and given it to the child. He had hoped that, raised together, they would form a bond and the animal would give protection to his heir. The two had grown together, but in a much deeper way than the King had anticipated. The wolf, known as Lylo, did move to his boy's beck and call, an obedient shadow always, but he also became a part of Gaven's very soul. Wherever Gaven went, he followed; whatever the prince felt, Lylo echoed the same emotions. It was even said that when the young man was wounded in his first battle as King, the wolf walked with a limp for several days after. Ari had never heard an explanation for how this happened, no record of sorcery, even in those days when sorcery was not so rare or so feared.

But Lylo lived long beyond the usual lifespan of a wolf in those times and only died when his boy was nearing his own sickly end at the age of sixty-four.

This famous pair was the first of many, the start of a tradition that began with old, royal families and slowly spread to countless others across the Capital and the surrounding regions. Most animas did not bond to their humans the same way that Lylo had. They did not always feel the pain or emotion of their soul partners, but they were still much more than a pet or a hunting mate. By custom, parents often chose wolves, big cats, or the occasional bear or bird of prey. These were fierce creatures, gifted to their children as companions and bodyguards. Every once in a while, one would come across an old seamstress with a songbird anima or a farmer with a weasel perched on his shoulder, but this was rare.

As the war carried on, families had grown to fear any unneeded curiosity or presumed connection to the Old Kings and animan pairs had become increasingly rare. In tiny villages like Nyin, far from the Capital and of little consequence in national affairs, animas had been few and far between even in the best of times. Now, they were practically a myth to the townspeople who had lived their entire lives within the village and its surrounding forest. Ari and Jagger were the fascinating exception, a strange pair that appeared unexpectedly every few months, dropping by for an hour or two before disappearing as quickly as they had come.

On this particular occasion, Ari came to complete a job. Reaching a small stream, she bore right and followed it, nearly keeping pace with the rapid current as she ran along, Jagger at her heels. They came to a fallen log that stretched over the brook and in a few quick strides they were both across, moving like weightless spirits over the rushing water.

They passed between two ancient and enormous oaks, and then suddenly the trees opened up into a clearing, revealing a village even tinier than Irlanda. The people here lived subsistent lives; they had little contact with the outside world, even when hunting or trading. Like Irlanda, half of the buildings had been razed to the ground at one time or another in the last fifteen years, but the Nyinans just kept putting them back up.

"Eyes open, Jag," Ari told her shadow, even though she knew he was always watching, always waiting to protect his girl.

The grey-brown cat just flicked his tail in response, staring around the open space with a focused gaze. Ari was not suspicious of the Nyinan people so much as she was worried that Tanthorn's men might have somehow beaten her there and be lying in wait. The likelihood of this was incredibly slim, but she never took chances.

Jagger let out a low growl as two small children came racing across their path, freezing in the middle of the street as soon as they spied the bobcat. The little boy, wearing nothing but a pair of summer trousers, tugged at his sister's skirt, gazing with wide eyes at the glowering woman and fierce animal. Curls bouncing, the tiny child shook him off, tottering towards Jagger with her hands outstretched. The growl grew louder.

"Don't touch him," Ari warned sharply, stepping around the children without a second glance. "C'mon, Jagger."

He followed her command, moving quickly aside and giving the little girl a final hiss and angry flick of his tail. Sharp stares came at them from all sides as they moved down the main street, passing gardens and vendors and tiny cabins. Ari ignored them and stalked by with her head held high and her pale grey eyes fixed straight ahead. She was aware that she looked especially unrefined, brown pants and leather boots splattered with mud and a gash across her left cheekbone where a low branch had caught her in the chase to Irlanda. Her dirty-blonde hair hung short, right around the nape of her neck, framing a face tanned and marked by years of sun and physical trial. Nothing about her person was especially remarkable, but the sharpness of her glance and the toughness evident in her small frame was nevertheless enough to draw the eye of passing villagers.

Moving determinedly, Ari and Jagger strode past a stretch of abandoned cottages, their empty windows like sad, gaping eyes. Weeds sprung up around the broken fence lines and pieces of glass glittered in the dirt by the road. Just beyond the forsaken homes, they turned left down a side street and skirted around a trio of huntsmen anxiously discussing the week's game, before finally, they reached a pub at the end of the lane, a large wooden building with a slanted roof and a small round sign posted by the door: *The Northern Bear*. Ari had always found this name amusing considering that Nyin was one of the southernmost settlements in the country and hadn't seen a bear for years, but the proprietor had inherited it from his father and everyone knew it was bad luck to change a name. *No Animals No Sorcerers*, read another sign beneath it. She pushed open the heavy door and Jagger followed her inside.

It was well lit for a pub, with several wide windows letting in the afternoon sun and three large oil lamps hanging from the low ceiling. Only a few villagers sat at the pale wooden tables: four men with large mugs in the corner and a handful of farmers eating a midday meal before going back to their plots. There was a bulky leather traveling cloak hanging by the bar, which was staffed by a dark-haired woman in a brown cotton dress. Every one of the patrons looked up when Ari walked in, pausing mid-sip or -bite to observe her silently. She saw their eyes linger over the lumpy calfskin rucksack, the watchful bobcat, and the long sword swinging at her hip.

"Leonor?" she asked the room, indifferent to their stares.

"Back cellar," answered an older man, directing a gnarled finger at the door on the other side of the pub.

Ari gave him a nod and headed across the room. The small

door swung open into a much darker hallway, illuminated by a single flickering lamp and cluttered with various odds and ends. A broom leaned against one wall and an old broken chair lay on the floor; a hammer had been tossed into the corner by someone with better things to do. The air felt thick, heavy with a sort of musky smell that filled Ari's nose and gave her the sense of being underground. Jagger's eyes seemed to glow in the long, gloomy passage, two bright orbs shining warily upon their grimy surroundings.

Ari could sense her anima's discomfort. They shared a dislike of small, dark spaces. "It's alright," she spoke softly, for herself just as much as for him. "The door's right down here."

Having passed several unmarked doors, she reached one at the very end of the hall. There was no handle and no sign, only a wrinkled piece of parchment tacked on, tilted a little bit left of center. The page had no writing, only the faded image of a thin blue dragon, twisted around into a circle so that its spiky tail met its clever face. Here Ari stopped, looked down at the bobcat, and then knocked once.

For a moment, there was no reply, and then the door and its dragon swept open and they were being ushered in by a short, thin man with beady eyes and long grey hair that hung wildly about his wrinkled face. He shut the door quickly behind them, dropping the latch and looking around as if, in that half-second, someone other than Ari and Jagger might have also managed to enter.

The little room was furnished very differently from the pub that acted as its front. The walls were built with thick stone bricks and the furniture was made of dark, shiny wood. On the back wall hung an ancient tapestry of such rich weave that one could tell in a glance it had been made in the Andoril guilds for some Old King or another. In front of this piece sat a long, narrow desk, with dozens of different drawers, each marked with a unique letter or symbol. Bright light from numerous oil lamps glinted off various gold and silver objects scattered about the room.

Ari recognized a few treasures from her past jobs. In one corner sat a large gold vase, rubies set into the handles. A collection of medallions was arranged on a tiny three-legged stool, and on the floor below the Andoril tapestry was a single silver goblet, the match to and inspiration for Ari's latest theft. These items were meant to appear haphazardly placed, but Ari knew that their owner spent a great deal of time admiring and displaying his conquests.

"I am doubling my price."

"It's lovely to see you," the little man responded drily, dark eyes darting to the leather bag that she still held close. He offered her an empty chair, though she had never once accepted a seat in his presence.

"Tanthorn knew someone was coming for them, and his men were all over me." She ignored the gesture and remained standing. "You said it would be an easy job."

"I didn't tip them off, if that's what you're saying." He looked nervous now, gaze jumping between the treasure and the big cat standing in front of him.

Ari paid no mind to his fidgeting. "I got inside, located the goblets, and as soon as I touched them, I was swarmed. I had to wound four of them and they still followed me nearly all the way to Irlanda."

He made no answer, drawing a chair out for himself and sitting down to rub his forehead thoughtfully. She had been working for Leonor since she began stealing and smuggling more than five years earlier. Greedy, cowardly, and only minutely more intelligent than the rest of his associates, the trader had made his fortune buying and selling stolen goods from his safe little hideout in Nyin. Nevertheless, he was one of the good ones - as far as traders could be - taking care to stay away from thieves with violent tactics and avoiding clients with questionable motives. As much as she found him exasperating, Ari relied on his business more than any of the other traders who regularly contracted her services.

"Leonor," she demanded, "I need more money for this job."

"Okay, I have a deal for you."

"You know I don't do deals. Just give me the money." A low growl came from Jagger's throat, rumbling across the room towards the trader.

"And you know *that*" – he pointed at the angry cat – "doesn't scare me." He spoke confidently although he still looked nervous.

Ari shrugged. "I'll just keep it, then." She hoisted the calfskin bag back up over her shoulder and turned to go.

"No, no, no!" Leonor was on his feet in an instant, reaching for the rucksack and prompting Ari to draw her sword and Jagger to lunge between them with hackles raised.

"Alright, alright, no one has to get jumpy," he laughed shakily, holding up his hands in surrender. "I'll give you six extra gold pieces but that's all I can afford. The rest you can make up with another job that I have arranged for you."

Now it was Ari's turn to be caught off guard. Heart thumping, her eyes narrowed suspiciously. "I swear on all the Old Kings, Leonor, if you gave me away again... I have asked you more than once *never* to share my name." She did not sheath her weapon.

Leonor gave a nervous laugh. "All three letters of it?" he quipped, then gave another uncomfortable chortle as Ari's look grew even stormier. "I didn't really. I just – I have an... associate... who has a big job. Needs the best. And I told him that was you."

Ari took another threatening step towards him, her sword still drawn. "Did you, *or did you not*, give him my name?"

"Alright!" he whined, his voice taking on a higher, slightly frantic pitch. "You caught me. He came asking for you. I only confirmed that you often worked my jobs." Leonor tilted his head, as if he'd just lost a bet. "He does know good work when he sees it, doesn't he?"

If the old man believed flattery would work on her, he wasn't nearly as smart as she had thought. Ari sheathed her sword, fighting to control her pounding heart. "I need more details."

"Meet with him and he'll tell you everything."

"I don't set up meetings or do jobs for strangers." She lowered the bag with the goblet and waited for Leonor to give her the money. He didn't.

"He's not a stranger if I vouch for him."

"Not good enough."

"After all these years of work, you still don't trust me?" He smiled now, comfortable that she wasn't going to run him through with her sword or set her bobcat on him.

Ari just looked at him.

"Hear the man out. I know you need the money."

At this, her eyes hardened. "What makes you say that?" she challenged.

A shrug. "Whispers. This is a score that could set you for years." He paused to consider this. "Or, for someone of your lifestyle, decades."

"I'm not interested. And I need my money now. I've been here long enough."

Shrugging again as if this was exactly what he was expecting, the little man reached into the desk behind him and pulled out a small pouch. "This is all I have."

Ari glanced inside to satisfy herself that he was playing fair. Seeing that he was good to his word, she dropped the rucksack to the floor, turned on her heel, and marched out into the narrow hallway. The dragon door swung shut with a bang, cutting off the golden-tinted light and leaving them in darkness.

CHAPTER II.

"Can you believe him?" Ari asked her anima as they walked through the forest, winding away from Nyin. She had an uneasy feeling, like the trader hadn't told her everything, like there was something more unexpected and unwanted awaiting her in the near future. Ari hated surprises of any kind, and one involving outside contracts sounded especially threatening. Her line of work wasn't exactly tolerated by the Malavi – or the Zaerans, for that matter – and she didn't like that Leonor was sharing her name with such little restraint. A successful thief made many enemies, and Ari had completed more jobs in five years than many of her older competitors had in their entire careers. Luckily, most people knew her only by a false name or a vague description, if that. She was good enough to stay out of sight and usually escaped before they realized that anything was gone.

It was for this reason that Leonor's reported rumors were concerning. The beady-eyed little man was either bluffing to sign her for the score – which he knew wouldn't work – or he had information. Ari trusted no human, but as far as trust went, Leonor was more reliable than most. She didn't think he would try to double-cross her, and more reassuringly, couldn't imagine what he would get out of doing so. If there was nothing to gain, he had no reason to deceive her. And he was too deathly scared of both Ari and Jagger to sincerely consider betraying them. She was the best thief he had, after all.

There was only one answer to the question plaguing her

as she hiked through the trees, relying on Jagger's keen senses to keep watch as she let her thoughts wander. If Leonor knew something but had no personal motives, someone else was setting him up, someone much smarter and much more powerful. Ari had heard of those types of traders, cunning people who trapped thieves into lifetime contracts after a single mistake or misstep. She would not go down that path, no matter what it took.

She could skip the next several jobs – keep her space and hope that Leonor forgot all about it by the time she came back – but here again, he knew too much. Ari had expenses beyond basic survival, a debt in the riverside city of Fraling that she had believed a secret until today. The creditor, a smuggler with whom Ari had a longstanding history, was getting impatient and threatening to betray her thievery to the Fraling Malavi. She was as well-hidden as anyone in the business, and his turning on her would likewise endanger his reputation – but the risk of discovery nevertheless disturbed Ari's peace of mind.

But how had Leonor learned about this? From the trader? If Ari's creditor had told him about the debt, there was no telling what else he might have shared. She had always believed his threats limited to professional games, but Ari felt a flutter of fear in her chest as the consequences of this possibility dawned upon her.

"What do I do, Jag?"

His response was a quiet hiss, but it did not mirror his girl's tired, irritated emotions; instead, it was a sharp alert, bringing Ari to a halt. Jagger had already stopped, every muscle in his slender body frozen except for his ears, which were quivering with tension as they flicked back and forth, listening to the vibrations in the forest floor. Now, Ari began to hear rumblings herself, the sound of muffled, irregular steps and steady breathing. Whoever it was, they were very close to her and Jagger's Hole. She thanked the stars for her anima and chided herself for letting Leonor's words distract her from proper vigilance.

Stepping carefully to prevent any unwanted noises, Ari turned back the way they had come and began to make a loop around towards the backside of the Hole. Jagger followed soundlessly. They slipped through the dense trees – old oaks and crab apples and expanses of rhododendron that wrapped around the forest so tightly it became impassable in some places. Large boulders began to pop up around them, with red and purple wildflowers springing from their ample cracks, and vines of thick ivy cascading over their sides and climbing across the soft dirt.

In the very heart of the Nyinan Forest, the Hole had been a fortuitous find. Leaving the village six years ago, Ari and Jagger had wandered for almost a month, sleeping in a cave or a secluded dell for a night, and then moving on to another spot the next day. After going in circles for weeks, Ari had stumbled upon the Hole, a small clearing protected on all sides by enormous grey stones, so concealed that it was almost impossible to find an entrance, even if you were looking for it. It was almost a cave, with an open ceiling and a soft, grassy floor, just big enough to fit Ari, Jagger, and a few possessions. After the first rainy night they spent there, Ari had fit the Hole with a sturdy wooden roof, made of long branches gathered from around the forest and fit down between the tall rocks so that, from the outside, unlikely visitors would be unable to find evidence of a human presence. Over this roof, she had placed a quilt woven from thin, tough rushes that she had collected along the Nyinan stream.

The Hole's advantages doubled as its drawbacks. There was only one real entrance, and therefore only one real exit. On this issue, Ari always attempted to reassure herself by accepting that her location was nearly indiscoverable and therefore not at risk. If trouble found them, it was possible to shift the roof and drop in from the top, but it wasn't easy to climb back out, leaving her trapped in the makeshift cave.

Reaching the back of the Hole, Ari decided that, regardless of whether she entered or waited for the creature to leave, she wanted to climb to the top and get a better view. She made a motion for Jagger to stay put and, placing her sword onto the rock to avoid noise, hoisted herself smoothly up onto the first ledge. Getting into position to continue the climb, Ari hooked the sword back into her belt and placed her right foot into a small crevice. She reached her left hand across the stone and wrapped her fingers around the top edge of the Hole, pulling hard as she pushed off with her anchored foot and easily swung her left leg over the crest of the boulder.

Now she was perched right on the top of the rock wall, slightly lower than the tallest stone at the front of the Hole, but still able to see everything ahead without being spotted. Ari peered over the front edge, knowing that there were plenty of leafy branches to hide her from view.

Before the Hole stood a large bay horse, a shiny-coated stallion with long, slender legs and a delicate face. The reins were knotted and thrown over his neck and he grazed calmly, oblivious to the woman watching him from above. Every so often he would take one or two steps, moving over to find a better patch of grass. The anxiety in Ari's chest loosened ever-so-slightly as she observed the unfamiliar creature; there was no one in sight, but it was clear that the rider was someone with money to spend. The saddle and bridle were of smooth black leather and the horse itself was a fine-looking animal, although not one Ari found appealing. She couldn't trust a steed that didn't smell a human and a bobcat ten yards away.

Still leaning over the edge of the steep grey stone, she scanned the rest of the area, looking for signs of her unwanted visitor. There were a few broken twigs and crumpled wildflowers on the left side of the Hole. It appeared that someone had been walking around her rock in search of something. Just as she was debating whether to climb down into the Hole, she heard the crack of a branch and a grunt of pain. Trying to locate the source of the noise, her eyes landed upon a brown hood, making its way slowly towards the clearing. With a start, she thought she recognized the man as one of Tanthorn's riders, and then realized that his cloak was of a darker brown and fastened by elegant silver clips, much nicer than those worn by her pursuers from that morning.

Though his hood covered most of his face, Ari could make out a blonde beard and a strand of golden hair poking out near his jawline. He was tall with an easy, athletic stride, and he wore soft leather riding boots that rose to fit just below his knees. She tried to get a good look at his hands, but they were concealed by a pair of brown suede gloves.

The man continued to wander the area, stepping silently about the rocks and trees as if searching for something, and Ari began growing nervous again. Unknown threats were undoubtedly worse than known ones. There was nothing in the middle of Nyinan Forest. Nothing except for her Hole. If someone were hunting around in this forgotten region, it wouldn't be without good reason, and, as much as she wished to believe that he was just a lost traveler, everything about his appearance said otherwise.

The man was bound to discover the entrance to the Hole sooner or later, and then their home would be compromised. It was critical that Ari retrieve her few possessions and get as far away as possible. Not one to foster attachment to anything, she was tempted to leave right then and there, but she thought of the many years spent in the Hole, all the time it had kept them safe, and decided that she could manage one last trial. Her only relics of her parents and Dav lay inside the hideout, along with her spare dagger and her hunting boots. It had taken weeks for her to save up enough contract money to afford the leather for the boots, and she was not keen to let them go.

The tall man made a soft sighing noise, just loud enough

to be audible. Strange, Ari thought, after he had been so silent this entire time. But he must have known that the falling branch would have given him away if he were being watched. As she looked on, he made his way over to the bay horse, untied the reins with a swift tug and leapt astride the enormous animal as if it were a small donkey. The stallion shook his head and then immediately settled under his master's command, looking all the more majestic and attentive for having a rider on his back. Ari couldn't help but be impressed.

Making one last observant sweep of the area, the stranger gave a subtle squeeze with his heel and steered the horse away from the Hole, trotting briskly through the trees and out of sight. Ari remained absolutely still, pressing her ear against the cool stone until she couldn't hear even the faintest beat of the animal's hooves. When the sound had finally died away, she inched herself back and leaned down to look at Jagger. The bobcat hadn't moved a hair since she had left him. His ears were trained in the direction that the man had disappeared, waiting as she had for signs that he was truly gone. After a moment, he twitched his nose and turned his head, blinking up at Ari.

"I don't think he found us," she whispered down to him, hoping that she was right.

Turning to face away from the rock, she slid over to balance on the lower ledge and then pushed off, jumping down to the soft earth. Jagger stepped aside to avoid her sword, which swung out and then back in as she made the leap.

"I wasn't going to hit you," Ari told him in exasperation.

He just looked at her with his wide, golden-brown eyes. After waiting to be sure that his girl was headed to the Hole, the cat ran around ahead of her, darting through the tiny entrance to inspect their home for signs of the intruder.

Not as quick as her anima, Ari stooped to enter, pushing aside the thin, flat stone and leafy curtain that gave the appearance of a solid rock face. The gap was only about three feet wide and barely four feet tall; Jagger could fit through the space covered by the vines but she had to move the rock and crawl on her hands and knees to squeeze inside.

Once within the Hole, Ari slid the secret door back into place and stood up to survey their space. It remained untouched. Even with the old rug she had bought in Nyin covering the earth, marks of a visitor would have been obvious. Her makeshift bed, a pad of woven rushes covered with a blanket she had taken from Dav's, was just as she had left it, and her soft leather hunting boots, broken in from endless hours of running through the forest, sat in their usual corner under an overhanging rock. She walked to a round stone, placed just where the rug ended by the foot of the bed, and pried it up from the ground. Underneath, sitting in a specially dug hole, were the spare dagger, an old copper compass, and a shiny golden cuff with one single sapphire set in the center. All was safe.

Sighing, Ari sat down on the floor and patted the space beside her for the anxious Jagger to relax. The bobcat lay next to her, pressing his warm body into hers and resting his furry chin on her knee. She stroked his head, drawing comfort from her anima's quiet presence as she felt him settle down and begin to purr. This wasn't over, but discovering the origins of the blonde stranger could be left for tomorrow.

Perhaps she would call an eagle to send a message to Fraling, to ask her smuggler how this information had gotten abroad. Though she was loath to speak with him, this seemed the best solution. There was only harm to be done by confronting Leonor again.

"We're safe, Jag," Ari whispered sleepily, but the bobcat was already dozing off, his purrs slowly becoming more and more distant until they stopped altogether. Smiling down at him, Ari leaned back and lay by his side, breathing in his familiar scent and feeling the slow thump of his heart against hers until she fell asleep.

CHAPTER III.

Standing outside the Hole in the early morning, Ari let out three long whistles and waited for a minute. She let the sound ring around the quiet forest and watched as two sleepy chickadees tumbled out of their nest in surprise, fluttering around before landing on a branch and staring at her with their angry bird eyes. She blinked back with satisfaction, knowing they would get even angrier, and was gratified to see the male puff himself up in defiance while the female zoomed grumpily back to the nest.

Jagger appeared, a rabbit held delicately between his teeth. He always hunted for his own food, and Ari for hers, although they had occasionally breached this pact when the situation demanded. Today, Ari had pulled some dried fruit and nuts out of her stores for breakfast. She hadn't had much time to hunt or forage lately, and the berries and mushrooms that usually grew right around the Hole hadn't done as well that summer. Together they sat and waited, eating their meals in contented silence as the Nyinan Forest woke up around them.

Dawn was Ari's favorite time of day. She took great pleasure in knowing that she was awake before the rest of the world, before the birds and the snakes and the squirrels. Before the trees had taken that first morning breath and the flowers had opened their bright petals to the slowly rising sun. Before the Irlandan farmers had started out to the fields or the hunters from Nyin had ventured one step from their little wooden doors. Jagger liked the mornings, too. It was easier to catch sleepy and unsuspecting prey in the early hours before they had time to get themselves acquainted with the new day.

Just as Ari was popping a pecan in her mouth and contemplating a grey fox slinking by in search of its own breakfast, she felt a change in the air, a subtle yet identifiable pump of powerful wings as they prepared to land. Jagger put down the remains of his rabbit and stood behind his girl, staring solemnly over her shoulder at the enormous golden eagle that had settled in front of them. The bird ruffled its long, silky wings into place and shot an equally serious look right back at Ari and her anima. Ari nodded slowly, dropping her eyes to the forest floor for a moment before fixing her gaze once again upon the eagle. After a careful pause, it returned the bow and dipped its razor-sharp beak to the earth in a calm, methodical motion.

Ari pulled a small piece of paper out of her pocket and offered it to the bird, who now took it without hesitation in one yellow talon and – with a beat of its eight-foot wings – departed as silently as it had arrived.

Jagger watched it disappear and then sat back down with his girl and his rabbit, satisfied that all was well. Hopefully it would only take two or three hours for a response from Fraling. Ari knew the eagle could make it there and back in less than that, but the question remained as to where exactly the man would be found and how quickly he could give her an answer.

Most of the contract thieves and smugglers that she worked with had decent relations with the golden eagles. They were proud birds, strong and brave and incredibly conscious of their status in the eyes of others. Eagles had been messengers for centuries, dating back some years before the reign of Old King Rinthorn. It was said that they could find almost anyone, anywhere, though Ari had never sent an eagle message to someone who did not already have a connection with the birds.

A human could not consider asking for a delivery without first building a relationship founded on mutual respect. People like Ari learned out of necessity to cultivate this kind of bond; the consequences of isolation and misinformation were severe in a thief's world. The richest traders and their thieves had whole networks of riders and messengers, but no horse was as fast as a golden eagle.

Having done all that she could on this front, Ari pushed thoughts of Fraling and the mysterious job from her mind. It was time to plan her next few days – or perhaps weeks, if Leonor was the only one who was going to offer her a contract in the near future. There was no way of knowing when the next job was going to come, something that Ari never minded except in times like these when she was anxious to avoid her most stable source of income and had an increasingly heavy debt abroad. In the lulls, she usually passed the time by collecting needed resources from Nyin or Irlanda, hunting, and mending her clothes and boots. Now, as the sun began to peek through the leaves, Ari stood and headed back into the Hole to assess what needed to be done. The bobcat followed, having deposited the unfortunate rabbit's bones discreetly among the trees, as his girl had taught him years ago.

Out of habit, Ari pulled the stone and vines closed behind her before settling down to consider the best plan of attack. As Jagger lounged in the center of the rug, watching, she opened each clay jar of provisions to inspect the quantity of their contents, ran her fingers over her riding and hunting boots, and checked her clothing and water flask for tears. The gear was in good shape, but she was running out of food. This would be easily remedied by a bit of hunting and a few days of roaming in search of new berry and mushroom patches. Not feeling hard pressed to accomplish any of this right away, Ari removed the rock by the bed and took out her spare dagger, laying it alongside her sword, her everyday dagger, and her hunting knife. She took a soft polishing cloth she had purchased in Irlanda, one of the few luxury items she allowed herself, and picked up the knife first. Ari never allowed her blades to go longer than a few days without a good polish and always made certain to sharpen them once a week. The little hunting knife only took her a few minutes, and then she was moving on to the spare dagger, a simple blade with a flat bronze handle that she had picked up in an attack on one of her first jobs. It wasn't an ideal weapon, not as wieldy as her other dagger and tougher to throw in a tight rotation, but it would do in a pinch.

The preferred blade was a bit longer, with a curved silver handle that fit just right in her palm. Ari had chosen it herself when she was fourteen and bartering in Tyson with Dav. Tyson was a sleepy fishing town at the other end of the river that ran by Irlanda, not known for anything except an annual market that drew craftsmen, farmers, hunters, and traders from all over. Twice, Ari had even seen nymphs there, though she expected that they were only visiting for the entertainment. Nymphs almost always preferred subsistent living to buying or bartering.

On this particular trip to Tyson, the last before Dav was killed, he had told her to pick out her own dagger.

"I already have one, and my sword," Ari had told him, shocked that he would think to spend so much on an unnecessary item.

"That one in your belt is just an ordinary blade," he had responded, ignoring her concern and walking through the endless rows of vendors with that confidence that Ari clung to as a most dear memory. "You want one that fits you just right, one that goes where you command and stays when it is not yet time to leave. And I know you love that sword." Here he had glanced down at her with a smile in his dark eyes. "But a good dagger is irreplaceable. Anyone can be decent with a sword."

"Few can be great."

"Right you are." He looked quickly around the area, searching for whatever it was he had in mind. "Tell me, what is one thing that helps to separate the good from the great?"

Young Ari had already known where her mentor was taking her with this lesson. "Skill with a dagger."

And Dav had pointed a triumphant finger at her before turning and disappearing into a crowd of men in green cloaks carrying bundles of fresh snow peas. Ari had been forced to duck under their huge baskets and weave between their legs, practically crawling on the ground before she made her way out and sprinted with Jagger at her heels to catch Dav as he turned another corner.

That was how he had always been. Expecting her to follow wherever he led, knowing that she would keep up, whatever it took. Everything was a lesson, but none of it really seemed like work. Dav was her hero as much as he was her teacher. If he said that something was, then so it must be.

So, Ari had picked the silver dagger, the one that sat in her hand like it was molded just for her, flew out of her grasp in the tightest spin she had ever thrown, and hit the center of the target every time. The show had impressed her onlookers, even drawn a bit of a crowd before she began to feel trapped by the shrinking space and growing number of people, and she decided to buy the blade and move on.

That day remained vividly painted in her mind, present every time she polished or sharpened the weapon, a reminder of Dav's lessons, his confidence, his faith in her. She had always preferred the sword, but gripping that blade changed things ever-so-slightly.

Dav had believed that she favored swordsmanship because of the weapon she had inherited from her father, but Ari knew it was more than that. It was a beautiful sword, a shiny silver blade with a gold half-basket hilt that curved in a kind of leafy shape around her small hand. Her father had left it for her several years before his death, having moved on to another weapon that he found more suitable for his purposes at the time. Of course, as a young child she had been unable to use or appreciate this sort of gift, but several years later she had taken to carrying it around Nyin with Dav, and on the occasional trip abroad if he would allow it. She was enamored with the object, with the art of sword fighting, the idea of all she could do with this weapon at her side. Ari loved the light but solid feeling of the long blade shifting in her hand, the way it tilted just so as she turned her wrist or took a smooth step forward. She liked to watch how the light played upon it as she sparred and hear the satisfying clash and scrape of metal-on-metal when her hand met another.

But more than all this was the feeling of power that she had whenever she had it in hand or swinging on her hip. Only true warriors could wield a weapon like this effectively. Sword fighting was the sport of kings and the job of soldiers, yet she, a young girl, was training to fence with the best of them. It was not an overnight transformation by any means, and the work was not all done before Dav left her, but Ari had a determination that went beyond that of most her competition, no matter how much older or stronger. Dav believed in her, and she would be a swordswoman, no matter what it took.

Just as she was finally moving on from the knives to her father's old sword, she felt Jagger tense and turned to read his expression. The bobcat had frozen, in the way only cats can, with his body so still that it almost quivered and you had to look closely to determine whether he was actually breathing. And then Ari heard it too, a shuffling, scraping noise, like when small animals climbed on the Hole, only much slower and much heavier. A terrifying thought entered her mind. She watched her anima move one ear backwards, tracking the noise as it crept up the rock above them. Jagger would tell her what it was. All was silent for a minute and Ari thought she could feel her heart pounding in her ears. *Please be a bear*, she begged. *Or even a nymph or a hunter from Irlanda. Just don't let it be that man.*

Suddenly they heard the sound of wood bending, creaking painfully under an unexpected weight; the visitor was testing their roof. Jagger jumped up and hissed, nostrils flared and ears flattened. He had smelled man. They couldn't stay inside any longer and wait to be trapped.

Sword still in hand, Ari grabbed her dagger in the other and shoved the rock door aside, rolling out into the clearing to land in fighting stance, with her feet spread wide and her sword held forward to deflect potential arrows. There was no way they could have escaped without notice from that perfect vantage point at the top of the Hole, but the man still seemed surprised to see them standing in the open.

"Who are you?" Ari demanded fiercely, gripping both blades and staring down the intruder who stood high above them. Jagger let out an audible growl from his place by her side.

The stranger smiled at this address, apparently more amused than terrified by her boldness. He wore the same cloak and riding habit, but this time his hood was pulled back to reveal a smooth, tan face with a strong jaw and bright blue eyes. His thick blonde hair fell almost to his shoulders and his satisfied grin displayed a set of perfect white teeth.

"You don't like to invite your guests inside for a cup of tea first?"

"Tell me your name." Ari did not lower her weapons.

"Ah, but you see, I know *yours* and that's the only one that really matters."

"I could pin you to that cedar right now," she threatened. An anxious thought made its way into the back of her head and she shoved it away, determined to focus.

The stranger twisted around to eye the tree that grew up behind the high rock face. He raised a brow at her. "Impressive."

"You tell me your name, or I do it." She flexed her fingers

around the silver dagger, cocking her wrist slightly in preparation for the throw. It was dangerous to challenge an unknown opponent, and it was certain he had something hidden in that cloak of his, but Ari was angry enough to take chances.

The stranger took a step towards the edge, apparently ignoring her ultimatum. Jagger hissed violently and angled himself to shield Ari.

"My name is Daerecles," the man said, inspecting the drop, and then jumping lightly to the ground in front of her. Ari was reminded of his agile leap onto the bay stallion the night before. This was not a man to be trifled with. "That shouldn't mean anything to you." He looked at her for confirmation of this. "People only know me if I want them to."

Now he was moving around her and peering into the Hole. "Shall we?" Daerecles smiled again and bent to crawl through. Ari was tempted to run him through with her sword right then but decided that the weapon deserved a more honorable use.

Begrudgingly, she slid it back into her belt and followed him into her home, no longer the sacred hideaway it had been only hours before.

"You can lower the knife," he told her, looking at the silver dagger still held at the ready.

Ari almost laughed out loud. "Do you think I started doing this yesterday?"

This elicited a nod and he opened his cloak, showing her a silky, royal blue tunic and tan breeches, a single sword hanging from his belt. Daerecles removed the sword and laid it at her feet.

"And the boots?"

He pulled a steely dagger with a short bronze handle out of his left riding boot and placed it alongside the first blade. "Satisfied? Shall we sit?"

"Did Leonor send you here?"

"Well –"

"Then you should know that I never sit. Now tell me what you want, and then leave my forest."

Daerecles considered her for a moment and then sat down himself, crossing his long legs and leaning back against the grey stone. He was an incredibly handsome man, but everything he said and did conveyed an easy surety that Ari despised. No one could behave with that kind of recklessness and survive in this world. If they thought otherwise, they were fooling themselves.

"They didn't do you justice," he mused at last, still eying her in casual interest.

Ari made no response, her face cold and unchanging. His gaze made her feel as if she were an object on display, her external existence put on hold for his strange, distant assessment. It was as if her sense of time had suddenly been bound to his and the only part of her that could continue independently was her frantically thudding heart. She both hoped that he would hurry up and speak, and feared what he would say when he did.

"I have been putting together a team to... recover something valuable," the blonde man began, drawing a circle in the dirt where the rug didn't quite reach the rock. "I sent feelers out to all the traders and smugglers I knew, searching for the best. I got your name from a few and went to Leonor. They told me he was the only way to track you down." Here Daerecles paused, like he was hoping she might chime in. She didn't. He flicked his eyes to the bobcat, who was standing in front of Ari with his burning golden gaze fixed on the intruder.

"Well, Leonor obviously had no success convincing you to take my offer – unsurprising, given that you had no information, and that old man is not in the least bit persuasive – but he did tell me where you lived." A devious smile. "Or rather, gave me a very rough estimate, which I managed to narrow down after some investigative work. It felt like someone had been around, and I could pick up the occasional track, but you've concealed everything very well." This was apparently supposed to be praise. "I had to spend the night a few miles away and wait for a sign, which you gave with that well-timed golden eagle message."

"You tracked my eagle." Ari felt a shudder of shock run through her. She had always considered a message by bird to be a practice of honor, safe and unreadable.

"You've never done it?" He seemed pleased that this insulted her. "I left my horse two miles out and walked the rest of the way in to discover how exactly you had hidden yourself in here."

"Your horse is an empty-headed pig that won't last a second in these woods if something decides it wants breakfast," Ari responded, in retaliation for having her eagle followed. "And all that work was wasted. I am not doing a job for you."

"Of course, as soon as I decided I wanted you," Daerecles continued, eyes glinting, "I had to abandon the team strategy, knowing you would never agree to work with a group."

This was true but Ari didn't want to give him the satisfaction of having done something right. "I haven't agreed to anything."

"I was confident that I could talk you around."

Glaring, Ari considered his relaxed figure as he leaned nonchalantly against the wall with his fancy boots stretched across her hard-earned rug. "I don't care what you're offering. I'm not accepting the job."

She had a very bad feeling about Daerecles and his mysterious deal. What kind of trader camped out in forests and forced his way into thieves' homes when he wanted to hire them? He was exactly the sort of man Ari tried to avoid. Too cocky. Too certain of his power. Ari had known enough of those men and did not care to know another.

Daerecles leaned forward and pulled a knee up, draping his arm comfortably across it. "What will your creditor say when he hears you can't pay him back?" he asked, his casual tone masking something more threatening. "What will all those people do when they learn *who really* stole and smuggled their precious treasures?"

For the briefest of moments, Ari felt The Hole spin around her, and something heavy and frantic gripped her chest, sitting on her lungs like she was drowning. *Let the anger become calm.* Restraining the urge to hurtle her dagger into his chest, Ari took a slow breath through her nose, jaw clenched too tightly to allow air in between her lips. Jagger's short tail flicked in severe agitation and he gave such a loud hiss that the blonde man actually looked startled for a moment.

"Get out," she said quietly.

"You have quite a skill for containing your emotions," he noted, the hint of a challenge in his voice. "It's a pity that your anima betrays them all."

"How *dare you* come here and threaten me." The words escaped in one single, steady breath, an icy whisper blending into the deep rumble coming from the bobcat at her side.

"I was hoping to go an easier route, but you're giving me little –"

"You pretend to be a great trader," Ari spat at him, "dressing in your silks and expensive leather and running around with that idiot of a stallion, and you're *threatening me? How dare you.*"

Although still in the same easy pose, Daerecles had lost the sparkling smile and his eyes were hard. "You have no idea who I pretend to be." He shook his head slowly. "I use the methods necessary to get what I want. I'm sorry if we don't agree."

"I can't imagine the day we would ever," she answered flatly, eyes blazing.

Now he patted the rug in satisfaction. "Fortunately, we don't have to."

"I am not afraid of you." She looked into his eyes to be sure he believed her. "I'm not scared of what you will do."

"Oh, I know that." Daerecles shrugged, that carelessly confident nature returning as if it had never left. "But you'll still take the job, and do you know why?" He did not wait for an answer. "Because, whether you believe in my threats or not, you need the money. Because thieving and smuggling is your life and as much as you tell yourself otherwise, you enjoy it. And because you're just a little bit curious about what it is that I could want so much to come all the way here and put up with a terrifyingly vicious woman and her growling bobcat."

Ari stared at him suspiciously, not any more comfortable with this than she had been with the threats.

"So, you'll take my deal," the man continued smoothly. "You'll agree to the contract and get what I want, and then you'll be rewarded with all the money you could ever need. And even better, we won't have to see each other again until the handoff."

"How did you find out about Fraling?" She had too many questions, too many unanswered worries twisting their way around her head. And she wasn't ready to give him an answer, though she knew that there wasn't much choice.

The change of subject didn't faze him. "I have my eyes and ears. The word among traders is you're hard to tie down, so I went looking for leverage."

"Who told you about the debt?" she demanded.

"A smuggler who knew you well. Said his name was –"

"I know his name," Ari snapped, furious. "What does Leonor know?"

"Nothing."

This was believable. The Nyinan trader would be easily wooed by a smooth talker like Daerecles. Ari nodded slowly, narrowed eyes searching the man in front of her for signs of deception. "And the objective?"

"A dragith stone. Stored in the Capital. Worth more than one man could imagine."

ALLYSON S. BARKLEY

"It's under Malavi protection?" He wasn't outwardly lying or cheating her, yet Ari could not trust him.

His brilliant blue eyes grinned at her. A smile was beginning to dance on his lips. "Not exactly."

Ari could tell that he wanted her to play a guessing game, but she was not in the mood to let him toy with her. She shifted the silver dagger into her other hand and waited. Daerecles glanced at her free hand as she flexed her fingers, grown stiff from clenching the blade so tightly. Noticing his gaze, Ari turned the motion into a wave directed at Jagger, who sat down immediately upon the command.

"Are you always so armed during friendly conversations?" He had assumed the same nonchalant tone but there was a hint of respectful resignation in his handsome features that satisfied Ari she had made her point clear.

"You have three minutes to explain the job or I'm not taking it," she responded flatly. The bobcat swiveled one ear sideways and Ari felt his muscles relax ever so slightly as he discovered her growing sense of calm. They were in charge now.

The man answered without hesitation. "The stone is located in the heart of the Capital. Malavi military style security but the holder is... We'll call him neutral." A pause and a searching look, which she returned with a fierce glare. "I estimate two weeks of travel time and three coming back. To account for the pursuers."

"I do almost all of my jobs without discovery," Ari told him, unimpressed by his presumed knowledge of her skills, "and I can easily make it in a week and a half."

Raising one blonde eyebrow, Daerecles nodded softly. "This job might entail some unexpected complications that will slow you down."

Now it was her turn to look skeptical. "Such as?"

"It is nearly impossible to foresee what, or who, you may encounter. But I warn you that the dragith is no easy catch."

"Yet you seem to believe that I can make it to the Capital and back, alone, without much problem."

"Ah." He pursed his lips and smiled apologetically. "Did I say you would be alone? I hope that wasn't misleading. You'll have one partner."

"No." Heat seemed to radiate from the bobcat at her side and Ari wondered if Daerecles could sense the tension in her anima.

"I'm afraid it's not negotiable," he said, with a careless wave of a finely gloved hand. "I've already signed the boy and he's on his way now to meet you in Principe, with the rest of the information you will need to complete the job. He's expecting you tomorrow morning at the Inn."

"If you force a partner on me, we meet on my terms."

He smiled. "Feel free to change the plans if you can get in touch with him. But I'll advise you that Ely is not as close with the golden eagles as you seem to be."

Ari was backed in and she knew it. She had given herself away with that eagle to Fraling; her creditor would know that she had the opportunity for a lucrative job, and more importantly, that something had made her nervous enough to contact him. Daerecles had played the game so well that she was left with no option but to take the job and do it the way he wanted it done. A small part of her wanted to fight this, while another acknowledged that it was not worth the trouble. "Fine," she told him shortly. "Now you can leave."

"I am so pleased that we could come to an agreement," he said lightly, getting to his feet and sliding his sword back into his belt. Ari watched as he picked up the little knife and slipped it into his riding boot, shifting his brown cloak on his shoulders and bowing low with a flourish. "Good day, my lady."

Daerecles squeezed out the door and was gone. Closing her eyes to hear better, Ari stood frozen in the middle of the Hole, straining her ears to catch every soft footstep as the intruder made his way out of the forest. After a moment, the sound died away and the birds began to sing again. Still silent and motionless, Ari gave Jagger a quick signal with her right hand, sending him shooting out of the Hole and into the woods. Now she lowered herself to the ground slowly, legs crossed, silver blade resting on one knee. It was five minutes, ten minutes, half an hour, and Jagger did not return. Ari did not move, all her thoughts focused on her anima tracking the blonde man through the forest, every heartbeat pulsing as if it were her own blood flowing through the bobcat's veins.

Finally, after almost an hour of waiting, she felt the tension ebb away, a sense of peace returning to her anima – to her. A few minutes later, the cat slipped back into the Hole and lay down by her side. Ari sighed in relief. Daerecles really was gone. Jagger blinked at her with his big golden eyes and lowered his head onto his paws, calm resignation mirroring her own discomfort. The situation had spiraled so far out of Ari's control that she couldn't see far enough ahead to plan a single step. And she hated losing control, hated it more than almost anything else.

"I guess we have to move out, Jag," she told her anima softly, running her fingers over the top of his soft head. Despite the insulting nature of the visit, she had to admit that Daerecles was right about the money. She was desperate to pay off the Fraling debt, and this contract would do that and more. Once the job was done, she and Jagger could be free again.

But there was something nagging at her, warning her not to ignore the trader's threats. *You have no idea who I pretend to be*, he had said. *I use the methods necessary to get what I want.* Who could say what kind of power this stranger held, what resources he had at his command? Even if he couldn't do more than spread her name, he had the potential to ruin her thieving career. She wasn't worried about the enemies she would make so much as the jobs she would lose. It was a small network, and word got around quickly when a thief had been compromised.

Denying her imagination any further rein, Ari gave Jagger a final stroke and slid her dagger back into her belt, standing up and looking around the little space. The Hole had been their home for almost six years now and she did not yet feel ready to leave it. But now that Daerecles knew it was here, they could never come back. Ari was hit with a strange pang of sadness for the life they were leaving behind. This job would only last two or three weeks, yet it felt different than the other times that she had ventured out for long contracts. Even if all went smoothly, things would not be the same when she returned.

Perhaps we won't come back to the Nyinan Forest at all, Ari thought as she began to collect her few belongings and pile them into a small suede bag. Her hideaway had been discovered, she couldn't trust Leonor, and she would have all the money she needed to survive for years. They could go anywhere.

Silently following her with his wide, serious eyes, Jagger watched his girl uncover the hole by the bed and remove her treasures. The cuff and the compass were wrapped carefully into her blanket and stored inside the bag. She considered the bronze-handled blade for a moment before slipping it down into her right boot and sliding the rock back over the hole. Tucking her hunting knife into her other shoe, she turned to contemplate her food stores, deliberately keeping her back to the anima in the center of the room. Ari couldn't bring herself to meet the bobcat's steady gaze, knowing she would see in his expressive eyes a look that would sting her heart. It wasn't his fault they were in this mess.

"I'm sorry," she said aloud, staring blankly at a clay jar of pecans. There was no answer and no movement, but then, Jagger only cared about her. If she had let him come on the Fraling job, maybe she would have avoided capture and the ensuing debt altogether.

Regret and remorse were useless emotions. Ari pushed these thoughts from her mind and went back to meticulously packing away her few possessions and meager supply of provisions. The Hole was only home because it provided shelter and concealment; they could find that anywhere. What mattered now was getting to Principe quickly and quietly.

She emptied the last of their stores into a goatskin pouch, tied it tightly shut, and dropped it into the suede sack with the water flask, blanket, and her hunting boots. Her sword hung from its usual place on her waist and she pulled her short, forest green cloak over her tunic and pants, drawing the hood down to shade her face.

"Alright, Jag." Ari motioned to her anima and he ducked out of the Hole, twisting his slender body to squeeze between the rock wall and the half open door. She followed after him without looking back. The chickadee pair was now wide awake and sitting in their tree, calling their chicka-dee-dee-dee calls and ruffling their feathers importantly as they watched the two creatures depart. Ari gave them a curt nod and hoisted her bag over her shoulder, ducking under a low oak branch as she strode into the thick of the forest. In one, two, three steps the leafy branches closed in around them and the Hole disappeared from view. Moving into a jog, Ari extended her silent strides, putting more and more space between them and their former home until the forest began to thin again and they reached the fields before Irlanda.

The pair continued on around Irlanda and over the river. Ari chose her second favorite crossing for this journey, a long, narrow log stretching across the churning rapids that served as a sturdy path for two creatures of such insignificant size. Jagger darted across first, his adept paws barely brushing the wood as he sprung over in three strides. Slowing to a walk, the girl hitched her bag up over her head and carefully placed her feet one after the other, confidently moving to meet the waiting bobcat.

As soon as she landed, they were off at a run again. Now they were entering dangerous territory. Everything beyond the river was open country, lands that Ari had never learned to trust as she trusted her forest, or even the two little villages of Nyin and Irlanda. Here roamed her enemies – the lurking, unknown foes who left her wary, but not afraid.

Ari had no real fears in the Southlands; it was the Northlands that Dav had taught her to dread, the teeming cities that he had taught her to avoid – the Capital, and Organa most of all. She and Jagger could not be seen in a city where they did not trust people with their names. Discomfort stirred once more in Ari's stomach as she considered that they were headed directly towards this danger, and then she returned her focus to the present threats.

Within thirty minutes, the trees had thinned to almost nothing, the rough edges of a greater wood. What now stretched before the girl and her anima were vast, grassy fields, filled with lush green and splashes of pink and yellow, and spotted with the occasional harvest shed or hunter's cabin. In the distance to the East rose the Parejon Hills: smooth, round mountains that gave off a hazy purple glow in the midday sun.

Ari's plan was to stick to the main cart path that led through the plain, keeping the Hills on her right and cutting straight towards Principe. She knew well where the city was located, having traveled by it many times, but she had never been inside. It was a strange sort of anomaly, sitting alone on the brink of the Northlands but disconnected from the events that embroiled that part of the country. No other city lay close enough to challenge Principe for dominance of that quiet region, and so it flourished, pampered by the rich, green fields and sparkling streams that trickled down from Parejon. On previous jobs, Ari had passed near enough to glimpse the rows of uniform rooftops, the polished metal gates, and the flashes of gold, silver, and bronze that ornamented the favored town. From far off, it felt still with a kind of silence that set her on edge. If she had to enter a city, she preferred one where she could disappear among bustling crowds. Principe was like something out of a legend from the Old Kings. It was too good to be true.

CHAPTER IV.

Dawn was just beginning to touch the sky when Ari arrived in Principe. Faint pink light gave a strange red tinge to the neat shingled rooftops and early morning shadows stretched from one smooth, grey wall to the next, painting a dark blanket across the silent cobblestone streets.

The city was sleepy in a privileged way that only such places knew. Principe managed to remain both small enough to be unimportant in politics, and wealthy enough to easily rely on outsiders for resources. There was no need to rise with the sun if your food was collected and delivered daily by farmers and hunters from poorer villages.

A few tired cattle herders led a small group of equally dull steers across the road as Ari paused to get her bearings. Neither the men nor the livestock noticed the woman and the bobcat standing in the dim light by the edge of the street. She watched the quiet little parade make its way around the corner and out of sight before moving on towards the center of town. There was not a single creature to be seen and Ari stayed in the shadows, head down, willing herself to remain a part of the nothingness.

As they approached the heart of the city, the streets became smoother and the buildings grew larger. Vast houses sprung up around them, surrounded by carefully maintained gardens and ornamented with golden finishes that threw the early light back into the sky in fantastic rays of orange and pink. Lavishly decorated storefronts advertised rare meats and herbs, imported silks, and the trade of fine gems.

The sun finally peaked over the sparkling bronze roof of the city hall, pulsing quietly before Ari's eyes and illuminating the central city square. It was a wide, open space, bordered by uniform shops and city offices that framed the grand hall rising up before them. Its grey stonewalls matched the rest of the city, but the glittering roof and the sheer expanse of the building gave it the impression of a silent, royal shepherd watching over his sleeping flock. Ari was struck by how little the city seemed to have been touched by the war. Where were the armed guards and paranoid citizens? Where was the destruction and fear? Perhaps it was too early in the morning for the truth to be awake.

As she considered this, she heard the clang of a bell. *One, two, three, four, five, six.* Now several small vendors were setting up shop on the gleaming cobblestones and three elderly women appeared with baskets ready to fill with fresh flowers and produce. Oil lamps flickered on as Ari and Jagger passed by the window of a linens shop and she automatically pulled her green hood lower over her face.

Off to the left of the plaza stood a freshly polished wooden signpost, clean-cut arrows pointing to the Market, the Stables, and the Inn. Ari bent right towards the Inn, Jagger close by her side. She wanted to get out of the open square before it began to fill with too many people. They walked briskly around the city hall and turned down a side street. The houses here were slightly smaller than the palatial structures before the square, but still carefully kept, with colorful window boxes and large mahogany doors, their round silver and gold handles set uniformly just left of center. At the end of the avenue sat the Inn, a long building with two tall floors. Ari could see bright oil chandeliers hanging from the ceilings upstairs. She hoped that the whole place wasn't done up that way and wondered why Daerecles had thought this a good spot to meet. It was too fashionable, too bright. People like her would only stand out.

Despite these concerns, Ari walked up to the front door and pushed it open. Though it appeared heavy, the dark wood swung inward easily at her touch, and the pair entered. Her first impression was of an entrance hall that, though large, was much dimmer than she had expected from the outside. Numerous lamps imbued the space with a trembling orange light, but the lack of windows in the spacious room diminished the impact to a feeble glow. Several doors lined the long walls, leading off to what Ari guessed were guest rooms, kitchen stores, and servants' corridors. The middle of the hall was filled with high, polished wooden tables that were carefully placed so as to avoid any crowding of the clientele. The chairs were of matching wood and studded with stones of a pale silvery blue. In a brighter space they might have been pretty, but in the weak light the fine stones seemed somehow bizarre and illogical.

There was only one other guest awake so early in the morning, a fact that Ari found pathetic, but convenient. The dreary-eyed young man, slumped awkwardly onto a table in the center of the hall, did not even look up as she entered. He took a tired sip from the mug in front of him and gave a great yawn, scratching absentmindedly behind his ear.

As Ari and her anima stepped forward into the room, an anxious man in a stiff blue coat came to greet them. Eying Jagger with discomfort, he appeared conflicted as to how to address the rough-looking woman in front of him.

"I'm meeting someone," Ari told him briskly before he could make up his mind. "You can leave us."

"Yes, ma'am, well – I'm afraid, I'm afraid we can't –" the man stuttered out awkwardly, "the bobcat –"

"Is this your first day?" Ari cut him off in a mocking tone, further exasperated by the realization that he was actually about to respond to this question. "The bobcat stays."

She turned away and stalked to the darkest corner of the room, not waiting to see whether he gaped in amazement or came up with an equally unimpressive response. Sitting down in one of the studded chairs, Ari motioned for Jagger to follow her example. He dropped to the ground and lay balanced upon his haunches.

The other guest looked over his cup at Ari with a befuddled expression, seemingly trying to determine whether she was real or a figure of his dreams. She glared back at him and he sank onto the table lethargically, nearly knocking over the dish as he dropped his head into his arms.

Another man in blue hurried out of one of the doors, motioning excitedly at a group of people to follow him into the hall. They appeared to be a family – a mother and father and two young girls, also accompanied by an old man who Ari presumed to be a grandfather or a servant. The parents and children all had thick blonde hair, that of the father and youngest daughter falling in large ringlets around their pale faces. Their skin was pale and smooth, untouched by sun or hard labor. They wore tunics of a soft green silk and the mother was dressed in a long, dark purple gown that hung tightly about her slim frame and accented her bright eyes. Only the elderly gentlemen sported a more modest huntsman's habit, with worn boots and a faded blue shirt.

It was clear that they weren't from this part of the country; Ari had never seen an entire family with such features in all of the Southlands. Traders, thieves, and soldiers came and went, but it was rare to see children so far from home.

They proceeded into the great room and sat around a table in the center, speaking in soft whispers as if they were worried that they would wake the entire inn. The older man, his face deeply lined and his remaining hair of a silvery grey, took a seat between the two girls, patting the older child on the cheek as he did so. As he turned to speak to the curly haired sprite on his other side, he noticed Ari and Jagger sitting in the corner. He made no noise, but Ari could tell that he had seen her by the way his eyes froze for a split second, fixing on her briefly before moving back to the little girl.

She felt a strange tightness in her chest, that sense that always preceded approaching danger. The look in his eyes was so familiar, as if he knew her already, even with the dim lighting and dark hood casting a shadow over her face. Jagger's furry hip pressed against her leg; he had moved to be nearer her.

Though the old gentleman hadn't spoken or signaled, now the woman was leaning to whisper in her husband's ear, glancing up at Ari as she did so. The younger man, who carried himself with an air to match his rich attire, followed his wife's gaze to the back corner, observing the girl with interest. Ari saw the situation spiraling out of control as the two daughters turned to learn what it was their parents were discussing. When the older girl gave a gasp of delight, Ari realized with relief that it was not her they were looking at, but Jagger.

Doing her best to look unapproachable, Ari lowered herself further into the chair and wrenched her eyes from the group of golden-headed travelers. The voices in the center of the room rose quickly; the youngest child seemed to be on the verge of tears.

"... she can have it in here!" the girl was whining unhappily.

"It doesn't matter what she's doing," her mother responded firmly.

"I want to go home!" was the angry response. Ari hoped that her unwanted partner would arrive soon so she could avoid witnessing the rest of this discussion.

"We'll go home soon," the woman said in a soothing voice that told Ari this was a lie. She wondered if they were fleeing the war as so many had before them. The little girls were in for a surprise if they were to live in the Southlands.

The child's next complaint was drowned out by a nervous exclamation from her father. "Ariana!"

Ari's head snapped up in surprise and she felt her anima

come to his feet.

"Ariana, come back here!" He was calling to his eldest daughter.

The girl was heading purposefully toward the back corner. Now that she was closer, Ari could see that she was only about seven years old, her shiny blonde hair falling in two long tresses down her back and her lively green eyes fixed on Jagger with excited interest. The bobcat tensed and backed into Ari, letting out a soft but steady hiss as the child approached.

"My sister wanted to bring Mixie, but Papa said we couldn't have pets here." The girl spoke as if Ari would understand completely, her voice high and sweet like a song.

Ari was opening her mouth to tell her to leave, but the little child raised her voice again as she reached the cat. "Did the inn man let you bring your tiger inside?" Jagger flicked his tail in irritation but the girl paid no heed. "I thought pets weren't allowed."

"He's not a pet," Ari told her, surprised at her own gentleness.

She touched her anima on the top of his head and he sat uneasily, the deep noise in his throat ceasing immediately. Perhaps it was those intense green eyes, or maybe the fact that they shared a name, but for some reason Ari allowed the little girl to stand face-to-face with Jagger and reach her hand out, ever so slowly, to brush his forehead. The bobcat tensed for a moment and then relaxed, blinking softly at the small, foreign human before him.

The girl's father had evidently been afraid that moving too quickly would frighten Ari into attack and was only then catching up with his daughter. "Ariana," he said sharply, "Get away from there."

Broad smile filling her pale cheeks, she ignored him. "Why is he with you if he isn't a pet?" she asked Ari, now stroking the cat on the nose. Her sister had begun to cry in earnest and the sound of her wailing was quickly overwhelming their mother's attempts to comfort her.

"Ariana." The man spoke to his daughter but looked at Ari, who straightened in the studded chair and shook her hood back to meet his eyes.

"He's my anima," Ari responded evenly. "He goes wherever I go."

The man raised his eyebrows and seemed to relax ever-so-slightly; his pale face bore an expression approaching respect. The little girl's pink lips fell open into a round 'o' shape and she finally tore her eyes from Jagger to look back at father.

"He's a real anima!" she exclaimed, as if he hadn't just heard Ari himself. "Like Grandpapa told us about!"

"You don't see many of them in the cities these days," he replied thoughtfully, still more focused on Ari than on his child, who had gone back to petting Jagger.

Ari just stared back at him, neither hostile nor welcoming. Though the child had distracted her for a moment, she was reminded once again of the business on which she had come. Behind the man, she could see his wife and the other girl, still fighting for control, and then the old grandfather, now watching the dim corner with unmasked interest. More than the pointed gaze, his sense of familiarity made her skin crawl with discomfort.

"What kind is he?" the girl asked. "Is he like Lylo?" She had turned away from her father once more to study Jagger carefully, as if she might find the answer to this question in his round, golden eyes.

Ari still didn't know why she had felt so kindly toward the young girl, but now anxiety was quickly overcoming her patience. The longer they stayed and talked to her, the more attention she would draw from the servants and the other guest, who would undoubtedly be joined by more breakfasters soon.

"He is being very gentle, but I think you should let him be now," she told the child quietly.

As Ari spoke, Jagger flattened his ears and took a step away from little Ariana's outstretched hand. Picking up on the change in tone, the man reached forward and took his daughter by the arm.

"It's time to go," he instructed smoothly, steering her back toward the rest of the family and continuing to whisper in her ear as they made their way across the hall.

The child looked back over her shoulder one more time, offering Ari a wide, happy smile, before grabbing her father's fingers and following him out of the same door from which they had entered. The woman and younger daughter went right behind them, still wrapped up in the same fruitless struggle. Last to go was the old man, taking a sip of his drink and standing up from the table with a slow deliberateness that struck Ari as graceful in its steady, sure manner. For a moment, she thought he was going to leave without another look, but at the door he paused and turned his head, meeting her eyes with a short nod. She didn't return it, but gazed back, watching as he passed through and disappeared again.

Breathing a soft sigh of relief, Ari pulled her hood back down over her face and waved Jagger down to the floor. The interaction had worn on her nerves and she was growing more and more impatient to get out of the Inn. As it had many times since Daerecles' visit only a day before, the thought presented itself that she might just leave and do the job without her mystery companion. How much easier it would be without another person to slow her down and worry her mind. But the trader had planned it well, leaving part of the information with this Ely so that there was no legitimate chance of her completing the contract without at least meeting him first. She wondered if he had been as thoroughly tricked and trapped by the cunning man as she had. At least that would put them on more even footing.

Just then, the front door swung open and a tall, skinny boy walked in, his short brown hair sticking up in messy tufts as he shrugged off a black hooded cloak and glanced around the entrance hall. He wore old leather boots that had been recently caked in mud and only halfheartedly cleaned. The nervous inn attendant approached him and the boy said something that Ari couldn't hear from the opposite corner, smiling as he spoke. The servant appeared relieved that he was neither threatening him nor accompanying tearful children.

As much as she wished she was wrong, Ari had no doubt that this was her promised partner. The young man could hardly be any older than her and he wore the pleasantly confused expression of a traveler in foreign territory. Even with the black cloak covering half of his belt and falling past his knees, it was clear that he didn't carry a sword, or even a bow and quiver.

She didn't say a word, just sat motionless in her corner, waiting to see how long it would take for him to find what he was looking for and what he would do when he did. The servant said something else and Ari saw the boy shake his head and motion to the back of the hall. The other man's eyes adopted their now-familiar expression of anxiety. He appeared to be preparing himself for another inquiry but the scruffy-haired boy walked away before he could speak.

Jagger flicked an ear back towards his girl as he saw the stranger approach. Ari still did not stir or speak, letting the anima discern her mood through feel and daring the young man to make the first move. Now she could make out his features more clearly: a face tan and freckled from the sun, with pronounced cheekbones that accented his thin aspect and drew her gaze to his soft brown eyes. He walked with an easy kind of lope, not smooth and athletic like Daerecles, but not exactly ungraceful either. It wasn't until he was mere feet away that he spotted the bobcat, who had hidden himself better under the table this time around. As quickly as he tried to cover it up, Ari's focused eyes caught the startled expression that flashed across his face. It was good to know that the trader hadn't revealed all her secrets.

"I don't suppose they're much accustomed to secretive meetings around here," he said, pulling out the chair across from hers and dropping down into it as if the exertion had taken all of his energy.

"Clearly," Ari answered flatly. She hated making banal conversation.

The boy looked at her with a strange, searching expression, put out by her curt response. "Elyrah Novian. But you can call me Ely."

"Ari."

"Short for?"

"Ariana." He asked too many questions.

"Well, shall we begin?" Ely seemed to think that she wanted to treat this as they would a trade in the market.

When she made no response, he continued, "I have the location of the dragith, and several contacts in the Capital. I have also been instructed to store the stone once we've taken it. My proposal would be to cut through the Parejon Hills to avoid the worst of the mountains and then head west to Falsa and on to the Capital." He finished in a breath and laid his hand on the table with hopeful firmness.

Allowing his words time to ring in the silence for a moment, Ari began calmly and quietly. "Here is how this will work: I am in charge. You do what I say, when I say it, and give your opinion only when I ask for it. We stay away from Parejon, Falsa, and any other highly populated region and head through the mountains, cross the Sonrein River and make our way through what's left of the Northlands before arriving in the Capital. The theft I will execute on my own and we will return by the same route to whichever exchange point Daerecles gives us at that time. I will keep the item in my possession at all times. Is that clear?"

Ely stared at her, his dark eyes widened in surprise. "This partnership might not –"

"There is no partnership." Ari cut him off sharply. "You are here because Daerecles gave me no choice, and frankly, I don't much care for any part of this job, so you're going to make it as easy as possible by staying out of my way unless you're needed. Understood?"

"You really think you can steal the stone without my help?" He wasn't as easily scared as she had expected, although that shocked look remained in his eyes.

"Are you a professional thief?" she asked drily, growing frustrated. "Because I've never heard of you. And I know what I'm doing."

Apparently struggling to format a response, Ely faltered at the sound of the low growl coming from under the table. The bobcat's temper ran in line with Ari's own. "Time to move out, Jagger." She stood up and swung her bag over her shoulder with ease, giving the boy a pointed look before marching across the entrance hall to the door. Her anima trotted silently at her heels, one ear swiveling backwards to determine whether Ely was following.

Seeing he had no choice, the young man got to his feet and headed out after them. By the time he had pushed open the grand front door and stepped out into the bright morning light, the pair was turning the corner at the far end of the street. Ely broke into a run.

Hearing his footsteps at her back, Ari stopped and turned. "You are being far too loud."

"You practically ran out of there. I was just catching up."

"Catch up more quietly. You're going to get us killed."

"In Principe?" His tone was incredulous. "I'm pretty sure I heard they pay off the Malavi and the Zaerans to leave the city alone."

Ari looked at him seriously, trying to keep her irritation to a minimum. They had many days of travel ahead. "This is a job, not a vacation. Nowhere is safe."

"Don't you think we should talk about this before we

start?" At least he was speaking in a whisper now.

"We've already talked." She turned to go.

"No, *you* talked," he corrected. "Don't you want to hear what Daerecles told me?"

Ari stopped once again and looked at him in annoyance. "There is no new information that could possibly affect the choices I make between now and nightfall. So, no, thank you."

"Are you going to tell me where we're going?" He sounded more resigned than irritated.

"Towards the Lanterbrun Pass. We won't stop until we've reached better cover." Already striding down the smooth cobblestone street, Ari turned her head to give him one last dark look. "Just try to keep up."

CHAPTER V.

Ari led them through the back streets until they reached the smaller of the two city gates and exited Principe unseen. According to her threatening advice, Ely stuck close and moved with acceptable silence, although Ari hoped for improvement as they entered more unpredictable territory in the following days. He did not complain, and hardly spoke at all except to comment on the unique purple tint of the tall grass that swayed around their knees as they pushed onward. Ahead, a swath of trees broke up the vast, empty plain. Unlike the journey to Principe, Ari did not feel comfortable staying on the road, and they waded along in the quiet, grassy void, not even a solitary farmer's hut in sight.

She kept up a rapid tempo, partly to reach the cover of the trees as quickly as possible, and partly because she wanted to test Ely, to see whether he could really keep up. His long legs and lanky stride made it an easy task; he never once fell back from his place a few yards behind her. Ari was acutely conscious of Jagger's position between the two of them, a wary reminder of the dangers of this unknown addition to their party. The bobcat always preferred to run in front of her when they were in this kind of environment, where anything could be lurking in the grass ahead. She wondered whether he was that mistrusting of the strange young man, or if she herself was subconsciously telling her anima that this threat was more dangerous than the creatures of the Trinidad Plains.

In truth, Ari was more irritated by his presence than she

was anxious. After all, she was quite certain there was nothing to fear from him. Ely seemed harmless, almost helpless when it came to surviving abroad. He was ill-prepared for hunting, carried only a plain steel dagger as a weapon, and ran distractedly, admiring the world about him too much to recognize the inherent dangers in passing through such an exposed and open space. Considering these flaws, Ari could not be afraid of Ely himself but rather of what his presence could do, of the possibility that his failure might also bring about her own.

They reached the little wood just before the sun began to set. It was a dense but empty place, filled with silent, bird-less trees and dark brush that crowded around their feet so tightly that Ari struggled to avoid getting stuck in the sharp undergrowth. The quiet was eerie, unnatural, and she didn't like it one bit. There were no rabbits and squirrels running out under foot, no cardinals and blue jays crying in the leafy forest ceiling, no soft pawprints left in the earth by wolves and cats stalking their prey. Now Jagger skirted around her and began to work in a zigzag pattern, exploring the path ahead in search of dangers, or perhaps in hope of signs of life.

They traveled about a mile into the forest before Ari decided it was time to stop. Reaching a small open space, tightly surrounded by thick rhododendron, she dropped her pack onto the ground and gave the bobcat a wave. As Jagger began to circle the clearing, Ari commenced a thorough examination of the area, checking for foreign prints, relics of human presence, and widow makers hanging from the branches above. Ely stood and watched them work, his own bag still slung over his shoulder as if he were waiting for permission to put it down.

Satisfied that it would do for one night, Ari crossed back over to her bag and sat down beside it.

"What are you doing?" she asked sharply, looking at Ely in annoyance.

"Why this place?" he responded with a question instead of an answer.

Ari frowned at him, but he was looking around at the dark, twisted trees, the shiny leaves bending over their heads in an ominous sort of canopy. At the feet of the rhododendron ran an endless expanse of prickly bush that seemed to fill the rest of the space so that they were wrapped in a nest of gloomy wood.

"It's one of the few open clearings in the forest," she told him flatly, wishing he didn't look so uncomfortable.

"No, why this forest? Why not the Plains?" Ely was still standing.

"We can't stay out in the open. It's too dangerous."

"And this place isn't?" Now he turned to look at her, waving a hand around as he spoke. Ari noticed with surprise that he did not look scared, as she had believed him to be, but sad, almost pained.

She shook her head. "This wood is sick. Nothing lives here, and no one will pass through. It is dark and unhappy, but it cannot hurt us."

As she said this, Jagger appeared from among the trees and lay down by her side, short tail wrapped around behind his girl and big eyes trained on the young man who remained standing before them.

"The fairies are gone."

Picking a burr out of the bobcat's coat, Ari paused and looked up at Ely. "What?"

"The fairies are gone," he repeated. "That's why it's so sick."

"The war has driven many creatures from their rightful homes and destroyed much of what once made this world beautiful," Ari said bluntly, returning to her anima's nettled back.

"How can you talk like that?" Ely sounded stunned, but Ari was glad to see him finally lower his pack.

"I've never gotten along well with fairies," she responded drily, plucking a particularly prickly burr out of Jagger's soft fur. "They're too moody."

"So you would rather see them killed by the Malavi?" Ely demanded, his voice rising in agitation.

"Of course not," Ari snapped back at him. "And if you knew anything about fairies or the war, you would know that these are not dead, because the war has hardly touched Principe or the Trinidad Plains." She made a point to keep a close eye upon the movements of both armies, given how much their presence could affect her work and safety. "The fairies left this forest to inhabit a bigger and better one when its previous residents were killed by the fighting, most likely west along the Trinidad River or east in the forests that surround the Blue Lakes. Like I said, they're temperamental little imps that are happy to take what is not theirs, even if it means great loss." Here she paused, unwilling to lose control of her temper. "And don't ever assume that it was the Malavi who did the killing. The Zaerans have spilled just as much blood."

Slipping off his cloak, Ely lowered himself to the forest floor and sat down right where he stood, across the small clearing from Ari and her watchful anima. "You have a very negative outlook on the world," he commented, all traces of tension gone.

Ari ignored this observation and pulled the final nettle off of Jagger's ear. "Tell me everything Daerecles shared about the job."

This abrupt change of conversation did not faze him at all. "The dragith is not just any precious stone. This one is larger than most, of a yellow-orange hue, tougher than diamond, and worth about three cities the size and wealth of Principe." He met Ari's eyes and his gaze seemed to be reaching for something, wondering what it would find. She returned his stare evenly, daring those thoughtful eyes to blink or look away. "It's not going to be easy to break in, or get out again."

"Where is it?"

"In one of the largest mansions in the Capital, three blocks from the King's Palace. The stone itself is in some kind of treasure vault. There are ten men guarding it and several dozen more in and around the house. There will not be any magical or non-human security..." Ely trailed off for a moment. "He isn't the kind of man to rely on anything he cannot control with brute strength."

"And the owner?" Ari asked, her interest piqued by this last comment.

"Jsepa Broun. The wealthiest neutral member of the central Capital. He pays off the Malavi in order to stay that way and meanwhile runs his own paramilitary force under the name Tannin Squire."

"I know," he added when Ari made a skeptical face. "I guess he has to keep up the front somehow."

"But everyone knows Broun is Squire?"

"I think it's common conjecture."

Ari mused silently, thinking darkly of all that she would love to do to a man like Broun. People like him were the reason the war continued on. With all his wealth, he could surely make a difference and help those remaining in the Capital, yet he used it to amplify the fighting and conceal what Ari considered to be worthless objects.

"And you said you have contacts in the Capital?" Ari questioned him, moving on to the most important issue at hand.

Ely nodded. "Three of them, yes." And when Ari said nothing, he added, "A silk merchant, a retired royal servant, and a professor."

"Are they trustworthy?" This she doubted. Anyone could be bought.

"The merchant and the servant, absolutely." He pursed his lips. "I'm not sure I could say the same for the professor."

Startled by his honesty, Ari had to gather her words before

proceeding. "I'll decide when we arrive. And if we've done everything right before then, there will be no need to ask questions and nothing to tip them off."

He nodded and they fell into silence for a few minutes as Ari turned these new details over in her mind. She was conscious of Ely's eyes on her but too absorbed in thought to care. Although she enjoyed a good challenge, this was the type of mission she always tried to avoid. The guards were only men, and probably dim-witted at that, but there were so many of them that she couldn't possibly take the stone without creating a significant distraction and leaving numerous casualties.

Ari's approach was one of stealth, shadows, and silence. She preferred to enter without breaking and leave no trace of her presence, save the mysterious disappearance of the select object. Of course, this was only possible in about four out of five jobs. A thief could not expect every contract to be easy. If she was attacked, Ari had no qualms about striking back. It just made things more complicated. Ely could serve as her distraction – he would surely draw at least five of the men away from their posts – but she could not trust him to hold his own in a confrontation. This again left her going alone, which was how she preferred it anyway.

"What can you do?" she asked, abruptly breaking the stillness that had settled around them. "Can you fight at all?"

"My father taught me how to throw a knife."

Ari arched an eyebrow in surprise. "Hit that tree with the broken limb." She pointed across the clearing at a tired looking rhododendron. "Right below where it splits."

"You don't believe me?"

She just looked back at him, waiting. Sighing, Ely got to his feet and slipped the dagger from his belt, squaring up to the target. With a deliberate look, he cocked his arm back and hurtled the blade from his fingers, releasing it with a smooth flick of the wrist. His form was not bad.

From her comfortable spot on the forest floor, Ari watched the knife bury itself in the tough wood, a few inches farther down than she had requested. "That took a lot of concentration," she observed.

Now Ely raised his eyebrows at her. "You gave me a five-inch target."

"It wasn't even moving," she responded, unimpressed.

Shaking his head, he walked over to the tree and yanked the short steel blade out of the wood. The trunk seemed to shiver, as if it didn't want to release the dagger just yet. Ely stood for a moment, facing the tree and fingering his knife, back turned to Ari and her anima. She got the strange feeling that he was waging a private debate, purposefully hidden from her sight.

"That's it," he said suddenly, turning back around to look at her. "I don't have any other skills."

Ari was quite ready to believe this, but something in his eyes told her this was a lie. He flashed a grin and, almost unconsciously, flexed his fingers and tucked the knife back into his belt.

"No other skills," Ari repeated. "And you're still alive at... what? Twenty-three?"

"Twenty-four," he said, apparently unbothered by her disdain.

No wonder you are so stupidly cheery all the time, Ari thought. *You're feeling lucky to have survived.*

She watched him a moment longer, and saw it again. "You're lying to me."

"What?" he said, confidence momentarily shaken. He was still smiling, but his gentle brown eyes were hesitant, cautious. "I am not."

Jagger took a step nearer Ely, gazing directly into his face. Ari felt how her anima opened his senses to Ely alone, how the bobcat absorbed the sound of his heartbeat, the smell of his sweat, the quiet vibration of the earth beneath his feet.

She fixed the young man with a withering look. "You are not like me. What are you?"

"What is that supposed to mean?" he asked, sounding almost offended.

"Are you part nymph?"

"What? No –"

"Centaur blood? ... Mermaid?"

Ely opened his mouth to reply but Ari cut him off again.

"No. No." Jagger felt it; Ari felt it. She narrowed her eyes. "You are a sorcerer."

"I am not a sorcerer," Ely protested, but once again, his eyes gave him away. Ari frowned, unwilling to reveal her surprise at this revelation. Sorcerers had not always been uncommon, but most had been killed or driven into hiding by the vengeful Malavi leadership. The majority of magically gifted humans had allied with the Zaera rebels when the fighting first broke out because the Old Kings had always respected their skills, though they held no special honors in the courts. The murder of the King and all of his party by the Malavi military coup had brought an end to both the revered leader and his benevolent treatment of the sorcerers. These days, it was very rare to witness a magically gifted person reveal their powers. Ari had not met more than two or three in all of her travels.

"My mother is a sorcerer, not me," Ely went on. "Only some of her powers got passed down, and I've tried to learn as much as I can from her, but..." He trailed off into silence.

"Would you be able to use it under attack?" She was studying him closely now, searching for something in his brown eyes that would spell out a realer truth than she could find in his words.

He shrugged. "I've never tried. Magic isn't meant for violence."

"Yes, it goes against the noble code of sorcery, I am aware of the rules, but –"

"They're not rules, they're –"

"I don't care what they are," Ari snapped. Jagger flicked his tail in aggravation. "I want to know whether you could use your magic in a pressured situation."

"I think so. I don't know – I –"

"You could or you couldn't?" she demanded, growing impatient.

The bobcat's golden eyes seemed to bore angry holes into Ely's face as he rapidly calculated his response. "Yes. I could."

Satisfied that she had received an answer, though not one she trusted in the slightest, Ari pulled a spare tunic out of her suede sack and stretched out beside her anima, folding the shirt under her head and closing her eyes. In her right hand she clutched the curved silver dagger.

***

Ely watched her for a minute, wondering if this was really the end of the conversation. But of course it was; the woman would put an end to it when she wanted. He had never met someone so mistrusting, so closed off, and yet so in command of her world. Ari possessed a fierceness that was startling in its intensity. It was clear she despised his presence, but Ely thought she probably would have treated anyone the same way.

Telling her about his magic had felt like a significant revelation – he had gone against his mother's strongest urging not to share his ability with anyone – and Ari had only asked him if he could use it in a battle. As far as Ely was concerned, Ari now knew everything he had to hide. He had a strong suspicion that it would take much longer to even scratch the surface of her many secrets.

Ely's thoughts were interrupted by an almost inaudible rumble from the cat at Ari's side. He blinked in surprise, so intent on the girl that he had momentarily forgotten about her anima. Jagger's wide eyes watched Ely distrustfully, daring him to look another moment longer. Unsure of how to respond to this animal that seemed to possess mind-reading abilities, the boy lifted his hand defensively and flopped down onto his back. The cat appeared satisfied and, after observing Ely for a few seconds, lowered his head onto his paws and let his orange gaze wander around the clearing.

Staring up towards the rhododendron canopy, Ely suddenly felt the weight of the situation settle over him in a heavy blanket that pulled at his eyelids and deadened his limbs. Slowly, and then quickly, he fell asleep.

***

It was still dark when Ari awoke, but she could tell that dawn was coming because the sky was beginning to buzz ever so softly with a gentle orange glow that signified the approaching day. Jagger shifted from where he lay alongside her, stretched head to tail so that their bodies were pressed firmly together. Feeling Ari stir, he lifted his big head and rolled onto his belly, blinking down into her sleepy eyes.

"We're going to make it into the mountains today," she whispered to him, voice coming out low and scratchy.

He stood up and, quickly touching his wet nose to his girl's cheek, trotted off into the dense wood. Ari hoped he would be able to find something to eat in this strange, sick forest. There didn't seem to be anything living but the twisted trees and endless thorny bushes. Knowing she would have better luck hunting in the mountains, Ari sat up and pulled her small pouch of food from the suede bag. The fresh game could wait for another day.

Popping a few blueberries into her mouth, she got to her feet and began to pace around the clearing. Once they left the forest they would have to cross more open plains, but closer to the mountains the space would begin to close up again, providing them with better cover. Though the Lanterbrun Pass was by far the easiest path, Ari had her doubts about the safety of the crossing. The wide valley, with its lush green pastures and plentiful water sources, was attractive to many travelers and the road was never clear. If needed, she knew several other passages through the jagged peaks of the Belem Range, but Ari hoped that their luck would hold out long enough to make it through Lanterbrun without a detour.

Remembering Ely with a grumpy sigh, Ari stopped her pacing and, looking about for the nearest rock or stick, spotted a black pebble, which she picked up and tossed at the sleeping boy. It hit him on the shoulder, jolting him into an upright position.

"Wake up and get ready to leave," Ari commanded, before he could splutter out any surprised protests.

Turning away again, she picked up her sword and pulled it out of its sheath, inspecting it for any unwanted marks or dullness. Daerecles had interrupted her polishing when he had climbed on the roof of the Hole.

"Is it even morning yet?" Ely asked, more awake but just as confused.

"It will be soon." The sword wasn't shiny enough. She hoped she had brought her polishing cloth.

"Is it wise to start traveling in the dark?"

There it was, at the bottom of her bag. Ari removed the blue cloth and sat down to begin polishing the long blade. "We're leaving as soon as Jagger gets back."

Ely gave up and just looked at her with a mixture of befuddlement and awe. Ari ignored him and slowly slid the rag up and down the side of the sword, which lay across her knee like a small child.

"You're going to struggle today if you don't eat something now," she told Ely without looking up. He still hadn't moved from his spot on the ground.

"Oh, yes, I know," he responded quickly, tearing his eyes

away from the glittering weapon in her hands and beginning to search through his own bag for the stores he had packed.

The orange light was slowly seeping into the blackness, turning it into a deep brown, then a softer grey tinged with the warmth of the sunrise. Ari was impatient for her anima to return, wishing that they had set off before the sky had opened itself to the sun, before the black forms of the knotted trees became green leaves and smooth, brown trunks. Just as she was debating whether to begin sharpening her sword, Jagger emerged from among the bushes, the remnants of a bony-looking squirrel trapped between his teeth. He dropped it carefully on the ground and looked at her expectantly.

"I don't need it," Ari told him. "Hurry up and eat."

The bobcat picked off the rest of the meat in a few deft bites, leaving the bones of the unfortunate creature in a neat pile. At a swift wave from his girl, he gave his paws a quick cleaning and stood up to carry the skeleton back into the bushes.

"What is he doing?" Ely asked, watching the cat with interest.

"Leaving no trace of our presence," she answered shortly. "Are you ready to go yet?"

"Just about," he replied, hurriedly arranging his remaining food and fixing his tunic.

Standing up, Ari held her sword straight out before her, twisting it side-to-side and looking carefully down the blade. Satisfied with her work, she slid it smoothly back into her belt, lifted her hood over her head, and picked up the suede sack.

"Let's go, Jag," she called into the bushes where her anima had disappeared with his bones. He trotted back into the clearing and, swinging her bag over her shoulder, Ari headed into the trees.

Ely opened his mouth to ask her to wait, but the young woman had already vanished into the maze of dark wood. Stuffing his cloak into his bag, he leapt to his feet and darted after her, sprinting to keep that camouflaged green cloak in sight.

Although the boy apparently believed he was running nimbly, Ari flinched at the sound of every crackling leave and snapping twig. Luckily there was nothing living in the forest. Any human enemy or native predator would hear him from a mile away. As it was, she rated her unwillingness to engage in conversation greater than the present need for stealth, and sped on without pause.

There were times when they had to slow to a walk because the forest grew so tight, the narrow branches crisscrossing over and around Ari's chosen path until it seemed they were being woven into a wooden birdcage with no escape. But as the little group continued on and the pale dawn became a bright, blue morning, the thick foliage began to open up windows to the sun. The trees thinned and the sharp brush turned to scattered patches of wilted greenery, allowing the travelers to pick up the pace once more. Willing them to make up the lost time, Ari pushed ahead and stretched her legs. They had to make it across the open Trinidad Plains before sundown.

Now Jagger ran out ahead of her, satisfied that Ely did not pose any real threat to his girl. Gliding along through the rapidly diminishing trees, he seemed to float in a sort of quiet bubble, his presence so silent that if it weren't for his legs propelling him along, it would appear that he did not move at all. Only his delicate tufted ears gave any sign of the hyper-alertness that hummed through his furry body. They swiveled back-and-forth, carefully listening for any sound that did not match the soft, steady rhythm of Ari's footsteps or the eager pounding of Ely's long limbs upon the earth.

The boy's strides were so even that sometimes Ari would forget that he was there, lose herself in the quiet of the earth and the comfort of Jagger's company, and let her thoughts fall silent to the whispers of the tall grass that seemed to speak of the mountains ahead. She would open her mind to these words, listen to their tales of eastern winds and approaching rain, feel a semblance of peace – and then a stick would snap behind her, Ely would suck in a breath, and Ari would grit her teeth to avoid barking angrily back at him. Eyes fixed on the path ahead, she would watch Jagger tense, so fleetingly that anyone else would have imagined it, but just enough that her spirit, so entwined with his, recoiled at its core.

They continued on like this for several hours, quickly breaking free of the sickly little forest and emerging into the bright day. The fields on this side of the wood were not much different from those closer to Principe. There were a greater variety of wildflowers, and the purple-hued grass was dotted with small, green bushes that sprung up along a haphazard stream running from the mountains. As they slowly neared the jagged peaks of the Belem, the Trinidad Plains began to climb into a steady slope that pushed up towards the base of the towering range. Spotting a place where the spring gathered into a small pool, Ari came to a halt and steered her company to the grassy bank.

"We'll rest here for a few minutes," she told Ely, dropping her pack to the ground. He followed suit, lowering his own bag from his shoulder and stooping to run his fingers through the cool water. Creeping to the edge of the grass, Jagger sniffed at the water before beginning to drink, lapping it up thirstily and then circling back around to stand by Ari as she knelt before the pool.

The water felt cold as she dipped her hand in it, sending little ripples across the shallow pond. Cupping her palms together, she scooped it up towards her mouth and drank. The cool liquid was soothing in her parched throat and she took several more handfuls before leaning back onto her elbows and tilting her head up at the sky.

Ely drank his fill and then flopped onto the bank, closing his eyes contentedly.

"We're not sleeping here." Ari's voice came sharply, stinging his ears with its bitterness.

His eyes flew open again and he sat up to see her watching him with a disapproving expression. "I wasn't sleeping."

"Never close your eyes when you're this exposed," she snapped. "You can relax when we find cover."

"Are you going to write down all of these rules, or do I have to memorize them?"

"Excuse me?" Ari had already focused her gaze elsewhere but she turned back to face him.

Ely was smiling. "Do you have a guidebook somewhere? Treasure hunting for the beginner?"

His grin really was obnoxious. "I don't think I've given you any rules that weren't common sense," she responded coolly, rolling her eyes and getting to her feet to pace the edge of the pool.

"Are we going already?" he asked.

"No." She pulled her dagger from her belt, then thought better and put it back.

"Don't you think you should save your energy?"

A muscle jumped in Ari's jaw but she ignored him and turned to walk along the other side of the pond. Jagger watched her carefully from across the still water.

"Have you ever had a partner before?" Ely wondered after a minute, indifferent to her cold response.

"We're not partners." She pulled the knife out once more, slowly running a finger along the razor-sharp edge.

"Okay." He shrugged. "Have you ever had a partner?"

"I prefer to work alone."

"Has anyone ever told you that you're really bad at answering questions?"

Ari's finger slipped on the end of the blade and she watched a drop of blood emerge from her fingertip. "Avoiding unreasonable and unnecessary inquiries is a finely-honed skill, equally important as hunting or sword fighting."

"See, you didn't answer that one either."

Bending over the water's edge, she dipped her hand in and swirled it in a circle, sending a faint trail of blood spiraling through the clear pool. Being around this boy was more aggravating than spending a day with Leonor. And it was clear that he was still expecting some sort of answer. Ari could feel his eyes on her even as she kept her back to him. It was astonishing that any creature could survive so long with the lack of tact that he possessed. Perhaps even more confusing was the realization that her responses seemed to have little to no impact on his cheerful mood.

"If you're not going to say anything useful, it's best that you don't speak at all," she told him at last. "You can write that in your rulebook. Now let's head out."

Making one last circle in the water, Ari shook her hand dry and stood up, meeting Jagger's eye. The bobcat was immediately by her side, waiting expectantly. At a subtle nod from his girl, he trotted away from the little oasis, pushing through the tall grass back towards the path. She followed behind, leaving Ely to catch up once again.

CHAPTER VI.

The next several hours seemed to drag on, or rather, they passed so quickly that Ari felt they were not making any headway at all. The sun hurried across the sky while the three travelers raced it on much slower horses. She was growing tense, the pressure of her own expectations making her grumpy and particularly anxious to get out of the open air. Picking up on Ari's stress, Jagger glanced back at the two humans behind him and lengthened his smooth stride to cover more ground. Ari followed his lead, pushing herself forward despite the many hours they had already logged that day. Ely's footsteps came from the rear in the same steady pattern, pounding the purple grass down into the soft earth.

As they moved on, the plains darkened with the evening light, turning a deep blue, almost black against the still-bright sky. Ari got the sense that they were running upside-down, with the sky in the earth and the earth in the sky, everything hanging by a thread so that they might fall at any moment. She wondered, if they did fall, whether they would land on the ground or fly among the stars until they were lost for good. It did not seem like it would be so bad to be stuck up there, as long as Jagger was with her.

Dav had always spoken to her of the stars, of the creatures that went to live there after life was done, and Ari had loved his stories, but never believed him. It was too dangerous to believe in anything that she could not see. What remained of the world was a battlefield, and she figured that there weren't many humans left who had souls worthy of the constellations anyway.

"Is that a camp?" Ely's loudly whispered question snapped Ari out of her thoughts.

"Let's hope not," she answered. But it clearly was. Even from a quarter mile out, the fire was bright and she could distinguish at least two figures standing under a tall tree with long, leafy branches. She and her anima slowed their pace and moved off the path simultaneously, instead tracking west of the unknown campers.

"They might be friendly," said Ely, his voice an irritating mixture of hopeful and confused.

Ari could hear every piece of grass that broke under his feet. "Or they might try to kill us," she hissed back. "Try not to move so loudly."

Near enough the fire to have a clearer view, Ari dropped down behind a bush with thick, spiky foliage. Ignoring the sharp leaves, she pushed her face through the branches to take a look at the scene before them. The two people she had seen from afar were still standing under the great tree: a pair of men with rough hunting attire and heavy axes resting on their broad shoulders. Now that she was closer, Ari could pick out several other forms, one resting against a smaller tree trunk and two more, both moving back and forth in a strange kind of rhythm.

"This way," she whispered to Ely, pulling her face back out of the bush and looking to make sure he was paying attention.

"Something's not right," he said, face screwed up in concentration as he strained to make out the figures in the distance.

"I know." Ari looked back at the two forms moving across the open space in their odd dance. "There could be more, so we'll keep our distance and stay low."

Ely nodded and Ari got up, back hunched and knees bent to keep hidden behind the silent purple sea. They moved in a unit, Ari in front with Ely following as discreetly as possible and Jagger an invisible presence at the rear. Only the top of the boy's head could be seen above the plains. In two minutes, they were reaching the edge of the same scattered wood that played host to the strange party to their east. The trees sprouted up suddenly, the first as large as the last, absorbing the tall grass into their vast shadows. Some matched the forests around Nyin and Principe, but most were great conifers, perpetually dressed in deep green needles that created a soft brown blanket when they fell to the earth.

The grass grew shorter as soon as they passed under the first branches. Now Ari had to count on the limited cover of the trees, which, though tall, were still only sparingly present. She hoped that the dim evening light would be enough to keep them hidden. The three men would not pose any real problem, but something about the other two creatures gave her pause. The way they moved together was so eerie, so unfamiliar, that she was certain some force, physical or magical, was binding them.

Spotting an especially wide trunk, Ari crept onward and positioned herself behind it, peering around at the scene before them. Ely imitated her and crouched behind a nearby tree.

The dancing flame from the campfire illuminated the faces of the three men, all tall and rough looking, with weather-beaten faces and heavy, forest-green coats. The two standing held their axes, one swinging his broad blade in a slow circle that caught the firelight. The man on the ground almost appeared to be sleeping, but Ari could see that his eyes were open, and saw his mouth move as he spoke to his companions. His legs were stretched out before him and his only visible hand rested casually on the hilt of a broadsword. Even in the unsteady light it was easy to tell that the make was sloppy, unsophisticated. The only thing these men had to their advantage was their strength.

"Those creatures in front of the fire," Ely whispered, "those aren't humans."

And then the flame flashed just as the two figures turned and Ari saw both of their faces, pale skin as smooth as a child's but eyes overflowing with years. Their noses were small and flat, barely protruding from their faces, and their hair parted perfectly down the middle into even sheets of raven black. Each of the creatures, female in appearance, wore similar clothing, a thin woven top and a loose skirt that stopped just below the knee. Their shoulders and arms were bare, but they did not seem to feel the chill of the late summer night air.

"They're nymphs," Ari breathed, struck by the fierce anger in the eyes of creatures who she had always seen to be so peaceful.

"What do we do?"

Nothing, she was about to answer, when something stopped her. Her voice froze in her throat and she put a hand up to silence Ely, who was clearly about to continue. There was another creature in their presence, and though it did not make a sound, Ari could feel its breath in the air and its eyes watching through the darkness. She turned slowly, putting her back to the tree and facing the empty forest.

But it wasn't empty anymore. As she peered into the woods, not one, but two men stepped forward, similar in appearance to those around the fire, no doubt a part of the same company. One carried a sword and the other a long, steel hunting knife.

"What are you young travelers doing out in these parts?" the one with the sword asked, his tone friendly but his eyes menacing. Ari's gaze darted to the fingers on his sword hand, which flexed and un-flexed upon the wide hilt.

"Traveling to Itswild," she said smoothly. "We have business with a trapper there."

"You two don't look cut out for the trapping life," the man laughed. His partner grinned darkly, taking a step forward with his knife held at the ready.

Ari could sense Ely's anxiety, loud and present, even without looking at his face. "We're tougher than you might expect," she answered, hoping her strength was enough for the both of them.

"Sure you are, sweetheart," the man with the knife sneered at her. Both hunters stepped forward again.

Casually pulling her cloak aside to reveal the blades in her belt, Ari made steady eye contact with the first man. "We're leaving. Many miles to go."

The sight of the shiny sword and silver dagger did not faze him. "You've seen our secret," he said, "And we can't have that."

"All we've seen is a group of fellow travelers sitting around a fire."

The man with the knife laughed. "Now, that's a lie." They had come so close that Ari could have touched them with the tip of her sword.

"Ely," she hissed, "run."

"But you –"

"Ely, *run*."

And he obeyed, taking off just as Ari unsheathed her sword and lunged forward to meet the blade of her opponent. Despite the man's strength, she parried easily, taking advantage of his poor form and the imbalanced weight of his sword. The satisfied look on his face changed to one of concentration as he felt the force of her parry.

The second man jumped into the fight when he saw his companion falter. Ari was prepared, pulling her dagger out with her left hand and blocking his strike as she dodged the wildly swinging sword of the other hunter. Before the first man could bring his blade back around, she had stabbed her own sword into his muscular thigh, twisting it a little bit as she pulled it back out. He shouted in pain and staggered backwards.

"That wasn't very nice, girl." The man with the knife leapt towards her angrily.

Once again anticipating his clumsy movements, Ari stepped aside and brought her sword to meet his knife. This was too easy. But as she countered his heavy strokes, she heard noises: voices, and the sound of approaching footsteps. The hunters' companions had noticed the skirmish.

Trying to turn so that she would be facing the newcomers when they arrived, Ari doubled her blows to her enemy's right side, forcing him to rotate in a slow semi-circle. She was getting ready to deliver the crippling hit when he pulled out a second hunting knife, equally unwieldy, but equally sharp. Now he came at her with both blades, recklessly hacking towards her arms, hands, and torso.

It was an unpracticed attack, naïve and immature, but paired with his great strength, the childish unpredictability made is almost difficult to counter. Ari was caught up in a flurry of blocks and deflections when her attacker's companions arrived, two of the men from the campfire, both armed with axes. Knowing there were only seconds to lose, she stepped back and let him come for her with arms outstretched, bringing her own sword up and slicing it across both of his hands so that he dropped his weapons. He cried out and she swung the blade around to connect with his abdomen.

"Careful about who you call sweetheart," she spat, kicking him in the knee so that he stumbled, doubled over, into the man that had just reached them.

The two newcomers did not try to bait her with taunts and instead pressed forward without pause, leaping upon her with their axes swinging. But Ari had had enough of this game, and enough of their boorish antagonism. She did not grant their attack the compliment of a single parry, spinning out and twirling under the heavy weapons with graceful ease. They swung, three, four, five times without response and then she saw her moment. Ducking the flying steel of one man, she sliced the thigh of the other and then whirled around back of both, digging her silver dagger into the primary axe shoulder of the first. The hunter with the leg wound collapsed to his knees, trying to hold the laceration shut with bloodied hands. The other man did not give up, grunting angrily and turning to face Ari again with his blade now in his left hand.

"Let me go," she warned him.

Ignoring her, he lunged with axe held high, leaving his torso completely exposed to her counterattack. About to take the easy option he offered, Ari changed her mind and instead jumped aside, finding his left shoulder with her sword to give him a matching mark. This time she plunged it a little bit deeper, sure to make him drop his weapon to the ground.

She slid her sword into its sheath and ran, certain that no one was following, but moving at breakneck speed nonetheless. Behind her, she could hear two of the men speaking angrily, their words impossible to make out in the ever-thickening forest as she quickly put more and more distance between herself and her attackers.

Jagger, she wondered, *where have you hidden Ely?*

Called by Ari's thought, or perhaps by the familiar beat of her heart, the bobcat appeared at her side, trotting along calmly, as if his girl hadn't just fought off four huntsmen. The only thing that betrayed him was the one ear he had trained on Ari, listening for sounds of the abnormal. There was nothing to scare him; their reckless blades had not even grazed her and she was barely winded, but Jagger always worried.

"I'm fine, Jag." Ari's voice was a low whisper, almost a hum that no creature but her anima could hear. His left ear joined the right in its steady back-and-forth swivel, shifting focus to the dark forest around them. They continued on for about three minutes and then the bobcat moved ahead. He led her into a thick cluster of trees, stopping in front of a particularly fat one, with low-hanging branches that intertwined into a kind of human-sized nest, full of brown-green needles clustered in spiky knots.

"Ely?"

The boy stepped out from behind the tree, bending down and pushing aside some long branches to emerge from his cocoon. There were several needles sticking up in his dark hair. Jagger flattened his ears unhappily at the sight.

"Your anima would not allow me to leave until you came back," Ely told Ari, a hint of annoyance in his voice.

"Good." She brushed her fingertips over the top of the cat's soft head.

"He growled and hissed at me," Ely protested. "He probably would have bitten me."

"Probably," Ari agreed. "Let's walk a little bit further and pick a place to camp for the night."

She waved Jagger to her side and looked about for the best way out of the tree nest. Brushing pine needles out of his hair, Ely followed after her.

"Did you tell him to do that?"

"I don't tell Jagger to do anything. It's a partnership."

"I don't believe that."

"That it's a partnership?"

"That you don't give him orders." The boy was keeping stride with her as she walked, doing his best to look her in the eye though she kept her gaze directed into the trees.

"Do you know how animan work?" she asked, tone bitter with condescension.

"Of course I do."

"Then we shouldn't even be having this conversation."

Now they had reached another tight cluster of trees, sufficiently far from the evening's combat for Ari to feel her chest loosening. She slipped her dagger back into her belt. "We'll rest here."

"Are you going to tell me what happened back there?"

There was one widow-maker in an old cedar above them. Ari inspected it from the ground, trying to decide if one strike with a knife would be enough to bring it down.

"Ari," Ely repeated, "what happened?"

She could definitely knock the branch out of the tree if she hit it in the right spot. Maybe it would be better to use her spare dagger in case it got stuck.

"You're not hurt at all," he continued. "It looked like there were several of them."

Pulling the bronze-handled blade out of her hunting boot, Ari cocked her wrist and hurled it, sending the knife into the tree in a spiral of shiny color. With a satisfying crunch, the dagger buried itself into the dead wood and then, slowly, a long, tired crack announced the divorce of the limb from the tree. The branch fell to the ground at Ely's feet, Ari's knife still lodged into the dry bark.

The look on his face was one of shock and awe. He knelt and wrenched the bronze dagger from the wood.

Ari took it with a curt nod. "I didn't have any problems," she said shortly.

Ely just looked at her for a moment, apparently grappling with what he had just seen.

"We will have a bit of time to hunt tomorrow morning if you want to find breakfast," Ari told him, dropping the knife back into her boot and pulling out her sword and silver dagger for cleaning.

"How many of them were there?" He had just seen the two blades, stained with traces of the fight, and his eyes suddenly adopted a sharper focus.

"Only four." Having wiped off most of the blood with a spare rag, Ari fished her polishing cloth out of the suede rucksack.

"Are they dead?" Ely asked her so bluntly that she stopped what she was doing and looked up at him.

"I don't think so."

"You don't think so?"

"I didn't exactly wait around to ask them how they were feeling," she told him brusquely, irritated by the string of judgmental questions.

"You don't know if they're dead?" he asked again, incredulous.

Ari didn't respond, returning her focus to polishing the knife.

"What, it does not matter at all to you whether you just ended the lives of four men?"

"It's not that simple," Ari snapped, feeling an unexpected flash of anger rise in her chest.

"Life or death is a pretty basic concept."

She spun around to face him, eyes narrowed. "Life or death is not the same as killing or not killing. You know nothing of what you speak."

For once, Ely was silenced. Ari wanted to sit down and work on her blades, but the beating of her pulse could not seem to slow and she was bothered by the boy's eyes still fixed upon her as she slowly polished the silver dagger.

"How many creatures do you love?" she asked, almost to her own surprise.

It was a minute before he could respond, caught off guard by the question. "My parents, my sister and brother. A few friends back home in Parejon."

Ari could tell he was ready to go on, probably prepared to list every person he had fancied, every fast stallion he had ridden across the Hills, but she did not really care about any of that. "My parents were killed when I was seven years old. Thieving and smuggling is what I do." Her voice was flat, brusque. "You can't survive in this business, or in this world, if you aren't prepared to make sacrifices."

Apparently struggling to balance the nature of this revelation with the tone of its delivery, Ely nodded slowly. Ari was once again surprised by how easily he seemed to accept everything she said.

"So, did you really live alone for..." He furrowed his brow.

"Fifteen years. No." Now she sat and went back to polishing with greater vigor.

Silence fell around them again and Ari could tell that he was hoping she would say more. She held the silver dagger before her face and inspected it for dull spots.

Realizing that she wasn't going to speak again, Ely lowered himself to the ground and looked at her thoughtfully. "Who did you stay with?"

"A man in Nyin," she answered without looking away from the knife. "Dav."

"What does he think about your thieving?"

Ari slipped the knife into her belt and laid her sword across her knee. "He's dead."

There was a noise as Ely's response was extinguished by this news. "I'm sorry."

"It was a long time ago."

The slender blade glistened in the dark as she ran the cloth back and forth along its sharp edge. Jagger sat down by her side, his eyes and ears trained on the deep wood around them. Something felt strangely familiar about the situation, as if replacing Ely with Dav would make it just another day in the forest with her mentor, hunting for boar or tracking a family of cougars. They would probably be joking about the fairies or looking for mermaid clans in the river. Dav always liked to introduce her to as many different creatures as possible. *You cannot judge another creature until you have met not one but many of them,* he would tell her. *You may find similarities in the places you least expect.* Ari had remained faithful to his words and found them to be true time and again. After all, it was the human race for which she held the greatest disdain, and she had met enough of those to permit herself to make a judgment. As for the mermaids, the nymphs, and all of the animals and magical beings, she respected them because they were a part of the world she loved.

"I live in the Parejon Hills," Ely interrupted Ari's thoughts, "in a city called Casina."

"I know where it is," she said flatly, hoping he was not about to embark on a complete retelling of his personal history.

"Have you been there?" His voice was eager, interested, and it made her sick.

"Once," she answered. The visit had been on behalf of a smuggling deal with a Parejon trader, a quick and effortless disposal of concealed goods and an easy road out. Her impression of the city was that of a smaller Principe. Not so wealthy, not so sparkling and silent, but nonetheless quite prosperous and content with its lot. The Hills, which were only hills in the shadow of the towering Belem Mountains, made navigation of troops less convenient and protected the Parejon towns from the very worst of the fighting. The war had hit, but not in the way that it had hit the villages in the rest of the Southlands and the bigger cities of the North.

"What business brought you there?" Again, the inquisitive tone made her clench her jaw in irritation.

"Vacation," Ari told him drily.

"You were stealing something."

"I don't have to answer any of your questions," she snapped.

"Do you think I'm going to tell anyone?" Ely asked her with a laugh. "I'm here on this job with you, taking something that's probably a lot bigger than whatever you stole in Casina. I'm not talking."

"I wasn't stealing anything," she responded, and it wasn't exactly a lie.

"Don't you ever think that your line of work might be a little... immoral?"

She scoffed. "Morals do not govern this world anymore."

"You don't have a problem with taking things that aren't

yours or hurting innocent people?"

"If it bothers you so much, what are you doing here?"

"Your parents –" He began, but Ari had had enough.

"My parents were innocent people, and that was back when there were laws and *morals*." She said the word with a sneer. "The people I've killed were trying to kill me first. Tell me how that's fair and we'll be getting somewhere."

The night was getting dark enough that Ely's face was no longer visible and Ari had to cease polishing her sword for fear of cutting herself. Through the stillness she could hear Ely moving around on the ground.

"Goodnight," came softly from across the little clearing.

Leaning back with her sword by her side and one hand in Jagger's fur, Ari closed her eyes and thought of the great mountains before them, a calm presence awaiting their hurried steps. It would be autumn in a few weeks and the deciduous trees would begin to turn, covering the lower slopes with a bright orange blanket. The higher altitudes would stay green, and then slowly the snow would creep down the peaks until it took the whole range and winter reigned for never-ending months. Ari loved the mountains. They were so predictable.

Maybe when she got Daerecles' money she would move into the Belem and live outside one of the mountain villages. Jagger would like that. With thoughts of a new Hole and life away from human cities, Ari fell into a restless sleep.

CHAPTER VII.

Ari awoke suddenly, heart racing and a shadow before her eyes. She sat straight up and looked rapidly around the clearing, certain there was something lurking in the dark trees. Wrapping her fingers around the blade that had fallen in her sleep, she reached out to locate her anima. The bobcat was already on his feet, body coursing with a hyper-alertness that told her she was not alone in sensing danger.

Getting to her feet, Ari turned slowly, trying to feel out the presence that haunted her uneasy mind. It was there, beyond the trees to the southeast, but she couldn't quite make out a form amidst the dark growth and violently crisscrossing limbs. She took another two steps forward, both sword and dagger held out with steady hands. Just as she reached out to probe the nearest branch with the tip of her sword, the tree parted with a rustle to reveal two bright eyes staring straight into hers.

Ari took half a step back in surprise, raising her blade to meet the pale chin that remained high with pride. The nymph did not even flinch when the cold metal pressed into her soft skin. Her eyes shone with an inexplicable light that could not have come from anywhere but within; the moon was nowhere to be seen yet it reflected in the wide, black orbs that gazed out of her smooth, white face.

"Someone must know –" she opened her thin lips and began, but each word got quieter, that sweet nymph voice quickly changing from a song to a raspy whisper.

What? Ari was about to ask, when she stopped herself. Harsh lines were spreading across the creature's skin, rapidly disfiguring her beautiful form into something tired and shriveled, unrecognizable. She was an ancient black walnut, a tree creased with the pressures of time and weather and human axes. As Ari watched, the nymph closed her big, black eyes and began to disintegrate.

First her hair came loose, then her fingers and arms and ears. Like a fallen log decaying into soft soil, the creature slowly dissolved into a million little pieces, ashes floating back down to the earth and coming to rest in a neat pile on the bare ground. Her hips crumbled away, and her legs, every little part disappearing until all Ari could see was the space where the nymph's eyes had stared out at her with that impressionable calmness.

For a moment Ari remained frozen in place, staring into the void where the nymph had vanished into earthy nothingness. She lowered her sword slowly, trying to order her frenzied thoughts. Dav had introduced her to these creatures, taught her about their ways and their strange cycle of life, but never had she actually seen one die.

They don't show any injury or affliction, nymphs. And it takes many evil strokes to end such a creature's life. Ari remembered this tale as if it were only a year ago, not wisdom imparted upon an awestruck seven-year-old. *Only when the pain is too much – when they have been wronged beyond relief, or the weight of old age has become unbearable – only then do they reveal all the wounds of time and go back to the earth. Never will you meet a purer being.*

At the time, Ari had thought this magical, peaceful. She had even dreamed of witnessing it herself, once or twice. The idea of nymphs returning to the nature from which they were born seemed wholesome and beautiful, enviable even. But what she had just seen was not beautiful or tranquil. The creature had appeared pained, suffering, far from peace. Few times had she witnessed a nymph camouflaging herself among the trees – or rather transforming to become one – but each time they had been young and healthy, bark smooth like their brilliant white skin and leaves full and green. Ari had no doubt that the wounds upon that poor being had been inflicted by human blades, likely those of the men by the campfire.

"Ari, what are you doing?"

She turned to see Ely sitting up and watching her from across the clearing. "Nothing." Realizing that she still holding the dagger in a defensive posture, she dropped her arm to her side.

"Is something wrong?" She couldn't make out his face but the tense set of his shoulders gave away his anxious confusion.

"No."

"Then why are you armed?"

"I thought there was something in the woods," Ari answered with annoyance. "There isn't."

"Okay." The boy shrugged and lay back down. "But you would tell me if there was, right?"

"Yes," she lied to shut him up. It seemed to work, because a gentle snore came from his side of the wood almost immediately. Amazing, she thought, that any being could feel so safe in such a place. Ari remained standing for another few minutes, looking and listening for any other signs out of the ordinary, or perhaps of the second nymph. Eventually she realized that none were coming, and she lowered herself to the ground.

"Here, Jagger," she whispered to her anima and he shifted to lay with his chin on her stomach. With the cat's short tail flicking back-and-forth before her eyes, she shut them and willed her racing heart to slow into sleep.

"You have fifteen minutes to find something to eat," Ari told Ely, shaking him awake, "then we're leaving."

"What's happening?" he asked groggily.

She didn't repeat herself. Although she had risen at the first sign of light, Ari had been awake for hours. In fact, she hadn't fallen back to sleep since seeing the nymph. Those eyes burned into her vision like the brand on Southland cattle, quickly fading from its original bold form into something much subtler but much more permanent.

Jagger was pacing back and forth, circling the clearing in a slow star shape that she knew was his reflection of her uneasy state of mind.

"Sit down, Jag," she hissed, a little more harshly than intended. He dropped to his haunches on the spot, a confused expression on his face.

"What's going on?" Ely asked again, now sitting up straight and watching her with a look to match the bobcat's. He was more alert but no less befuddled.

"Fourteen minutes," Ari snapped.

Yawning, the boy got to his feet and stretched his arms out, swinging them round, back-and-forth with a wiggle of his shoulders. Apparently feeling more awake after the completion of this routine, he gave her a nod and strode into the woods.

Ari looked back at Jagger, hoping to share her disgust, but he was still watching her intently. Shrugging, she strapped her blades into her belt and headed off in the opposite direction from that which Ely had gone.

The early morning here even better than in the Nyinan Forest. The trees were prettier, older, more complex. The animals were diverse and beautiful; large, furry squirrels hopped across her path and fat birds of every color and shape wheeled from the bushes in surprise as they found the silent hunter suddenly upon them. She passed tracks left by long-legged foxes and all variety of porcupines and possums. If Ari continued much further, there was no doubt that she would encounter evidence of cougars and wolves.

This was a privileged land, a forest that thrived in the

protective shadow of the mountains, carelessly enjoying the fruits of the rivers that cascaded from their peaks. Not only did the Belem protect their environs from the elements, but from the harsh, scorching wars of men. No army wanted to traverse those jagged peaks, even to access the Lanterbrun Pass. It was a fruitless effort, a waste of man- and horsepower that could do nothing but suck away time, and life. Ari had to admire the mountains for this. They were a watchful mother to the lands at their mighty feet. She could smell the freedom in the air, in the scent of the late summer leaves. It pulsed through the earth with a power that only grew stronger as the ground began to climb.

A twig snapped and Ari froze. There was an animal shifting in the undergrowth. Listening carefully for more movement, she pulled her dagger from her belt and, with the knife poised at shoulder height, crept towards the source of the noise. As she neared, a rabbit shot out of the brush, racing for shelter. It wasn't fast enough. In a flash, Ari had flicked her wrist and let the blade fly from her fingers to find home in the small creature's soft belly. The hare fell still on the spot.

She bent and scooped it up without a pause, removing the knife and grabbing its furry feet with her free hand. The little rabbit felt heavy in her fingers; it had grown plump off the rich summer forage. Her anima appeared in front of her, quieter than all the prey and predators of the forest. A black weasel hung from his powerful jaws and he was calm. Breathing deeply, Ari smiled at him. All was well. The nymph was nothing to worry about.

They jogged back to the little clearing together. Ari pulled out her hunting knife as she sat and quickly began skinning the hare, while Jagger stretched out beside her and ripped into his breakfast with deliberation. It had been several days since they had eaten a good morning meal together.

Ari's moment of peace was interrupted by Ely's less-than-stealthy return.

"You were unsuccessful," she observed.

"Well," he began somewhat sheepishly, "fifteen minutes is not much time."

Ari looked down at her own catch and then back at him. He was a useless man. "Here." She sliced the skinned rabbit in two and tossed him half. "Eat this."

"I don't need it," he protested, looking somewhat shocked to have a slimy piece of meat thrust upon him.

"Eat it," Ari repeated.

"It's raw."

"So?"

"Is it safe?" Ely was still eyeing the carcass with uncertainty.

"Jagger is eating raw meat."

"Jagger is an animal."

"And you're too superior to stoop to such a level?" she responded flatly.

"No, that's not what I meant –"

"Eat it. Now." Picking up her own half again, Ari cut off a smaller piece and took a bite. Of course, she preferred cooked meat, but when there was no time for a fire, a good catch could always be served raw. This was something else she had learned from Dav. If it was good enough for the predators of the forest, it was good enough for any huntsman. And right now, they definitely could not afford to light a campfire and wait around for their new enemies to find them.

"This isn't as bad as I thought it would be," Ely commented through bites.

Standing up and swallowing the last of her breakfast, Ari put her hand on her hip and stared up through the opening in the trees above them. Would it be too bold to assume they could make it into the coniferous forest tonight, perhaps take shelter in one of the mountain villages? If she was clever she could probably borrow a pair of horses from Itswild or Darlin. It was always a shame to steal from honorable people, but desperation often called for such measures. If the situation did present itself, she would be careful to take horses and not mountain unicorns. She had no desire to witness the wrath of the mountain men.

"Ready?" Ari asked, looking back at Ely, who was chewing the last of his rabbit with a concentrated expression. He nodded. "Jag." At her word, the bobcat took the weasel bones in his teeth and leapt to his feet, disappearing into the dark brush, only to reappear within a minute, breakfast remains gone.

"Alright," Ari breathed aloud, gathering her belongings and her thoughts, "We're heading out."

CHAPTER VIII.

It was hardly twenty minutes before Ari could feel the earth moving beneath her, building into a steady incline as they traveled on. If they could make it safely through the Lanterbrun Pass they would miss the very worst of the climb, but even the easiest route would require them to travel fairly high into the mountains.

Mountain treks had always been her favorite. In the mountains, everyone was on equal footing. The great peaks broke you, pushed you to the furthest of your mental and physical capabilities, empowered the worthy but exposed the weak. She just hoped that Ely belonged in the first category.

The air was crisp and clean, touched with that fresh morning smell of cold, and souring summer leaves. This part of the forest was preparing for autumn. As they passed, more and more wildlife awoke, beginning their daily routines of hunting, foraging, tending to their young. Jagger's ears were on full swivel, rapidly flicking side-to-side to catch every breath and footstep that caressed the quiet morning. Alternating between a rapid walk and a steady jog, Ari drove them forward, enjoying the burn in her calves and the mountain air in her lungs. Perhaps it was just his long legs, but she had to admit that Ely could keep up. She wondered what he did back in Parejon that could possibly have prepared him for the distance they were covering.

"Ari?"

She waited, knowing that he would speak whether she

wanted him to or not.

"Where exactly are we going? I mean, I don't mind following, but I like –"

"The goal is to make it into the coniferous part of the Belem Forest by sundown, if not over the ridge and into the Lanterbrun Pass."

"And from there?" His footsteps grew louder as he shifted his concentration from running to speaking.

"With luck, we make it through the valley and then over the other edge of the Belem, before crossing the Sonrein River and arriving in the Capital after three nights in the Northlands. Two, if we can acquire some horses."

Her brusque tone quieted him for a moment as he considered this. Ari did not understand why she should have to explain the plan more than once. Preparing to tell him to save the conversation for later, a movement from Jagger forced her to withhold her words. The cat flicked his short tail excitedly, ears trained forward with wary curiosity. Coming to a silent halt beside him, Ari motioned at Ely to do the same.

The great Belem trees held the earth together in an elegant pattern, deep roots twisting and reaching across the soft, grassy soil like something stitched into an ancient royal tapestry. Between these giants sprouted countless smaller trees: saplings and yearlings and those striving to reach as high as their great-grandparents. A peculiar cluster of young roots and branches blocked Ari and Ely's view of the space ahead, weaving a wall of bending limbs and sweet flowering ivy across the path.

A gentle nod was all it took to send Jagger forward, and he disappeared through the bright green brush, moving so smoothly that the plants hardly shifted against his silky frame. Ari was right behind him, pushing one of the larger branches aside and ducking under a cluster of yellow flowers. She emerged into the open space and came to an immediate halt. Before her stood a huge mountain cougar, coat washed out into a light brown from the summer sun, and ears flattened in angry anxiety.

"Dear Old Rinthorn," Ely breathed over her shoulder.

"Don't do anything to scare her," Ari whispered back. "Let Jagger see how she will respond."

The cougar hissed uncertainly as Jagger took a step towards her, his tail low and his head bowed respectfully. Flicking one ear forward, she stared him down for a moment before scrunching up her nose and lowering her head in an unsteady truce. Ari suddenly became aware that she was holding her breath, and let it out in a long, low sigh.

"I've never seen a big cat do that," said Ely quietly.

"It's because Jagger is an anima," she responded, a steady whisper. "He has a stronger connection to other living things. They respect him for that."

Before Ely could speak again, Ari held up her hand. The cougar had now turned an expectant gaze to the two humans. Stepping carefully forward, Ari knelt on one knee and offered her palm, outstretched, to the suspicious creature. In response, the cat took a soft step to meet her, reaching out with her enormous head to place a soft, wet nose in Ari's hand. Her breath was warm, searching upon Ari's skin, and the touch of whiskers sent a ticklish chill down her arm.

"I am honored to make your acquaintance," Ari told her somberly. The great cat stared back at her, deep brown eyes so wide, so profound that Ari could see her own reflection swimming in them. How small and insignificant she looked.

Now Jagger looked to Ely, who stood watching with amazement by the tangle of vines through which they had passed moments earlier. "Ely," Ari spoke when she saw that the boy was not picking up on the bobcat's signals. "It's your turn."

"What?"

"She wants to meet you."

"Um, alright." He moved uncertainly, as if in his awe, he

could not quite remember how to walk.

"Stand here." Stepping aside, Ari motioned for him to take her place before the great cat. She spoke in a soft tone, gently placing her hands on Ely's wide shoulders and pushing him down onto his knees. "Kneel and bow your head."

He did as she said, holding a hand out to the cougar, who waited patiently. As soon as he was still, she moved to meet him. Ari thought she seemed more eager, perhaps now feeling that they would not harm her. The creature pressed her muzzle into Ely's hand as she had done for Ari, her wide, intelligent face fitting perfectly into his long fingers. Ari could see a visible shudder of excitement run through his body.

"You can look up now," Ari whispered. "Tell her you are glad to meet her."

Raising his eyes, the boy smiled at the huge animal before him. "It is a pleasure to meet you." His expression was so entirely joyful that Ari almost found herself smiling too.

In his keen attitude she was reminded of her younger self, a small blonde child who had met her first wild creature on a journey through the Northlands at the age of six. She had come across a lone male wolf, still in his teenage years and searching for a pack to lead.

At this point, Ari and Jagger were about the same size, the bobcat infinitely stronger and more physically adept, and she had struggled to even approach the wolf with her anima's nervously protective presence. She remembered wandering off from the campsite, leaving her father who was preoccupied with a golden eagle message he had received moments before. With her anima, Ari had skipped through the forest, one of the small Northland woods that was now gone, burned to the earth by the fires of human war. She had found paw-prints and followed them, intrigued by the tracks that were so different from Jagger's, so narrow and sharp in the dark soil. Crossing paths with one another, they had both frozen in place, Ari and the wolf, eying each other with curiosity but not mistrust.

Her anima had stepped between them immediately, turning his body sideways to stop the girl from moving any closer to the wild beast. Annoyed, Ari had tried to push him aside, wanting desperately to approach the animal, to introduce herself and to see how his wiry hair felt beneath her tiny fingers. She and Jagger were too deeply connected for him to hold out too long, and ultimately his protective instincts had succumbed to the sense of adventure beating in their intertwined souls. Instead of blocking her path, he had led the way and bowed his silvery brown head before the young wolf. Ari remembered being so thrilled that she could hardly breathe.

Then a moment came when the wolf had nodded back and looked to the girl and, without knowing what to do, she found herself stepping forward to meet him, kneeling and extending a tentative hand towards the great silvery creature. That animal had not been as hesitant as the cougar today. He was still young, still braver and bolder than he would later learn to be. With one long-legged stride, he had approached the little blonde child and sniffed her outstretched palm, then placed his entire forehead gently into her hand.

Ari had searched her brain for the polite thing to say, gripped by the strange feeling that the wolf was waiting for her word. "I am honored to make your acquaintance," she had told him at last, her sweet voice taking on as serious a tone as she could muster. She had recalled her parents using a similar line when meeting diplomats from other cities within the kingdom.

The wolf seemed to appreciate this, and in an act that Ari had not often seen repeated, he had sat down onto his hindquarters and then dropped to his belly, allowing the little girl to stand by his side and run her fingers through his fur. Though it had looked thick and stiff, it felt as soft as Jagger's coat, silvery grey hiding a layer of deep black underneath. At his hips, the hair swirled backwards in a kind of curled tuft that Ari had found absolutely fascinating. It was there, playing with the wolf's silky cowlick that her father and his advisor had discovered her.

"Ariana," her father had whispered softly, careful to keep his tone calm and relaxed so as not to startle the beast at her side. "I would like you to come with me."

Ari believed she had jumped at his voice, so engrossed had she been in the animal before her. "Look, Papa! Jagger and I met a friend!" she told him without taking her eyes off the wolf. But he was already sitting up, already pulling away from her soft child's hands and stepping back from the tall man and his soldiers. Trusting as he may have been, there was a difference between a little girl and a band of grown men. In the blink of an eye he had vanished, leaving no trace except for the few silver hairs that clung to Ari's velvet traveling cloak.

"Goodbye!" She had waved as his fluffy tail disappeared into the wood. "Goodbye!"

"Ariana." Her father had wrapped her into his arms, breathing in the smell of her bright golden hair. "I told you not to wander off alone. It is very important that you listen to me."

"But I made a friend," she had protested.

"You're too young to be out here alone," he had answered. "You must always have an escort to keep you safe."

It was no different, really, from what her parents had said all her young life, but she could not stand to hear it. Why couldn't she do what she wanted? Why couldn't she and Jagger look out for themselves?

"And you," her father had continued, wagging a finger at Jagger, "how could you let her get this far from the camp?" He always preferred to admonish the furry cub rather than his daughter. Jagger had borne the consequences of many a broken palace treasure back in Organa.

The bobcat had just stared back at him, completely

unperturbed by this scolding. From the moment of Jagger and Ari's bonding, his heart and soul had been entirely hers. If his girl wanted to walk around the forest, then so did Jagger. If she wished to escape the palace and wander the city streets, he would be right there by her side.

The encounter with the wolf had been the first of many meetings with the wild beasts of the world. It had given her a thrill unlike anything else; her childish heart began to beat with the knowledge of this new creature, with the feeling that she now knew the wolf as she knew the neatly paved streets around their home in Organa. She had wanted little more than to roam through the forests and plains of the Northlands and search for more wolves, birds, leopards – anything she could find.

It was not long after this incident that her family had moved to Nyin, and her parents had been killed. Dav had raised her differently – protecting her, but also teaching her to explore and learn the ways of all living things. He had seen Ari and Jagger's natural connection with the creatures of the Nyinan Forest and had encouraged her to continue meeting as many animals and magical beings as she could.

"The more we know of them, the more we understand how the world works," he would say, "and the more harmoniously we live within it." It was only men who brought evil, Ari had come to understand; from the other species that walked the earth, they had nothing to fear.

"Is this your first time meeting a wild animal?" Ari now asked Ely softly, watching him as he slowly stroked the cougar's face.

"I've come across them in Parejon," he murmured, "but never like this."

"You won't forget it," Ari told him, thinking of her wolf, so many years past.

"We should get going soon." It wasn't clear whether Ely was muttering to her, to the cougar, or to himself.

"Yes," Ari agreed.

There was silence for a moment.

"Will she remember this?"

This was a question she had asked herself many times. Dav said no, that those moments were but blinks of an eye in the lives of creatures like the old cougar, who knew the world so well. One encounter did not change how they understood the universe. But Ari had to argue that it was precisely this reason that they must remember. That their great understanding of life came from countless interactions with that life itself, with every being that passed through the forest or plains or water that they inhabited. Perhaps she just didn't want to believe that she was so easily forgotten.

"I don't know," she said.

Ely was still captivated by the beast before him, and Ari knew that he hardly heard the words she spoke. "Ely," she probed, "we need to go."

"Alright." It was like speaking with someone unconscious.

"We need to go now," Ari said, a little bit more firmly. As little as she cared about the young man, it was hard to tear him away from this moment.

The great cat seemed to get the message before Ely. She was growing tenser; Ari could see how her ears were beginning to flick back and forth anxiously and her mind was already moving ten steps ahead, thinking of her departure and where the next dangers would show their angry faces. Now Ely sensed this and glanced back at Ari.

"Drop your hand and step away slowly," she advised him. It was never good to overstay such a generous welcome. He did as he was told, as careful as if the creature were about to burst into flames. With one final blink in the humans' direction, the cougar slipped away, silent and graceful even in her enormity. Ely stood frozen, staring off into the trees where she had disappeared.

"We're moving on." Now Ari had no patience for waiting

around. They had a lot of ground to cover by sunset. She turned from him and headed back onto their path, following the angle of the earth up towards the distant peak of the mountain.

Ely was quiet for the next two hours. It was clear his mind was elsewhere, back with the golden-faced cat in that little vine-walled room. Ari was thankful for this, as it allowed her to unleash her thoughts and turn everything over as the party rushed towards their destination. Uncertainty gnawed away at her troubled mind, a constant reminder that she did not have a real plan, not yet. Ari was as talented an improvisation artist as anyone, but that did not mean she enjoyed this sort of work. She liked to know where she was going, what she was doing, and how she was going to do it. As things stood, she was relying upon Ely to find Jsepa Broun's stronghold, and she would have no idea how to execute the job until she had properly scoped out the place. Right now, she had no choice but to operate one day at a time.

The ground beneath Ari's feet was becoming rougher and stray boulders began to appear among the rapidly-dwindling summer trees. The oaks, walnuts, and rhododendron gave way to the sturdy winter plants that could handle this harsher environment year-round. Pines and firs slowly and surely began to crop up among the lichen-covered rocks, and red and purple mountain flowers lifted their hardy faces to the sunlight streaming in through the deep green needles. The light danced across the bright earth in a tranquil geometry, spinning its way through the crisscross of sharp branches into soft golden triangles that shifted and dissolved upon the grey rocks and bold green grasses. The path seemed to open before them, though it was not really a path at all. The trees bent out of the way and the random stones became almost ordered as they moved onward, following a natural stairway up and up and up.

"Had you met another cougar before?" Ely's spell was broken.

"Two or three." *None so large or so beautiful as the female today*, Ari thought.

"Do they always respond to you and Jagger like that?"

"They're quite suspicious. Normally they're gone before you can get close."

They came to a stream that skipped happily across the slope, pouring down over a large boulder into a gurgling pool of crystal-clear water. Jagger paused to take a drink as Ari stepped up onto a sizable stone and jumped across.

"But other creatures are more receptive?" Ely asked, following her over the stream and landing on the other side. "You've met many?"

"The smaller cats and forest beasts are often curious," Ari said, "and the birds I can approach easily, even without Jagger."

"I feel like I have a strange kind of connection now, like I could meet any cougar and know him or her as a friend." Ely's voice was thoughtful, his tone sounding like the look he had given Ari before leaving the cougar.

"Each being that you meet enhances your understanding of their kind and of this world," Ari answered matter-of-factly. "The more you learn, the better you will live."

"How do you know so much about all of this?"

"About what?" Pausing for a moment, Ari studied a pair of prints set into the mud. The shape of the pads looked like those of a wild dog from the Southlands, but those creatures hardly ever ventured this far into the Belem Forest.

"The animals, the land, fighting and hunting..." Ely looked down over her shoulder at the tracks. "Did you have a childhood, or did you just... train?"

Only a few feet away another sort of mark began, surprisingly clear even as they continued over the firmer earth further from the stream. "These tracks are from Sonrein horses. They're bred bigger than most, and the humans there use iron instead of aluminum in their shoes." Ari knelt and examined the semicircular imprint more closely, hoping for a sign that would tell her how recently these horsemen had ridden through. It was not right for them to be in this part of the country.

Sniffing at the tracks, her anima let out a low growl. Ari felt her heart pick up. "They're still close," she breathed, laying a hand on Ely's arm to silence any speech or movement.

They were all still for a moment, slowly breathing in the hushed forest air. Even the animals and the trees were motionless, as if they, too, were awaiting what would happen next. With dagger drawn, Ari advanced once more, senses on full alert. Maybe it was just the attack from the huntsmen still pulsing through her veins, but the whole forest suddenly seemed dangerous.

The pale grey stone passed by, as did the mossy green undergrowth and the thin conifers that walled their trail. Nothing moved and nothing signaled danger, and the small party continued on. It lasted for almost forty-five minutes, this silence, reverberating about the air like the unspoken hum of rain before a storm.

"Don't you think it's safe now?" Ely finally whispered.

"Don't speak," Ari ordered in response.

She could still feel a foreign presence, Jagger's nose and ears sending nervous alerts to her heart in rapid fashion. It was enough that she herself felt uncomfortable, but if her anima sensed an enemy, there was no room for error. In Ari's caution they had slowed their pace, but even so they passed into the coniferous forest, where the only trees were hardy evergreens. The ground was a bit harder and the rocks were more diligently blanketed by lichens and mosses. All around, the grass and undergrowth became a scrubby red-green, stiff and spiky like the coat on a dirty sheepdog. The wildflowers persisted, but now different types sprouted up among those from before, the higher altitude blossoms taking over where the low altitude plants could not maintain their brilliant red and purple hues. The entrance to the Lanterbrun Pass was so, so close. If only this unwanted pack of horsemen would stay away long enough for them to make a clear escape.

"Ari, I think –"

But Jagger's reaction to the noise behind them had tipped her off and she was already spinning to face the arrows that came flying through the pines. "Take cover!" she urged Ely as the first one went to ground right by her left foot.

"They're over here, too!" he called back, diving behind a cluster of firs.

And it was true; five men had circled them, all mounted on massive chestnut horses, all bearing sturdy bows. Jumping out of the way to avoid a second shot, Ari drew her sword and stood firmly in the center. There was nowhere to hide.

"Lower your weapons and state your intent," she challenged, glaring around at them. "We have brought no harm upon you passing through this wood."

"You do the same and perhaps we might talk," one of them shot back.

"Bold words for someone so outnumbered," another muttered from behind her.

"Three to five is hardly outnumbered," Ari retorted flatly.

The men sat lightly on their mounts, maroon riding habits fitting smoothly about their thin but muscular frames and soft leather boots rising to meet their knees. These were skilled riders and warriors, not like the hunters from the night before. All but one had the blonde hair of the Sonrein men, with fair skin and bright eyes. The one outlier wore a hunting cap, but Ari could plainly see a reddish beard darkening his pale cheeks. It was he who now spoke.

"There are suspicious events happening in this part of the country. We have been sent to investigate and report anything that we find unusual or threatening."

"And what is so unusual about a small band of travelers?" Ari argued.

"We are hardly threatening," Ely added, finally stepping forward to join Ari and Jagger.

The redhead raised an eyebrow at Ari, with her sword drawn and Jagger poised to strike. Several of the other men laughed.

"Allow us to go on our way and we will not cause any trouble," Ari demanded, praying that they did not get into a second scuffle in less than twenty-four hours.

"They seem pretty unusual to me," the man behind her said.

"And very threatening," a second added.

"Yes, I believe we shall take them back to camp, gentlemen." Redbeard gave a nod and the five horsemen nudged their steeds forward, closing in on the three travelers.

"This is purely a formality," he told Ari casually, "so please cooperate."

"Ely," her voice was low and urgent, "now would be a good time to see how you work under stress."

"I'm not –"

"Do you want me to kill them all or do you want to do something about this?"

"On the count of –"

"Now!" Ari and Jagger lunged forward in one motion, the girl swinging her sword up to slice through the waiting bow of the rider on her right. The bobcat went for the legs of a second man, leaping and digging his claws into the shiny brown leather. Before the man could react, Ari had cut his bow with her blade and was throwing herself behind the nearest horse to avoid an arrow aimed at her head.

"Ely!" As far as she could tell, he still hadn't moved. Jagger threw himself upon Redbeard as his stallion came thundering towards Ari. The man cried out and pulled his bow but Ari's knife found home in his shoulder before he could set the arrow on Jagger.

Another horseman was approaching from behind, bearing down on her with bow taut. Suddenly, there was a burst of light and a high-pitched whistle and the horse reared – so forcefully that his unprepared rider fell to the ground, bow still in hand. All around them, the beasts were rearing in terror and one more rider dropped. Turning, Ari saw Ely standing where she had left him, hands outstretched with a blaze of fire floating above them. It was unclear where the sound was coming from, but it was working.

"Hold that for one minute longer!" Ari shouted over the shrill noise, scooping her dagger from the ground where Redbeard had dropped it. With the knife back in her belt, Ari grasped the reins of the nearest loose horse and leapt into the saddle. "Grab the other one!"

The sound dissipated immediately and she urged the horse onward. There was no time to wonder what kind of horseman Ely was; she could only hope that being from Parejon he was a good one. Hearing only one set of hoof beats behind her, Ari turned quickly in the saddle to look. It was Ely.

The huge chestnut shifted uneasily beneath her, anxious after the skirmish and unsure about his new rider. "Good boy," she cooed, and watched his ears flick back to her voice, felt his muscles slowly relax into a more comfortable rhythm. She let her hands slide up and down on his neck, giving him the rein to stretch out and extend his already-lengthy stride. They needed to put some distance between them and the Sonrein men before leaving the horses. Their tracks were so visible that they would be easily followed as long as they were mounted.

"What about Jagger?" Ely pulled up beside her, standing effortlessly in the stirrups as his mount galloped beneath him. He was clearly an experienced rider.

"Jag can track us. As soon as we lose the horses, he'll catch up."

"You never answered my question," Ely went on, voice raised over the heavy sound of hoof beats. "Did you ever get to be a child?"

"You're going to run into a tree if you don't pay attention," Ari responded, steering her own steed around a cluster of bushes with some pressure from her right calf.

"Is there anything you're not good at?" Ely avoided a pile of boulders and then jumped a small log without interrupting the stream of questions.

"Many children have grown up too quickly amongst the destruction and violence of the war."

"There is growing up too quickly and there is skipping childhood. I had a half a childhood, at least," Ely protested. "And my mother has been in hiding for most of my life."

"You live in Parejon," Ari responded flatly.

"Do you think that the war has not affected us? People have died, disappeared, gone into hiding. Our tradesmen cannot barter outside of the Hills because it isn't safe and the armies have destroyed so much. Four years in a row we had no wheat or corn crop and countless families nearly starved to death. The Malavi demand our livestock, our horses, and we must give them over."

"I did not say that it hadn't affected you." Her tone was even, emotionless. "But you cannot pretend that Parejon has experienced the same consequences as the Sonrein Plains, the southern coast, or any of the smaller villages scattered across the Southlands."

"My point is that every part –"

Ari had let him go on, hoping he would wear out and end the conversation, but she could not listen any longer. "I don't need a lecture," she snapped. "I am perfectly aware of what the war has done."

Unperturbed, Ely flashed her a smile as if she had just complimented him on his riding. "I know you are."

Ari pushed her mount forward with a hard dig of her

heels, guiding him ahead so that she passed Ely and opened up a few lengths between them. Cool air rushing into her lungs, she breathed deeply and the rhythm filled her chest. *One, two, three. One, two, three.* The stocky chestnut beat such a balanced tempo that Ari felt it could almost put her to sleep, if she were not thinking of pursuers and dragith stones.

Up ahead she saw the trees thinning to nothing, ceasing to plant their roots and stretch their branches just a few hundred yards before the crest of the hill. They had come clear east of the Lanterbrun Pass. It was time to leave the horses and continue on foot.

Ari raised her right arm in a signal to halt and brought her stallion down to a trot and then a walk. "We let them go here." It did seem a shame to lose such fine horses and tack, but mountain men would not look well upon stolen animals.

"I thought you didn't like spending so much time out in the open?" Ely looked towards the empty mountain, a suspicious expression dancing in his eyes. "The horses will get us through faster."

Already dropping to the ground, Ari quickly began removing the saddle from her steed's broad back. "We won't be in the open for long. Itswild is just over that hill."

"Can the mountain men really be trusted?" Ely followed her lead and slid down from his horse, unhooking the girth in one smooth motion.

If she had been in a better mood she might have laughed. "They're more dependable than any other people."

"They hate foreigners," Ely protested, pausing with his hand on the stallion's crownpiece to look at her in bewilderment.

"They dislike those who do not share their values," Ari corrected. "Let's go."

She smacked the horse on the rump and watched it trot off through the trees, veering northwest until it had disappeared over the far ridge. Ely's mount followed, eager to keep up with its companion, and soon they had both vanished with little trace but the hoof prints in the brown earth. The saddles Ari took and dropped into a divot in the land, a ditch that must have once been a small brook, now dried by the summer sun.

"Where did you learn all of it, really?" Ely trailed behind her. "Who taught you?"

Dragging a dead branch over to the hole, Ari hefted it onto the pile of tack, the shriveled leaves forming a secretive blanket over the evidence of their presence. "A good man."

"Did he also teach you Rinthorn's Rummy and tell you bedtime stories? Or did he skip that part?"

"He taught me that folly does not dull pain. Work does. Training. When the world goes up in smoke, we do best to channel our anger into productive outlets."

Ely grabbed several more branches and scooped up a pile of mountain flowers to drape over the little mound. "Sword fighting. Throwing. Tracking."

Ari gave their handiwork one last glance. It would have to do. "Sure, if you want."

Above them, the tough red grass gleamed in the bright afternoon sun, so near and so bold beneath the circle of great peaks that loomed all around. That mountain seemed only a small hill, a tiny part of the larger formation that stretched up to touch the sky with its stony fingers. As far as they had come, the mountaintops remained distant, frozen into the heavens by icy white snow and encircled with perpetual cloud. To Ari's eye they were absolutely still, but she knew that those quiet glaciers were at that very moment giving way to torrential waterfalls that tumbled down the slopes of the mountain in a monumental roar. It was fascinating how something so silent could be so powerful.

Chapter IX.

Jagger rejoined Ari and Ely not long after they buried the saddles and together they walked quickly up the grassy, treeless slope. Other than the thin, worn path that ran along and then over the ridge before them, there was no evidence that they had entered mountain man territory. Ari admired how the entire village lay hidden in plain sight. She worked hard to cover her tracks. These people did it effortlessly.

The Belem had operated as a semi-autonomous region even before the war and neither army – the Malavi nor the Zaerans – had dared to attack the mountain villages since. It was not worth the time and resources to climb to those heights only to be defeated by skilled warriors trained to fight in the mountain terrain. And the mountain men never ventured far. There was little point in battling them when they had made no efforts to oppose the civil war waging outside their protected realm.

As Ari, Ely, and Jagger passed over the hill where the path dropped off, the entire village came into view. Scattered across the next three rolling peaks, Itswild was high enough to remain nearly untouched by outsiders but low enough that it missed the worst of the mountain weather. It crept up and down the sides of the gentle valley, settled and silent, blending into the mountain. The tiny wooden dwellings were constructed with a dark-as-night and hard-as-rock black walnut, hauled up from the base of the Belem decades earlier. Stacks of thin rock served as stilts, piled between the wooden bases and the earth to protect the people from heavy winter snowfalls. The roofs were made of thatched straw, sticks, and reedy stalks, and secured over the humble homes with more stone, or thick wooden beams.

Looking out over the little community, Ari could see where their path split and wound its way through the structures, connecting houses with the occasional barn or store cellar in a practiced, deliberate manner. In between the buildings, the summer grass had grown long and rough. It was a tall, reddish kind of scrub that alternated between lanky sprouts and short, scrappy tufts of sharp brown buds. Ari watched several figures moving about. A group of young girls carried baskets down one hill while a small boy flew after them, calling out something inaudible. Several men walked through the center of the village with bows and axes in hand; they appeared to be preparing for a hunt. Off to the east, a woman rode a black mountain unicorn up the far hill towards a lonely cabin.

"Is that...?" Ely began, eyes on the same figure.

"They're known for their black unicorns," Ari confirmed. "They breed them like any other people would breed horses or white unicorns. Prized beyond anything else."

"I didn't know it was true," he said, tone hushed.

"They say that the dark ones are stealthier, less proud, easier to manage. I've never ridden one, but I'm sure it's true." She watched the woman and her unicorn disappear behind the little hut. "The mountain men are too smart to waste their time on any beast as ridiculous as a white unicorn."

"You don't approve of many creatures in our world," Ely noted, a smile in his voice.

Ari turned to look him in the eye for a moment. "You don't know me very well."

The smile did not disappear, but his eyes grew more serious and he gave her a nod. "Shall we?"

Turning back again, she was surprised to see that they were no longer alone. While they were talking, four creatures had approached through the infrequent pines, making their way towards the travelers. Jagger stepped cautiously in front of his girl, ears fixed on the young man and the three black unicorns that trotted easily up the steep slope.

The man rode the beast in the middle, a tall and muscular creature with a pretty head and a curved nose. Her horn was a smooth silver that caught the late afternoon sun in a subtle glimmer. On each side was tied another black unicorn, both slightly smaller, less muscular. Ari guessed that they were only two or three years old, probably still in training. The one on the left had a coarser head and a stocky build, but the other was particularly pretty, with finer features and tiny, chiseled ears that were trained on the foreigners with great interest. Her coat was a powerful black, so bright in its darkness that Ari could not help but wonder if the rider hadn't rubbed oil on it before taking her out.

"That is a fine filly," she called out as they grew nearer. "And she looks clever."

"As clever as they come," answered the rider, who – now that he was within easy speaking distance – looked to be only about twenty-five years old, with the same dark hair and dark complexion of all the mountain men. He had deep brown eyes, and an early beard covered his strong jaw. From the young man's seat alone Ari could easily observe his mastery of horsemanship, as well as his distrust of the strangers.

"We are not here to discuss unicorns." She cut right to the situation at hand. "We would like food and a place to stay the night. We can pay."

The young man nodded, giving his mount a short check on the reins as the animal lifted a hoof to move nearer Ari's anima. "Are you being followed?"

"No," she answered honestly.

"Just for one night?"

"Yes."

"Come with me." Without waiting to see that they would,

he turned the three unicorns in one even rotation and headed down the hill.

Ari started after him, with Jagger by her side and Ely bringing up the rear. Hurrying to keep up with the powerful animals, they strode quickly into the village, passing four or five houses and a two-unicorn barn before they came to a stop outside a medium-sized home with a narrow stone stair leading to the door. The young man swung his leg over his mount and slid down between her and the pretty filly, tying the mare's lead to a hitching post by the wall. The other two unicorns seemed content to stand by her side.

"Wait here," he told Ari, and leapt up the steps, disappearing inside.

Silence settled around them once more as they stood outside the cabin. A general quietness pervaded the very step and breath of the people that passed, and, though the village was busy, it felt still.

They had waited for a minute when Ari could feel the questions coming. "Don't speak until I'm done here," she cut Ely off before he could begin, "and *don't* touch the unicorns." Turning, she found him with a hand outstretched, inches from the filly's soft neck.

"How did –"

"Stand still and be quiet," she ordered. He stepped away from the animals.

At that moment, the door swung open and an older man emerged, followed closely by the first man, who Ari could only guess was his son. They shared the same dark, handsome features, serious faces with wise, searching eyes. The often-told story was that mountain men trusted no one and cared for little but their own survival. Ari believed this, but she had seen traces of an inquisitiveness in their speech and expression that betrayed a deeper interest in the outside world than they often let on.

"Samorin tells me that you wish to be provided with food

and lodging for one night." The older mountain man eyed Ari carefully, sizing her up without shame. He fingered the hilt of a long knife, fastened into his belt and lashed three times around with wide straps of calf leather.

"He does not lie," Ari answered, meeting his eye confidently.

"And you are running from enemies?" Over the man's shoulder, his son was also watching Ari closely. She could feel his gaze even as she maintained eye contact with the older villager.

"No."

"Why should I take your word?"

"If I were running, I would not count on others to keep me hidden."

At this, he paused for a moment, then dropped his hand from his dagger and made a motion to Samorin, who turned and slipped away around the back of the house. A slight smile seemed to dance in the man's eyes as he spoke. "Have we made acquaintance in the past?"

A memory of riding into Itswild with Dav flashed before her. Young Ari sitting so keenly upon her spry little gelding, watching her mentor barter with the mountain men for various furs and goods, exchanging talk about black unicorns and winter weather. Listening to the stealthy silence of the village life, admiring the beauty of the mountains in the fall.

"I do not believe we have." It was another lifetime.

"Does your companion speak?"

"Only when absolutely necessary."

This elicited another half-smile and a short nod. "Samorin will show you to your lodgings."

Upon his father's word, the son appeared again, a small cloth sack in hand. "This way."

They walked a minute along the same worn path through what could best be called the center of town. The houses were a bit closer together, a bit older. Along the top beam of each home, just under the thatched roof, were carefully carved messages, phrases in the ancient mountain tongue that spoke to locals and travelers alike of tradition and honor. Various mountain men stood outside or walked between the modest dwellings, boys carrying logs and buckets of water, women leading black unicorns around the small stables, old men talking quietly by an empty hitching post. Some of them looked up and watched the small party as they passed through, but most betrayed no sign of recognition or interest.

Glancing back to be sure they were still following, Samorin turned off to the left, taking a path that wound out of the busier part of the village and towards a somewhat secluded cabin. There were fewer houses on this side of the town, which was built upon a steeper hill than the rest of Itswild. Together, they approached a tiny cabin with a stone roof. Its stilts were tilted shakily upon the uneven ground and the black walnut lumber appeared worn and weathered. Samorin stepped to the front stair and pushed open the narrow wooden door, motioning for Ari to come inside.

"This will do for the night," he told her. "And here is a bit of bedding to make it more comfortable."

"It is sufficient," Ari agreed. "Thank you."

The cabin was small, but there was a sturdy wooden table in the center and two low beds pushed against the far wall. By the door sat an empty bucket and a coil of rope. The afternoon light streamed in from the lone window on the western side, throwing convoluted rays across the smooth, wood-paneled floor. Flicking his tail thoughtfully, Jagger slid between her legs and entered the house, turning a quick circle around the room with his ears and nose working furiously to assess the temporary quarters. Satisfied, he blinked at Ari and came to a halt by her side.

"Your anima is not very trusting," Samorin noted. Animan were not tradition in the mountain villages, and he was watching the bobcat with an intent expression, as if he could

ALLYSON S. BARKLEY

read his mind by looking closely enough.

"Neither am I," Ari returned.

Shifting his gaze back to her, the young man met her eye for a long moment. "Trust is a fickle force. They say that, here in the mountains, we are cold because we are born without it. I'm not sure that it isn't worse to be born with it and lose it along the way."

"Perhaps you are right," she responded evenly, "but survival in these times rarely lends us such a generous choice as to keep it near our hearts."

There was something of interest in the young man's eye now, something more than suspicion or concern. His aspect softened, became bolder. "If you would like, you may come to supper at sundown in the Eating House."

Ari only nodded in response, slipping her sack from her shoulder and setting it down onto the wooden floorboards of the tiny cabin. Without another word, Samorin stepped through the entry and sprang down the steps.

"Am I allowed inside now?" Ely asked as soon as the mountain man had skirted by him and hurried off up the path.

Motioning briskly for him to cross the threshold, Ari sat onto the nearest bed. It had been months since she had slept on a mattress.

"How do you feel about becoming a mountain woman?"

She tossed him one of the spare blankets.

"He fancies you," Ely continued, "Samorin. You've caught his eye."

"Nonsense."

"It is not. Any clear-thinking man would tell you the same."

"Not only is that false, but it has nothing to do with our job." Ari spread her own blanket neatly across the bed. "Keep your ridiculous ideas to yourself."

Ari shook Ely awake two hours later. The sun had just

114

disappeared behind the nearest Belem peak and through their lone window she could see a pale evening settling over the land. Ely had fallen asleep almost immediately, but she had sat wide-awake upon her bed, thinking and cleaning her blades with Jagger by her side.

"You must polish those every day," Ely observed as he sat up to see the sword and knives lying across the old blanket.

Slipping them one-by-one back into her belt and boots, Ari ignored him. "I'm going down to the Eating House. Come along if you're hungry."

He swung his legs over the edge of the bed and bent to lace up his boots. For a moment, Ari stood and watched his long fingers as they fiddled with the string and tied it into a swift knot. She thought about how several hours earlier those same hands had conjured fire out of thin air. The world was a strange place.

Seeing that Ely was ready, she turned on her heel and strode out of the house, stomach eager for a well-cooked meal. Her anima's nose twitched in anticipation as he fell into step alongside her, bright golden eyes gazing upon the little village with cautious interest. All around them, people were leaving their homes and heading towards the center of Itswild.

"Watch carefully," Ari whispered to Ely. "It is a privilege to witness a supper in the Eating House of a mountain village."

He looked at her with new interest. "What do they do?"

"This meal is the time when the whole clan comes together. They come to eat, of course, but also to discuss matters of their people, to share stories – on occasion, they hold contests and games." She paused for a minute, thinking of how Dav had loved to tell the stories collected from his visits to the mountain villages. "I was allowed to take part once, when I was young."

"You supped in Itswild?" he asked in surprise.

"Yes," Ari answered. "Many years ago."

They were approaching the core of the village now, and

more mountain men had appeared on all sides, filling the narrow paths and casting numerous glances in the foreigners' direction. Ari fell silent, wishing to keep a low profile. They would attract enough attention as it was.

Low, dark, and perfectly circular, the Eating House lay just before them, a large round building constructed from heavy black walnut pillars and sturdy panels stretched in between. The roof was nearly flat, hardly more than a gentle slope up to a raised hole in the woven thatching. Dav had told her once that they replaced it every year, that three workers labored continuously throughout the summer so that a tight blanket of vines and rushes could be laid over the hall by wintertime.

The entryway was similar to the doors of the old homes in the center, though much wider and several feet taller. Ancient script made its way across the top of the frame and wound down the right side. On the left, there were faded images: an army of men, a unicorn, and a man and a woman standing with arms outstretched to the noble creature. Only the unicorn remained bright, the charcoal black of its smooth coat glistening as if the paint were fresh that day.

Ari, Ely, and Jagger were ushered in with the crowd of mountain men, pushed gently yet deliberately through the door by the patient hordes. The ceiling hung higher than might have been expected from the outside, and the bold flame in the center of the room made the dimness on the edges of the Eating House feel like a darkness that Ari found comforting. Stationed around the fire were vats of fresh, warm food, already being served and shared by countless villagers. Those who had received their food were dispersed about the hall, standing in the light or taking shelter in the shadows, sitting on one of several long, curved benches or carving out a space on the soft dirt floor.

It was to the dark back of the room that Ari headed, Jagger at her heels and Ely following closely behind. As she prepared to sit, she felt a pressure on her elbow.

"Compliments of the Elders." Samorin held out a bowl of stew, hot steam rising in slow wisps to evaporate in the air between them.

Ari met his dark eyes with a nod. "Thank you."

Pulling a package from his belt, the young man glanced down at the great cat standing between their feet. "For your anima." He slipped the brown paper off and offered Jagger a large piece of meat.

The bobcat sniffed at it in hesitation. "It's alright, Jag," Ari told him, and he accepted it gently in his powerful jaws.

Seeing that his gift had been well received, Samorin took leave of the group and returned to the center of the Eating House. Ari sat and watched him walk over to a party of young men who stood just right of the fire. All wore similar tunics and breeches, with fine, worn riding boots, and they spoke with a familiar sort of stance, as if they had known each other for many years. Two of them had long swords strapped to their belts; one had a quiver slung over his shoulder, though there was no bow to be seen. A fourth was smiling at the man next to him, a cup of something in one hand. Several of them glanced across the hall to Ari when Samorin arrived, but they continued talking and eating without pause.

To the left of the young men was a group of five older villagers, three women and two men, who sat upon painted stools with bowls of food in their hands and serious expressions upon their faces. Halfway hidden behind the fire pit, the orange and yellow flames leaping up and down in a dark dance, their countenances seemed to reflect back the light that flashed into their eyes. In the flickering darkness, Ari could see every line and wrinkle, yet they were beautiful in their wisdom. They were the Itswild Elders, the council that led the people in all matters of life. These were the masters of farming, of the mountain unicorns, of building, of trade, of war. It was at the nightly suppers that they made most of their important decisions.

As Ari looked on, a young woman approached the Elder on the left, knelt before him, and spoke into his ear, motioning anxiously with her hands. The old man, his remaining hair snow white against his tanned skin and his once strong fingers now knotted with age, nodded slowly as the villager went on, then placed a gentle hand on her arm. With what seemed to be no more than three or four words, he sent her on her way, a relieved smile upon her face. As soon as she had gone, three men approached the Elder. Before they could speak a word, he pointed to the ancient woman on his right and they knelt before her. Ari watched them explain, one after another, their problem, and saw the Elder consider and then answer with steady surety. Just like the young woman before them, this small group stood and left, satisfied.

This process was repeated many times over, mountain men coming one after the next to tell the Elders their troubles and solicit advice. Sometimes it seemed that they were making decisions, and in these cases, the Elders often turned to their fellow councilmen to confer, but most frequently it appeared to Ari that the men and women simply wanted guidance, reassurance, a dose of the wisdom of their people.

"Are their leaders elected?" Ely's voice came low over her shoulder.

She turned to look at him for a moment. His eyes were glued to the scene by the fire. "I believe they are selected by the previous Elders, before they step down. Then the town must agree to their appointment."

As she spoke, the atmosphere in the Eating House was changing. The steady babble of voices shifted into an excited buzz and people began to move about, adjusting to make space in the middle of the room. The curved benches were pushed back so that they formed a neat circle and the food was whisked away without a word. A small girl stepped into the center, dragging a wooden tripod anchored by a stone base. It made an absentminded line in the dirt as she stumbled across to the far side of the hall, finally stopping with a sigh before a plain wall riddled with pockmarks. With a start, Ari realized what they were about to do.

"Target practice." There was a smile in Ely's voice.

Only one small X marked the narrow wooden post; there was no space for error. "It's brilliant," Ari whispered.

"He's coming over here."

"What?" Her heart seemed to give a small, involuntary jump.

"Samorin is coming to speak with you," Ely said. "I'd bet a mountain unicorn that he will ask you to sit up front."

Sure enough, the mountain man was making his way to them, weaving in and out of the people and shadows to reach the other side of the Eating House. The flickering firelight danced across his face, tracing over his thoughtful eyes and solemn mouth.

At last, Samorin arrived before them and held out a hand towards Ari. "You have a seat with us, if you would accept it." His tone was formal as before, but there was a hint of curiosity, of hanging onto the silence in expectation of her answer.

Ari stood from their bench and he smiled, then turned and made his way back across the room. Trailing after him through the throngs of villagers, Ari had almost reached the front row when she paused and looked back. Ely had not moved from his spot by the wall. She motioned for him to follow, raising her eyebrows in question. Looking resigned, he got up and strolled, as she was beginning to believe only Ely could, across to them.

"We're their guests," Ari hissed at him as they sat between Samorin and the young man with the quiver. "We do what they ask of us."

"So far, they've only asked anything of you," he responded.

"Maybe you should try harder."

"Try harder?" Even at a whisper she could hear the

laughter in his voice. "In any other company, my social etiquette would be far superior to yours. But for some reason, they seem to feel more comfortable with your reticence and reserve. I am fairly certain that if it weren't for you, I would have been shot or driven out before I could speak a word to them."

Ari shrugged. "Maybe."

"And that is exactly why you fit right in here," he said with a good-natured sigh and slow smile breaking across his boyish face. Rather than respond, Ari turned to Samorin, who was watching them with interest.

"Is it a contest?"

"Shooting, and then throwing," he answered, his voice low and smooth.

"What does the winner receive?"

He shook his head. "Honor."

Ari gave a small smile and shifted around to watch. There was no announcement to mark the beginning of the competition, yet suddenly a woman was standing opposite the target, many yards to the other end of the Eating House, and the trial had begun. She shot and missed near right, then the boy on Ely's left, now holding a bow, shot far left, and another man aimed too high. One by one the competitors aimed and released, sending the arrows in a star-like spray around the skinny post. Finally, one older woman hit her mark, then a man struck just by her shaft. There was an audible noise of support and approval each time that these two stepped up and sent their arrows home, the pair of them exchanging three rounds before the woman missed left. She nodded respectfully to the man and went to sit in the second row of benches. With hardly any indication of pride or feeling, the winner turned one slow circle to kneel before the Elders. The Elder in the center stood, knobby knees cracking in the now-hushed silence, and held out her hand to the man. At this motion he came to his feet once more, lifted his bow to his shoulder, and disappeared into the crowd.

"Will you place a bet on my knife?" Samorin spoke over the voices that had suddenly sprung back into the hall as this first game finished.

"I prefer not to wager upon anything until I can count its worth proven."

"She makes a fair point," one of his sword-wielding friends commented, stopping before their bench on his way to line up for the contest. "I would not bet on any of us without a trial."

"The men and women of Itswild are noble fighters and marksmen," another put in evenly. "Any fool will have heard of our skills with knife and arrow from the back of a mountain unicorn."

"But tonight, you do not shoot from the back of an animal," Ari answered flatly. "You shoot from the solid, still earth beneath our feet, at a target which will not move no matter how hard you may wish it."

"That only makes the job simpler," the young man replied, his dark eyes gazing keenly at her.

"For some," Ari said.

At this, the conversation was over, and the young men moved along to take their turns in the competition. Now Ari watched even more closely, eager to see how they displayed their skills with a dagger. Archery was a fickle art that she had practiced enough to feel sufficiently competent, and then promptly abandoned. She had never understood the utility of a weapon that could be exhausted so quickly.

But blades were different. Though sword fighting was Ari's great love, she considered anything that shone and spun through the air to be worth study. The most unexpected being could often be the greatest swordsman, Dav used to tell her. There was a nobility in confronting your enemy face-to-face, in being forced to duel for the right to continue onward, the right to return for one more block or parry. There was a nobility in fighting with a blade, and a thrill.

The gentle hum of voices continued as various villagers attempted their shot at the target and the crowd of those waiting to try became thinner and thinner. Only two had hit it, and one knife was just barely holding on to the corner of the post. Now Samorin stepped up, face set into a serious expression, his eyes locked upon the tripod and his jaw grimly set. Planting his feet carefully, the young man bent his arm back, cocked his wrist, and released his knife in a smooth motion. It sailed over the top of the post, clipping the edge and sending the blade clattering into the wall and down to the ground.

Ari gave him a nod when he had retrieved the weapon and returned to his seat. "Try holding on a split second longer."

His eyes narrowed for a moment and then he looked thoughtful. "You take a turn."

She opened her mouth to protest but received an elbow in the side from Ely.

"We do what they ask of us," he told her with a smile.

Breathing deeply, Ari stood and glanced over to the Elders. They were all watching her. The woman in the center held a hand palm up toward the shooting point, as if waiting for Ari to take her place. There were only four mountain men left and none of them hit the target. After dozens of attempts, only three remained lodged into the ancient wood.

The noises of the Eating House shifted once more and the hum became a nervous sort of rumble, the sound of anticipation, of three hundred questions fighting for air to breathe. The buzz continued as Ari stepped up to the line drawn in the dirt, as she slipped the silver dagger from her belt, and as she drew her arm back and then flicked it forward without more than a glance at the narrow target. The whispers only stopped – extinguished with such a silence that one could almost forget there had ever been noise – when Ari's whirring blade dug itself handle-deep into the very center of the target.

The thud of the silver knife seemed to reverberate over the hushed crowd. Trying not to visibly clench her jaw, Ari focused on the curved handle that pointed at her from across the hall. She hated this kind of quiet more than she hated incessant babbling. Jagger shifted from where he sat under Ari's seat, unsure whether he should stay put or move to shelter his girl. With a subtle flick of her finger, she urged him to remain.

The stillness went on for what felt like many minutes, though Ari knew it was mere seconds. Then a voice came from the doorway behind her.

"Throw another one."

She turned slowly to observe the speaker. It was Samorin's father, standing by the entry with his hand on his own knife and a serious expression in his dark eyes. "Throw another one," he said again.

So, Ari pulled the bronze-handled dagger from her boot and faced the target once more. The flat blade found home just left of the first shot. Without waiting for another word, she took her hunting knife from the other boot and let it fly into place on the other side of the silver dagger. The three blades stared back at her in a neat little row, still as the mass of mountain men who watched her with mounting interest.

"I believe we have a winner," Samorin's father said, low voice carrying through the quiet room, "as long as the Elders concur."

"Come, child." The woman in the middle spoke in a way that beckoned Ari forward, pulling her from her place before the target. The Elder held a hand to her, reaching out in expectation of a response. Knowing she had no choice, Ari stepped closer and placed her fingers over those of the ancient leader.

"Sit here."

She complied, perching upon a stool that someone had drawn up as the Elder spoke. The silence was breaking up into respectful chatter that grew slowly louder as the formation of the hall shifted once again to remove the shooting range and fill the space left in the middle. For the first time since the silver dagger had left her fingers, Ari allowed herself to look around the room.

The older mountain men remained seated, but children and young adults sat around the fire or stood at the back of the hall, facing toward the center in patient anticipation. The youngest girls and boys waited in great excitement, eyes lit by dancing flames and youthful reverence. Men and women like Samorin's father conversed calmly throughout the Eating House, clearly expecting the start of something, but lacking the eager focus of their children and grandchildren.

Though they all appeared occupied, many villagers continued to look Ari's way while they spoke and moved about. As she let her eyes roam the scene, the young woman felt a presence approach from behind.

"I believe you were missing these."

"Thank you," Ari answered Samorin shortly, taking the three knives and sliding them back in her belt and boots.

He sat on the ground by her left hip. "That was impressive."

She made no response and he did not elaborate. Slinking quietly through the crowd, Jagger came to sit by her feet. Ari could feel his anxiety about the mass of people and the concentrated attention. They both breathed a sigh of relief as his warm hip pressed against her calf.

"In the year of the First Winter, our people were suffering," a voice began, worn – but not tired – with age. Ari glanced around in search of its owner. "The wolves came, the harvests disappeared, and then, there were the wars from the East."

Some of the talking continued, but this was confined to the far corners of the Eating House and most of the mountain men turned quietly to look upon a hunched little man, hair silvery with years, who spoke with his eyes gazing down into memory. "The wars brought thousands of soldiers. On foot they came, and on horseback from the Zrignigh Range, with their flaming arrows and poison blades. Even as our people banded together and fought to repel the attacks, we were falling, one-by-one, to the terror of the eastern threat."

The young children were entranced, eyes stretched wide as he continued on. "The Elders conferred for days, but amidst the fighting and the starving and the chaos, they failed to find a solution that would see our people through to the other side. Hope was fading when one man, Gramm, son of Hauwil and father of Liliaja, went high into the Belem and roped a wild Pegasus." At this, there was an audible breath from the cluster of boys and girls on the floor. "In the dead of night, he rode the creature of our mountain skies, carrying nothing but a single candle to light his way. This candle was lit with the fire of our people, which Gramm had taken from the Eating House for his journey up the mountain. It was a magical fire, visible only to the honorable mountain men, who now saw their world illuminated by a light so pure that they nearly fell to the earth in awe.

"But Gramm called for them to stand and fight, to drive away the enemy under cover of a darkness which oppressed all but themselves. So, from all sides, they wailed upon the Zrignigh soldiers, recovering the territory they had lost until, at last, this evil presence had no choice but to retreat and leave the village to peace." Here the storyteller took a deep breath, almost like a sigh of grief. "The people were shouting with joy, so relieved to be rid of the battle, so grateful to Gramm for his great deed. But, although the flame was magical, the candle was not – and as he flew, it grew slowly smaller until it was gone. When it finally extinguished, the land and the sky fell once more into darkness and that brave man was unable to navigate his way home. The Pegasus, shy as the creatures are, became afraid and threw Gramm from its back. Though the people searched for weeks, they never found his body.

"Today, we use his star to guide us home," the ancient little man concluded quietly. "Brighter than any other light in the sky, it reminds us of the sacrifice that one must make to lead as a hero, to hold aloft a flame that might save all, but will ultimately drop the bearer into darkness. No fire can survive forever and one day even the greatest, especially the greatest, must be extinguished."

Ari slipped out of the Eating House as the storyteller began his third tale, an account about a renowned black unicorn healer and a stallion that could run faster than an arrow could fly. She stood outside the round building for a moment, breathing in the cool summer night air. There was a chill over the mountain that spoke of an early autumn, reaching up into the peaks before it touched the low earth of the valley. It felt good to be alone, even briefly. Jagger trotted about the empty village center, sniffing at the beaten dirt path and swiveling his tufted ears back-and-forth with the sounds of the night.

"You put on quite the show in there," Ely said, coming out of the hall to stand by her side. "I think they'll probably give you a star, too."

"I would have to die first," she returned flatly.

The moon was so big and round up here, but the mountains somehow made it look even further away than it had appeared from the plains.

"It's an interesting thought, that candle. Providing life to others at the cost of your own existence."

"Or it's just a candle."

"I suppose you don't believe in Pegasi either." Ely looked away from the moon to study Ari's profile. She did not meet his eye.

"They lived in these mountains once, and in the Zrignigh Range above the lake. But that was hundreds of years ago. No one has seen any sign of them for centuries." Now she turned to face him. "The Pegasi are gone."

Another figure exited the hall to join them and Ari motioned at him. "Samorin will tell you the same," she said to Ely. "As much as the mountain men love to talk of the Pegasi, they know there is no chance they will return to roam this earth."

"It is dangerous to believe in something that cannot be seen," Samorin spoke softly. "You cannot trust a being that is nothing but a legend."

"So, there is no one here who still believes they are up there somewhere?" Ely asked, gesturing with his hand up towards the nearest peak.

"Children," the Itswild man answered, "and those blinded to the present because they are consumed by the past."

Ely made no response but Ari could see him purse his lips in the dark. "We must go back and sleep," she said to Samorin. "Tomorrow is an early morning."

"I will walk with you," he responded. "They are not speaking of anything that I have not heard many times."

"May I ask what they now discuss?" Ari inquired as the four of them began to make their way toward the little cabin.

"The war. The movements of the Former Military and the Rebels. The destruction of the crops and the trade in the Sonrein Plains."

"The mountain men have not been involved in a war for two hundred years."

"And they will not be involved in this one," he replied, "but that does not mean we should not be aware of how it will affect our people."

"You are all capable soldiers," Ely protested. "Combined, the mountain villages could create an enormous impact on the movement of the battle. Why not fight?"

"For whom would you say we fight?" Samorin's tone was almost disdainful. "Who can be trusted when it is impossible to track their plans or their motives? We must look out for our own people. Itswild and her neighboring villages have passed centuries in peaceful neutrality. There is no cause to break that now."

"But this is not just any battle," Ely pressed on. "This war has gone on for fifteen years! Thousands have died needless deaths!"

"Ely," Ari cut him off coldly, "Do not be rash."

"The mountain people do not involve our villages in unnecessary violence." Samorin's low voice hardly wavered but Ari picked up a new coolness in his tone. "And there are rumors..." He trailed off and no one spoke for a minute, the dirt crunching under their boots the only noise in the dark.

"The Elders have received word of a new force," he said at last, as they neared the crooked wooden house, "a third party to counter both the Former Military and the Rebels. Our scouts do not know where they are based because reports come from all sides of the country, hazy whispers at most."

"There have been such rumors before." Ari stopped at the bottom of the stone steps and turned to face Samorin.

"Yes, but they say this is different. They are stronger, or more organized, I suppose."

"There is no power strong enough to combat the Malavi army," Ari said definitively. "Or the Zaerans."

"Apparently someone disagrees."

"You both have such pessimistic eyes for the world," Ely observed, more calmly now.

"Practical," Ari corrected brusquely. "And it's time to get some sleep."

"The Elders have extended their welcome to you," Samorin said as Ari started up the stairs. "You may return freely as long as you come in peace."

She paused with one foot on the stone, then turned and extended a hand to the young man. "Give them my thanks."

Taking her hand, he pressed it briefly and gave her a searching look. "Perhaps we will see you again."

Ari pulled away and went into the cabin, feeling how the warmth of his hand slowly slipped from her fingers back into the cool air.

"So that's it?" Ely asked when the door was shut and the sound of Samorin's footsteps had died into the night.

"What is?"

"No more words for your friends and admirers?"

Shrugging her cloak off, Ari unhooked her sword from her belt and laid it carefully at the foot of the bed. "They are not my friends. No more words are necessary."

"Would it not be proper?"

"This is thievery, not diplomacy." She unlaced her boots with an aggressive yank and dropped them to the wooden floor. Jagger stood uncertainly by the side of the bed.

"You're not quite as frightening as you seem," Ely said after a minute of quiet.

Ari patted the mattress next to her and the bobcat jumped up to stretch out by her side. "I suppose I need to work harder then."

"You don't have to be frightening, if you don't want to be."

"I do if I want to survive."

"Survival isn't the only thing that matters."

Ari looked at him with ill-concealed disdain, unsure that she had ever met a naiver being. Silence fell again and she laid her head back onto the mattress, staring up at the flat boards that crossed perpendicular to the stone ceiling. Curved lines ran across the grey rock in a strange, spider web pattern. She thought about how near and real the ceiling was in comparison with the distant and intangible mountain sky. She thought about how they filled that tiny wooden hut, how they were so big for a moment but so small as soon as they stepped outside of its walls.

"You did well today – with your magic." Her voice was a whisper. Maybe Ely was not even awake.

"I didn't know if I could do it." He was.

"Well, you can."

"Thanks."

"Goodnight, Ely."

CHAPTER X.

It was one of those clear early mornings where the sun's light rose to the sky before the moon had time to sleep. Cloudless and pale blue, but softer than it was cold. The stony peaks above Itswild were ringed in a fog that was rapidly dissipating to reveal each sharp point with startling clarity. Sometime in her sleep, Ari had decided that stealing horses would not be wise, especially given the reception they had been given the night before. Either way, the Sonrein horses had allowed them a bit of extra time and she figured that their riders had made it far enough down the Lanterbrun Pass that her party would be safe to drop into the valley for the next stage of their journey.

Now they were on the thin path that wound its way out of the village, starting up the slope before curving back down through the trees and into the wide green basin below. Ely had been quiet as they got up and packed their things, and even as they walked quickly towards the forest he seemed to be lost in thought, or rather focused intently on something that existed in his eyes alone. Ari continued on, relishing the strength she felt following their grand meal in the Eating House.

As soon as they began the descent into the Lanterbrun Pass, the undergrowth took on a new shade of green, brighter and brighter as they neared the valley. Around them, small brooks and streams found their crooked way down the mountain, runoff from the great glaciers that gripped the uppermost summits with icy fingers. Somewhere on the slope, an aspen planted its colonizing roots and sprouted up among the pines until those, too, disappeared and gave way to the even grey of that steady tree.

"Do you think we'll make it through the Pass in a day?" Ely asked as they skirted around a particularly thick clump of aspen up-shoots.

"Most of it," Ari answered. "We'll enter a few miles in and likely have to camp about four miles from the far Belem ridge."

"I suppose that is assuming we don't take any detours."

"The Lanterbrun Pass always requires luck."

A hare went darting across their path and Ari felt Jagger tense in anticipation of his favorite meal. *All yours, Jag.*

He flew into the brush after the animal and she and Ely moved on alone. This part of the forest was similar to the region at the base of the Belem, lush and filled with fauna of every type. The birds were louder here than they had been in the other parts of the mountain, and Ari spotted at least six different species in the first mile of their hike down to the canyon.

Her anima returned to their company after only a minute gone, a mangled half of the rabbit hanging in his jaws. Ari experienced a flood of contentedness as he rejoined them, her heart feeding off the satisfaction that he now felt in his own.

"We will reach the valley within the next half of an hour but we'll keep to the eastern side, near the forest cover in case of unwanted company."

"Late summer is the ideal time for traveling," Ely noted. "Everyone will want to pass through the mountains before winter arrives."

"We must hope that we have picked an unpopular day."

Ely glanced up at the sky, now quickly transitioning into a perfect shade of blue that stood vibrant against the pale aspen branches. "Not every traveler will be hostile," he said hopefully.

Focused once more on the path ahead, Ari did not respond.

The widespread violence had greatly thinned the population, weeding out the weakest. Now, there were too many years of war and chaos between their world and that hardly-remembered peace for most travelers to be friendly. As far as she was concerned, the only people who were crazy enough to journey away from the safety of their homes were the ones dangerous enough to be a threat.

They reached the bottom of the chute in twenty minutes, exiting the wood into a big green valley with steep rock walls that only opened for the occasional narrow passage, such as the one through which they had come. The edges of the Pass were spotted with clusters of trees and bushes, which concentrated themselves around the small springs that gurgled calmly across the grassy plain. On either side of the valley, waterfalls tumbled down the stony cliff faces: some small streams and others roaring bodies of water that splashed into wide, clear pools below. After a few rainy days these falls would be even more numerous.

The Lanterbrun Pass was a strangely flat region amidst rolling hills and jagged peaks, a spot of smooth perfection that stretched on until it came to a halt at the huge mountains that formed the far ridge of the Belem. The rock slopes seemed to frame the back wall of the range, leading the eye to the great climb ahead.

There was a path that ran straight down the center of the valley, cutting it in half with a precision spoiled only by a short bend over one errant stream. This trail, clear and well-worn though it was, they avoided. Ari kept her company out of sight as promised, darting in and out of the trees along the eastern wall.

"Can I ask you a question?" Ely panted as they slowed after a particularly quick crossing from one bit of forest to the next.

You just did, Ari was tempted to respond.

"If this is the best place to keep cover," he continued,

"won't there be others doing the same?"

Ari was about to answer when she heard a noise and saw Jagger freeze. There was something else moving in the woods. Their section of forest was thin; only about a dozen yards separated the rock from the open plain. Whatever moved nearby was taking little care to hide its presence and it passed so close to the edge of the brush that it might as well have ridden on the main path. *Humans*, Ari quickly decided, hearing the slow hoof beats press into the earth and the voices begin to rise to her ears. Centaurs were much stealthier in such small numbers and much louder in large numbers. Nymphs and fairies did not ride, nor did they possess hooves.

Ari raised a hand for Ely to stop and remain silent, then she crept a few steps forward to try to catch sight of their company. There were only two: a man and a woman, both dressed in blue and riding dark bay horses. She saw a flash of white socks through the trees. It was difficult to catch a thorough image of the man, but the woman she saw, with a head of silvery grey hair and a pinched face. They walked their horses slowly, as if this trip was merely vacation and they had nothing to do but enjoy the sights and sounds of the Pass. The stiff riding uniforms said they were on duty, but to Ari they appeared a pair of friends traveling at their leisure in a time before war.

"I don't suppose they believe we'll actually find anything out here," the woman was saying to her partner, her tone doubtful but not pessimistic.

"They've got to check all their bases," the man answered, "be sure we didn't miss anything, right."

"I will not be the one to complain," she laughed back.

"Nor I."

"Though I do wonder sometimes where they have the proof," she continued. "I surely never hear these rumors until we're told. Baffles me where they get them."

Ari strained her ears to understand more, but the riders

were getting further away and she was afraid to follow them too closely. A little news was never worth an unwanted meeting; after so many years of war, the small shifts and new quarrels felt almost meaningless.

"There is some young man who's told them, is what Boldin told me." The man paused for a minute and Ari felt that she could hear them both thinking while their horses stepped on, further away, further away. "But I also heard that the leader himself came to them and announced his intentions."

"Seems a wonder they would all make it out alive," the female rider replied with a laugh, and that was the last Ari heard, just a few chuckles fading into the lush emptiness of the valley.

"It sounds like they are looking for that third army that Samorin mentioned," Ely said when Ari had crept back into thicker cover and they had resumed their trek towards the far ridge. She did not tell him that she had been thinking the same thing. Over the last fifteen years, there had been many attempts to oppose the two-party contest that ruled their country, fruitless efforts to present an alternative to the reckless destruction. Things always turned out the same way.

"We need to be more careful," she told Ely. "They were very loud, but we will not be so lucky the next time."

Their path continued unobstructed for many hours after this, the valley stretching on seemingly without end. They followed the same pattern, staying well within the leafy shelter as long as possible and hurrying the short treks that passed through open air.

There was a peaceful silence over the Pass, the kind that Ari liked despite herself. Dav had taught her that a traveler could never trust such an easy road, and she had experienced her share of ambushes to prove as much. Nevertheless, Lanterbrun gave her less anxiety than most plains and gorges. Perhaps it was the ample cover, perhaps the fact that arrows from the high rock walls would doubtless go astray, but she felt safe, or as safe as she ever did on the road.

As the sky darkened, Ari tried to remember the last time she had slept through the night when on a job. She supposed that their night in Itswild had been fairly restful, but that was not the same, considering they had been in a cabin. Only with Dav had she ever felt comfortable enough to close her eyes and drift off into dreams. Not the light dreams of a midnight nap, but the deep, complex visions of a true slumber.

When in her Hole, she had sometimes dreamt of the stars, and she would see herself running through the sky, leaping from one bright orb to another until she landed on a light all her own, and looked down upon the earth turning below. She would see Dav then, and her parents, and many other creatures all living out lives of simple pleasures and simple problems. It was fascinating. She would stand and stare, entranced by their comings and goings, unable to tear her eyes from this world that so resembled her own yet was so incredibly different. All the little pieces moved in silence beneath her gaze, and though she was distant, she felt terribly near.

Other nights, she would dream of running through the forest with Jagger, or fighting her way through dozens of soldiers on a contract. Sometimes there were golden eagles that came with messages that, when opened, became pouches full of silver pieces or water or pebbles. Once she saw herself riding straight into the Old Palace and slashing the throne over and over with her father's sword.

But more often than not, it was the same dream of Dav, walking toward her with his hand outstretched and that quiet but subtly playful look upon his face. And he would nearly reach her, each time so close that she could just grasp for his fingers before his expression froze into one of pain and he fell in slow motion, onto his knees and then his face, nothing visible except that small red mark that crept wider until it was a large circle across his broad back.

An involuntary shudder ran through Ari's body and she felt Jagger brush up against her legs, trying to comfort her. She shook the image from her mind. It was important that she focus on finding a safe campsite for the night.

As they neared the northern Belem ridge, cave-like formations began to appear along the rock wall. Ari looked closely at the shape of the stones, the way that each hollow ran out from the slope, into the valley. Some stood like neat little cabins and others tumbled down in haphazard circles, often gathered about small pools or feeling the wash of the falls over their smooth shoulders. Ari avoided such ideally-placed hideouts. They would immediately attract other travelers, and the noise of the water would mask the approach of unwanted visitors.

Finally, after almost an hour of walking and searching, she stopped in front of a small grotto, far from any trails out of the valley and hardly large enough for two humans lying side-by-side. The full trees held their branches in a gentle curtain over the entrance and several bushes crouched around the edge of the rock. It would do for a night.

Jagger trotted ahead and sniffed about the area, peering suspiciously at each corner of the tiny cave with his ears on rapid swivel. After three circles around, he turned his head to blink softly at Ari.

"We will rest here tonight," she told Ely, marching forward to drop her satchel by the opening. She ran a hand over the rock. It felt rougher than it appeared and the dark underside held a trace of that dampness that never really left mountain caves.

Ducking inside, Ely passed by her outstretched arm and laid his own bag upon the cool ground. "I have been thinking," he said, as he sat down and leaned against the wall, "And I have decided that those riders were looking for the second rebel army."

Ari made a noise in her throat but did not answer. She wanted to tell him that he was wrong, but an anxious beat in her heart held her back. There had been years of fighting and burning and destruction, but something had been different the last few months. She had seen it in the anxious faces of the soldiers and felt it in the emptiness of the Nyinan Forest. Though the skirmishes between the two armies had indeed been fewer and farther between, Ari could not call it peace. It was something more like silence, a tense, apprehensive stillness that she knew was building – building up until it exploded over and the fires reached all ends of the earth. It felt like everyone was watching and waiting and the world was frozen in a terrible standoff, all of them refusing to act until someone else made the first move. What were they waiting for?

Someone must know... The nymph's broken voice rang in her ears and Ari saw another flash of those fierce eyes. A part of her desperately wanted to ask, *What? Know what?* and another part wanted to ignore it all. She and Jagger could spend their lives running free of the world.

"It seems most likely that they're searching for the army," Ely continued on. "What else could they really be looking for?"

"The Zaerans," Ari answered flatly. "Or your missing Pegasus." She sat with legs crossed and pulled the suede bag into her lap.

"I'm being serious."

Feeling around for a moment, she found what she was looking for and placed the small bundle on the ground before her. "So am I."

"What is that?"

"Nothing," she told him brusquely. The golden cuff glittered in the folds of the old blanket. Grasping it carefully between two fingers, she turned her back to Ely and held the bracelet to the waning light. The journey had not yet damaged it, but Ari had conducted inspection several times over the past several days, anxious about it jostling around with the other items in her sack.

The old copper compass was dull in contrast, heavy in her hand and beaten with years of use. "You never know when you might need to find your way home," Dav used to say. Ari had always thought this strange, considering that he preferred to follow the stars.

The stars were always seen and never forgotten.

CHAPTER XI.

They descended quietly down the Belem just the way they had come up, watching the flora shift as they moved to lower and lower altitudes. The pines gave way to aspen, which gave way to oaks and rhododendrons and various maples that spread long, smooth roots out among the brush and wildflowers. As the afternoon approached and the land flattened, the trees began to thin out and the grass grew shorter and sparser until it was a strange, unfamiliar browned leaf. They were moving through the forest, passing the same smooth, grey stone and tall, leafy trees, until suddenly they weren't.

Ari froze in her tracks.

"No," Ely breathed, coming to a halt by her side.

The forest was gone, burned to the ground, so scorched that even the rocks looked dead. Nothing moved, and an empty whisper drifted over the dry land like a lost soul searching for its home.

A rumble began to stir up in Jagger's throat and Ari felt her skin crawl. The sky was a pale, sick yellow, a stark contrast against the blackened earth. Here and there, murdered tree stumps and ashy branches poked their spiny bones up above the flat, lifeless expanse. The destruction seemed to stretch on for miles, though Ari thought she saw a spot of trees in the distance, standing against the horizon like tiny green poppies in a desert.

"How..." Ely seemed to be searching for words.

Ari did not answer because she knew that "how" was not really what he was asking. *Someone must know...* But it did not matter who had done this; it just mattered that it was done. The Malavi, the Zaera Army – they all had the same power-hungry goals and the same violent effect in the end.

"We have to keep moving," she said. "Keep your eyes open." She started on again, picking up the pace so that they moved at a brisk jog, and then a steady run. Chin up and gaze fixed on the land ahead, she moved determinedly across the burnt earth, but inside her heart was pounding twice its normal beat and the dry heat seemed to seal her throat shut. The dead brush and blackened dirt crunched loudly beneath even Ari's silent feet, the land's incessant reminder of the horrors it had witnessed.

Of course Ari knew of the fires. From the first days of the war, both armies had burnt farms and villages for refusal to comply, or for what they claimed to be strategic reasons. She had seen many with her own eyes, come across them in her travels and on jobs, even watched some blaze across the plains with their wicked orange flames that jumped and spread faster than any beast could run. But those had been smaller, or years gone. This was fresh; she could smell it on the air and feel it under her boots. Weeks, maybe even days old. The ash still leapt and floated about as they ran and the sky was tinged with memory of the flames. She knew that the bones they passed were not only those of trees, but also of foxes and birds and squirrels. She saw something that must have been a bear. And worse, dozens and dozens of figures that she tried desperately not to see. There was no time to think of these things. There was nothing they could or should do but hurry on. Perhaps some of the fairies had escaped and would return one day, to rebuild what they had lost.

Ari could feel Ely creeping up behind her, feel how he quickened his pace to pull up at her side, but she matched him and stayed ahead. She had to run. She had to get out of there so that she could breathe again.

They did not stop until they had gone several miles, crossing the man-made desert at a pace that, ordinarily, Ari would not have dared to push. She slowed briefly about forty-five minutes in, then sped up again once they had all had time to catch their breath. Ely was silent and Jagger ran with every muscle taut; she could feel her anima's discomfort in her chest, could see his ears pinned back against his head. Finally, those distant green poppies became bushes, and then tall trees, made taller against the empty sky. They marked the edge of the Sonrein River, which had apparently kept the fire from spreading past the huge swath of land it had already conquered.

The sound of the water reached Ari's ears as they approached, loud and lively in spite of the deathly silence that sat upon the plain. *It must be deaf*, Ari thought, *or it would know how ridiculous it sounds.* Green sprouted up all along the near bank, small brush and shoots of grass that were beginning to fight for rebirth. On the other side were the trees that she had seen from afar, full and almost bright, but just tinged with remnants of the fire. They formed a neat row along the riverbed and behind them ran several more rows that grew stronger and healthier the further they grew from the ash. After that, the Northlands fell into a flat plain that stretched on for about two days' walk to small, rolling hills.

The Sonrein Plains were not like the Trinidad Plains, and though they were greener and richer with flora, Ari did not like them as much as she did her beloved Southlands. The sky always looked too dull and empty here, even though it held the same stars, the same moon and sun. It was growing late, but the pale air had not yet darkened and the moon was huge, a great yellow orb that hung so low over the flat earth that Ari thought the birds, if there were any birds, would hit it with their wingtips. It did not seem heavy, or ready to fall, but simply waiting patiently, resting right upon their heads with a strange watchfulness. Perhaps it was the same, but she had never seen such a moon over her Plains.

Finally tearing her eyes from the pale light, Ari stepped to the sharp edge of the riverbank and looked up and down. The river rushed at least two yards below the lip of the bank, a great blue current babbling its way around dark rocks and driftwood eddies. She tried to remember how and where she had crossed the Sonrein last. She hated thieving in the Northlands and had not been to this part of the country in several years.

"Can we ford it?" Ely asked, staring into the whirling water apprehensively.

"It's too strong, and it is another hour downstream to find a shallow crossing."

"So how do we cross?"

Ari's eye caught on several boulders about thirty feet upstream. "Over there."

They walked quickly up the river and approached the edge once more. Here, the roots of an old tree bent over the rim of the land and made their twisted way down to a great black rock that protruded from the water. The branches and trunk of the tree were completely gone, burnt away by the flames. Ari tested the orphaned roots with her foot. They would hold her weight as long as she moved quickly.

Grabbing the thickest part of the root with her right hand, she placed her left foot in a crevice about halfway to the rock and swung herself down so that she landed with the other foot on the smooth boulder. It was slippery from the rapids and she had to steady herself a moment before letting go of the tree and turning slowly to face the water. The next stone was only about four feet away, but the rushing current made the landing critical.

"You should have let me go first," Ely said, right as she was about to jump.

Ari wobbled and then regained her balance. "Don't interrupt me when I'm about to leap across a river," she snapped at him.

"I'm only saying that I have longer legs. I could go over and help you."

Gritting her teeth, she ignored this offer. "Wait until I get across."

"One minute!" He cut in yet again, and Ari thought she might hurl her knife at him.

"I *told* you –"

And then suddenly the river froze into solid ice before her feet. Ari turned slowly to face Ely. His face was pinched in concentration and his hands shook as he held them with palms outstretched.

"Hurry," he whispered, as if talking too loudly might break the spell. "I'm not sure how long I can keep it like this."

Wary, but unsure of what else to do, Ari placed one tentative foot upon the ice and then another, and quickly darted across with Jagger at her heels. As soon as they made it, Ely let out a breath and the water flowed back into the river. He followed Ari's tracks and climbed down onto the first boulder, then leapt to the second and third with ease, ignoring the powerful current that thundered around the slick rocks.

"Good," she said when he landed on the northern bank. "Let's go."

Ely nodded as he fell back into step behind her. Ari ignored the flicker of a smile that touched his eyes.

The trail they now followed was a winding one, twisting around dark green bushes and small pools, each surrounded by their own miniature woods. Small springs wandered over the land in a lazy, nonchalant pattern, cutting haphazard ditches through the quiet earth. The grass was tall and thin, and waved slowly back-and-forth as a light breeze drifted over the Plains. When the travelers passed through, it sprung back into place as soon as their feet lifted from the ground.

Now that the fiery desert was far enough behind them, Ari felt comfortable slowing to a walk. It had been a long day.

"So," said Ely, as if he was about to begin an interrogation, "you never told me how you got this job."

"I didn't," said Ari.

"I suppose I just don't see you working well with someone like Daerecles." The young man pulled even with her.

"It pays well."

"So you offered your services?"

"No."

He looked over at her, eyes somewhat narrowed. "He conned you into this."

Ari frowned at his choice of words. "No one *conned* me into anything."

That easy smile flashed across his face. "Lucky for you, then. He certainly tricked me into it."

"It was more like a threat," she said crossly.

"Ah." Ely looked over at her quickly. Ari glared at him. "What could anyone possibly threaten you with?" He looked genuinely perplexed. "I don't mean to offend, but if you don't have family or –"

"I do what I must to earn money and stay away from trouble," she told him coldly. "There is nothing else to discuss."

"My family has been hard on money for years, with the war and everything." For whatever reason, he was feeling particularly talkative. "Daerecles arrived in Casina and came to my mother's cabin... How he found it, I don't know, but he was sitting there, talking with her when I came with that day's rations. He told me he had a job that would pay enough gold pieces to last us years."

There was a pause and Ari watched him searching his memory for his family, for Parejon. She wondered if Ely knew something she didn't, something about Daerecles that could help her get out of this mess. Jagger, trotting ahead of them, flicked his tail gently.

"Of course, the job he explained to my mother and me was not the one he really hired me to do. Something about collecting messages at the Blue Lakes. I should have known that it was not legitimate, as vague as he was." Ely shook his head, the remnants of a smile still etched across his shadowed face. "As soon as we stepped outside, he told me what he really wanted, but I couldn't back out after promising my family the money. And..." He trailed off for a moment. "He knew my mother's secret – and mine. He didn't threaten us, but... it would have been too big a risk."

"He's crooked," Ari said quietly. "But smart."

"Are they all like that?"

"Traders?"

Ely nodded.

"They all have a deceitful streak or they would not be in the business. Some are as honest as thievery will allow, others as dishonest as the world will."

"But you have never worked for Daerecles before?" It was clear that he knew nothing.

"I had never heard of him," Ari answered brusquely, "and even if I had, I would not have gone near one of his contracts."

A growl came from the bobcat. Ari could feel his displeasure. He did not like the memory of the golden-haired man any more than she did.

"Don't walk beside me," she told Ely. "It makes us easier to track."

CHAPTER XII.

Should she allow Ely to help her with the theft? Could she trust his abilities to do the job and stay out of trouble? Could he keep himself alive? They had been hurrying across the Sonrein for almost three days and these questions continued to form a constant circle in Ari's mind. She hopped over a ditch and heard her boot squelch in a solitary mud puddle on the other side. It was difficult to determine exactly how Broun would be holding his treasures without knowing any more about the man himself. Normally she could scope out the site and complete the assignment within twenty-four hours, but the Capital was bigger, busier, trickier. As they approached, the warlord could be engaged in any manner of activities that would make her job even more complicated.

"When you use your magic," Ari called over her shoulder, "is it strong enough to remain once you have gone, or does it vanish immediately?"

The majority of the last two days had passed in silence and Ely seemed thrown off by the fact that she was actually starting a conversation. It took him a moment to respond. "To be completely honest, I have not often conjured anything meant to last," he answered after a minute. "I believe it could hold up for a little bit, after I've left."

"What is a little bit?"

"One or two minutes." He did not sound entirely decided on this number.

"Are you certain?"

Ari heard him stumble on a rock that she herself had only nearly avoided. "As certain as I can be without testing it first."

"Which of your contacts is located furthest from Broun's mansion?"

"The servant. He lives in a cottage on the southwest edge of the city."

"How are you acquainted?" The small hills that surrounded the Capital were taking clear shape on the horizon, and Ari could feel her legs tiring from the long days of travel. On the way back, they would definitely steal some horses.

"He was an old childhood friend of my father who left Casina to work for the King when they were about our age. They kept in contact and visited several times a year. They were like brothers." There was a sadness in Ely's voice that gave her pause.

"But now?" she asked.

"The coup changed many things," he said, and his words did not carry as they had before. "The Malavi have made the journey dangerous and association with such people... unwise for a man who has a family to protect."

"And you think he will still welcome you after all these years?" She did not bother to mask the skepticism in her tone.

"Like a son," Ely answered confidently.

"Showing up unexpectedly, unannounced, that won't cause any suspicion?"

There was a pause behind her, the kind where Ari could hear the words ready to break over his tongue several times before he finally spoke. "I think, to be safe, we should have a story."

"Of course we will have a story," she said scornfully. "You do not arrive anywhere in this country without a story, true or fabricated."

"I mean that it cannot just be anything," Ely responded cautiously. "Not if we are to stay with an old royal servant in

---

a Capital run by Malavi forces."

"Say whatever it is you are trying to say."

"We cannot be tradesmen or merchants. That tale is too easily proven false."

"And so?"

"We are newly married." He spoke somewhat quickly, as if by talking faster he might trick her into mishearing his words. Their feet made a steady rustle in the tall grass. They were getting further and further away from the rich, river-fed land and entering the drier, browner region of the Sonrein Plains. Every so often, they passed a swath of scorched earth, grass and brush burned down into a blackened ash that drew streaks like claw marks across the wide, yellow plain. Immediately to the east stood an old, abandoned inn. A broken cart lay tipped on its side by the front door.

"No."

"What other reasonable explanation can we give for our travel to the Capital? It is customary for the bride and groom to visit after the wedding."

"It was customary fifteen years ago. It is not customary during wartime."

"Do you have a better idea?" When Ari did not answer immediately, Ely continued, "It would seem natural that, on such an occasion, my father would send us to see his oldest friend. We pay our respects, tour the city, and leave. It gives us a chance to request lodging with ample excuses to be gone most of the day."

"We are not dressed as bride and groom."

"Like you said, old customs are not always practiced these days."

"I have never met your family, and hardly seen Casina."

"We'll call you taciturn," he answered, a smile creeping into his voice. "That shouldn't be too difficult."

Quickly running out of objections other than the general disgust she felt upon consideration of this plan, Ari could no longer continue to protest. "Alright," she said after a minute's thought, "but we do this my way, and we do not leave anything out."

"As you wish, my lady."

"Don't speak like that," Ari snapped.

Jagger picked up the pace and his girl followed, breaking into a run so that her footsteps beat her thoughts steadily into the ground.

"We'll stop here tonight," said Ari. "And no fire. We are too close to the city and the Malavi soldiers are always patrolling."

"They wouldn't attack two travelers at camp," Ely said, though it was more of a question than a statement.

"It would not be the first time."

The land where they now stood was even more yellowed and barren than before, a dry wasteland that stretched seemingly without end to the east and west, and to the north only broke as it reached the small hills that hid the Capital. Nothing moved, and only a few hardy plants poked their broken limbs up from the firm earth, which was covered with a short, stubbly brown grass that chafed uncomfortably against Ari's legs as she lowered herself to the ground.

She thought she remembered it being green, overgrown with reedy bushes and wildflowers, but those childhood recollections were so distant that she didn't know if she was imagining it. In any case, it had not been so since the war started.

"It didn't use to look like this," Ely said, as if reading her mind. "I remember coming with my family when I was young." He sat beside her and picked up an old, dried stick, scratching the tip into the dusty earth. "Bright green, like the region near the Sonrein River, as far as you could look. And so many animals. I saw my first centaur here."

"In the Plains?" Ari looked up at him in surprise.

He nodded. "A delegation was on its way to the Capital

from some forest in the East – I don't remember where – but they stopped and spoke with us."

She watched him sketch a lopsided circle into the dirt. "Did your family travel often?"

"Some. My father is a farmer, as was my mother. She worked as a healer in the city, too. Before the war." He drifted off into thought and Ari wondered, just for a moment, what it was like to have a family in wartime.

"I only ask," she said, when he remained pensive, "because we need to be sure not to say anything suspicious."

"Oh. Right." Ely glanced up from his circles. "Well, we traveled when we could, I suppose. When the high season had passed and my parents fancied a trip."

"You have a brother and a sister?"

He seemed surprised that she remembered this. She watched his eyes blink wide and then settle back into the same thoughtful expression.

"My brother is seven years younger than me – sixteen now. He was born right before the war... It's been hard for my father to raise him without my mother. Dinar, my sister, she left a few years back." Here Ely furrowed his brow and looked down at his lap, then back at Ari. "She didn't want to do it anymore – provide for the family and worry about our mother and all of that. She is so smart and strong and it killed her to just wait around, so she left."

"Where is she now?" Ari's voice was even, matter-of-fact.

"I haven't seen her in four years," he answered softly. "I got a letter once."

For a split second, Ari felt something like anger well up in her chest, and then it was gone. "So you helped in the fields?"

"Since I was young, though not with real seriousness until I was about seventeen."

She raised an incredulous eyebrow. At seventeen, she had been on her own for a year, scored her first contract from Leonor, and traveled a good bit of the Southlands.

"I had a lot of other things to do," he said, perhaps guessing where her train of thought had taken her. "I am the main provider for my mother because it's too dangerous for my father to visit often. After him, Dinar was in charge of the farming."

Each time Ely mentioned his sister, his words seemed to bend towards bitterness, just for a moment. He glanced down at his hands and then back at Ari with a fresh smile on his face. Her chest felt tight and uncomfortable.

"What is your brother's name?" She asked abruptly.

"Tomaas," he answered, and then went on, "You see, the thing is, I always felt closest to Dinar."

He was suffering from another talkative mood. Ari averted her eyes and once again watched his circles loop through the dirt.

"Maybe because we were already seven and ten when he was born, maybe because we knew the world before all this, and he didn't. Tomaas and I are still close," he put in quickly, as if Ari might be concerned that this was not the case, "but Dinar and I always knew each other... She was so restless and I was the only one who could understand her, talk to her and make her see where we were, remember the world around us. It was like she was in the clouds and it was my job to pull her back down."

The thought crossed Ari's mind that Ely, too, lived somewhere in the clouds and that maybe his sister's ignorance had rubbed off on him along the way. If Ely was grounded, she did not want to know what Dinar was. Leaning back, Ari rested her head on Jagger's furry belly, a gentle pillow on the otherwise rock-hard ground. Dav used to joke about how lucky she was to have a cushion when other travelers had only wishful thoughts for company.

"Did you have any siblings?" Ely interrupted her musings.

"No."

"What professions did your parents hold?" He was still

sitting up, now twisting the stick absentmindedly back-and-forth between two fingers.

"You can tell the servant anything you like about me," Ari answered flatly. "I'll just go along with it."

"I was thinking about our conversation earlier," he began, and Ari rolled her eyes at the sky. "It is something to do with your work, isn't it? The blackmail Daerecles has on you."

Jagger flinched as Ari sat up abruptly. "It is none of your business," she snapped.

"Ah." Ely nodded knowingly. "It's that bad?"

"What makes you think anything of it?" she demanded.

"Well, you are clearly upset," he told her matter-of-factly. "And while you have been consistently hostile to me since we met, it has been a cool, collected hostility. This," he said, gesturing at her face, "is not cool and collected."

Ari glared at him. "If I tell you, will you stop asking?" Other than his absolute uselessness, she knew there was nothing to fear from someone like Ely.

He grinned. "Fair enough."

"I have a debt to a man who helped me escape capture in Fraling. A trader from the Blue Lakes sent me there for a job and it went badly. I needed him to get me out. No one else was supposed to know. Even the trader never found out."

"And you can't pay the debt without this contract?"

Ari pursed her lips. "Perhaps I could, but Daerecles did not make that an option."

"What, does having a debt taint your thieving reputation?" He seemed genuinely curious.

"What do you think?" she asked coldly. "I don't want to deal with the rumors Daerecles could unleash, and this job would pay for it all, the absurd interest fees included. It was not a hard choice to make."

"What is his name?"

"It doesn't matter." Jagger flicked his tail in annoyance.

"Why are you so determined to keep names private?"

"Why are you always so curious about them?"

"I'd like to know to run the other way if I come across a man that scares you this much."

"He doesn't scare me," she said, a bit too emphatically.

Ely shrugged, as if he wasn't sure whether to believe her. "I'm not a part of your underworld, but I know that he must have more on you than just money."

Jagger was still, tense as a stone against Ari's hip. "He's called Icario."

"Alright; Icario. And he is some dangerous trader?"

"He is a smuggler. And you would, in fact, do well to run the other way if you meet him."

"Noted," Ely said, sounding satisfied.

She looked at him closely. "If you ever share this information with another soul, I will find you and you will pay for it."

He grinned. "Your secret is safe with me."

CHAPTER XIII.

From afar, the Capital city looked beautiful – it was beautiful. It stood like a polished stone on the side of the biggest hill in the plain, not particularly high, but enough to give it the ostentatious appearance of sitting upon a pedestal and looking out over its surroundings. A small river ran through the middle, cutting below the Palace and the old center to divide the poorer neighborhoods from the bustling hub that grew richer as it climbed the gentle slope. From where Ari and Ely stood, the three main bridges were like tiny brown lines drawn across the dark water and the Palace towered above, a cool, spired edifice of indifference.

Ari had always been impressed by the uniform buildings, the neat brownish-red shingled rooftops with their stone sides and cobbled walkways. It seemed improbable that the city still looked this way after centuries of life, that even when people added a new cottage here or a bakery there, they always followed the same model. She figured that there must be a better way to build houses now, but perhaps the people of the Capital were more concerned with keeping up appearances than they were with making progress.

When Ari had visited as a small child, the city had been magical. So clean that it sparkled, filled with people and creatures of all shapes and sizes; it was a young girl's dream. Soldiers trotted through the streets on shiny-coated horses, their shoes clip-clopping on the stone pathways. Gaggles of nymphs and centaurs darted in and out of secluded alleyways while the King passed through on his unicorn, a fine cohort trailing behind. On one occasion, Ari saw a small river dragon. And among these beings were humans, busy with bartering and politics and crafting clothes or tools or carpentry. People of the Northlands and the Southlands, from the villages around Nyin and the Trinidad Plains and the Parejon Hills. Travelers from the East, from the Blue Lakes and Fraling and even farther off places that Ari still had not seen.

"It is not the same the second time," Dav had told her before they entered when she was eleven years old.

"This is not the second time," little Ari had felt the need to correct him. "I went twice with mother and father."

"It is not the same," he had said again, unperturbed by her attitude.

She remembered trying to discern what exactly he meant by this, thinking long and hard as they approached the city from the south, staring up at the high roofs on their mountainous perch and wondering how it could have changed. Of course, the Capital had not changed. It was Ari who had changed, who in her eleven years had already become older and wiser than many had the burden to be at any age. The brown shingles still gleamed in the sun and the cobblestones still felt smooth and pure beneath her feet, but she saw new things, she saw more. It was a movement of minds, of arms, of business that now passed before her watchful eyes. It may not have been magic, but it was still knowledge, and it was still secrets.

Though she had returned once more with Dav, it had been years since her last visit, and Ari had the distinct thought, now, that the rooftops did not sparkle. As they grew nearer, following the wide, stone-paved road that led to the southwest entrance, she began to see that maybe it was not her jaded mind that dulled the city's brightness. The few cottages that lay along the outskirts were quiet, some even shuttered closed. Their walls looked grimy and charred, the small yards either overgrown or completely barren.

"I feel..." Ely did not finish his sentence but Ari knew what he was trying to say.

As they walked by one lonely home, an old man stared out at them with mistrusting eyes, not ceasing from his raking of the untidy yard. Wayward leaves and broken stalks slipped through the wide fingers of the metal instrument, which grated harshly across the hard, dusty ground. The sound scuttled through the still air and sent a chill down Ari's spine.

She actually felt relieved as they approached the city gate. At least with more activity they would not be so exposed to such empty eyes.

The city wall was a formality more than an operational structure. It wrapped around in a steady, weaving sort of pattern, up-and-down over small hills and the contours of the land. At some point, three hundred years earlier, it had been taller and stronger, a new addition to the stronghold that was the Capital. Now it fell in graceful ruins, knocked down by time and – being only symbolic – not picked up again by the inhabitants. A mile or so within this stony ring there was another, even older wall, and yet another across the river, circling only the Palace and the most ancient buildings. It seemed so natural, like the rings on a tree, a sign of growth and old age. Ari thought about how trees only showed their rings when they were dead and wondered if this said anything about the once-great city.

Noises of life and afternoon bustle reached their ears now that they approached the gate, a solid metal piece that hung open importantly, flanking the stone street. The structures within the wall were significantly bigger and cleaner than those outside, though this did not mean much. They remained modest, tired, and dead. People hurried about with baskets and boxes and carts pulled by stocky little ponies, doing business and conducting trade as they had every morning for the last several hundred years. But there was still an air of anxiety, a sense of quiet that pervaded the busy street despite its initial appearance. The shoppers did not remain outside longer than necessary. Ari saw several young women run into a house and shut the door as soon as they had picked up a bushel of carrots from a vendor across the way.

Stray dogs, ribs poking through shaggy hides, trotted across their path and sniffed at an overturned butcher's stand that looked as though it had been abandoned days ago. The starving creatures turned up their noses and meandered away from the rotting meat. Ari could feel Ely glancing at her, trying to catch her eye, but she stared ahead, focused on the eerie scene.

Her instinct screamed that she and Jagger should not be seen together, but logic told her that no one here would notice, that these people were too deep into a terrible present to think of a mostly faded past. Still, Ely's eyes made her anxious, like his attention might encourage more.

"Do you want to go to Randal's house first?" he asked her in low tones, seeing that she was intent on ignoring him.

"I want to get off these streets," she answered. Jagger flicked his tail anxiously.

"Follow me."

Ari had no choice but to comply, glancing over her shoulder to be sure they were not being trailed. There was hardly a soul in sight; the rush of the morning market had apparently come and gone.

"Be sure to avoid a direct route," she told Ely shortly. "Anything out of the ordinary will cause suspicion here."

"Nothing is ordinary in this city," he replied, but he took a sharp turn to the right anyway.

She realized as they walked that she had never really studied Ely from the back. He strode along with that same easy lope, but somehow, she felt like she was watching a different person move before her. This stranger had similar curls, but they stuck out at new angles and his broad shoulders looked stronger. He walked with greater confidence.

They twisted and turned through the little streets, gradually moving further west along the edge of the city. Sometimes they would track several blocks with the old wall in view, then they would head back towards the center for a few minutes and lose sight of it completely. It was about half an hour before Ely slowed and came to a halt on the corner of two quiet side streets. Diagonally across the intersection was a florist's shop that had been shuttered closed. A burnt streak smeared across an image of yellow and red tulips.

"He lives there." Ely pointed at a tiny home sitting next to the shop. The windows were dark and two ripped wicker baskets lay on their sides by the front stoop.

"Do you think he is home?"

"Almost positive." She noticed that his eyes betrayed concern even as he spoke with steady surety. Perhaps he had not expected such a changed city.

Each of them looked both ways down the street before stepping across to the little cottage. Ely rapped three times. They waited. For almost a minute, there was no response, and then Ari saw a flicker of movement in the window. Stillness again.

The dark wooden door swung open with a heavy grinding noise, revealing a tall, thin man with snow-white hair and bright green eyes. As soon as he recognized Ely, his eyes lit up and his lips broke into a wide grin. He was missing two teeth and his skin hung somewhat loosely about his bony frame, but his aspect radiated a great warmth that Ari found startling.

"Elyrah!" The man stepped forward and embraced Ely as if he were a small child. "My boy... Come inside!"

He ushered them in without taking a second look at Ari or her anima. The front hall was small and cramped, but a few feet back it opened up into a cozy sitting room that was lit by a brightly burning fire. The curtains were drawn shut over the back windows as well, giving the room the feel of a campsite at nighttime.

As they sat upon chairs conjured up by their host, Ari had a chance to observe him more closely. In the better light, she now saw that he was not so old as she had first imagined. He looked aged by care and hunger rather than time. His face was etched with lines of worry; a permanent wrinkle sat above his eyebrows and the bags under his clear eyes told her he had experienced more than one night's poor sleep. Scattered among the white hair were a few stray strands of raven black, the last remnants of the young man he had once been.

"Tell me, my boy, what is it that brings you and your companion so far, to the Capital?" He was gazing at them intently, expression piqued with interest.

"Father and I thought it was appropriate that I introduce you to Ari, my wife," Ely answered, and the last word he spoke with just a trace of hesitation. Ari hoped that the old servant did not notice this.

If the man thought this strange or surprising, he did not betray it. "Oh, my dear!" he exclaimed. "I am honored to meet you. Randal. Randal is my name."

He offered Ari his hand and kissed her fingers gently with a bow of his head. She blinked in surprise and forced a small smile. Ely looked nervous.

"I have heard only the kindest things," she answered politely.

"Is that so?" Randal raised his eyebrows and tilted his head at Ely, who nodded. "Well. You must stay here the duration of your visit. That is, unless you already have finer lodging prepared?" He chuckled but did not wait for an answer. "And how is your father?"

"He does what he can," Ely answered. "We are luckier than some, but Parejon is not what it once was."

The briefest second of tense quiet fell between them before the older man said, "I suppose nothing is."

"We all miss our visits." Ari saw the meaning in Ely's eyes

as he bit his lip into an apologetic frown. "My father, too. Truly."

Randal leaned forward in his chair and placed a bony hand on Ely's knee. "I do not need an apology, my boy." He smiled. "And Dinar? Is she as wild as ever?"

"She is well," the young man answered.

Randal nodded slowly and looked back to Ari. "Are you from Casina, too? How did you two come to meet?"

"I'm from a small village in the Trinidad Plains," she responded, because this was somewhat truthful. "I was passing through Parejon and met Ely there."

"In Casina?"

"Yes –" began Ari.

"No," said Ely. They glanced at one another and she had to stop herself from gritting her teeth.

"What he means," she continued, as sweetly as she could muster, "is that we were just outside the city when we first crossed paths."

"Ah," Randal hummed thoughtfully, "a chance encounter."

"You might say that," Ari replied.

"What is the city like these days?" Ely asked, somewhat too quickly though his tone remained casual.

Again, the man did not seem to notice anything strange. "This being the first time you have seen the Capital in nearly fifteen years, I would think you could answer that for yourself."

This seemed to embarrass the young man to a certain extent, and Ari spoke up to relieve him of the uncomfortable silence. "How do you pass your days?"

"Oh, this and that," he said. She could tell he was less comfortable talking about himself than he was them. "Squire and the others run the city as if it were their own private quarters. Demonstrations and parties every other week. We try to keep indoors."

"Tannin Squire?"

Randal gave her an odd look. "The same."

"Even in the Southlands we hear talk of your warlords," she said shortly.

Ely caught her eye and then looked away.

Ari addressed Randal once more. "Do you know if they are holding any sort of special event today or tomorrow?"

"There is a party every night this week at Jsepa Broun's mansion."

Ely was silent. Ari's heart leapt and a dozen new ideas filled her mind. This could be exactly the opening they needed.

"Ari wants to see the city today," Ely cut in abruptly.

"Of course, my boy, of course!" He stood and gave a vague wave of his arms. "Do not feel obligated to keep an old man company all day. The morning is quite young, I believe."

Nodding politely, they followed his example and stood. Jagger circled behind Ari's legs and peered at Randal warily. For the first time, their host seemed to acknowledge the anima.

"Noble lineage?" he asked Ari. "I do not think I heard your family name."

"Traditional parents."

Randal just smiled knowingly. Ari felt her skin crawl with discomfort.

"We will be back," Ely said.

"*Are* you of noble lineage?" Ely asked, when Randal had waved goodbye and shut the door behind them.

"No." Looking about the still-empty street, Ari automatically checked the weapons in her belt.

"Randal asked about your family name –"

"I have no family," she snapped. Whatever happened, she could not go back inside that cottage.

"So, you have no ties whatsoever to the Old Kings?"

"We need to get into that party," Ari said.

"I can get us in." His confident tone surprised her.

"How would you propose we do it?" She was skeptical.

"Talk, and if that fails, a little magical distraction."

"Vague and unreliable." Coming to a decision, Ari turned down the lane and started towards the old city center.

"I know what I'm doing," he protested, keeping stride. "You cannot bully your way into one of these events. And you definitely cannot fight, unless you want to injure half the guests and get captured before we even lay eyes on –"

"Do not speak of it in public," she hissed. "And stop looking around so much. The more you make eye contact, the more likely you'll be remembered."

Ari was moving at such a pace that they had already reached the second wall. The streets had remained so vacant that she had not bothered to slow down, but now they were entering a busier part of town and she had to alter her trajectory. As the homes and businesses grew larger, vendors and merchants filled their stands and shop windows, and the red-brown rooftops began to look less dilapidated.

Nevertheless, the streets lacked that shine that Ari remembered so well. A permanent sort of dust seemed to have settled over the smooth cobblestones, as if the rocks were rusty pieces of metal. The animals that trod back-and-forth moved slowly, wearily, and their riders and drivers were no more enthusiastic. Though the citizens appeared busier, they drifted about with the same trembling anxiety as those on the outskirts of the city.

After passing several textile and clothing shops, Ely motioned for Ari to pause. "We need disguises if we are to attend to this party tonight."

She looked about the square. Two old men were arguing outside a fish market. It was a wonder that they could pay anyone to travel this far with good fish.

"I suppose they would not be disguises so much as costumes, or dress clothes," Ely continued when she did not reply immediately. "There are plenty of stores around here."

"I want to see the building first." Perhaps they were arguing over the last fish.

"And then we buy something?"

"I have not decided."

"We cannot go dressed like this." He was clearly finding this conversation somewhat ridiculous, but Ari did not feel like accommodating his mood.

"I will decide how we dress," she answered coolly. "Take me to Broun's home."

'Home' was certainly not the right word to describe Jsepa Broun's palatial mansion. It was more like a small village, sprawling, reaching out hungrily to overtake the other buildings. Ari had the brief thought that all of Nyin might fit inside of it.

They had passed over the river and through the oldest wall into the central district, watching the buildings grow bigger and grander as they went. Here, finally, Ari saw the Capital that she remembered. The gleaming gates and well-kept streets, shop-front glass so clean, it was invisible. Gold and silver glinted in the rising sun's light and every so often they passed a mansion that was set with a variety of precious gemstones. Soldiers dressed in the Malavi military blues were posted at every corner, and glimmering white unicorns stood waiting with fine black carriages outside of the massive houses.

This was the only part of the country that had witnessed almost no war. After the initial coup fifteen years ago, the wealthy Former Military and paramilitary leaders had quickly taken control. Power had shifted hands a few times, from one general to another as they mysteriously resigned or grew gravely ill. Occasionally, word traveled around about small conflicts within the top officers, but nothing ever changed. It was military rule after all. A matter of strength, not intelligence. Passing control from one weak-minded soldier to the next did little to alter the livelihoods of the average merchants and farmers forced to give up their goods and rebuild burnt homes year after year.

But those people lived in the Sonrein Plains or the Southlands, not in the Capital city and certainly not within the innermost wall. Here, the war was like the distant murmur of an earthquake, its effects largely unseen. Nothing but the feeling that everyone was waiting for that earthquake to hit them next. For fifteen years, the city center had remained decadently, oppressively peaceful.

The Old Kings' Palace rose up above it all, its thin, pointed spire sticking into the cloudless sky with calm confidence. The grey-white walls stood firm as ever, smooth and solid against the speckled colors of the city. The tall, golden gate was hidden from their view, but Ari could picture it as it had once shone and sparkled. She imagined the Malavi generals sitting on the King's throne and felt revulsion rise in her throat. Pushing the image aside, she turned back to the mammoth house.

As the most influential member of the wartime Capital elite, Broun had taken the biggest home and decorated it to his lavish tastes. Ari did not need Ely's direction to identify it.

"Sickening," she muttered to herself.

Ely started to reply and Jagger cut him off with an angry hiss.

Four armed guards stood outside the tall, black gates: big, bulky men who looked almost exactly as Ari had pictured them after Ely's description. Inside the high fence was an expansive green yard that seemed strange and out of place in the middle of the old city. The hedges were manicured into perfect cubes and set off by well-groomed flowerbeds of all shapes and colors. Strolling about these gardens were several more soldiers – and those were only the ones that she could see from the front façade.

The front door was curiously small and ornamented with all manner of gold and red stones that flashed in the midday light. The only visible windows were no lower than the third or fourth floor and cut into long, thin pieces that gave the expansive building a sense of stretching upward to reach the high Palace towers behind it. Steep and slanting, the roof cut up and down in multiple sharp ridges, with no place to stand except for three flat sentry points that were occupied by more armed men. Broun had planned his security very thoroughly; she would not be able to scrutinize the full perimeter of the building in advance of the job.

Though it was not her place to do so, Ari questioned the value of so reckless a mission for so trivial an object. It might indeed be worth some investigation to learn more about the trader who was so intent upon acquiring this particular precious stone.

"Can we really achieve anything by staring at it?" Ely whispered, though they stood far from the soldiers at the entrance. "We are going to have to wait to get inside tonight."

"I just need to think," Ari said between her teeth, biting her lip in concentration. The street was not void of activity, but every person that passed between them and the giant house seemed eerily silent, as if they were afraid to speak so near the heavily fortified complex.

"We should really go purchase our dress clothes," Ely went on, apparently ignoring her.

Ari tried to picture an exit strategy. During the party, there would be more people and more open doors, but it was also likely that there would be more guards. Invading Broun's home would put her on the wanted list without question, but hurting any of the guests would be another thing entirely. This she wanted to avoid. There had to be a way out that would circumvent the main halls, where the party would surely be located.

"They'll notice us staring," Ely spoke up again.

"Come on." Ari led them away from the house and down another street, searching for another market or shopping area. She needed space to think. "Do you know where 'Malavi' comes from?"

Ely locked into step beside her. "The name of the general who led the coup, wasn't it?"

She shook her head. "His name was Murivic. 'Malavi' was the old word for 'army.' In the ancient tongue."

"Where did you learn that?"

"I've always found it humorous," Ari said. "They so despise being called Former Military, and yet they named themselves 'military' as it would've been called in days past."

It was only a few blocks before they came across a bustling avenue with dozens of vendors and sparkling display windows. People moved about with baskets and boxes, dodging in-and-out of stores with determined expressions. On most of the storefronts, the owners had hung small signs banning sorcerers, or magically-gifted beings in general. Ari wondered how many of them were afraid of magic and how many were simply afraid of the Malavi.

Ely stopped her in front of a squat wooden door with a yellow dress painted on the upper panel. In the long window Ari could see racks of various fabrics and piles of fine shoes lined up along the sill. She frowned at the thought of shopping.

"I'll find what we need and we'll get right back out of there," Ely said when he noticed her face.

"I can do it."

"No, you really can't." He looked at her in amusement. "This is one area where I do have more expertise than you."

Looking grumpily at the rows of silks in the shop window, Ari made a huffing noise and did not reply. Ely took this as a sign of consent and stepped forward to enter the store. As he placed his hand on the door, he paused. "Maybe you should stay outside."

"Excuse me?" She arched her eyebrows in annoyance.

"Unless you're hiding something from me, we have very little money. I'm going to try to bargain the price down. You need a little bit of charm in these places."

"You are joking."

"If you make a scene or act suspicious they won't want to serve us. It will just be ten or fifteen minutes." Shrugging apologetically, Ely turned and pushed the shiny gold handle inward, disappearing behind the rows of fabrics and rich gowns.

Ari took another look at the little street, feeling simultaneously peeved and relieved that she didn't have to enter the cramped building. People continued to pass by, occasionally glancing over at her and Jagger where they stood. She walked across the street and headed left towards a small market, where a butcher and a vegetable vendor were both setting up stands and quickly drawing a crowd of shoppers. Approaching with the rest, Ari let herself blend into the mass of Capital men and women with their busy expressions and arms full of new purchases. Up ahead, she saw a row of forest green storefronts with small windows and moved silently, purposefully towards them.

Once upon a time, she had known a few thieves in the Northlands. If Icario was not to answer her, perhaps one of them would have some information about Daerecles. *I am likely grasping at stars.*

The leftmost storefront had a picture of a mallet and a beveller printed on the window, just under a faded name that Ari could hardly make out: *Daria's Leather & Goods*. There was a large wooden table to the right of the door, standing empty of anything but a pair of blunt scissors and some useless leather scraps.

While Jagger remained outside, hidden from sight by the wooden stand, Ari pushed open the door and stepped in quietly. The space was simple and consisted of little more than a countertop and a pair of shelves with leather products displayed haphazardly about them. There was no bell or chime to signal her presence, and only one other customer inside, an older man waiting impatiently by the counter. Ari pretended to be engrossed by the set of boots and the traveling pack with matching knife holster on the shelf nearest her; she let her eyes roam the cut and stitch work until the other customer had left with a few choice words for the proprietor, who he apparently deemed to be late on numerous orders.

The owner was a silver-haired, middle-aged woman with deep brown skin and suspicious eyes. Her blue work apron draped in folds over her slim frame, which was only partly visible behind the counter. She looked Ari up and down once before demanding, "What do you want?"

"You don't believe I am here to purchase a new travel kit, then?"

"A woman like you?" She smiled ironically and put her callused hands on her hips. "You and your anima are trouble. I'd like you out of my shop."

Pursing her lips, Ari looked back at her stonily. "We bring no trouble. I only wondered if you knew of a Jaklyn Frie. Near here, perhaps."

"Never heard of her. Will that be all?"

It being clear that this had led to a dead end, Ari nodded, thanked her, and left the store. It had been a long shot; Jaklyn was the only thief she knew who might still be around the Capital, and that was a slim possibility at best. Sticking her neck out any further was not worth it for a little information on Daerecles. Not just yet, anyway.

As Ari and Jagger stepped back out into the street, a woman with an osprey on her shoulder walked by, nearly tripping over Jagger as she hurried to get into the quickly-forming line at the shop next door. Looking ready to snap something angry, she stopped with mouth open as she saw the girl and the bobcat before her. Her lips closed slowly and she gave Ari an almost imperceptible nod, looking her in the eyes with a meaningful expression. Ari inclined her head slightly and then turned away, her anima following behind. Wishful camaraderie was not a sufficient excuse for betraying her identity. She made a more determined mental note to leave Jagger behind for the theft that night.

"Ari." She tensed at the sound of her name from over her shoulder. "I got everything."

Ari turned to see Ely holding three boxes in his long arms, two rectangular and flat, one taller and shaped in an elegant sort of oval. They were a simple duckling yellow, with bands of silver painted around the top and bottom edges.

"Why do you have so many?" she asked with distaste.

"One for me and two for you," he answered.

"What's the second one?"

"Your shoes."

"I don't need shoes."

Now he raised his eyebrows at her. "Yes, you do."

Not wanting to have the conversation in such a public space, she turned her back to him and strode away, knowing he would follow.

"I can get away with shining up my boots but you're going to attract a lot of attention in those," Ely persisted, easily keeping pace. "I promise I picked the most comfortable pair."

"Fine."

"Fine, what?"

"Fine, Ely. Now be quiet until we arrive."

He obeyed her orders and stopped pursuing the subject. They passed through the smooth streets, silently dodging the groups of shoppers, travelers, and merchants who filled the wide lanes with their hustle and bustle. Jagger fell into place at the rear, concealing himself in their shadows, which were cast long by the early sun. Now, few people seemed to take notice of the great cat gliding, well-hidden, through their midst.

Ari continued on, watching for anything out of the ordinary, any strange look or questionable behavior. She walked cleverly, melting – as years of thievery had taught her

– into the surrounding world. Following whatever seemed to be the popular current, she led the small party past rows of lavish mansions, through a fish market and an armory, and around the edge of a large square that was filled with an ironic combination of flower vendors and armed guards. Irritated by the thought of having to wear a gown and dress shoes, Ari spent her leftover thoughts considering the most effective ways to conceal her weapons in the inconvenient clothing.

Ely stayed by her side the entire time, quietly mirroring her steps and trying to avoid eye contact as he had been instructed. He did not ask where they were going, even though it was clear that they were not headed back to Randal's cottage.

It was about twenty minutes before Ari slowed to a stop in front of a tall, refined-looking building with a narrow, rounded door. The decoration was simple but elegant. The grey stone matched that of the surrounding buildings, and neat brown shingles slanted over the roof, which slid down and curved over the top of the wall in a graceful sort of bow. To the right of the door there was a small sign, the words hammered with gold leaf into a dark wooden panel:

Swordsman's Lodge... This is a reputable establishment.
Failure to treat it as such will not be tolerated.

The door swung open before Ari could place her hand on the knob. Before them stood a tall, curvy woman with bright blonde hair that was tied up into a tight bun on the top of her head. She had pasted a winning smile onto her pale face, but her eyes were mistrustful and Ari got the feeling that she was expecting them to cause some sort of disruption.

"We would like a room for the night," Ari said calmly, motioning for Jagger to sit and remain still.

The woman's eyes flickered down to the cat and then back to Ari. "Of course," she said sweetly. On the knob, her long fingers flexed twice as if she would have preferred to shut the door in their faces, but instead she pushed it further open and beckoned them forward.

Following her inside, they entered a long, narrow passage with a cathedral ceiling that stretched up to spectacular skylights. On either side of the hall were a dozen identical doors, each framed by a simple, dark mahogany trim and set with a curved silver handle. The woman turned at the fourth door on the right and raised a hand to open it. It swung inward before her fingers had grazed the metal.

Down another long hall they went, this one with only one door at the far end. There were no windows here, but a strange glow resembling sunlight seemed to emanate from the yellowy-gold walls and floor. Like the first door, this one opened without a touch and they were ushered into one of the strangest rooms Ari had ever seen.

It was circular, with an enormous domed ceiling almost entirely covered in skylights that sprayed out from the center point in a star-like pattern. The walls were a silvery marble, completely smooth and unblemished, and on the floor were dark marble lines that bent into the center to give the inhabitant a sensation of the ground collapsing into a very symmetrical sinkhole. All around the edge of the hall were tiny doors, about twenty in total, perched thirty or thirty-five feet above the sunny floor. Each door had its own set of steps, which, as they all climbed from right to left, added to the impression of a downward spiral. Ari had the feeling that she was standing in a very large birdcage.

"This way," the woman said in the same singsong, cheery voice. Perhaps she was the bird.

Her heels clicked sharply on the cool marble floor, echoing around the hall. Jagger padded silently along beside Ari, and she felt the buzz of tense interest in his lean body. She wondered if he felt caged, too. Halfway across the room, the woman paused and turned to look at them. One hollow click trailed into the emptiness and disappeared.

"One room?"

"We're married," Ely blurted out. Ari tried not to wince.

The hostess gave him a haughty, disapproving look and nodded. They continued on. Their room was on the far side of the grand hall and the stairway, identical to all the others, carried them to the door, which Ari found was actually not so small now that she was standing before it.

"Everything you need is inside. Pay on your way out in the morning." With this cool salute and another forced smile, the woman left them to find their way into the room.

"This place makes me nervous," Ely said as soon as they had shut the door behind them. "There are no people here."

"Calm down," Ari told him flatly, heading down the small entryway to explore their lodgings.

"Did you see? It was empty! Like walking through a tomb!"

His dramatics were lost on the young woman, who was inspecting every nook and cranny of the space, which turned out to be more of a suite than a room.

"Why are we here?" Ely asked the question she had been expecting for the last hour. "We cannot afford this."

"We won't stay long. We cannot risk entering Broun's home two nights in a row, so we'll have to steal it on the first try and head directly out of the city. Your friend's home is too modest and too far from the mansion. We need a better base, and we most certainly cannot be seen walking all the way from the outer city in dress clothes."

"You don't plan on paying at all." The tone was somewhat accusing.

"No."

They had come upon a small dining space with an array of food and drink laid out across the table. A crystal chandelier hung from the ceiling above and sent diamonds of white light spinning across the walls. Ari pulled out her hunting knife and cut a piece of meat off a large flank that sat adorned with peas and strange purple leaves.

"We used to stay at the Inn Debouryne sometimes," said Ely wistfully.

Ari almost sliced into her finger. "I've never heard of it," she replied a bit too quickly, turning away to hide her shock.

The young man hardly noticed. "I don't know what it's called these days. I'm sure the Malavi have changed the names of every building named for the Old Kings and their descendants. It was a nice place, just inside the second wall."

The name of an inn meant nothing. It would be her fault entirely if she let her emotions give her away.

"Jag." Ari motioned at her anima and he took the meat in his jaws. "Eat something now," she told Ely, "but not too much or you'll get sick tonight."

Heart still pounding, she left the boy and the bobcat in the dining room and wandered farther down the suite's narrow hallway. At random, she picked the second-to-last door on the left and went inside. It was small, square, and unadorned except for a plushy armchair and one small image that hung on the right wall. A cavalry roared across a battlefield, its enemy hardly in sight. At the forefront of the painting stood two figures, one mounted on a majestic white unicorn, the other standing by his side with hand raised to offer a message.

It was clear that the proprietor had chosen this piece because it seemed, at first glance, to be a neutral Former Military scene. The protagonists wore the blues that the army had always worn, from the days of the Old Kings through the civil war. The man on the unicorn wore no crown or coat of arms, and the messenger looked to be an ordinary servant doing his civic duty. But Ari knew, even with fifteen years between her and that old life, that this was not an ordinary post-coup scene.

The man on the unicorn was not a captain or a general. He was the murdered King's father, a renowned leader whom Ari recognized from the portraits in the Old Palace. It was only twice she had been inside the great castle, but she would never forget those bright blue eyes, which she had stared at for what felt like days before her mother had gently tugged her away.

The largest portrait used to hang in the hall leading up to the throne room, wrapped in a grand golden frame that seemed to young Ari a work of art in and of itself. The Old King was portrayed mounted in that painting as well, though on a grey stallion rather than a unicorn. The horse stood, fiercely proud, on the edge of a cliff overlooking the Capital, whose miniscule rooftops and square streets sprawled in every direction below. The fine animal and the shining sword hanging from the man's hip were impressive enough on their own, but those eyes had fascinated Ari more than anything else. Turned away from his country to face the viewer, the Old King had stared solemnly out of the frame, eye contact unwavering.

In the image in the tiny square room, the same eyes looked down at the servant, who Ari knew to be a trusted diplomat, the man who had filled her father's position before him. Both figures had shining blonde hair and full shoulders; the white unicorn held one knee up in a strange, posed position. Even so many years later, all she could see were those eyes, those blue eyes.

"Ari?"

Her hand shot to her hip and then dropped slowly back to her side.

"Sorry, I didn't mean to scare you." Ely seemed embarrassed.

"What do you need?" she asked, a little too sharply.

"I put your gown and shoes in the bedroom. I'll change in the room across the hall."

"Okay." She did not turn away from the painting.

"That man looks familiar," Ely said.

Ari remained silent and he left the room.

Chapter XIV.

Ari looked at her reflection in the long mirror. The woman in front of her was hardly recognizable. Her pale blue gown rose high to meet her slender neck and cut in so that her tanned shoulders lay completely bare. The soft, silky fabric clung tightly about her breasts, then dropped down from her slim waist to the floor in loose, wavy folds. She turned to observe the rear of the dress, which remained open to display a browned back with three scars that marked a claw-like path across her spine.

On her feet was a pair of woven silver slippers, soft and tight to her narrow arches. She had to admit that Ely had chosen the shoes well. Ari ran her fingers through her short, dirty-blonde hair, trying to determine if she was the same girl that she saw in the mirror. Her light locks fell in a smooth wave about her face, softer and straighter after brushing it for the first time in weeks. Those cold grey eyes did not look so hard and the blue dress seemed to reflect a new light into them. For a moment, she saw an image of a small blonde child, light on her feet and quick to dirty any decent dress her parents forced her into. Ari hadn't worn such a fine garment since she was seven years old.

"You look lovely." Ely's voice made her jump and the little girl with the bright eyes vanished. Unclenching her jaw, Ari made eye contact with him in the mirror as he stood looking over her shoulder. His face held a strange expression.

"Here." He draped a thin white veil around her shoulders,

covering the scars on her back. She prayed that he did not ask how she had gotten them.

"Are you ready?" she asked, even though he clearly was. He wore a deep navy tunic over long grey pants, cuffs shining with a silver thread and several finely-set stones. His cloak was also grey, but darker, and it shimmered as if it couldn't quite decide on which color it wished to be. He had washed and combed his wild hair so that it stuck up slightly less than usual, sitting in a jaunty tuft at the front and giving further character to his cheerful, boyish face.

Ely looked around the room. "Where's Jagger?"

"He's staying behind."

"I think you should wear your bangle," he said, as if this were the next logical step in the conversation.

Ari narrowed her eyes. "What are you talking about?"

"That golden bangle you always take such good care of." He pointed at her suede sack where it lay open on the floor. "You got it from your parents, didn't you?"

"I'm not going to wear it on a job," she said.

"This might be your only chance to wear it," he answered matter-of-factly. "They didn't give it to you to keep in a bag all your life."

"Just go meet me out front," Ari told him.

With one last look at her, Ely walked out, that now-familiar loping stride carrying him from the room in a few easy steps. When he had gone, Ari turned to her bag and knelt down to pull out the spare shirt. Unrolling it, she found the gold band, shining innocently in the lamplight.

She thought of her parents' faces, figures that she did not often consider now, so far were they from her recent memory. She tried to picture her mother's dark curls and soft, slender hands, her father's wide smile and big blonde beard. The memory was fuzzy, a recollection that had become idealized, caricatured over time until she could only see certain distinct elements. The maroon cloak her father always wore or her mother's tall leather riding boots. The feeling Ari would get in her chest when Irena laughed, something she had done seldom enough for those moments to stand apart as the times of greatest joy and comfort.

And always there, in the background, was Zaid, her father's top advisor and closest friend. She could hardly remember her parents without seeing his face or hearing his voice. He had been there every day, a second father to her until he had murdered them.

What Ari remembered most now was the fact that they were gone, that her parents had chosen their King over their child and left Ari in favor of the man who would kill them for a bribe. Dav was the only one who had ever been willing to do whatever it took to keep her safe, to stay with her forever. And he had been taken, too.

Ari looked at her tired hunting boots, sitting in the corner by the mirror, a stark contrast to the shining luxury that surrounded them. What was she doing here, in this gown, these shoes? Everything felt wrong and out of place. For a moment, she wondered if this is how her life would have looked had they survived, had the coup never happened. Remembering the blonde child with the soiled dresses, Ari shook her head at the boots. That little girl would never have grown into a princess.

But whether she wanted it or not, this was the only way to get the dragith, to get Daerecles' money and leave everything else behind. Feeling a warmth enter the room, Ari turned to face her anima as he came to stand by her side.

"Don't I look ridiculous, Jag?" She stood up and realized she was still clutching the bracelet. "What would they say if they were here now?"

The bobcat blinked calmly up at her, such strong feeling in his wide golden eyes that Ari was hit with a wave of guilt for leaving him behind.

"You don't exactly blend in here anymore," she told him

softly. "This city is a dangerous place for us."

He gave a slow flick of his tail, still observing her with great intensity. It was hard to feel anything but settled with his steady presence so near. Ari slipped the golden cuff over her hand and slid it up her wrist. It fit perfectly. Strange, that in all these years she had never once tried it on.

"It doesn't mean anything," she told Jagger. "It's just jewelry." Bending down, she pressed her face to his for a slow second, then pulled away. "See you soon."

She took one final look at her strange reflection in the narrow mirror. It was almost pretty. Sliding the silver dagger into the waist of her dress so that it was hidden by the folds of the fabric, Ari grabbed her sword and marched out of the room to find Ely.

"Here," she said when she discovered him by the door, thrusting the weapon into his hands. "Put this under your coat."

He looked at her in confusion. "Won't people notice?"

"No, because it will be under your coat."

"What if I want to take it off?"

"We are not going to enjoy ourselves," Ari snapped. "We're going to steal something."

"It might look somewhat out of character if –"

"You already made me wear this ridiculous outfit and I'm leaving two of my other knives behind," Ari cut him off. "If you can't carry this for me, you will stay here and I will come up with a new way to finish the job on my own."

Holding up his hands in submission, Ely opened his cloak and slid the blade into his belt. "Okay?"

"Let's go."

***

As soon as they stepped outside, they were rushed into the flow of several dozen other partygoers who hurried up the wide avenue in the direction of Broun's mansion with pretentious importance. Instinctively, Ely reached out and grabbed Ari's hand so as not to lose her in the crowd. She twitched as if to pull away, but he held on more tightly.

"We're a couple," he hissed out of the corner of his mouth, and for whatever reason, she let it be. Her fingers, though small, were tough and calloused and they felt strong against his palm.

After a few minutes of silence between the two of them, their even foot-beats muffled by the sounds of excited voices and noisy carriages, Ely dared to glance down at the young woman who walked by his side. She strode on purposefully, directing them around and among the mass of people so that they blended in even as they moved ahead in the crowd. There was a strange jump in her grey eyes that he wondered if he was imagining. He wondered if, maybe, forced to wear that "ridiculous outfit" and venture into the open with only one weapon, Ari might actually be scared. He wondered about the secrets that haunted her and the pain that he heard her reliving most nights in her dreams.

Her pale eyes turned on him and their accusing glare pushed his gaze immediately forward. She did not speak but he knew what she would say. *Never look back. Always look ahead.* He felt her hand clasped in his and decided that she could not possibly be afraid.

***

The house was already teeming with people. Finely dressed guests were milling about the gardens or making their way through the front doors, which once again, Ari noted to be oddly small. Having stashed their bags in an unwatched hedge two blocks over, she felt very empty-handed.

A long line curved its way out from the doors, filled with women and men talking about dinner and worrying about their clothes as they waited to enter. Flanking them were fat potted shrubs that rose almost to Ari's chin and sprouted strange orange blossoms at their edges. Ely tugged Ari into the queue behind a trio of men dressed in matching green tunics.

From their place in the line, she watched as the guests ahead of them presented slender cards to the soldiers at the gate. The men glanced at the papers and then waved them through one-by-one.

"I don't think 'talk' is going to be enough," Ari whispered to Ely.

"It does not appear so," he replied quietly. "Can you follow my lead?"

She eyed the large men on either side of the entrance, and the dozen more stationed on the rooftop and about the lawn. The line shifted forward again. "If this doesn't work, I'm breaking in without you."

"One, two, three." There was a small pop and the bush to their right caught fire.

"Oh! Oh, my stars – Tomm! Tomm, the shrub is on fire!" The woman directly behind Ari and Ely began to shriek, grabbing her husband's arm and waving at him as if he were responsible for putting out the flames.

"Do not *shove* me, Willah. What do you expect me to do about it?"

The woman clutched a small purse – too small to fit the invitation card. Ari glanced at the soldiers and back to the couple.

"Guard!" The fire had grown quite tall and the man began to yell, too. "Guard! Will you do something about this?!" He took his hands out of his pockets to beckon the soldier over and Ari saw her chance.

As the bulky gatekeeper made his way to them, she stumbled into Ely and then tripped into the couple, who were now two of dozens fretting over the flames.

"Pardon me, sir," she apologized, blinking up at the

husband. "What a ruckus."

He ignored her and continued to shout at his wife, the guard, and the rest of the crowd. Ari turned away and looped her arm through Ely's, steering him towards the open gate.

"He's with me." She offered Tomm's invitation to the remaining guard and smiled. "We're just married!"

The soldier nodded and they passed through. Ari pulled her hand from Ely's.

"They know we're here together."

"That wasn't bad teamwork." Ely was grinning.

"We need to locate Broun, if possible."

"He's about sixty years old, medium height and build," Ely told her in a whisper. "Probably surrounded by a lot of guests and likely wearing something very expensive, though it won't be Malavi military attire."

"Everyone is wearing something expensive," Ari said.

He smiled again. "Fair point."

Continuing on, they passed over the yard and through the narrow front door. There were guards here, too, and they gave Ari and Ely bored, brooding looks as they crossed the threshold into the house. All of Broun's men seemed to be big and bulky, heavily muscled about the arms and chest and equipped with long broadswords. Though she could not see them well, Ari suspected that the soldiers on the roof were likely armed as they had been that morning: with blades, and bows as well.

The inside of the mansion was no different than could be expected from observing the exterior. Ancient, expensive tapestries hung about the high-ceilinged wall and tall marble columns rose up from the floor, where they were ringed with precious metals and stones. Ari and Ely entered the main hall almost immediately upon stepping foot within the building. There were tables placed around the room, set with glittering white cloths and piled high with all manner of food and drink. Servants milled about the space, which was already filled with guests and quickly growing even more crowded. In the center, there was an open area, which Ari took to be a dance floor.

"We should split up," she said, turning her face to Ely so that her words would reach his ears alone. "If you find Broun, or see anything strange or useful, let me know."

"But how do we locate it?"

Internally, she thanked him for not saying the name aloud. "I'll worry about that."

"Try to look like you are having fun," he said and turned away from her to wander off into the crowd, disappearing among the colorful, sparkling figures that flitted about in thoughtless enjoyment.

The noise of the party remained at a constant babble. Strands of music wove in and out of the excited voices, but the flutes and violins could not match the man-made sound that filled the large hall. It was sickening, how carelessly joyful they were, these humans who knew that they were in the home of an evil, destructive man, yet continued on without pause. Eating, drinking, laughing, talking with sophistication of frivolous things. There was a time for happiness, even amidst war, but there was also a place, and a way to celebrate it.

Try to look like you are having fun, Ely had said. Ari made a concerted effort to rearrange her face into a pleasanter expression. She wished Jagger were there and then immediately pushed that thought from her mind. It was dangerous to feel such emotions when it was so crucial that her anima remain hidden.

After a moment, Ari walked in the direction opposite from that which Ely had gone, drifting among the guests and studying every corner of the grand room. She tried to ignore the bright colors and rich foods and instead let the conversations and whispered words fill her mind. Along the outside wall, there were five doors in total, each monitored by armed guards who the guests seemed to avoid. Women gathered in small groups about the columns, eying the people on the dance floor and talking in hushed tones. She heard nothing of interest from them and tightened her circle inward, passing near the tables of food. Conversation here was more mixed, but it was fleeting, as guests passed through and wandered off again. After spending several long minutes listening to two people arguing about the Malavi tactics on the Southern Coast and only gaining a greater distaste for the Capital elite, Ari moved on once more.

"I say they all had it coming." A woman in a bold red gown took a sip from her glass and shrugged carelessly. "As I understand it, they were all corrupt. King Ilhro most of all."

Despite herself, Ari slowed to eavesdrop.

"Even so," said a man on her left, "it seemed awfully harsh the way they died." He tugged anxiously at his black and gold coat and glanced around.

"Don't look so anxious," a second man chimed in. He was quite young and carried himself with a self-assured air. "They are not listening that closely here."

Ari picked up a plate from the table next to them and began to slowly layer it with food.

The man in the black coat shook his head quickly. "You did not hear? They raided Seku and Rinah's home last week."

The other two guests cast their eyes down respectfully, as if mourning a fallen soldier, before resuming the conversation.

"All I mean," the woman repeated, "is that they were corrupt! They were keeping more than their share. My wife" – the two men, for whom this was apparently not a new topic, sighed in unison – "was there, you know. The day they took Ilhro. He did not even defend himself against the accusations."

"But let me pose this to you," said the younger man. "Consider that they had removed the King only, leaving the others alone. What then?"

Idiots, Ari thought, about to walk away.

"You know as well as I that the throne goes next to the

King's son." Still fighting her better judgement, Ari froze with her plate just above a large lamb platter.

"Ilhro didn't have a son."

"I know that." The man with the black coat seemed irritated now, as well as anxious. "Then it passes down through the line of Princes."

"Organa – Medeinot – Vuccine – Falsa," the woman recited the names like a schoolgirl. "What is your point?"

The young man clearly found this to be little more than an amusing intellectual game. "Perhaps the Organan Prince might have been better. Or if not him, the Lord of Medeinot."

Ari set the plate down abruptly and stepped away, losing herself in the crowd again as the woman in the red dress began to rant about how each and every one of the Princes had deserved to die.

Try to look like you are having fun. She found a small gap between two large circles of people and squeezed herself between them, hoping that her presence was moderately inconspicuous. She let her eyes rove the hall once more. Several couples were moving out onto the dance floor. All three of the green-suited men from the line were gathered at a table nearby, talking with great enthusiasm.

"May I ask you to dance?" a deep voice spoke in her ear, and Ari felt a warm hand press into the small of her back. It was all she could do not to spin and kick him in the stomach. Remain calm. Remain relaxed.

"I'm afraid I don't dance," she answered coolly. Maybe if she did not look at him he would walk away.

"A drink, then?" Now the man had shifted around to her front, his hand still cupping her back, sliding over the edge of the veil so that it rested against her bare skin. They were standing so close that Ari thought she could feel his heartbeat.

And suddenly her own heart stopped. She felt it pause mid-thump and then leap ahead, pounding double-time. A feeling of icy cold was steeling over her whole body and she wanted nothing more than to be far away from the man who stood before her.

He wore a rich red satin tunic, tucked into black pants with a wide leather belt that featured an intricate golden buckle, a dragon at its center. Gazing eagerly down at Ari, his bright eyes seemed to pop out of his thin, sharp face, his cheek and jawbones so pronounced that she had the brief image of a skeleton leering out of its coffin. He was still waiting for an answer.

"Yes, that would be fine," she heard herself responding, just so he would let go and step away. Her voice was hollow, vacant, an echo that reached only the outer ear and then vanished before Ari could be sure she had actually spoken. She had a vision of herself bursting into dust like the nymph in the forest, and fought to keep her hand by her side, away from the dagger at her hip.

The man nodded and released her, disappearing into the crowd in search of the provisions. His departure seemed to break the ice that had covered her brain. Now her entire body was coursing with a strange, frantic energy. Where was Ely? Ari spun in place, frantically searching for him among the throngs of partygoers. Suddenly he was before her, placing a hand on her arm to stop the twirling.

"What's wrong?" Upon his face was a look of deep concern.

"That man," she said, and for once she was almost at a loss for words, but she had to speak because if she did not tell Ely, she knew that her wish for Jagger would be too strong and the anima would come running.

"It's him," she began again, and when Ely looked understandably confused, continued, "That's the man who killed my parents."

CHAPTER XV.

As soon as Ari spoke, her eyes went cold again and her body was still. Ely automatically dropped his hand from her arm. His heart gave an anxious flutter in his chest and he wondered how – if what she was saying was true – Ari could be so calm.

"I need you to explain," he said slowly, deciding that this was better than releasing the string of questions that, by now, he knew would only irritate her.

Eyes roving calculatingly about the hall, Ari pursed her lips and, for a moment, Ely thought she might ignore him altogether. Then she spoke quietly. "I saw him nearly every day of my life until we moved from Organa to Nyin. He was my father's partner in service to the King and they worked together, traveled together, raised their families together. Then he saw an opportunity for power and he took it."

"So, this man..." Ely struggled for the words to answer, confused by her blunt delivery and composed demeanor.

"Zaid Moharine."

"Moharine. He killed your mother and father."

"Yes."

"And you are sure it is him?"

"He hasn't changed." She was not present in their conversation. She was somewhere else, somewhere across the hall or across the country, or in another time altogether.

"Ari," Ely said, because the situation had suddenly become much more complicated, "we need to focus on our mission.

Did he recognize you?"

"Not yet," she answered, eyes finally coming back to rest on the boy's worried face.

"Ari..." he said again.

"Don't look so nervous," she snapped. "They will think something is wrong."

"What do we do?" Ely made a conscious effort to slow his racing heart, but it did not seem to do much good. He had a bad feeling about this.

"We follow the plan." It was becoming clearer that, though Ari appeared calm, the encounter with Moharine had left her deeply unnerved. "I'll talk with him only as long as I must, and then I'll make my way out of the party, in search of the bath, I suppose. Have you located Broun?"

Ari's gaze was once again flitting around the chamber with such rapidity it was almost dizzying. Though she had asked a question, Ely was not sure that she was listening for an answer. Of course, ignoring him was only habit at this point, but given the circumstances he thought that perhaps he deserved a bit more attention.

"I think so. I was just going to investigate that side of the room when I saw you..." *Spinning*, he was going to say, but instead he let his words trail off.

"Well, hurry and identify him!" Ari whispered angrily. "And then find me in the back halls, because I'll need my sword."

"How am I supposed to find you in this massive house?" he asked, his own irritation mounting as she continued to snap at him.

"Make up an excuse, use your magic, figure it out," she answered flippantly. "I'll be heading towards it."

"But –" Ely's next query was cut short by the sight of a tall, gaunt man in a red tunic striding across the room, two slim glasses in his bony hands.

"Go," Ari commanded. He went.

***

Zaid did not seem to have noticed Ely leaving as he arrived, and he handed Ari her drink with a gentlemanly bow of his head. She took it without offering so much as a smile. The touch of his pale fingers on hers made her want to scream. Staring fixedly at the clear liquid in the glass, she did her best to ignore his eye contact.

"It is very brave of you to wear such an article tonight." His pointed tone startled her and she glanced up to see him gazing at her gold cuff, an alarmed look on his face.

"I don't understand what you mean," Ari told him coldly, both because she did not want to betray anything and because it was the truth.

"There are many who would not recognize that symbol, but I can guarantee you that none who do will take it lightly."

"I can assure you," she repeated, looking away once more, "that I am not aware of any significance."

He grinned menacingly, baring slightly crooked teeth. "You may hide behind such claims because you are young and ignorant. But I warn you that I am the only person in this house who would recognize that band and say nothing, out of respect for past sacrifices."

For a moment, Ari's confusion overcame her vengeful anger as, mind racing, she searched her memory for the golden cuff. Though Zaid did not seem to associate it directly with her parents, the bracelet clearly meant something. It had been a mistake to let Ely talk her into wearing it. She felt an unfamiliar pang of regret in her stomach.

Past sacrifices. There was no doubt that Zaid was talking about those killed in the coup. Or perhaps this was only her projection onto what might have been a completely offhand comment.

"I don't mean to upset you," Zaid said when she did not

respond. "It will be our secret."

Her anger was rising, rising from her toes to her stomach and then to her neck and head and the tips of her ears. Or rather, it was not rising at all but spreading out from her heart, her burning, boiling heart, to reach every part of her being. He thought he was being generous, forgiving her the sin of wearing her dead parents' jewelry, he thought he knew what secret he was keeping. She yearned to tell him to whom he spoke, and then to run him through with her father's sword. *Ely has my sword,* she thought. *Why did I let Ely keep my sword?*

Still watching her carefully, Zaid was clearly beginning to find it strange that she was not speaking. Ari knew that her facial expression lay somewhere between extreme irritation and ill-contained fury, probably nearer the latter. She needed to remove herself from this situation before she made a mistake.

"I'm feeling a bit queasy," she told Zaid in a clipped tone. "If you'll excuse me, I must step outside."

Though he had given her more space since returning with the drinks, the older man now stepped close and placed a cool hand on her shoulder. Ari took a slow breath.

"Think before you turn foolish thoughts into foolish actions," he warned, voice hissing into her ear so that she could feel the words like fire scorching the side of her face.

Without looking back or acknowledging him, Ari pulled free and strode away. Her pulse was quickening with every thought or image that crossed her mind. *Focus, focus, focus,* she willed herself. *There is a job to do.* The job was the most important thing.

Having thoroughly lost Zaid in the crowd, she looked around for her next step. A servant stood by the edge of the dance floor, eyes wandering lazily around the room in a relaxed, mildly interested manner. He pushed a lock of raven black hair from his eyes and nodded deferentially at a man in a gold-threaded robe walking by with a short, red-haired woman on his arm. Ari made a direct beeline towards him.

"Excuse me, sir." Ari placed a hand on the young man's arm, trying to keep her expression as earnest as possible. "Do you work here normally, or just for the night?"

Smiling generously, the servant nodded at her, sending a fruit arrangement sliding sideways across the tray he balanced in one hand. "Yes, miss, I am here every day."

"Would you direct me to the bath?"

"Make your way out of those doors and take a left. There is a chamber second from the end of the hall." With his free hand, he pointed at a pair of wide double doors, one of which was propped open by a burly guard.

"Is there any part of the house to which access is restricted?" Ari asked nonchalantly – and when he looked wary, added, "I just want to be sure not to wander somewhere I'm not allowed. It is such a big, confusing house, don't you think?"

The man was immediately appeased. "Of course," he told her kindly. "The eastern wing is off limits to anyone but Mister Broun and those select few with his permission. So, avoid the hall to the right when you pass through the doors."

"You have been most helpful," she assured him brightly.

Blinking abashedly, he gave a little bow. "It was my pleasure."

Ari took an apple from his platter and glided off around the edge of the dance floor towards the doors.

The guard at the open door was a stocky older woman, dark hair streaked with silvery grey and weathered face marked with an assortment of scars and sun freckles. She frowned at Ari as the young woman passed by, her gaze following her down the hall for several seconds before deciding that she really was headed to the bath. When Ari had nearly reached the end of the hall, she turned to be sure that she was not being watched. The guard had gone back to observing the party. Reversing direction, Ari walked silently to the other end of the long corridor, toward the eastern wing.

There was strange lighting in this part of the building, and it made her feel more comfortable with her task to think that she was moving in partial darkness. The oil lamps glowed brightly where they hung all along the ceiling, but the stonewalls were so dark that they seemed to consume part of the light. There were few decorations here, only the occasional oil painting of a dim face or a brown battlefield, none of which stood out in the weak haze of the lamplight. At the end of the hall was another door, which Ari was sure opened up to the eastern wing. Her heart thumped, Zaid's skeletal face filled her mind, and there was no time to think about her next move. She pushed the door open.

Before her was an almost identical hallway, except that it was really two hallways and, unlike the first, each of those two were guarded. The passage to the left was filled with soldiers; the one on the right had only two.

"This area is off limits for guests," one of the men on the left called, noticing Ari in the doorway.

She had only seconds to make her decision. At first glance, it seemed obvious that the most valuable items would be kept behind the rows of armed guards, but Ari had seen this before. It was a rudimentary but effective trick and her years of thieving told her that the dragith was more likely to be protected by fewer, more skilled soldiers to deceive the thief into attacking the more heavily guarded area. But in this case, she thought, Broun would not be expecting an attempted theft. There was no reason for him to play these games unless he knew something, and Ari doubted that Daerecles, as clever as he was, would have given them away. Who else would be insane enough to steal such a valuable object from the country's most secure paramilitary fortress? She made her choice.

"I'm sorry," Ari answered calmly, now striding forward to

meet the mass of men who blocked the left corridor. "I was just feeling so light-headed in there with such a crowd. I had to remove myself for a moment." She rolled the shiny apple about in her palm.

"There are other places where you can rest. You are not allowed here."

"Might I just wait and eat my apple in peace?" she asked them mildly. "I'll even let you share a slice. It must be so dull standing back here all day."

By this point, Ari had reached the guards and stood only a yard from the man at the front. They all watched her with wary curiosity. Paramilitary soldiers were always so dense, she thought. Hired hands and nothing more. Some of the men at the back were eying her up and down, gaze roving over the pale blue dress in mounting interest. She shot them an angry look, but it did nothing to lessen the stares, so she pulled the silver dagger out of her waistband.

"Whoa!" The man at the front stepped forward hastily. "You can't have that in this house."

Ari moved smoothly out of his reach. "I only want to cut my apple. Didn't you want a piece?" She looked serenely up at him.

He faltered once more. None of them spoke for a moment while she slit the smooth skin of the red fruit with her blade, which glinted in the flickering lamplight.

"I wouldn't mind a taste," one of the soldiers behind him spoke up at last.

There were probably ten or twelve of them. Not a big problem if she had her sword but, as expected, Ely was nowhere to be found. Something told her that it would be foolish to act now. Something more desperate whispered that there was no time to waste, that all she had to do was to finish the job and then she and Jagger could run very, very far away from Zaid's bright eyes.

"Come here," she said, holding up a slice of the apple in

her knife hand.

Three of the men moved past the front row of guards to stand in a semicircle around her and as Ari lifted the apple she tossed the white shawl into the air and raked her blade as forcefully as she could through their broad midsections. Before they could react or even double over in pain, she had kicked the man in the middle backwards into his companions, setting off a domino effect of bodies falling and stumbling behind him. By now, the two on either side of him were clutching at their wounds and did not move quickly enough to stop her from darting between them to follow the path of fallen soldiers. Jumping over the first two, Ari used her dagger to lash out at the men who tried to block her way. There were still five left standing and they fell upon her with their broadswords in such a manner that she knew they did not consider her a serious threat. It was a lackluster attack, but without her sword or a second knife, she would not make it far.

Where is Ely? Ari dodged one, then two swinging swords and thought that maybe she should have listened to the second voice instead of attempting this worthless attack improperly armed. Managing to avoid another blow, she plunged the dagger into one guard's thigh and watched a blaze of light illuminate the dim corridor, searing past her line of sight with intense speed. A second beam shot past and Ari realized that it was not a light, but a flame.

"It's sorcery!" one of the guards shouted, panic in his voice.

Another ball of fire whirred through the air and hit the man nearest Ari in the shoulder. He cried out and dropped away.

"Get out of the way, Ari!" came Ely's voice, strong, excited, commanding.

She moved aside. Three more blasts came in quick succession, each striking one of her attackers.

"Keep them down!" she called over her shoulder, already moving further down the hall. "I'm going in!"

There was no time to pause and make sure that he could handle this task; Ari was certain that more men would be on the way soon and this was already a bigger mess than she had hoped for, no matter how reasonable that hope had been. Sprinting down the passage and cursing her choice of attire, Ari tried to arrange her thoughts. The dragith stone would not be in a lofty position in Broun's treasure room. Rather, if he followed the pattern of most rich and powerful hoarders, it would be shoved into a back corner, covered with a fancy velvet cloth or stored in a simple box. With so much security out front, there would not be anyone left in the room, perhaps one at the most. She prayed that the room was small.

It was. There was no guard. And the dragith was not on prominent display. In fact, Ari realized with a lurching in her stomach, it was not there at all. She ran frantically around the room, which was conveniently tiny, though packed with all manner of valuables. She tried to convince herself that it might be hidden in a secret vault or stored underneath another treasure, but she could not. She knew that it was not there. It was in the other room. Ari had been fooled by the oldest trick in the book. How had Broun known they were coming?

Ari ran back out of the chamber, silver dagger clutched tightly in her left hand, the right feeling uncomfortably empty without her sword. A fire, blazing up like a wall before her eyes, stopped her in her tracks.

"Let me through!" she shouted at Ely, who was beginning to sweat with the effort of maintaining his magic. "It's in the other room!"

"What other room?"

"Let me through!"

"What about these –"

"Let me through, Ely!"

The wall vanished, leaving only steamy wisps of hot air in

its wake, and the men ran towards her. Now they were almost all wounded in some way, clutching at their own smoky burns or dagger-induced cuts but still brandishing those clunky broadswords with righteous indignation.

And Ari was angry, too – angry that someone had known about the mission and angry that she'd let Broun trick her and most of all angry that Zaid could put everything at risk. She let her anger overflow and moved through the attacking soldiers with something that could almost be called ease, skirting blows and dealing her own so forcefully that they actually began to fall back, ten against one. And she didn't even have her sword.

"Follow me to the right-hand passage and warn me if anyone attempts to enter after me," she ordered Ely, who was trailing behind her, stunned.

"You don't want me to come in?"

"Picking up a rock doesn't require two people," she snapped without slowing down.

He began to jog to keep pace with her; they were leaving the pile of groaning guards behind.

"Just keep them all out and give me..." She paused. "Keep the sword."

"Thanks," Ely said in surprise.

"You need it more than I do."

The two guards at the end of the hall had drawn their swords and were stepping up to meet the thieves. "Stop there!" one said firmly, holding out his weapon in what was supposed to be a threatening stance.

Ari did not bother to answer this, meeting them instead with her silver dagger, which was imbedded in each of their thighs before they could speak another word.

"Stay there or the next one hits higher," she told them.

"She isn't joking," said Ely.

The second treasure room was slightly more spacious than

the first, but no less cluttered with ludicrous objects. Despite this, Ari knew immediately that the dragith was there. Her well-trained thieving senses guided her to a nook on the left wall, where something that looked to be a small box was draped with an ornate tapestry. Moving around an ivory table laden with several piles of precious stones, she reached the box and threw off the cloth. It was plain mahogany underneath, carved with a little half-bloomed rose on the top. She reached to pry it open but the silver clasp stuck, as if glued shut. After a brief effort, Ari tucked the box under her arm and turned away, already calculating their escape from the mansion.

"Did you really think you would make it out of here with the stone?" The voice was sickeningly familiar, grating on her ears like a nightmare on sleeping eyelids.

Zaid Moharine stood before her, sword balanced lightly in his hand, eying her with a wary sort of amusement. How stupid was she, to enter and search the room without even noticing his presence? He must have been right by the door the entire time. Glancing quickly around the room, Ari assessed her options. In a room this small, it would be nearly impossible to escape without contact. And, oh, how she wanted to kill him.

"You are not getting out of here without me," he laughed as he watched her look about. "I will be leaving with you – whether I drag you out of this room dead or alive is entirely your choice."

"The problem with clichés," Ari told him coldly, "is that the speaker usually fails to perceive any outcome other than the one he expects."

Zaid laughed again and Ari's skin burned with hatred. Ely was probably too far away from the doorway to hear this conversation, to know that she was not alone. She couldn't remember ever wanting to kill anyone before.

"Didn't you know we were expecting you?" he asked

derisively. "Is it not common knowledge that we have inside information on nearly every Rebel plan?"

Caught off guard by his flawed assumption, Ari hesitated. "I told you already –" Then it dawned on her; they had been expecting someone. Someone other than her. "We have Former Military information, too," she said quickly.

"The Malavi are a government," he corrected. "Not military."

"You are no government," she spat, unable to stop herself. "A government stands for people, not power. It does not murder out of blind ambition and it definitely does not have to hide itself behind rows of soldiers because it is too afraid to shoulder the responsibility it has stolen for itself."

An anger that Ari had never known was crashing down around her, an anger not stemming from his nauseating statements or revolting countenance, but from the knowledge of what he had done, suddenly so tangible in his presence before her. Never had she allowed herself to consider his betrayal as something so real. Never had she stopped to think about what it truly meant to her. It had all been so distant, muddled in her seven-year-old brain. But now Zaid stood there with that self-assured expression plastered upon his pale face and the reality struck Ari with incredible force, burning and boiling up until she thought she might explode from the sheer heat of it. Only the tiniest fragment of judgment kept her from letting it run away with her.

There was some sort of recognition hitting Zaid, a dawning idea that reflected out of his bulging eyes. He spoke more carefully. "You have awfully strong opinions for a Rebel pawn."

"You have a lot of confidence for a murdering traitor." It was out before Ari could think on her words and she immediately regretted it. If they were to make a clean escape, he could not recognize her. If she was to go on living as she had, he could not recognize her.

Too late. "No," he said softly, staring at her with widened eyes.

She stared defiantly back, self-reprimand fueling her lividness.

"Ariana –"

"Don't you *dare* call me that."

"I believe I would have heard if you had maintained your title all these years. Even in wartime, news of Starlen's long-lost daughter would no doubt reach many ears."

"You are sick."

Her heart was pounding in her head, her ears filled with the noise of her own blood rushing like it could fight this fight for her. This was a dream. This could not be real.

"Do you actually work with the Zaerans or is this just a job?" He was mocking her now. "Is this what you've spent your life doing? Running around as hired mercenary to the highest bidder?"

Thump-thump, thump-thump, thump-thump.

Somewhere in the back of her mind was Ely's voice calling for her to run, to get out of there because more guards were coming, but that voice was faint in comparison with the rage that continued to build up in her chest, filling her eyes and ears and mouth.

"Hired mercenary to the highest bidder?" Her words came out so softly that if it weren't for the acidic tone, they would have been lost even in the tiny chamber. "You have no right to speak to me about anything, much less about selling my honor for personal gain."

"I was faced with an impossible choice –"

"There was no choice!" Ari cut him off, voice now jumping from a hiss to a shout. "Killing your best friend and his wife is not a choice! It is the will of a monster."

Zaid almost looked put out by this. "Is that what you think of me?"

Thump-thump, thump-thump.

"Were you hoping for hugs and kisses?" she retorted bitterly.

"If not me, it would have been someone else," he began, and then added quickly when Ari's mouth fell open in shock at these words, "I had my own survival to think about. I recognize that you may not agree with my past decisions, but I have a job to do now, and I cannot let you leave with that stone."

Thump-thump.

Now she really could hear Ely saying something about moving, something about four more men on their way.

"I have to bring you in, but I don't have to kill you." Zaid waved a pale, bony hand. "Perhaps we can keep your lineage quiet. If they find out who you really are, even I will not be able to protect you." He spoke as if he were someone of power, and not a pathetic imposter. "The Malavi cannot risk someone of your status bringing the rebel groups together behind you, not when they are building something –"

"*If you don't get out of here right now,*" Ari interrupted, unable to stomach another word, "*I will kill you.*"

"Unarmed?" He laughed. He was either blind to her knife or not taking it seriously.

"With my bare hands."

"Your father was a dear friend," he said, as if this was supposed to make it better somehow.

"Yes, you have taught us all what friendship really means," she snarled.

"I thought of you as a daughter, still think of you –"

"Stop!" Ari's voice cracked with angry emotion. "Don't say another word!"

She took a step toward him, shifting the silver dagger into her right hand. "Move out of the way."

"Ari!" Ely's shout came clearly down the hall this time. "We need to leave now!"

"Starlen and Irena did not choose this life for you," Zaid

said gently. Like she was a child that could be talked down.

"No," Ari agreed, "they didn't."

She let the silver blade fly home to the man's chest. His eyes widened and he dropped to his knees with a grunt. As Zaid swayed unsteadily, Ari moved forward and retrieved her dagger with a harsh yank. The growing bloodstain hardly showed through his tunic, only half a shade darker than the ostentatious color of the silk.

"This is not justice," Zaid murmured feebly, perhaps surprised that the golden-haired princess had grown up into a cold-blooded killer.

"I don't care about justice." Ari wiped her knife on his sleeve. "I learned that from you."

CHAPTER XVI.

As soon as she exited the treasure hold, Ari saw that they were not alone. Ely had drawn her sword and erected another flaming boundary between their end of the corridor and the oncoming guards, who had more than doubled in number. He looked relieved to see her. He was running out of energy.

"Keep that one moment longer," Ari ordered briskly, "and pass me my sword and belt."

"What took so long?" he asked, tossing her the items and then biting his lip in concentration as the right side of the wall flickered out and then back up again. A few drops of sweat slid down his face.

"Moharine."

"He's in there?" The fire died completely at this news.

The soldiers took this chance to rush forward before Ely could conjure anything else, but Ari had already strapped her leather scabbard belt around her waist and drawn her sword.

Without a word, Ely grabbed the dragith box from her and clutched it tightly with both hands. "I'll keep it safe. I promise."

She nodded at him. "Follow me out."

They flew down the hall as more guards charged at them from all sides. Ely's magic seemed to have exhausted itself for the time being and he kept to Ari's wake, letting her do most of the fighting, as she preferred it. It was almost no time before they made it the length of the eastern wing and arrived at the doorway with the silver-haired guard. Sensing that a less-conspicuous exit would be near-impossible at this point, Ari made the snap decision to take them straight through the party. Now, though her heart still pounded, it beat a steadier rhythm; this was what she knew.

A scream went up as soon as they burst from the dim passage into the brightly lit dance hall; Ari had knocked into one woman, and Ely was sending a servant flying into two men with overflowing dinner plates. Once again, they clasped hands, but this time it was the young thief who reached back to find her companion and pull him along behind her through the chaos.

Come find me, Jagger, she was thinking. *Come find me. Come find me.*

If the scene before them had been reenacted in silence and then frozen in time for an artist to paint, perhaps altering the shocked and terrified faces to conjure a prettier picture, it would have formed quite a pleasing image. Bright silk skirts of every color twirled wildly out of their way, men in dashing coats and trousers threw their arms up in surprise, and all around them jewels and glasses and plates of food flew out of startled hands to find home, first in the air and then smashed upon the marble floor.

The benefit of this surprise escape was that, in their shock, not one of the guests attempted to stop or even slow them. In fact, most moved out of the way to avoid the fleeing pair, and – because the guards were several seconds slower – had readjusted by the time the burlier pursuers were making their way through. Ari shoved the soldier by the front door out of their way before he realized what was happening, and they were free – or as free as they could be out-of-doors but with an entire army on their trail.

The cry had gone up, and dozens of men and women were filing out of the mansion and its surrounding buildings, armed with swords, axes, and bows. Ari and Ely had a head start and the benefit of a busy square of people, but somehow, she doubted that Broun's soldiers would be very shy about firing arrows upon innocent civilians.

Come on, Jag.

"We can't leave without our things," she told Ely out of the corner of her mouth. "We must retrieve them quickly and keep moving."

They took a sharp left around the next block, and she could see their chosen hedge at the end of the street. A yell about reinforcements echoed down the lane after them, followed by a knife that came skittering out of the sky, bouncing across the cobblestones near Ely.

Ari laughed aloud. "Pick that up."

He did and just then the bobcat appeared, a silvery streak in the dark night. His girl could sense the anxiety that swept his agile body, and she bent to brush the tip of an ear as he fell into step by her side.

Reaching the long hedge, Ari pointed for Ely to remove their bags, then turned quickly to watch for their pursuers. "Hurry," she instructed. They were coming. Nearer and nearer, they were coming.

Belongings in hand and over shoulder, they took off once more down the street. Ari, with the sound of heavy footsteps in her ears, focused on the gaps between the people and carriages that blocked the open road. Ears on a swivel, Jagger darted lithely around obstacles as they hurtled onward. An arrow came flying from somewhere behind them, narrowly missing his girl's left arm, and he let out a loud hiss. Suddenly, Ely was grabbing Ari's hand and pulling her down a side street.

"What are you –?"

"Better cover!" he shouted over the cries that went up at the sight of this detour.

She yanked her fingers out of his grip. "We need –"

"– horses!" he finished for her, still yelling to be heard through the racket that followed them down the narrow lane.

"They'll be mounted soon and we won't have a chance!"

As soon as the words left his mouth, Ari heard the unmistakable click of hooves on cobblestone. They exchanged glances and sped up. Without a word, Ely motioned to her and she followed, turning down yet another, smaller path. Wedged between tall, square homes with flat red roofs and blank-looking windows, it grew narrower and narrower until it was gone altogether and the buildings opened up into a wide plaza. At the far end sat an exquisite stable, a pale, wooden structure with two long wings stretching out from a central dome.

The two sentries standing outside the open aisle were completely unprepared for the group that now came flying at them. They had barely raised their sabers when Ari disarmed the one on the right and ran him through the leg with her sword. The other fell to the ground at Ely's well-aimed punch to the face.

"Grab that one," Ari ordered, pointing at a black gelding that stood saddled and hitched in the aisle.

While Ely ran to untie the horse, she pulled a bridle off of a rack by the barn door and looked around for another mount. The rest of the stable was now filled with horses in varying stages of hysterics. Ari picked the nearest stall and quickly undid the latch, sliding in calmly and holding her palms outstretched to the nervous mare.

"Want to get out of here and go on a run?" she cooed to the animal, a pretty dappled grey with fine legs and a plump belly.

"They're coming, Ari!" Ely's voice rang in a strange, empty echo, up to the high beams of the ceiling.

The mare pinned her ears and stepped sideways. There was no time to waste with making her feel comfortable. Keeping up a steady stream of conversation, Ari moved to her and placed a hand on her withers. The horse tensed, and then relaxed slightly as Ari continued to rub her shoulder reassuringly. Seeing her opportunity, she reached to pull the mare's head down and slid the bridle over her ears.

"Ready, pretty girl?"

Eyes still wide, the horse breathed heavily and snorted, shaking her head at the flowing blue gown that Ari still wore.

"Damn it," the girl muttered to herself, realizing that the dress proved a hindrance in yet another important area of her work.

Without a second thought, she bent and ripped a slit all the way up to her thigh, hoping this would be enough for her to sit comfortably on horseback.

"It'll have to do, princess," she told the horse, who was now standing stock still as if she were waiting for something to push her anxiety over the edge. Ari needed to get her outside before that happened.

"Ari!" Ely called again, and she heard shouts in the square.

"You bought the dress," she retorted, though she knew he could not hear her.

Now she dug her left hand into the mare's thick black mane and half-pulled, half-leapt to throw herself over her back. This was enough to set the terrified horse in motion. She took off with Ari still hanging on sideways, skirt billowing and sword banging against her dappled shoulder. Ely looked ready to rein his horse in, but the mare blew by him and up the street.

"Come on!" Ari shouted back at him. "They're here!"

And they were. Soldiers were pouring out of the lane where Ari and Ely had been only a minute earlier, some on foot but many now on horseback as well, tearing determinedly after the thieves. Shutters snapped shut around the square and down the street as the air filled with the sound of angry shouts and orders directed at troops to "Close off the exits, cut off the main road, and chase them down!"

Arms and abdomen burning from the effort of holding on to the galloping mare, Ari let an arrow zing over her horizontal frame and then gave a forceful jerk on the only rein she could grab. The animal veered to the left, twisting Ari sideways so that she was facing forward. Swinging her right leg all the way over, she pushed herself into an upright position and grabbed the reins with both hands.

There was an immediate change in the horse's demeanor as soon as she felt the strength and ease in Ari's legs and seat. Though still moving at a flat sprint, the mare flicked an interested ear back to her rider and softened her hold on the bit. Breaking one of her own rules, Ari turned to check behind them. Ely was about seven lengths back, but the soldiers were gaining on him. There was a big house with long window boxes coming up on their right, the second story just high enough for her to reach on horseback.

"Stay left!" she called back to him.

Without looking to see that he had followed her order, she unsheathed her sword and hacked into the wooden bolts that held the boxes in place. Three of them snapped and the boxes went crashing down on the heads of their pursuers.

"Good one," came from behind her, closer now. Ari did not look back again.

Now that they were both mounted, Ely and Ari began to pull ahead of the Malavi force, putting greater and greater distance behind them as they galloped on. The hooves of the grey mare and the black gelding pounded their fleeing rhythm into the stone streets, and three seconds behind came the thunder of dozens of Malavi horses in pursuit. As they ran, more shutters swung shut, curtains dropped, and locks clicked into place. The people were retreating into their homes, doing their best to shelter themselves from whatever was coming. Ari did not know how long it had been since there had been any real action in the Capital city, but even through the padlocked doors and darkened windows, she could taste the fear that leaked out and over the silent cobblestones.

"Do you know your way out?" Ely asked loudly, raising his voice to be heard over the hoof beats.

"I think so," Ari answered honestly, because she was not certain that she knew the fastest path out of the city.

"Do you want to follow me?"

Two arrows soared over their heads in quick succession. The grey snorted in surprise and then pinned her ears as Ely's steed drifted too close to her. Ari ticked the left rein and cooed reassuringly to the horse. One ear flicked up and she ran on.

"Can you keep that animal moving fast enough without someone to chase?"

Ely smiled. Digging in his heels and tilting forward almost imperceptibly, he urged the gelding into an even quicker tempo and pulled ahead of the mare, who tensed angrily.

"You and me both," Ari whispered, tightening her leg to settle the irritated horse, "but sometimes we have to let lesser beings take the lead."

"Don't listen to her, girl," Ely called over his shoulder. "We lesser beings are the ones that'll keep you sane."

"Less talking, more focus," Ari said, but she could hardly keep the smile out of her voice.

Already past the innermost wall and coming upon the second barrier, Ely slowed ever so slightly, seeing a wide hay cart placed perpendicular to their path. After a split-second hesitation, he wheeled off down a tiny lane to the right, barely making it around the corner without clipping his knee on the window box of a squat brown cottage. Ari followed suit, though with a smoother turn, and found herself in an even narrower space than expected. The cottages converged upon them from both sides, coming so close together that she was not sure they would make it through mounted. But Ely charged ahead, surprising her with his boldness. She pulled her feet up so that her knees were even with the mare's withers, balancing carefully on the galloping horse's round back.

"We won't make it through the wall on a main road!" Ely shouted, leaning left to avoid a low awning. His bag banged against the side of a building.

"Can we jump out?"

Behind them, Ari heard a cry of surprise, followed by one of pain and several angry yells. The soldiers had just reached the lane and realized they could not fit, resulting in a collision between the horse at the front and the one immediately to its rear.

"There's a low point this way! But get ready, it comes up fast."

Ely was not exaggerating. Ari could see the last house on the street and then, immediately beyond it, the base of the crumbling wall, which rose up directly in front of them. Even here it was massive. She dropped her legs and sat back to collect her horse, letting the black gelding pull ahead into the open space. Then Ely was flying over the wall, torso tilted in perfect form; in three strides, Ari was also in the air, soaring over what she knew was close to five feet high and holding her breath that there was nothing to trip up a smooth landing on the other side. There wasn't. They were away, and even though they had a whole third of the city to make it through before the final wall and the Sonrein Plains, she knew that it was too late for Broun's men to catch them now.

Ely let loose an exhilarated whoop as Ari gave her mare the reins and allowed her to pull even with the gelding. Grinning, the boy shook his head at her in disbelief. They had done it.

"What does this say about me?" he asked with a laugh. "Does it always feel this way?"

Ari just steered the grey into the lead once again.

They did not slow up until they were about three miles out of the city. The black was foaming at the mouth and even the spirited mare was growing weary. They had run until they could run no longer.

There was no sign of pursuers over the vast expanse of

plains, only that quiet stillness that seemed to pervade the tired, burnt earth no matter the time of day. The high city appeared smaller and smaller each time Ari glanced back, and then one-by-one the bright white lights that illuminated the peaks and towers extinguished themselves until there were only a few left to shine upon the lonely Palace. The adrenaline from the chase was ebbing out of Ari's body and she felt a sudden wave of exhaustion hit her like a rock wall, or a rainstorm. It was exhaustion, and something else – something more fearful. Jagger was still moving at a run somewhere behind them, trying to catch up with his girl.

"We need to stop," she said abruptly, reining her mount back to a walk.

Ely looked about how she felt, curly hair plastered to his head and eyes squinting wearily into the dark night. He stared back at her as if not entirely comprehending what she had said.

"They will send another group after us in the morning," Ari said, blinking to clear her mind and settle her thoughts. "We need to sleep so that we can rise and ride out early."

"Right here?"

They both looked around. There was no shelter for miles and the reedy grass that did stick out of the dry earth was rough and yellowed in the cold moonlight.

"Yes."

Unwilling and unable to question her further, Ely slid wearily down from his horse. Unbuckling the leather girth, he removed the saddle and laid it carefully on a barren patch of ground. The gelding sniffed at the saddle curiously. In the near distance, Ari's anima continued on.

With both horses un-tacked and standing calmly side-by-side, Ari and Ely stretched out on the dirt.

"You don't think they'll wander off?" Ely asked, staring up at the starry night sky.

"They're too tired, and we're their protection out here."

"That's what I was thinking."

He was silent for a minute and Ari hoped that he had fallen asleep. She knew that she could not sleep tonight, but at least she could hope for a quiet few hours of rest.

"There is a lot you have not told me," he interrupted her quiet.

"How did you know there was a stable there?" she asked, voicing a question that had been on her mind and ignoring his comment.

"A hunch. Some childhood memories." He brushed the inquiry aside and continued, "Where were you born?"

"Organa." Jagger materialized out of the dark, his grey-brown coat a pale arrow in the moonlight, and made a circle around their little camp, flicking his tail anxiously. Ari waved him down.

"You told me you had no connection to the Old Kings. But your parents were civil servants." As much as he tried, Ely could not hide the surprise in his voice.

"My father was," Ari told him flatly. "So were many people in Organa." A small, but prosperous city on the outskirts of the Capital, Organa had been known as the home of the King's court. Until the coup, almost the entirety of its population had worked for the royal government.

"And Moharine?" Ely asked. Ari did not know why he was so concerned with everything.

"His partner." Ari continued to hope that he would lose interest and go to sleep.

"Did you and your mother travel with them?"

"I went sometimes, she always."

"He never realized it was you?" Now Ely's tone was slightly more careful, probing.

"He did," she said, and the air felt cold on her face, which stared up at the stars, and her bare shoulders, which were still exposed by the awful blue dress.

Ely sucked in a breath. "So he let you leave?"

"No."

This time there was no question. "You killed him."

"Yes."

In the pause, Ari could hear him grappling with this truth. "How can you be so calm?" he finally burst out.

"I was not aware that there was a proper etiquette for these circumstances," Ari intoned drily.

"You just murdered someone," he said, both emphatic and bewildered.

"And he murdered my parents," she snapped in return. She did not understand why he didn't hate and fear her now, and this only made her angrier.

"Anyone," Ely answered, "that has to kill to get what they want has mistaken priorities." He was so measured, his shock tempered by an optimism she could not begin to comprehend.

"I must have entered the wrong profession."

"Is this a joke to you?"

"No," Ari told him firmly. "It's real life. And that is exactly what you do not seem to understand."

"Just because you see the world one way does not mean that we all do." It sounded like maybe he was looking at her, but Ari continued to watch the stars flicker. She took a quiet breath and counted the stars in the constellation right above her. *The Lion. One. Two. Three. Four. Five. Six. Seven. Eight. Nine.*

"What I do is not a game," she answered slowly. "Every contract is a risk. People are angry, scared; they trust no one. They do not hesitate to injure or kill. And if I slip up and the wrong people discover my identity, they will track me down." A brief pause. "I have many enemies."

"I wonder why," Ely muttered, but his tone was more good-natured now and he did not speak again.

Soon, Ari could hear his breathing slow into sleep. Lying there on the rock-hard earth with her blue gown covering her legs like a blanket and Jagger resting by her side, she thought about the lights in the sky. If Dav was right, and her parents were up there, she wondered what they were thinking now. Would their stars be shining brighter tonight? Or would they be dulled with grief?

Starlen and Irena did not choose this life for you. Perhaps not, but the little girl Zaid had remembered had not wanted a life of courts and diplomacy either. The white of the stars made their dark carpet almost blue and, before Ari's tired eyes, the blue shifted gently into a morning purple. The stars blinked out one-by-one.

CHAPTER XVII.

The two horses had hardly moved a muscle when Ari rose and stretched her arms above her head. There was no sign of the sun other than the subtle lightening of the sky, and even her anima blinked wearily up at her, worn out from miles of travel the night before. With her companions still asleep, Ari rummaged through her rucksack and pulled out her usual tunic and pants.

She turned away from Ely's sleeping form and slipped out of the party gown, shivering at the feel of the cool, silky fabric sliding down around her legs. Other than a few small cuts and scrapes, she had made it through the evening's events unscathed and was relieved to see that Ely and Jagger had done the same. She pulled her top over her head and fastened her pants and belt with a satisfied sigh. Never had she been so glad to put on her riding boots. The gold cuff she removed last and tucked carefully back into the folded fabric with Dav's compass. As she stowed it away, a glint of metallic light shone, taunting, into her eyes. It might have given her away, might have betrayed their mission – and her survival. It could not be trusted.

There was a nicker, and Ari turned to see the grey mare awake and watching her with interest.

"I wish I had some food or water," she whispered to the horse. "I'm sorry."

The animal flicked an ear forward-and-back uncertainly then stretched out her neck to sniff at the rucksack and Ari smiled. She liked this horse. Hopefully she could keep her around for a few days.

"Do you want some walnuts, princess?" Reaching into her bag, Ari removed the little leather pouch with her dwindling food supplies and offered the mare a handful.

"Have you named her, then?" Ely was sitting up with his legs crossed, watching her. His bag was open and he'd laid the dragith box on the ground in front of him. Ari searched his face for remnants of the previous night's conversation, and found nothing.

The grey brushed her soft lips over Ari's open palm, inhaling the nuts. "What?"

"Princess?"

Wiping her empty hand on her pants, she turned to face him. "I didn't name her."

He shrugged. "Looks like you've named her."

"Were you going to open that?" Ari motioned at the box.

"I thought it would be easier to carry. Smaller."

Ari nodded. He reached for the clasp and popped the lid. She raised an eyebrow but said nothing about her failed efforts to open it the night before. The yellow-orange stone shone bright in the morning light, giving off a hazy glow that seemed almost to emanate from within.

Ely picked it up. "Interesting," he commented vaguely.

"I'll carry it," Ari told him, holding out her hand.

He placed the stone in her fingers and held up the box, which Ari now saw featured a dragon's head, not a flower, as she'd thought. "I suppose we'll leave this behind, then."

"Are you ready?" she asked, slipping the stone into the pouch on her belt.

"Ready to get out of this wasteland."

"Dressed like that?"

Glancing down, Ely seemed to remember for the first time that he was still wearing dress clothes. "I guess not."

Ari popped a few walnuts into her mouth and then cinched

the pouch shut and dropped it into the suede sack. When she looked up, Ely was pulling a shirt down over his chest.

"I wish we had stopped to say goodbye to Randal," he said, running a hand through his dark hair and looking about absentmindedly.

This was too ridiculous a suggestion to warrant a response.

"I mean, obviously there was not much time." The boy saw his boots on the ground and bent to pick up the right one. "But it would have been nice. I suppose I could write him a letter once I am back in Casina, but we don't often send regular post these days. The Malavi are always intercepting the messengers."

Ari waited impatiently while he began to lace his shoes.

"You said your father worked with the Organan government. Did you ever meet the Debouryne family?"

Ari's heart skipped a beat and she was glad that Ely was distracted by his boots. "A few times, yes."

"My parents spoke so highly of the Prince," Ely said absentmindedly. "They liked how he handled the trade deal with the Parejon Hills. Was his name Starling?" He straightened up and shook his head. "No, that's the city. Starlen. Prince Starlen."

All Ari could do was breathe and hope he would move on, which he did, his face now quite serious.

"Did Moharine say anything that suggested they would send troops out after us?" Ely spoke Zaid's name quickly, like he could make it not exist if he rushed over it. Ari forced herself to breathe evenly.

"Of course they will," she answered, brow furrowed. "Men like that do not let such valuable objects go freely."

"You don't believe that there might be any other reason for them to search for us?" He busied himself with packing his bag, shifting things around as Ari hesitated.

Zaid's words about the Zaerans infiltrating replayed in her

head. She saw the rows of soldiers stationed as decoys in front of the first treasure room. "Why would you ask that?"

"I only thought it was an awful lot of men they sent out," Ely said casually. "Seemed like an entire cavalry."

"It was," Ari said thoughtfully, turning away from him to stroke the grey on the nose.

"An entire cavalry?"

"A lot of men."

"So, you think there is something going on?" he asked, and came to stand beside her.

"Saddle up," she answered. "It's going to be another hard day."

"I don't need the saddle, if you want it," Ely said, motioning at the piece of tack where it lay on the ground. "You rode bareback yesterday."

Stepping to the grey's shoulder, Ari shook her head. "She's an easy ride."

Ely picked up the saddle and set it over the gelding's narrow back, then cinched the girth with a quick, effortless tug at the billet strap. "I'm not going to just forget about this. You cannot keep ignoring me when you don't want to talk about something."

Ari sighed. "Give me a leg up?"

Ely laced his fingers together and held his palms out by her knee. In one smooth motion, she placed her left foot in his hands and, with a little boost, swung herself onto the mare's back.

"How is Randal with the golden eagles?" she asked, after nodding in thanks.

"What?"

"Is he familiar with the eagles? As messengers?"

"I'm – I don't know." Ely stood awkwardly with one hand in the gelding's mane, paused in preparation to mount.

"Okay."

"That's it?" He seemed almost annoyed that she had no

further response to his lack of knowledge.

"Well, I was going to offer to send him a message," she said tersely, "but there is no point if he cannot receive it."

"Oh." Ely looked at her curiously, still standing with his fingers over the horse's neck. "Thank you."

"We need to hurry," Ari told him. The sun was going to show itself soon. The sky already looked a lighter pink.

Ely pulled himself into the saddle and reined his horse into step alongside the grey mare. Breaking into a brisk trot, they left their campsite behind and began the journey across the Sonrein Plains. It would only take a day to make it to the river and then on to the edge of the Belem. They would need to find a shallow crossing if they wanted to keep the horses with them, and Ari had a feeling they would need the animals to get as strong a head-start as possible.

The stiff grass made a crunching noise as the horses' hooves thudded over the dry ground, pounding the dusty earth into an even trail of half-moon prints. Jagger loped comfortably along beside them so that they made a line of three abreast. As they rode, Ari scanned the sky for signs of golden eagles, hopeful that when their little party grew nearer the forest they would be able to send a message to Daerecles. This part should be easy for someone as practiced as she was but something was off. It nagged at Ari like hunger in the pit of her stomach.

"He thought I was with the Zaera army." She voiced her thoughts aloud. "Zaid did."

"Why?"

For a moment, she was halfway startled by Ely's response. Normally her musings were for Jagger alone. "They were expecting a Zaera attempt to steal the dragith."

Now he took a moment to respond. "So there are other people after it. People other than us."

"People other than Daerecles," Ari corrected.

"Right."

"That is what I'm worried about."

The mare skittered sideways to avoid a waving piece of brush and knocked into Ely's mount before Ari could settle her. Pinning his ears, the gelding snapped at his companion. "Be nice to Princess," the young man said soothingly, checking the left rein and giving a bit more leg. "She's sensitive."

Ignoring his use of her pet name, Ari continued, "We don't want even more parties on our tail."

"The Zaerans won't know it was us," said Ely hopefully.

"That is not the sort of reasoning I like to rely upon."

"Okay, so we have to be more careful," he spoke slowly at first and then said quickly, "But it's alright because soon we will hand it off and be done."

"It does not add up." Ari's thoughts were jumping ahead, and she hadn't really been listening to him. In her mind, she saw the dying nymph's bright eyes and heard Zaid's words echoed over and over again.

Didn't you know we were expecting you?

"Why would the Zaera Army want the dragith?" Now he was catching up.

"I don't know." And she did not, but still she ran through every scenario in her head, desperately trying to conjure up a logical solution.

"They don't need money." Ari was beginning to regret her thinking out loud. "And they have no use infiltrating the Capital at this point. They would need to take more of the country before they could conquer the city."

"Let's wait on this discussion until I can think more," she said coolly.

Ely fell into a thoughtful silence, absently tugging at his steed's head every time the gelding veered too close to the irritable mare. It was several hours before they spoke again, and when they did it was only for Ari to confirm that Daerecles had not given Ely any more specifics about the hand-off point. In that time, they quickly crossed the upper half of the Plains and the sun found its way into the open sky. It shone warmly upon their faces, casting ever-shorter shadows that flickered westward as the horses' thin legs cut back and forth over the land. As they neared the river, the noise of the water grew loud and their surroundings became green again. The mare began to tug at the bit to reach the fresh growth.

Ari turned them west along the bank while the rest of the group followed wordlessly, searching for a low point in the surging river. They found it about half a mile down, a shallow pool where the powerful stream slowed and collected into a quiet pond. The black gelding balked when the cold water touched his belly, but the mare charged forward, prancing into the river with her head held high and her fine legs stirring up little whirlpools with each step.

"That's a girl," Ari told her with a smile. "Take a drink."

She dropped the reins so the horse could stretch her neck down and inspect the water. Snorting excitedly, the mare blew ripples across the surface and then plunged her muzzle several inches into the river only to come up with a nose full of water. Ari laughed out loud and the grey pinned an ear, then shook her head and began to drink greedily.

"Don't make fun of Princess," Ely said. His horse had finally made peace with the water and was gulping it down several feet away. "You'll offend her."

"She doesn't have a name," Ari responded, but she was still smiling down at the dappled neck.

Just then they heard a fierce, desolate cry, an avian screech that flew over the barren plains to reach their distant ears, where it was only barely muffled by the brief swath of life.

"What –" Ely began but Ari shushed him and took a deep breath.

She let out three long whistles, each louder than the last. As she did so, she collected the mare and urged her onward. They crossed the river and climbed up the southern bank, which the grey jumped with a somewhat spastic motion that sent Ari sliding backwards. When they had reached level ground, the young woman brought her to a halt and stood listening.

"What is –" Ely tried again, but again she cut him off.

"Wait."

And so they waited, all five still, silent. A minute passed, then two, then three. After four minutes, Ari was ready to take another breath and try again but just as she opened her lips, the air moved. Massive wings stretched above their heads and then descended from the wind to the tree-covered earth. Moving quickly, Ari slid from the mare's back and crouched before the bird, bowing her head low. This golden eagle was less trusting than most, and it watched her carefully for a long moment before gently dropping its wings to its sides and acknowledging her with a subtle tilt of its sharp beak.

Letting out a breath of relief, Ari dug through her bag for a slip of paper and scratched a message onto it. The golden eagle hesitated, and then stretched out a taloned foot to take the note. As soon as the paper was in its grasp, it raised its wings once more and lifted into the air, sailing off to the southeast in a long, sweeping curve.

"Is there anything you can't do?" Ely asked good-humoredly when the eagle had disappeared.

Raising a disdainful eyebrow, Ari ignored him. "Hopefully we will hear from Daerecles by tonight, or tomorrow morning at the latest."

She mounted again, and they returned to a walk and then a trot, moving away from the roaring body of water and through the last of the green land before the miles of scorched earth that Ari knew was coming, and dreaded. She tried to keep the anxiety out of her mind so as not to worry her horse, but the grey was already growing skittish in nervous anticipation of whatever her rider feared.

"He knows the eagles, too?" Ely asked, chewing on his lip and gazing back at the final row of half-burnt trees.

Ari thought of Daerecles tracking her golden eagle and frowned. That was treachery she could not forgive. "Yes."

The only sound now was the crunch of hooves upon the desolate earth, which had quickly shifted from valiant green to burnt black. Even the black gelding became jumpier, nostrils flaring open and ears spinning quickly to catch every frightening detail of the dead scene before them. The irony, Ari thought, was that there was nothing left alive to harm them, but she supposed that the very fact of death was enough to set any living creature on edge.

It did not seem appropriate to talk and they remained wordless. Without notifying Ely, Ari pushed her horse into a canter. He followed. As they sped up, their feet kicked up more ash and dust, a strange mixture of dark and light that filled the air they left behind. Moving forward to avoid this cloud, Jagger settled into place beside Ari, legs reaching out to cover ground as quickly as he could. He seemed almost to blend into the grey air, more of a subtle shadow than a tangible being as he glided through the ashy haze.

Ari's mare snorted and shook her pretty head, choking indignantly on a particularly thick puff of burnt debris. Opening her mouth to calm the cross animal, the girl swallowed her own mouthful of dust and began to cough, further startling the grey.

"Maybe we should slow down," Ely suggested when Ari's horse let out a succession of crow hops that brought her dangerously close to trampling the bobcat. "She's right to be upset. I can't breathe, or hardly see a thing."

The ash continued to stir from the earth, rising to coat the air and settle over their quickly-greying clothes. Eyes watering, Ari nodded and they both reined their mounts back to a walk. The dust hung in the wind, seemingly still, frozen into the sky like rain that had been paused mid-storm. Only this was not cool water, but rather harsh, grimy remnants of life that scratched on Ari's naked face and caught in her hair and eyelashes. They had to be close. She hoped they were close. But in this strange, thick cloud it was nearly impossible to make out even the highest peaks of the Belem Range and Ari had the feeling that they could be walking in circles and she would not know it, so disconnected was she from everything but Jagger, Ely, and the two horses.

The feeble sun, a yellow-colored twin of that silent white moon from several nights earlier, shot the occasional ray through the ashy sky, illuminating small spots upon the blackened ground or reflecting through the debris like a dirty kaleidoscope. These patches of light did not make Ari feel any better. Instead they provided flashes of daytime that was just as quickly sucked back into the perpetual greyness, leaving the travelers with an even more desperate feeling than before.

"At least we know we're safe here," Ely said, and Ari could tell that he was only talking to fill the eerie void that surrounded them. "No one could possibly see us well enough to attack."

"We can't exactly see them either," she responded dully, wiping ash from her eyelashes with the back of her hand.

"I feel like I'm stuck in a very grey snowstorm," he declared cheerfully.

Silently, Ari considered whether she would rather die from frostbite or from suffocation by hot ash. At the moment, freezing to death sounded more appealing.

"Who's there?" A muffled voice called out through the floating debris. Ari held up a hand to halt and they all froze. "Come this way!" the voice commanded, and it sounded like a woman, though she could not be sure.

A horse nickered a few feet away. Ari felt the grey mare tense to respond and gave a quick check on the reins to silence the noise. The animal chomped angrily on the bit but did not whinny back. There was the sound of a few tentative hoof steps, then a rider's boots hitting the cracked earth. A whistle on some kind of instrument. In the distance, an answering call.

Ari's heart seemed to have slowed just as the ash in the air had frozen in time, beating only once every few seconds, or maybe every minute. She kept her body relaxed, calm so that the anxious mare would not react. It was imperative that they were not seen. The boots were approaching. To move or to remain in place?

But this was not to be Ari's choice. A figure began to take shape in the dense air, quickly turning from shadow to flesh before their eyes. It was a woman, short and stocky with a young face and keen eyes that fixed upon Ari like a predator upon prey. A long whistle hung around her neck.

"Who are you?" she demanded.

"Travelers. We are leaving the Capital after visiting an old friend."

"The Former Military claims that two thieves stole from them last night. A young woman and a young man. The girl was said to be short, thin, blonde..." She peered fiercely up at Ari. "Now, I don't see any blue dress, but I figure you might have changed since then."

"And you're with the Malavi, are you?" Ari asked of her, maintaining a flat, neutral tone. The woman did not wear the typical army blues; instead, her grey tunic and pants recalled a Zaera soldier.

At this, the woman crinkled her nose in disgust. "Of course I'm not with the *Malavi*." She said the word like it was poison, or a disease that could infect upon the slightest mention. "We're Zaerans."

Ely opened his mouth to reply and Ari immediately cut him off. "What is your interest in two casual travelers?"

"We do not condone the Former Military's goals but we may still desire their methods."

This peaked Ari's interest but her gaze remained impassive. "What is it that these reported thieves stole that could be so valuable to both armies?"

There was fear and confusion jumping in Ely's eyes, but

the soldier was so focused on Ari that she did not notice. "An object of great power," she answered snappishly. "But I'm sure you already know the item of which we speak."

"I am not one to play games," Ari told her coolly. She was now thinking of the second whistle that had answered their challenger's call and wondering how much longer they had before more Zaera soldiers joined them.

"They also reported that the boy had a fine sword." The woman's eyes narrowed even further, gaze piercing Ari's person with determined severity. "That blade on your hip looks an awful lot like the one described."

"You're going to arrest us based on an account, which is probably hazy at best, that one of us has a sword?" She could hardly keep the incredulity out of her voice.

"Are you saying that you are opposed to complying with the Zaera mission?"

Again, Ely was on the verge of speech but Ari did not allow him the chance. "Absolutely. We will not comply without cause. It does not matter who you say you are."

"Who we *say* we are?" The soldier was practically spluttering with rage.

"Ari –"

"We're going, Ely."

"Don't you dare take one step!" the woman threatened angrily. She began to blow frantically on her whistle.

Ari did not reply, but instead turned her horse away and urged her into a trot. There was no chance that the soldier would catch them on foot, or even if she took the time to mount her horse, but Ari wanted to get as far away from them as possible. The whistle continued to sound, squealing in her ears and causing the grey's eyes to roll around in her head. Faster and faster it blew, and the sheer speed and volume seemed to make the ash fall more rapidly, swirling around them in a terrifying vortex of grey sky and earth.

Now there were definitely others approaching; hoof beats

wove in-and-out through the muffled quiet of the ash storm, drawing nearer. Glancing over her shoulder, Ari was startled to see that Ely was not with her. She clenched her jaw, unable to roll her eyes without filling them with dust and flakes of ash. If he got himself lost out here, there was no chance of her finding him again. The thought crossed her mind that it would be easy to leave him behind now – that she had the dragith, that she could probably move even faster, and certainly quieter without him in tow. But then she remembered his wall of fire in Broun's mansion and the promise of money for his family.

"Ely!" she called, against her better judgment. "Ely!"

"I'm right here!" The boy materialized right by her side, appearing like a ghost out of the grey haze. He posted slowly in the saddle, concerned eyes flitting between her and the seemingly empty air behind them.

"Oh – don't –" Her words were lost in a coughing fit, which nearly doubled her over in its force.

"I'm trying to think of something," he said, raising his voice as a series of whistles went off once again.

Ari was coughing too hard to answer immediately. Tears made dark tracks through the ash on her cheeks and Jagger began to lope anxious circles around the two horses, who continued to move forward at a brisk trot.

"Are you alright?" Ely asked. "I'm thinking that I might be able to..." He murmured something under his breath and suddenly the air before them cleared; the swirling debris flew out of their path and built itself into two walls on either side.

A strange noise was coming from the empty air, a rushing sound, like wind whipping through a mountain pass. The young man was holding one hand out, with fingers flexed as if he were pushing a heavy door, while he kept the other gripped tightly on the reins of the black gelding. Behind them, the storm did not let up.

This time, Ari did not wait to see whether her companion

could hold the spell. Too desperate to get herself and her anima out of that horrible, dead desert, she pushed the mare into a gallop and they ran forward into the wind tunnel. She had forgotten what clean air felt like and this was heavenly, like cool water on a parched tongue. She took one, two, three deep breaths of fresh air as they rushed ahead, gulping it down in gratitude, and in fear that it would soon be gone. The footsteps, shouts, and whistles of the Zaera forces had disappeared yet they galloped on, not slowing until it was green earth, and not magic, that dispelled the dust.

Breaking out of the burnt plain, Ari still did not pause, did not even deign to look over her shoulder at the wall of twisting ash that rose up under that meager yellow sun. There was no Capital behind the dirty cloud, no shining Palace to spot among the hilltops. The sunlight sat atop the grey expanse like watery paint on a soiled canvas.

"Would it have been so bad to comply with the Zaerans a bit more?"

They were sitting in a small, fire-lit cave, facing each other from opposite sides of the dark cavern. After hours of traveling into the forest, Ely had spotted an expanse of rock with a sizable cavity and, with Ari's approval, they had hitched their horses and built a fire inside. It should have been somewhat relaxing, sitting by the fire with freshly washed faces and sore legs grateful for a rest. But the flames reminded Ari of burning ash, and a feeling of unease had settled in her chest.

"We now have two armies after us," she said evenly.

"But the Zaerans are not like the Malavi," Ely protested. "They fight against the forces that initiated the coup. They're not bad people."

"Bad people?" Though she tried to fight it, there was a catch in her voice. "If they're not good people, what are they?"

"What do you mean?" She had caught his attention.

"It has never been about right and wrong. The Zaerans

claim to be our liberators, but in reality, they kill as many civilians and destroy as many livelihoods as the Former Military does."

"That's a strong statement," he answered, looking at her closely.

"It's the truth." Ari met his eyes for a moment and then turned to the feeble fire, picking up a burnt branch to poke at the flames.

"Is this about what happened in Nyin?" The question was posed casually, but there was a tension in Ely's voice that made it clear he understood the risk he took in asking it.

***

Ari didn't respond for a minute, still stoking the fire with her blackened stick, staring deep into the embers as if in search of the right answer.

"We always knew what the Malavi wanted, what they were trying to do and how they were going to do it," she said at last. "But the Zaerans have never made it clear what they wanted. They say they're fighting the Former Military regime but that's all we've ever been told. What they really want is power. I have seen what they do. I have felt the..." She seemed to be searching for the words. "I have felt the fear, and the desperation, in those settlements, those regions under Zaera rule. They are no saviors. They show up in helpless villages, in ruined cities, and demand loyalty without cause. And if people don't give it, the Zaerans kill them."

She paused, deep in her own thoughts and oblivious to the effects of her speech on the creatures sitting around the small fire, which she continued to tend. "They tear across this earth like it is theirs to burn," she said softly, so softly that Ely had to strain to catch her words. "But it's not theirs. It's not anyone's."

He watched her, stunned into silence by this address,

which was so uncharacteristic of the woman he was slowly coming to know, always so brusque and blunt. Though Ari spoke in a whisper, there was a heat behind her words that he found startling. He wanted to ask her more but those few sentences felt like a gift, and he was afraid to push her too far.

Jagger hadn't raised his head from his paws, but he observed Ely closely, with a kind of quiet curiosity, sensing Ari's strange mood. The anima was stretched out by the fire, back legs resting against his girl's thigh with a comfortable, loyal warmth. His big yellow eyes reflected the dancing flames as he stared down the human opposite.

Ely noticed the big cat watching him, and something about Jagger's uncertainty gave him courage to continue. "Were you there when it happened?" he asked, voice low, gazing across the fire as he tried to make out the expression on Ari's face.

"When they died?" Her voice still carried the same gentle tone, a sweet whisper that flickered in rhythm with the orange flames.

He nodded. "Yes."

"My parents moved us to Nyin because they knew what was coming. They stayed long enough to get me settled in, and then they left. They said it was a short journey, a job my father had to do for the King."

Ari paused and stroked her anima's smooth coat, taking comfort in the steady rise and fall of his flank. "Even at that age, I had heard enough to understand that they were in danger. So I wasn't really surprised to hear that they had been killed. Maybe that it was so soon, or that it was Zaid who did it, but not that they were gone."

She shook her head, and it seemed again that she was speaking more to herself and the quietly crackling fire than to Ely as she continued, "I got the news and it felt like it was so far away, like if I didn't have any proof, it couldn't be real. I almost hated them for that, for leaving me to live in this empty void without them. Dav was the one who really raised me. I had my parents for seven years, him for nine, and that time was more important... What is there to learn from peace and plenty, really?" She asked this without expecting an answer, glancing up quickly to check the reaction of her audience.

Ely sat as if frozen in place, worried that if he even breathed too loudly he would break the spell.

"The war had begun when I moved in with Dav. He taught me the basics of everything I know. How to hunt, how to fight, how to move without being seen. He taught me to learn from the past, not to dwell on it. You learn from the pain and the failure. And then you do better, so that you never have to feel that again. You train until you are the best hunter, the best warrior. And then you will be safe. We were prepared and we were strong. Together. He wanted us to be ready in case the fighting ever reached Nyin. He didn't think it would."

Here she stopped again and took a slow, deep breath. The bobcat blinked reassuringly. "When my parents died, it was news from afar. When the Zaerans came to Nyin, they killed him right in front of me."

Now, after minutes of gazing at the fire, Ari looked up at Ely and stared directly into his eyes. "I can still see it, every detail like it was yesterday. They asked if he supported the Malavi, and if he supported the Zaerans. He answered 'no' to both and they stabbed him in the back."

The silence in the cave was overwhelming, so still that all three creatures could feel it pressing down upon them like a heavy weight about to crack.

"It was winter." Ari broke the quiet at last. "It took me a whole day to dig the grave."

Chapter XVIII.

Ely was not entirely sure what he thought would change after the night's conversation, but whatever it was, it did not occur. The next morning, and indeed for the rest of the day, Ari was even more taciturn and aloof than usual and when he did dare to speak to her, she issued a snappy, irritated reply. Though he knew that it was foolish to think he could fully understand her behavior, his thoughts invariably wandered into deliberations on her state of mind.

It seemed clear to him that her closed manner was the result of those years of pain, which she had managed to channel into incredible determination, a willpower that verged on mechanical indifference. If the run-in with Zaid Moharine had caused that sudden shift in character last night, Ari had apparently managed to push the encounter far enough from her mind to resume her normal hostile behavior.

He glanced over at his companion, who had once more refused the saddle and sat tall on Princess' bare back. Ari's face was arranged into a stoic, emotionless expression, nothing more than a hint of thoughtfulness in her cool grey eyes. Her anima trotted alongside her, an equally silent figure in the shaded green of the wood. It had been several hours already since they entered the thickest expanse of forest along the base of the Belem, and still Ari steered them eastward with no sign that she might soon turn their course back into the mountains. As the undergrowth had become increasingly tangled, she had slowed their relentless pace down to a walk, and it was at this speed that they now continued, silent except for the steady tread of hoof beats on the grass.

***

Ari fought to keep her mind trained on her surroundings. She made a concerted effort to feel the movement of every muscle in the horse beneath her, to hear every rustle in the forest around them, to smell the drift of summer honeysuckle on the wind. It was only through this fierce exertion of will that she could force Zaid from her thoughts. Zaid and her parents. Her parents killed prematurely, unjustly, far away. She had always felt a strange kind of resentment towards them for dying, for foolishly trusting in other people who were always bound to act on their own evil interests. But now Zaid's wide eyes were in her head and that anger was gone, turned into a deep sadness. Zaid's choice. Her loss.

And Dav – how Dav was ever-present in her conflicted soul and mind, chipping away at her resilience with reminders of his every word and lesson. His memory both encouraged her and drove her insane. There he was, telling her to be strong, to remember what he had taught her, to remember that she was smarter, quicker, more skilled than the rest. And there he was dead. There was that red-black circle and that empty face, eyes like the sky without its lights.

She fought back the pang of hurt and grief that threatened to overwhelm her, told herself that she must focus on now. The forest was calling her and its dangers were great, especially now that there were others on their trail. The Malavi, the Zaera forces, and who knew how many more. Ari would remember this and collect her thoughts, and then some familiar-looking rock or particular species of tree would remind her of him and that knife would enter her heart once more, piercing through its incessant beating with such vigor that she had to stop herself from gasping aloud. It was a real, physical pain, so powerful that it clouded her eyes and stopped the breath in her throat. Why now, after so many years of solitude, did it hurt so badly?

See that stone there? she heard him saying. *That green lichen is edible. Remember that when you're hard-pressed for food.*

Never burn rhododendron or oleander for firewood.

Be careful about standing upwind and upstream.

Look at how the eagles fly with their eyes on the world; we must do all we can to imitate them.

Danger. There was danger everywhere.

Do you remember the nymph we met in Tyson? Do you remember what she said?

They had a few hours of light left.

The greatest swordsmen are those who need it to survive.

She had killed Zaid. She had killed him with the silver dagger.

Skill with a dagger separates the great from the good.

Why hadn't she killed him with her father's sword? That would have been more appropriate revenge.

Trust no others but always trust yourself. When that is not possible, trust Jagger, for he is the best parts of you.

Ari blinked hard and took a deep breath. The dark green of the wood seemed close and real before her tired eyes and she suddenly noticed how near she came to the branches that wove their way around her head and shoulders. Looking down at Jagger, she saw that his eyes were also following her, calm as ever but filled with watchful care. Dav was gone. They had survived six years without him; they could continue to do so without wallowing in such weakness and grief.

Never look back. Fortune favors those who learn and look ahead.

There came a rustling of leaves and they all halted. The great golden eagle had landed on a branch in front of them, Ari's paper curled up in its sharp talon.

It took you long enough, she thought, but did not share aloud for fear of disrespecting the regal bird. Daerecles had certainly taken his time.

She nudged the mare forward and reached up to accept the message from the eagle's outstretched foot. As soon as it was in her fingers, the bird lifted its wings and took to the air. Ari quickly unrolled the paper and let her eyes rove over its contents. At first glance, all she could see was her own note, scrawled in a hasty, messy hand. The page had been stained with what looked like splashes of mud, though they streaked across the cream-colored surface in a strange, deliberate pattern. She considered it for another moment.

"Is there something wrong?"

Ignoring Ely, she dropped her reins and scratched at one particularly thick blot. It flaked off under her fingernail, leaving a pale, brown mark that covered the words "Starling. Blue Lakes. Caution."

Ari stared at these words for a minute. The handwriting was easily legible but slanted in an awkward curve off to the side of the page, like the script of someone who was normally very neat but wrote in a great hurry. They had not specified a hand-off location, but she had understood, perhaps mistakenly, that it would be in the Southlands. Even without enemies on their trail, it would take nearly three weeks to reach the Blue Lakes and the travel would not be as easy as it had been thus far. How had the trader ended up all the way out to the East? And why – Ari looked at the writing once more – did he urge caution? For a thief, caution was more natural than breathing; there was no need to remind her of that unless he knew that they had encountered problems, or believed they would face more.

"Starling is north of Konchot?" she asked, stuffing the message into her pack.

"On the edge of the Blue Lakes, yes," Ely answered curiously. "Why?"

"That's where we're going." Ari clucked at the mare, who started forward eagerly. It was time to get out of the forest and take the chance on open land, where they would move much faster.

"To *Starling*?" His tone was shocked.

"Apparently Daerecles has relocated."

"The Blue Lakes are hundreds of miles from here!"

"Did you make him promise the hand-off would be in the Southlands?"

"No."

"Then we're going to Starling." Ari liked to have flexible meeting points in the off chance that there was a complication, but now she was feeling irritated that she had allowed this particular location to be quite so vague. If the job were not going to pay so well, the trip would hardly be worth it.

Ely gave a harsh, sharp sort of laugh. "Easy for you to say."

Ari had never heard him speak like this and she was momentarily shocked. "What?"

"I have an aging father, a sixteen-year-old brother, and a mother in hiding back home. I can't spend two months running around the country in search of that damned trader."

"Go home," she told him indifferently. "Maybe Daerecles can deliver your share of the payment later."

He stared at her for a moment and then he grinned and the nervous frustration was gone as quickly as it had come. "I can't let you off that easily."

"Then stop complaining."

"I've never been to the Blue Lakes," said Ely.

"Please be quiet."

"Did you hear that, Princess? She said 'please!'"

"Quiet, Ely."

"Is it true that there are dragons in the mountains?"

Pursing her lips, Ari ignored his stream of commentary but did not ask him to stop again. She thought about how every person under the sun had a way of coping with the chaos and the pain. She thought about Ely and his endless, infuriating optimism and wondered how, in such a dreadful world, he'd come to be the way he was.

Slowly, they made their way to the edge of the north Belem wood and Ely's words filled her mind like the steady buzz of crickets at night, painting over Zaid and Dav until all she could see were the darkening trees and the stars popping out one-by-one in the velvety blue sky.

Ari had been counting down the hours – the minutes, really – until they were caught. Not 'caught' in the literal sense. Rather, she worried about any discovery or encounter that would further complicate their increasingly lengthy journey. Yes, they had a pair of armies on their tail, but what concerned her most – what nagged at the back of her mind – was that these two large but cumbersome groups would somehow multiply into many. She still did not understand the purpose of the dragith or its appeal to the Malavi and the Zaerans, but if they did seek it as some kind of weapon, how long would it take before others joined the hunt?

Although the fighting had been limited to the two armies in the first couple of years after the coup, the people had soon realized that nothing was going to be accomplished and the country had descended into lawlessness. That was not to say that individual cities had no rule or order. Everyday citizens still went about their lives as they had always done, whenever that was possible. But out on the road, and even in the back streets of the quietest towns, gangs of mercenaries and huntsmen prowled with savage aggression. Sometimes they took sides or declared themselves an alternative to the two-party struggle, but more often they were simply small groups of people taking advantage of the anarchic state for personal gain.

It was bands like these that Ari feared. They would pop up when least expected and least wanted, more concerned about money and territory than strategy or principle and thus quicker to attack than either the Malavi or the Zaerans. She guessed that the huntsmen holding the nymphs had been part of one of these groups, or else mercenaries hired out by a Malavi army that was growing more desperate every day.

It was with these thoughts on her mind and worries in her heart that she was prepared when, to their right, the edge of the forest came alive and six men burst from the trees. Ari felt it coming before the first one had even emerged.

"Heads up!" she yelled at Ely, who looked startled by her cry and then grasped the situation as the band of riders broke from the tree line.

Ari knew immediately that this was going to be a tougher escape. The men on their heels had fresh horses and they had been waiting – whether for them or for any unlucky traveler, it was unclear. Nostrils flaring and tail swishing angrily, the grey mare felt a chase brewing and lunged into a gallop. But Ely's mount did not have the spunky attitude that Ari's did, and days of travel wore on his tired limbs more than competitive nature fueled them. The boy was an excellent rider, but there was only so much he could do with an exhausted animal.

About to pull her own horse back to match his pace, Ari had a different idea. The riders came surging up around them, swords already pulled.

"Go for the girl!" they called to each other. "The girl has the stone!" This was not a chance encounter.

"Ely!" She pulled a walnut from her pouch and tossed it to him.

He snatched it out of the air with a convincingly emphatic motion and the men let up an excited cry. The fact that it was the wrong color and size did not seem to cross their minds. Without another look at Ari, they moved to surround Ely while she sat up and hauled on the reins to slow her enthusiastic horse. They dropped back behind the group. She drew her sword.

"I hope you're okay with contact, princess," Ari murmured.

But she did not have to wonder long. She let out the reins and before she could urge the mare forward, the animal had bolted into the mix of her own accord, ears pinned in defiant determination. They blasted their way through the back row of riders and Ari let her blade fly, slashing about with such precision that the men were taken completely off guard. Her legs were pinned against the riders on either side of her, but she willed herself to keep her balance and gripped as tightly as she could. The man to the right caught a blow to the ribs and slid sideways, toppling off his horse like a rag doll. Wanting to move into this space, Ari shifted her sword to her left hand and reached for the reins, but as she moved to do so, the mare took her own prerogative and lunged for the horse on their left, slamming Ari against the other animal. Knocked off balance, she grabbed a fistful of mane and pulled herself into the grey's neck, bringing her sword up in time to block an energetic strike from her opponent. Just as their blades met, the mare took a bite out of the other horse, chomping down with such vigor that the animal threw its head up in pain and pulled away from the fray.

Taking advantage of the other rider's vulnerability, Ari attacked, connecting with his sword arm and slicing through the reins for good measure. Ahead of them, Ely was doing his best to dodge the other three riders while the fourth dropped back to engage with Ari. Desperately trying to get to Ely, she made the split-second decision to steer the mare straight into the oncoming horse, this time ready for the impact. The horse's shoulder slammed against the man's leg and he let out a cry of pain.

Not as easily deterred as his companion before him, he came back at Ari with a sudden slice of his sword that, much quicker than expected, caught her in the elbow before she could parry. Jagger, who had been running alongside them, let out a yowl of anger just as Ari spun her sword around that of her opponent to send it flying upward. She punched him in the face as hard as she could and heard her knuckles crack upon the contact. Without pausing to see whether he would hang on and continue to pursue her, she nudged her horse away from his and into the skirmish ahead.

Ely now had two men on his left and one attempting to cut him off in front. His horse was frothing at the mouth, its muscled chest heaving with exertion. Armed with nothing more than a knife, the boy could hardly put up a fight. Weaving back-and-forth at rapidly shifting speeds, he was doing his best to throw them off with horsemanship alone, but as Ari pulled even with them she saw that he was bleeding profusely from a gash on his left cheek and had a second wound on his thigh.

"Get out of the way," the man furthest left snarled at her when, sword still drawn, she steered her mount alongside his.

But he had not witnessed the fight that had occurred only two lengths behind him and was not expecting such a vicious attack from the slim, shorthaired woman on the dainty-looking mare. They were locked in a duel before he realized what was happening. Their blades hummed eagerly back and forth, each blocking the other's every move while the man to Ely's immediate left was getting increasingly accurate with his attacks.

"Stop messing with him and help me out!"

"I – am – not – *messing*," she shot back at Ely, each word emphasized by an increasingly vigorous stroke with her sword.

But by the third blow her enemy was outmaneuvered and by the fourth he was on the ground, left in the dust by the ever-smaller pack of horses and their struggling riders. Just as Ari dispensed with him, the one out front was able to get his horse in position to block Ely, pushing him left at an angle nearly perpendicular to their previous course so that he and the rider on his other side were wedged between Ari and the lead man. Despite the change in direction, they continued at a gallop. The sound of hoof beats and heavy breathing filled the air and the rest of the world was gone, fallen away to leave the four of them locked together and roaring across the earth.

"You *were* messing," Ely told her through gritted teeth, swinging a fist at one man and then ducking low to avoid the sword of another. "We need to get out of here!"

"Give it up!" the rider on his right ordered. "You're outnumbered!"

"Outnumbered?" Ari's indignation at this falsely ambitious proclamation was enough to end it.

Seizing the next open opportunity, she threw herself onto the horse that ran between her and Ely, wrapping her wiry arms around the surprised man and stabbing the silver dagger into his midsection. Caught up in the excitement, the grey mare had continued to run alongside them, but shifted away from the group as Ari pushed the rider off his horse and took the reins in her own hands. Her legs were not long enough to reach his stirrups but she had been riding for several days without a saddle and even this felt like a luxury. She pushed her startled new steed forward as urgently as she could.

"Drop back," she hissed at Ely, hoping their final opponent would not hear.

He did not. As Ely brought his horse to a sudden stop, she and the other man collided in the vacuum, bodies and horses meeting with such disordered force that Ari thanked the stars she was no longer riding bareback. And while she had been prepared, the last rider was not. He fell like his comrades before him, nursing a hemorrhaging shoulder and limping after his mount, who was trotting nervously towards the now-distant tree line.

"I was right," Ely said, looking halfway validated and halfway astonished.

"You really were not."

They slowed to a canter and then, when Ari felt certain that none of the six men could pursue them, to a trot. The grey mare was still bouncing haphazardly in their wake, head high and nostrils flaring with adrenaline-filled agitation.

"Then tell me: does my presence really serve any purpose or are you humoring me?" There was a playful kind of smile on Ely's face that was marred only by the leaking wound over his cheekbone.

"You were a good diversion."

"Ah, so – why are we stopping?"

Ari had brought the new horse to a complete halt and was rummaging in her pack. "Perhaps next time I will use you as bait," she told Ely drily, feeling strangely content. "Now that you've revealed your magic to the Malavi, you might be just as wanted as I am." She came out with a short coil of rope, which she fixed into a lasso.

"If you take that horse with us," Ely warned, "she gets to keep her name."

As the grey mare swung round to their right, Ari let the rope fly. It settled over her crown, caught on one ear so that she was only halfway hooked. The horse gave an excited shake of her head.

"Come here, princess, pretty girl," Ari cooed. "Let me fix that."

She gave an encouraging tug on the lasso, trying to maintain a soft touch so that it would not slide off the mare's delicate head. It took no more than that. Whether she was taking to the fierce little rider or just wearing down after miles of work, the grey pranced over to fidget by Ari's side. The woman reached out and quietly pulled the rope over the free ear and down her dappled neck.

"Alright." She nodded at Ely, who was giving her a curious look. "We ride as long as it takes to find proper cover, and then we stop immediately. It's dangerous to go too far with these wounds untended."

"I'll be alright." She did not like his expression.

"You don't know that."

Now he was smiling at her again. "You have a soft side."

"I'm not worried about you," she told him flatly. "But if you pass out from blood loss, I'm going to have to carry you to shelter and that would be very inconvenient."

Ely was shaking his head, the same grin plastered across his bloody face. "You kept Princess," he said.

"You should stop calling her that. You'll get attached."

"Right." He was still smiling. "I'll get attached."

They walked on, all members of the party moving more slowly as the adrenaline drained away and the weariness set in. After a few minutes, Ari turned them back towards the edge of the forest once more, searching for a place to make camp. The stars, no longer full and bright, were disappearing under a wispy grey cloud, made blue by the late-night moon. It felt like rain.

"How have you kept yourself a secret all these years?"

"What?" She looked away from the tree line to meet Ely's eyes for a moment.

"Anyone could see that was not the first time you've been in a fight like that." He peered through the darkness at her blank face. "News travels."

Frowning, Ari turned back to her search.

"I just don't understand why no one knows your name," he said when she did not speak.

"We do not exactly run in the same circles," she replied coolly. "Half of the thieving world could know me and you would not have the smallest idea that I existed."

"That's not the reason." He waited.

"Because I don't want them to." As she spoke, she realized how much she sounded like Daerecles and felt an inkling of respect for the secrecy of the arrogant man. "Any mission that involves contact is a failed mission. It is far better to escape unseen."

"But you can't do that every time," he pressed on.

"No."

"So how is it that we don't all hear tales of the young Southlands woman and her anima beating the toughest soldiers and huntsmen at their own game?"

"Who decided it was theirs?"

"What?" Now he was on his heels.

"First rule of combat: as soon as they draw their swords, it's your game."

Having spotted what she was looking for, Ari pressed her mount towards the forest. The branches were lower here and the two riders had to duck to avoid getting caught.

"Teach me to swordfight."

Ari did not respond right away. She pushed a leafy cherry branch out of her face and tugged on Princess to follow more closely. The rope hooked on a stick and she stopped to shake it loose.

"It is not a skill that one can learn overnight."

"I know that." His tone was eager. "I just need to learn the basics."

"It takes years –"

"Just get me started," he interrupted. "That is all I ask."

She pursed her lips. "You don't have a sword."

"We will cross that bridge eventually." Ely flashed her a charming smile.

Sighing, Ari slid from the saddle to land between the two horses. He stopped his mount behind them and looked at her expectantly.

"Get down," she told him. "We're sleeping here for the night."

Her right elbow was beginning to throb and she knew that his wounds were worse. Though he tried to hide it, he winced as he swung his leg over the back of the saddle and hopped to the ground. Ari quickly hitched her two horses to a wide cedar and removed the tack from the new horse. Then she dropped her pack on the ground and stood to go.

"Stay here and watch the camp."

Ely had no chance to reply before she had vanished among the trees, heading straight down a little hill that was peppered with strange purple-colored shrubs and ancient cherry trees. The slope bottomed out after only a minute or so, collecting into a happy stream, which bubbled along in quiet contentment. Ari knelt and dipped her arm into the clear water. Though it was now quite dark, she could see the spring turn brown as dirt and blood swirled away from her submerged limb, which stung with a searing pain upon contact. Fingers now clean, she felt for the cut with her left hand. Not deep, just uncomfortably located. Nothing that a little fresh air would not fix.

Now she pulled a rag from her pocket and held it out by a corner, letting it sink slowly into the water. When it was fully saturated, she got to her feet and walked back to the spot where Ely and Jagger waited.

"Come here," she ordered the boy, who was sitting on the ground and watching Jagger's tail flick back-and-forth, back-and-forth.

He looked somewhat like one waken suddenly from a heavy sleep, but he complied. Following her direction, he perched himself on a log about three feet high, so that they came eye-to-eye.

"Be still."

Ari pressed the wet cloth to his face, gently at first and then harder, testing to see how much pressure she could apply before he protested. He did not move or make a sound, the only sign of feeling a general whitening of his already pale face. It was only now that Ari saw her knuckles beginning to blacken from the punch she had thrown in the midst of the struggle.

"Feel how I hold it?"

Ely nodded.

"Take it and keep it just like that. No more pressure, no less."

He raised his left hand to cover hers and she slipped it out from under his, so that the pressure was maintained constant. Ari did not ask to look at his thigh; she simply moved to inspect it, probing cautiously at the place where the blade had sliced his trousers. A flood of relief broke in her chest when she saw that the wound was not deep. Face and arms could be dealt with. A leg injury would severely cripple their mission. This wound would require no more than cleaning and the time to heal, though of that they had little. It was the kind of cut that she would grit her teeth and ignore until it sealed itself back together. Hopefully Ely could do the same.

"How is your arm?"

Ari looked up to see him watching her intently, brown eyes gazing into hers with care and concern. She suddenly felt their closeness, made even more intense by the pressing nightfall, and a sense of anxiety thumped in her heart. Breaking eye contact, she glanced down at his bloody leg and then stepped back.

"It's fine."

"Can I look at it?"

"I already did." She had not moved from where she stood a half step away from him, and she met his eye once more, daring herself to discern what it was in his look that seemed so old, so familiar.

Ely laughed. "Tell me you can examine the back of your own elbow and I'll admit that you really aren't human."

He motioned for her to come to him, and for whatever reason, she obliged. Turning so that he could inspect her arm, Ari let him run his fingers along the wound, prepared to steel herself against the painful discomfort that was sure to come. But his touch was light, gentle, and it did not even sting as he bent and unbent her elbow to watch the gash stretch on her tanned skin.

"I just want to be sure that you are not going to break more skin moving your arm around," he explained. "Any kind of injury takes longer to heal when it is located near a joint."

"Right. Are you done?"

His hands fell away from her arm at the hard tone. "Yes. You'll be fine."

"I could have told you that."

"You did," he said, and then paused for a moment. "Did you see any yellow willow by the water?"

"There was one a few dozen yards downstream," she replied, striding over to where her pack lay on the ground.

Ely slid off the log and moved across their campsite. "I'm going to get some leaves."

"What?" Eyebrows raised, Ari stopped with her hand in the bag.

"Crushed yellow willow leaves have healing properties," he said with a casual shrug. "They help the new skin grow in faster."

"Are you sure?" Dav had never taught her this, and Ari still considered his knowledge of healing to be almost completely infallible.

"I used to help my mother sometimes, when she was still a healer in Casina." Ely seemed unconcerned by her lack of confidence in his expertise. "It was mostly common illnesses, or injuries from working with animals or in the trade shops. We never had to deal with many battle wounds, but the technique is not all that different, is it?"

Ari just looked at him. She wondered how many more times he would surprise her like this. "I do not understand you."

He gave a short laugh. "That does not surprise me."

"We'll finish this job soon," she told him, not sure why she was continuing this conversation. "So you can get home to them."

"I know," he replied with a smile. "I am not worried."

"Why not?"

This question, however cynical it was intended, did not seem to faze him at all. "I don't have a choice." He shrugged. "There is no time to weep and fall apart when people are counting on you. Without my sister, I'm the only one who can help them."

Ari heard that strained tone in his voice again and noticed that he hadn't actually said his sister's name. "Were they angry with her?" she asked, because this was simpler than asking Ely how he felt.

"Sad," he answered. "Scared. If they were angry, they didn't show it. It is easier to be silent and solitary and filled with rage, but each day they choose joy, and risk loving others, even those who might leave us. My mother likes to say that hope is not simple, but it is worth the work. The beautiful moments are what carry us through the ugly ones, aren't they?"

Ari studied his friendly, open face for a moment as she considered his words. His brown eyes were gentle and earnest, looking back at her expectantly.

"Well, anyway," he continued, starting to fidget a bit under her scrutiny, "I'll go find the yellow willow."

"Be careful," she said without thinking.

Ely gave her another curious look and strode into the trees. Ari pulled her polishing cloth from the pack and set to shining her blades. The silver dagger caught a glance of moonlight through the closed treetops, shining like diamonds on the curved hilt. Jagger came to sit beside her and she worked the rag back and forth until the weapon shone all on its own.

CHAPTER XIX.

"I'm ready to learn."

"No."

Ari had felt the rain coming as she was hunting for their breakfast that morning, watching less and less light drift through the branches. One raindrop and then another until it was a steady drizzle, hovering like a great avalanche ready to roll down the mountain. It had pressed lower and lower until the leaves began to drip and the forest floor became slick with dark rain.

The storm had unleashed itself by the time they left their camp and they had been forced to travel all day long through an unceasing downpour. The rain seemed to keep enemies at bay, but it left Ari feeling tired and water logged, not eager for a training session.

But Ely would not let up. "Please. I'll be so much more helpful to you if I know what I'm doing."

"One lesson isn't enough to know what you're doing," she told him crossly.

"What else are we going to do with this time?" Ever so persistent.

"Rest. In case you haven't noticed, we've been on the road for over a week."

"In case *you* haven't noticed, our journey just got a lot longer. If you won't train me," he added with a touch of humor, "I'll have to fill the time some other way. Perhaps we could discuss the function of the stone, which you seem so keen on ignoring."

"A thief's job is not to bother with the uses of an item but simply to acquire and transport it."

"There are legends, you know," Ely said, as if he hadn't heard her at all. "My mother used to tell stories about talismans with wild powers. Summoning hurricanes or great fires – you know the tales. There has to be some truth to them, doesn't there?"

"I don't care what the dragith does," Ari lied. "It is likely just a pretty stone." In truth, she was becoming more anxious the longer their journey dragged on. It was clear that the dragith's mysterious power called to many dangerous people; she worried that these first attacks were just the beginning.

Ari looked around, contemplating their newest campsite. The grey mare seemed to have broken the branch to which she was hitched, but she had not moved more than a few yards off from the other two horses and was watching the woman with fixed interest.

"You're always watching," Ari whispered, getting to her feet and moving to the horse. She glanced over her shoulder to check that Ely wasn't listening. "Do you like the name he's given you, then?"

The animal blew quietly through her wide nostrils, deep eyes considering Ari with haughty respect. She flicked an ear forward and then back as the girl reached to untangle the broken stick from her lead.

"You do seem rather royal, don't you?" She stroked the grey's soft nose. "You would be quite the lady if you weren't so... tough."

Smiling, Ari thought of the mare careening sideways into the significantly larger horses during the fight the night before. There was something very endearing about her hardheaded nature. Remembering Daerecles' brainless stallion, she regretted once again that she did not know more about the trader. But it was useless to worry now; it was unlikely she would have another chance to ask around about him until they reached Starling, and at that point it seemed a worthless endeavor.

"Ari?" Ely had not forgotten her. "I'm serious about this."

She turned around, frowning. "How are your wounds?"

He lifted a tentative hand to feel for the wound on his face.

"Be careful that you don't open that up," Ari reprimanded him, quickly crossing to kneel by his side. "Let me look."

Obediently, he dropped his arm and let her peer at his face. The cut was still fresh but beginning to set into a crooked red scab. It would heal nicely as long as it did not get infected in the next day or two.

"How does it look?" He watched her eyes expectantly.

"Did you use more of the yellow willow?"

Ely nodded.

"It's looking fine." Stepping back, Ari slid her sword from its scabbard and tossed it to him blade-up. He grasped it out of the air with surprise, looking at the weapon as if he had never seen such an object in his life.

"Throw me that stick."

"What?"

"Throw me that stick by your foot," she ordered him, irritated.

He did as she asked, still holding her sword out away from his body as if it might bite him. She caught the stick, which, at a decent two feet in length, had broken off from an oak branch and seemed to be quite solid.

"First of all, don't grip it like that and don't hold it away from you. It is part of you; it exists to do your bidding. Act like it." She stepped forward and nodded at him. "Now come on."

"Sorry?"

"Let's see what you can do."

"Fight you?" Ari received a certain sense of satisfaction from his absolute befuddlement.

"Yes."

"Me with a sword and you with a stick." Ely could not believe his ears.

"I would rather not part with my sword but I'm afraid you wouldn't last long unarmed."

"Isn't this unfair?"

She raised a disapproving eyebrow. "Should I drop the piece of wood and beat you with my bare hands?"

Silenced, he took an uncertain step towards her, then two more, raising the sword as he went. She nodded encouragingly and he slashed it through the air, once, twice, three times. She dodged each attack with ease, not even raising her branch to defend herself. On the fourth, she decided to mix it up and hit back, delivering a light parry that surprised Ely, who hesitated before his next move. She waited. He brought the sword back again and she blocked that too, but this time punished him for his indecision, and slid the stick up the blade so that it flew back towards his face and he had to increase the pressure to avoid cutting himself. As soon as he did so, she let her force fall away and the sword went plummeting downward to leave his mid-section exposed. Without hesitation, Ari slammed him with a blow to the stomach – and then as he doubled over, one to his sword hand so that he dropped the weapon. She kicked it up with her toe and caught the hilt with her left hand.

"Okay," Ely wheezed. "Okay."

"Stand up," she told him coldly.

When he did not immediately straighten to face her, she raised her sword to his neck. "Stand up."

"I'm up, I'm up!" He held a bleeding hand out in submission.

"Never take your eyes off your opponent's weapon, no matter where they hit you."

Eying the tip of her sword where it pressed into his chin, Ely nodded slowly. "Point taken. Release me?"

She lowered the blade and slid it into place on her right

hip. The boy looked confused.

"You are not touching this again until we fix your feet," she told him flatly.

"What's wrong with them?" he asked defensively, quickly glancing down to be sure that they had not suddenly turned blue or morphed into hooves.

"They don't move." Narrowing her eyes, Ari considered him for a moment. "Mirror me."

She took a step forward with her right foot and Ely did the same. She moved her left back and he followed so that they stood inches apart. Wordlessly, Ari placed a hand on his right hip and pushed him away from her so that they had switched diagonals. Now she took two steps forward and then one back, and each time he echoed, like a dance in which they fit together, one foot forward and one foot back.

"Understand?"

Ely nodded.

"You can only get by standing flat if you are wielding an axe or some other commoner's weapon. Sword fighting is all about angles." She jumped towards him and he leapt aside. "We create the angles we want and we steal those left open to us."

Ari moved swiftly left and Ely stepped into the place she had been. "But we must remember that those angles are on the ground. Not in the air. If I duck, and you swing, you're dead."

"You fought off those men on horseback with your sword," Ely said as he jumped back to counter her next move, "but there was no footwork there."

"There are still bodies. The animals are the moving pieces and we have to combine our angles with the ones they give us. It's tougher than fighting on foot."

Continuing in their dance, Ari and Ely darted back and forth around the twenty-foot space, watched only by the group of animals that looked on with varying levels of interest. The black gelding and the new horse had long since fallen asleep, but Princess glanced up every so often from her patch of grass to check the progress of her peculiar new mistress. Jagger paced around the area with a focused glare, simultaneously patrolling for enemies and monitoring the weapon-less fight until at last, he decided their camp was safe and flopped down upon the ground to devote his full attention to his girl.

It was a few minutes after this that something changed in Ari's expression and she began a more rapid procession of forward steps, pushing Ely backwards in a spiraling circle until he was upon the bobcat. Oblivious to the animal's position, he went tumbling backwards with a grunt of surprise. Jagger flew out from under him, hissing so loudly and angrily that his girl had to go to him and stroke his ruffled head.

"It's my fault, Jag," she whispered. "Shhhhh don't be angry."

Ely rubbed his lower back with a grimace.

"Angles exist on all levels," Ari told him scornfully. "You have to pay attention."

"He wasn't there a minute ago," the young man protested.

"That argument won't work when the reinforcements arrive and you have ten more soldiers to duel. Learn to use your environment to your advantage."

"Jagger is *your* environment," he told her. "If I had tried to push you into him he would have moved."

Ari knew what Dav would say, could hear his words echoing about her head, as they always did. *Do not dwell on the pain. Let your anger at this failure drive your blade, your feet, your very senses until it is no longer anger, but calm.*

"Complaining makes you weak." She sat and waved for her anima to lay by her side. "If you do not take credit for all that goes wrong, you cannot take credit for all that goes right."

Ely wiped the contemplative frown from his face and stepped forward again eagerly. "But we're not done, are we? I want to learn more."

"We have done a lot." Rummaging around for the remains of that morning's kill, Ari gave him a thoughtful look. "We'll save the next lesson for tomorrow."

He looked like he wanted to say something else, but he kept his mouth shut and nodded, all signs of discontent gone from his boyish face. Running a hand across his sweaty forehead, he walked over to the horses. Ari watched as they nickered softly and gathered around him, all listening to murmured words that did not quite reach her ears.

"When did you start training to fight?"

"Seven."

Ely did his best to hide his incredulity. "When you moved in with Dav?"

It was the first time he had broached the subject since Ari had told him about this history and the hesitation was noticeable.

"Yes."

"Was it his idea or yours?"

For a moment she did not answer. She had never considered this before. The start of that new life had seemed so natural in many ways that nothing had been a decision – more like a logical link in the chain of their lives.

"Both, I think. He knew how much I loved this sword." She fingered the golden hilt, running her thumb over the edge of the leafy basket. "I was always playing with it, dueling my imagination. And one day he was there."

She lost herself in her memories, trailing off into a silence that stretched on for several minutes before Ely broke it. "Where?"

"What?"

"Where was he?"

"In front of me. With his sword, ready to fight."

In her mind she could see that morning, could see Dav

stepping out of his cabin with his old silver blade, wider than the average weapon but not thick enough to be a broadsword. She remembered the noise it made when it whirred through the air, a heavy slushing sound completely unlike the song of her lighter saber. She could hear the clinking of their two weapons, growing ever louder and fiercer as she aged and their practice sessions shifted from playful duels to vicious fights. Despite all the times Ari had gone too far and hit him, Dav had not once touched her with his sword. Looking back on it, she supposed that this was the reason she had so often emerged victorious; he never would have dared leave even a scratch upon her.

The horses' hooves squelched in the mud leftover from the rainstorm. It had been another slow day and they were all growing restless and tired of sloughing through puddles and slick undergrowth. Ari was back on Princess, who now wore the other horse's saddle and had, for the past four hours, continued to toss her head each time mud flecked up to her delicate muzzle.

"I think I can see mountains," Ely said suddenly.

Ari was ready to reply that, of course he could see mountains – the Belem were only seventy miles behind them – but then she saw what he was talking about. A rocky crag rose up in the distance, somewhat faint on the horizon but there nonetheless. It was unlike the Belem or the Parejon Hills or even what Ari remembered of the mountains north of Konchot. Rough and grey, from where they stood the entire surface did not appear to have a single spot of green.

"That should be the Norrte Barre Cliffs," Ari mused. "We've come farther north than I intended. I've never been here."

"The start of the Aermosa River?"

She nodded. "It begins just beyond the rock. Dav once told me that there was a passage through the northern part of the Cliffs. A sort of trail. When we get to the other side, we may be able to travel by water for a bit, but I'll have to decide which will be faster." Peering out across the gently rolling hills, Ari considered the prospect of leaving the horses behind. "He never took me here after the war started. They say it has become a very volatile region."

Ari could tell that Ely's interest was piqued at the mention of Dav. For some reason this did not bother her as much as it should have.

"The Zaerans left this part of the country to the Malavi forces years ago," he said. "It can only be so volatile now."

"But you saw those Zaerans in the Sonrein," Ari replied, looking back at him. "They were much closer to the Capital than they've been in ten years, and not by chance."

"We're going to be followed all the way across the country, then?" Ely spoke with a kind of resigned energy in his voice, as if he had already accepted it and was moving on to his usual overly positive thoughts.

Thinking of Daerecles' hurriedly scribbled note, Ari nodded in confirmation. "Yes."

"My mother told me a story about the village at the birth of the river," Ely began as they cued the horses into a trot. "I think it's called Aerme, after the water. There used to be a community of sorcerers living there."

The mud splashed underfoot as they moved quickly across the saturated earth. "They'll all be gone then," Ari told him bluntly. "And lucky if they made it out alive."

Ely ignored this and continued, "She said that travelers coming over the Norrte Barre Cliffs fell and injured themselves so often that the sorcerers organized a rotation to watch the eastern face and rescue them. They were the Guardians of the Barre."

"We will have to cross without assistance," said Ari.

"Maybe," he replied, but there was something in his voice that told her he had hope.

The sky was that clear, bright blue that so often appears

after a heavy rain, a color that shouts of short-term memory and blissful ignorance. Every puddle and blade of grass glistened under the yellow sun, reflecting the light up into the air so that the atmosphere seemed to shine with the whiteness of a snowy afternoon. Falling into silence, the travelers listened to the happy chirping of the birds and the hum of the gentle breeze over the open land. If they weren't wanted by nearly every man and woman in the country, it would have been almost peaceful. The calm was beginning to eat at Ari's nerves and she yearned to be out of that wide, exposed space.

"I think it has dried enough to run, don't you?"

Startled that she was asking his opinion, Ely blinked and looked out across the hills. "If you let me pony that horse. Princess might eat him alive if you let her go."

Shrugging, Ari tossed him the rope and urged the mare into a canter and then a gallop, Ely and the other two horses right on her heels. The wind whipped up around them and tears stung in her eyes. Princess let out a triumphant whinny as Ari loosened her grip on the reins, and the mud and water splashed a trail of movement in their wake. They tore across the land, pulling the great Cliffs nearer and nearer with every stride.

CHAPTER XX.

The Cliffs were much bigger than Ari had expected. Even as they arrived in the dark of night, she could see that the rock face rose up past the reach of the moon. Much of it was a vertical wall, a sheer boundary completely insurmountable by any creature without wings, but to the North she could see that it flattened slightly. It was in this direction that they turned, hoping against hope that they would find the rumored path.

After twenty minutes of searching, however, the trail was beginning to seem more and more like a legend of the prewar years. Though the Cliffs became a more reasonable slope, there remained no clear path over which they could pass without scrambling over loose boulders and climbing several very steep sections. There would be no chance of getting the horses over the ridge.

"We have to leave them here."

"There has to be some other way around." Ely was not eager to continue on foot and Ari could not blame him; the horses had made the last stage of their journey much easier. But there was no time to lose, and no better way.

"We'll waste an entire day trying to find another path. They stay here." To emphasize her point, she swung her leg over the mare's back and dismounted.

Sliding down himself, Ely patted the gelding's dark neck and looked over the saddle at Ari. She could hardly see his face in the night but she knew it was not pleased.

"We should leave them somewhere with better food and shelter," he said firmly.

"We should not do anything for them," Ari shot back, her impatience with his naïveté growing by the second. "They're safer than we are out here."

She had dropped the grey's saddle by the rock wall, and now stood with her hand on the mare's throatlatch, ready to unhook the bridle. Despite what she said to Ely, she never liked leaving horses alone in an unfamiliar land.

"If you're going to let her go, just let her go!" Ely told her vehemently, voice rising in anger as he pulled the gelding's saddle off a bit too forcefully.

Turning away from him with a cold look, Ari slid the bridle over Princess' pretty head and gave her a stroke on the nose. The horse blew softly on her hand. For a moment she stood still, uncertain, and then she turned and began to move off into the night, walking in the direction of the now-distant forest. The other two animals nickered excitedly and, as soon as Ely released them, trotted away to catch up with the mare. Hearing her companions' quick hoof beats, she shook her head and jumped into a canter, kicking out and shaking her head playfully. The boys thundered after her and all three disappeared into the darkness.

Avoiding Ely's angry stare, Ari hiked her bag up on her shoulder and faced the steep façade of the Cliffs. Climbing would be more difficult at night but it had to be done, for the sake of time if nothing else. She started up the slope, which was scattered with large, uneven stones and boulders that steered her first left and then right in a crisscrossing pattern upwards.

With Ely behind her, she made slow progress, half-walking and half-climbing, testing each step for loose rock. At moments, the slope smoothed into what could almost be called a trail, which took them onward at a faster speed for a few minutes until another large boulder blocked their path and they had to find a way over or around. As they got further up the cliff, Jagger moved to the front, picking out the smoothest tracks with confident four-legged agility. The three of them traveled in relative silence, a cold distance maintained between the humans and no noise but the crunch of their feet on the gravely hill and their breathing, heavy with exertion.

Only a few dozen yards from the summit, the last semblance of a path ended; a wall about ten feet high rose up before them. All three of the travelers stopped and looked at it.

"We can climb," Ari determined after a moment of consideration.

The moonlight illuminated the contours of the rock, revealing several bumps and ledges that would serve as feasible footholds. She felt the bottom section with her hands. It was rough and solid, not prepared to break away and send them down the mountain.

"Be careful," Ely told her as she began her ascent, Jagger poised anxiously at his side.

Placing her right hand as high as she could reach, Ari stepped each foot up, one at a time, onto the nearest ledges and pushed herself higher. With her left hand she stretched for a crack another two feet up and half-pulled, half-pushed to drag her right foot to the next available crevice. She was almost there, just ready to pull herself over the lip of the rock, when it crumbled beneath her fingers. The layer at the top fell away, a loose stone in her hands, and with a gasp she went tumbling backwards.

Ari simultaneously braced herself for the impact and desperately grabbed at the rock wall to avoid it. But instead she collided with Ely, who caught her clumsily and staggered into the rock, leaning away from the steep slope that would have sent them both dozens of yards down the Cliffs. Together, they fell to the ground, arms and legs tangled in a messy heap.

"Are you alright?" Ely wheezed as Ari extracted herself and pulled her sword from her belt to check that it had not been nicked or damaged.

Jagger made a quick circle around his girl, tail twitching rapidly. She stroked the top of his head and he blinked his wide golden eyes once, then turned away and hopped up the side of the wall.

"If only it were that easy for all of us," Ari intoned drily.

"Maybe we should find another way over."

"We'll be fine." She brushed off Ely's concern and then added with the hint of a smile, "I think I got rid of all of the loose gravel anyway."

"I'm taller. I'll go first and then help you up."

"I can do it," Ari told him firmly, sliding her sword back into her belt. "I don't need help."

"Just because you don't need it doesn't mean you can't make things easier on yourself. At least let me give you a boost."

She glared at him, and then sighed. "Fine." A pause. "Thanks."

"You're welcome."

"For catching me."

He shrugged. "It was instinct."

With that, Ari stepped into his hands and he lifted her into the air so that she could reach the top of the rock, which was now smooth and solid, cleared of all the extra debris. It was mere seconds before she had scrambled over the edge and onto the flat ledge above.

"Keep moving," Ely told her. "I'll catch up."

So Ari continued on, scaling the last few yards in no time at all to reach the very top of the Norrte Barre Cliffs. It was a wide, flat table that, in the blackness, stretched on infinitely. The moon shone upon the surface but even in the pale white light it looked somehow shadowed and the wind whipped over the plateau from the East, hitting Ari as soon as she got to her feet. It swirled about like an angry spirit, spinning and howling at the woman who dared traverse its sacred plain in the middle of the night.

But the breath of the sky was not the only noise that reached Ari's ears. It took her a moment to discern exactly what it was that disturbed the tumultuous peace upon that high rock, and it was only as Ely finally crested the hill and approached her that she realized.

"We made –" he began just as she shoved him to the ground and two arrows went whistling over their heads.

A growl rumbling in his throat, Jagger's hair stood straight on his back and his ears flattened against his head. Raising her head from the ground, Ari stared out into the night, searching for a sign of the archers. Another hiss came from her anima right before a third arrow whizzed by, and she flattened herself to the rock once more.

"They've been waiting for us," Ely whispered, his voice near to her ear.

"Or they're aiming to kill anyone that makes it onto the Cliffs."

"Is that supposed to be comforting?"

"We need to find them."

"What?" he exclaimed, the whisper cracking in his throat.

"If we don't engage, we are not going to make it."

"They can't see us in the dark."

Ari turned her eyes to him. "Has that stopped them from nearly hitting their mark?"

He had no response, so she nodded into his wide eyes and they began to crawl on their elbows and knees towards the origin of the arrows. As they moved, Ari slid the silver dagger from its scabbard and passed it to her right hand. The wind continued to rush around them, screaming into their ears and tearing at their faces. With eyes half-closed, Ari concentrated as hard as she could, listening to Jagger's heartbeat for any disturbance in the steadiness of the earth and the shift of human scent on the wind. The rough surface was cutting into her arms, and she could feel the nearly-healed gash on her right arm break open again, warm blood seeping into the traveling cloak she had pulled over her tunic.

They were getting close and Jagger knew it. With his furry side pressed against hers, Ari could feel how her anima grew tenser with each step, directing his attention with increasing precision towards the southeast. There came a moment in most fights when the initiator had to make a decision that would determine the course of the battle, no matter how great or small. Now was that moment and Ari had to judge how to proceed. She could not leave it up to the bowmen, whoever they were, to set the pace for the approaching conflict.

So Ari made her choice. She whispered instructions to Ely and then they both rolled out in opposite directions, tumbling over the plateau to flank the figures that had appeared under the cold light of the moon. The wind howled and she leapt to her feet and howled with it, a high scream that wove into the air like a terrifying song. Across the flat rock, Ely did the same, emitting a terrible shout just as Jagger yowled and shot up the middle, straight toward the group of archers.

They converged upon them before the five men could discern exactly which way to turn, and the ensuing arrows flew wide of their rapidly moving marks. Ely had drawn his dagger and Ari her sword and the bobcat threw himself upon the nearest man with claws out and teeth bared.

While the men were not bad with bows, it quickly became apparent that they were less qualified with their blades, and by the time Ari had sent Jagger out of the fray his opponent was severely crippled. As soon as the archers realized that the young woman was the more talented warrior, three of them flocked to her and she had to double her efforts, trying to find her way in the shadowy dark and the wind. Meanwhile, Ely had managed to fend off the wounded man and was locked head-to-head with the fifth archer, who swung his axe with aggressive abandon.

"Who are you?" Ari spoke as she dueled three of them at once.

None of them answered her. Each time she drove one back, another was on top of her and they had spent hours, days maybe, on top of that rock, adjusting to the wind and the rough surface. They were silent ghosts, expressionless and mechanical in every way except for their combat, which operated in a haphazardly determined manner that contradicted – and yet, reinforced – their stoic comportment. Though they were difficult to keep at bay simultaneously, Ari's skill was far beyond theirs and she was never in real danger. Darting in and out of their slashing blades and dealing her fair share of blows, eventually she caught one man in the chest and he fell away. A second, she stabbed in the leg with her knife and kicked to the ground, just as Ely knocked his enemy out with a blow to the head.

It should have been easy then, the three of them and only one man left to fight. But the archer Ari had just pushed away received a surge of energy and was on his feet, hurrying with great speed towards Ely. And she saw the man coming from behind, saw Ely turning to face him, ducking with his knife held tightly in his right hand. The other bowman was coming at her but she leapt aside and swung her sword through the air, mentally wincing at her own reckless form. The man wasn't ready for this, and the blade cut across his abdomen and forearm, drawing a low cry of pain and forcing him to drop his weapon. Ari flew past him, tearing across the open rock towards the lanky boy and his opponent.

Ely's attacker was coming down with his axe but Ely was able to dodge the first swing, and Ari could see that he was coming back with his dagger pointed at the man's chest. Before the blade could connect or the archer could finish his second swing, she was between them, slicing her sword upward to block the heavy weapon. With a single smooth motion, she had thrust the wide blade skyward and brought her own sword back down, spearing it straight into the man's midsection. She did not pause, yanking her sword out and spinning away as he fell.

"Hey!" she yelled, almost colliding with Ely. She grabbed his arm and pulled him behind her. "Next time you get that close to me, I'm going to hurt you."

"You would –"

"When I'm *fighting*, Ely," she snapped, letting go abruptly and jogging ahead on her own. "If you stand right next to me, I'm going to think you're an enemy."

"Why did you do that?" He kept pace with her as she hurried purposefully across the plateau and away from the scene of the battle. His fingers were still wrapped around the dagger in a vice-like grip, but Ari wasn't sure that he was aware he was holding it.

"Do what?"

Ely's face was concerned, confused. "Step in for me. I had it handled."

"I'm not so sure you did."

Out of the corner of her eye, Ari saw Ely open his mouth and then close it again. He fell into step behind her, glancing down at his hands and quietly slipping the blade back into his belt.

They headed for the eastern edge of the Cliffs, an invisible boundary that existed only by the fact of its nonexistence. They were all treading carefully. When at last they reached the end of the flat expanse of rock, Ari saw that it was even steeper than the western wall that they had climbed an hour earlier. The cliff face cut straight down, in some places even curving inwards and giving way to what sounded like waterfalls, raging down the vertical sides of the mountain into the Aermosa River below.

"Wow," said Ely.

And Ari said nothing, but the severity of the drop, the void of empty space ahead, and the strength of the falling water left her stunned. How could they possibly find a way down?

"The archers had to get up here somehow," the young man mused, as if reading her mind.

She held up a hand. "The water has to get down."

"The water? No, I –"

"Look for a hole." She was already striding off along the edge. "Some kind of tunnel."

It was only a few minutes later that she heard Ely's voice calling her. "It's here!"

Turning to make her way back to him, Ari saw that his body was now two-thirds of the way underground, obscured by the dark stone so that only his head and shoulders rose up into her line of vision. He had a hand on the lip of the tunnel opening and another pressed against the inside of the rock. As she drew nearer, she saw that this was keeping him from slipping down the hole, which was not a tunnel so much as a chute, worn completely slick with years of rainwater and footsteps. Ely had wedged his lanky body into the narrow entryway so that, as long as he didn't move a muscle, he would not go careening down into the unknown depths of the Cliffs.

"I stepped down to see where it went," he explained, somewhat embarrassed, "and it is a lot more slippery than it looks."

Ari raised an amused eyebrow but did not reply. Instead, she bent to peer inside and study the available traction. There was not much to see in the darkness, but two small crevices, worn into the rock by repeated use, convinced her that this was the path for which they had been looking. If the archers could navigate it, so could they. Ari motioned to Jagger and he slipped between Ely's legs and down the hole, silvery coat disappearing almost immediately into the black depths of the rock.

After a moment's pause without any sound or signal from

her anima, Ari nodded at Ely. "It should be clear, just make your way slowly." She looked him up and down once, remembering his wounded leg. "Try not to fall and break anything."

"It's nice to know that you're always so concerned for my wellbeing," Ely told her drily, studying the tunnel for a minute before shifting his weight onto one foot to begin the descent.

She ignored this snide comment. "Find that niche down on the left."

He did so, and slowly, surely made his way deeper into the chute until Ari could no longer see or hear the grinding of his boots against the cold stone. When she was satisfied that there was a safe distance between them, she began her own journey downward.

As soon as she lowered herself into the hole, she felt a blast of cold, damp air. It was not uncomfortably humid but chilled her body like fresh mist from a fountain. Even under her cloak, she felt the hair on her arms stand on end. Perching on the smooth rock, she braced her hands against either wall and let her feet slide down to search for the holds to which she had directed Ely. She reached them without problem, but as soon as she had shifted down she realized that she had a new challenge. The lip of the tunnel blocked out any remaining light from the moon and her path was plunged into darkness.

Ari lifted one foot and suddenly felt the other slip sideways. Unable to see anything, she reached for where she believed the wall to be, grasping about for something to hold. There was nothing there, and her balance was failing, betraying her lithe frame to the depths of the water-worn chute. Then, just as she was preparing for a long, bumpy ride down to whatever was at the bottom, her left hand found a crack and her body stopped. Ari was trembling, adrenaline coursing through her veins as her muscles strained to be still, be still, be still.

With a deep breath, she shut her eyes. The pressure of the

darkness ebbed away and she felt how she floated in the empty space, which her senses now filled with rough edges and rocks jutting into her expectant fingers. She lowered herself to the steep floor and felt along the bottom and sides of the chute until she found a helpful crevice, then slid further along in search of the next. Again and again, she worked her way downward until the stone floor began to flatten into a gentler slope and she found that she could stand in a genuine tunnel.

There was an increasing sense of lightness hitting her face, and a dull roar, a rushing noise that sounded like the waterfalls over the Cliffs. But it couldn't be; they were not yet outside the rock. Ari opened her eyes. It was still dark, but not pitch black, and the reminder of moonlight gave vague shape to the passage in which she now stood. As her vision adjusted, she heard the crunch of Ely's boots on the wet, gravely rock. Underneath the louder noise, there was also a gentle dripping, water falling in delicate droplets from the tunnel walls around her. Reaching a hand out to inspect the stone, she was surprised to feel that the entire passage was heavy with water. Little rivers ran down the walls and droplets beaded up on each protruding bump or crack. The air was still cold, and it still felt fresh.

"This is incredible." Ely appeared around the corner ahead, his figure no more than a silhouette before her. "You made it down quickly!"

When she did not respond, he continued, "You have to see this."

Ari followed him onward, listening to the sound of the rocky floor churning under their feet and the *drip, drip, drip* trickling down the walls. Over it all was that steady roaring, which grew and grew until it thundered through the mountain like a herd of horses stampeding over a dry plain. Her ears were filled with the sound, a pounding and a whooshing all at once, the kind of noise that is not only heard, but felt in every bone.

Just before they rounded a final corner, Ely turned to look back at her, a brilliant grin upon his face. "I've never seen anything like it."

And neither had she. The narrow tunnel opened up into an enormous cavern, an underground tower that stretched and twisted its way high into the stone above them. From some unknown point at the top there came a massive white waterfall, cascading past them into the infinite darkness below. The water took a snaking journey downward, shooting into a corkscrew pattern that whipped about glassy smooth rocks and then swirled twice around before dropping out of sight. The sheer force and volume of the falls created a heavy spray that blasted Ari in the face and left her short hair dripping. For a moment, she stood staring, awed by its beauty, and then her anima pressed up against her leg and she looked down into his wide, golden eyes. His hair stood on end, ruffled wet by the torrential mist.

"Alright," she said aloud.

"There's a path down this way," Ely told her, pointing off to the right, where a narrow track followed the cavern wall out of sight.

"Jag?"

The bobcat headed off down the trail, quickly but carefully testing the footing as he went. They followed in his wake and found it to be reasonably navigable, treacherous though it appeared. Moving slowly and clinging close to the rocky wall, Ari and Ely made their way lower and lower into the Cliffs. The corkscrew falls continued to plummet past, occasionally splashing up onto their path or spraying them with a jolt of water as they turned a sharp corner.

All the way down, they kept quiet. This was not for fear of discovery or for lack of things to say, but for the sheer noise that surrounded them. The pummeling of the water into the earth was multiplied by the depth of the cavern, so that the sound seemed to beat at the travelers from all sides. It might have been overwhelming, but instead Ari found it to be soothing, like a drum hammering a march to the rhythm of their footsteps. She felt strangely safe.

Ely's hand found her shoulder and she turned to glance at him. "Look there," he mouthed, or maybe spoke, but she could not hear over the water. "Light."

She had already seen it, the moonlight streaming through somewhere high in the cave, but she nodded anyway. "We're close," she mouthed back.

Ahead, the water twisted off to the left and disappeared out of sight. Their trail cut into the rock and became another tunnel, smaller and lower than the first, pressing them deeper into the ground until Ari thought that they must have passed below the water, and in fact she could hear it rushing above and over them. But then the trail became damper and a cool mist drifted back to them as they walked, minute after minute growing stronger until it became an actual fountain of water, a heavy curtain that blocked the path and brought them to a halt. Beyond was the outside world. Ari knew this because the darkness that squeezed through the sheet of water was not the heavy, oppressive kind of darkness that one felt indoors or underground, but the kind of darkness that was merely a temporary absence of light.

She stepped to the edge of the rock, which seemed to drop off where the water began. Below her lay a wide pool, churning vigorously under the pressure of the falls and then rippling out into eventual silence. It was a twenty-foot plunge at most. She twisted her head to peer upwards. The cascade began a few dozen yards above, pouring from its rocky home like a river suspended in orbit above the rest of the earth. As far as she could see, there was no path down.

"We have to jump," Ely shouted in her ear. He had moved to her side and was staring down into the water below.

Nodding, Ari pushed the dragith stone deeper into its pouch and tied the strings with an extra knot. "Try to get as far out as you can," she yelled back. The roar of the waterfall was so loud that she was not sure she heard her own voice.

And then they were jumping, all three of them leaping in one wild motion to blast through the white curtain and out into the night. They seemed to hang in the air for a moment and then went crashing down into the depths of the pool.

CHAPTER XXI.

The morning came too quickly, a bright early sun bursting through thin willow leaves to assault Ari's sleepy eyelids. She awoke to Jagger's soft nose on her cheek and opened her eyes to see his round, furry face looking down into hers. He was happier now that he was dry. She smiled.

"Good morning." He blinked.

Jagger had found them a good spot under a wide-armed willow tree and she had rested well, despite knowing they were in the middle of long-held Malavi territory. Maybe it was just that. Without a real Zaera threat in the area, the Malavi would keep to the towns and patrol by day.

As Ari packed up her things, she checked them all once again, turning every item over to ensure that it was dry and unharmed. The dented copper compass shone dully in the morning light, no worse off for the unceremonious bath. She ran a finger over its face and watched the arrow swing southeast as she tilted it in her hand. Boots, food stock, polishing clothes, and her cloak and weapons were all in good condition. The golden cuff she stuffed back into her pack before her stomach could flip.

They had put so many miles behind them, and somehow their journey was just getting longer. Ari thought of Princess and the two geldings, wondered if they had found their way to safety in the forest.

Something seemed to have lifted from her chest in the night and she was not afraid of the storm she knew was brewing on every side. Let them come; she could do anything with four fresh hours of sleep.

"Ready?"

Ely nodded, taking a last look back upstream. The waterfall was long out of sight, but it still made its presence felt, trembling in the earth.

They made quick time following the tree line down the river. In fact, it was hardly "down" at all, but rather a flat expanse of white pebbles that stretched across an open area over which the river flowed in various strains. In some areas it was deep enough to form one wide channel; in others it became like a beautiful, twisted braid of smaller streams that wove out and in until they came back together a few hundred yards downriver. The water glistened a bright, almost turquoise blue over the white stones, and it was so clear that, even from afar, Ari could see every little detail of the river floor. To their right, the Norrte Barre Cliffs rose up in a long, determined wall, complimenting the tranquil purity of the scene.

The plant growth around the river was sparse and new. Beeches cropped up along the gentle banks and river birch and ash trees interspersed themselves all about the quiet forest that spread out from the water. Every so often, they passed another old willow that had managed to dig its roots deep enough into the rocky ground or stretch its long, weepy limbs to reach the water from where it stood further up the bank. On the Cliffs' side of the river there was little tree growth – shadowed by the high rock, they had no chance for long life – but in the low cracks and crevices there could be seen many varieties of flowers and wild berries. Red lobelia sprouted from the sandy base of the wall and pure white snowdrops bent over the edge of a little braided spring, nearly invisible upon the pale pebble shoreline.

"Ari." Ely's voice fell soft on her ears, dreamlike in the manner it seemed to work its way into her thoughts.

"What is it?" She knew she sounded irritable, but his voice was disrupting her focus.

"You didn't want me to kill that bowman." It was a statement, not a question. "That's why you intervened."

Ari was silent for a minute. She could hear his breathing, the calm kind of breathing that happened when someone was sleeping, or thinking deep thoughts.

"Keep your eyes open for tracks, Ely," she told him gently.

"You don't have to protect me," he said quietly.

"I wasn't," she said, a bit too quickly. "Once you kill a person... it changes you."

As they continued on and the sun grew higher in the sky, Ari began to notice signs of human presence. Along the river, a trail became more clearly defined and every so often they passed what appeared to be abandoned campsites. Coming around one sharp bend, the travelers found themselves facing a small wooden structure – a humbly built dock with a fraying rope that floated limply in the clear water. There were no boats, but as she bent to inspect the ground, Ari discovered fresh footprints. They looked to be flat and wide, the shoes of sailors or fishermen who had approached from the forest and stomped around the little dock for a few minutes before disappearing into the water.

Rising to continue along their path, Ari felt an uncomfortable sensation come over her. Her skin prickled and her eyes automatically darted to the bright wood behind them. There was no one there. It would be impossible to avoid discovery in such a spacious forest.

"What is it?" Ely asked, now looking around in imitation.

"Nothing." She shouldered her bag and started off once more. "I thought someone was watching us."

"We must be near Aerme," he said, and Ari could hear that note of optimism sliding back into his voice. "Maybe there are people nearby."

"Let's hope not." The calm she had felt earlier that

morning was falling prey to her agitated conviction that they were not alone.

"It is not always a bad thing to interact with other living creatures."

Ari wondered how many times they were going to have this conversation. "When you live this life, it is."

"That must be lonely."

Unwilling to engage in this debate again, she glared at him and then cast her eyes about the forest one more time. Empty.

"There's something in the water," Ely said suddenly. "Is that... a fish?"

Ari turned to follow his gaze. She saw a flash of a silvery fin beneath the water. Smooth, shiny scales sliding by out of sight. Something long and golden twisting around with the currents. Then a voice rose up, silky and crystal clear like the very waters of the river, beautiful and colorful, entirely unique.

"Shall we consider it an insult to our looks or your brains that you cannot tell the difference between my sister and a fish?"

Ely's mouth fell open. A mermaid had emerged from the river, elbows propped saucily on a wide white stone that tilted down towards the water. Her purple tail was of a bright metallic sheen beneath the gentle current and her thick brown hair fell down around her smooth shoulders in perfect waves, seemingly dry though she had only just risen into the open air. Like most mermaids Ari had seen, her skin was pale, almost luminescent, and her mesmerizing face seemed to shimmer in the sunlight. She eyed the boy with a disapproving, though somewhat amused look, twirling a strand of hair through her fingers as she arched an eyebrow condescendingly.

"Well?" A second mermaid, the one with the silvery tail they had seen moments earlier, popped to the surface. She pushed her long blonde hair out of her face and glared at Ely with angry green eyes.

"I am so sorry," he told them both sincerely, looking flustered.

Ari watched his cheeks flush with embarrassment as he shifted nervously forward and then back again. "It certainly speaks badly of him," she assured them serenely. "The man has not seen much of the world."

The mermaids did not appear any more pleased to be speaking with her than they had been Ely, and the brunette actually looked vexed that Ari had entered the conversation. The blonde swam to her friend's side and leaned over the edge of the rock, peering suspiciously up at the young woman.

"Then you tell me why he is now journeying through a region controlled entirely by human Military forces and empty of disinterested travelers for close to a decade."

"I can speak for myself," Ely began, but stopped when all three turned withering glares upon him.

"It would be equally fair to question your presence in these waters," Ari challenged the mermaids.

They studied her a minute, searching, musing. She felt the same sort of sudden, intense scrutiny crawl over her skin, their brilliant eyes fixed so steadily upon her that she had to remind herself to breathe. Burying her discomfort, Ari stared straight back, cold grey eyes gazing into their greens and blues. Ely watched in silence.

Something in the mermaids' expressions softened and the blonde even let a smile play across her lips. The purple-tailed mermaid rested her chin on her hands and considered Ari with an intrigued look.

"The people of Aerme do not bother us," she said at last, "and though it has not always been so, all we know of this Military regime now is peace. Our sisters have suffered in rivers and seas across the country. We will not give up that which is still good."

"They leave you alone."

"She's a clever girl," the blonde told her companion

sarcastically.

"Look how fast she catches on," the brunette replied. They both giggled, and their laughter bubbled into the air like music.

Ari knew enough of mermaids to accept their attacks without insult. She had only spoken with their kind a handful of times throughout her life, but their reputation preceded them. Unlike nymphs, whom ignorant travelers might take for their land-bound cousins, mermaids were lively and energetic, exuding a vivacity that often became antagonistic, even vicious when they were provoked. Their spirit and strength were not to be underestimated. Confined to the water, they had much less influence upon the ongoing war than most other creatures, human or otherwise, and Ari was not surprised to learn that they remained in the Malavi territory for its stability. She could not blame them.

"Is there an entire population living here?" she asked.

"In the northern half of the Aermosa," the silver-tailed mermaid answered.

"What's in the southern half?" Ely jumped in eagerly and both of the mermaids laughed again, their beautiful eyes shining with amusement.

"Fresh water mermaids do not pass time in brackish or salt waters," the brunette told him archly. "We are not accustomed to the backwards ways of our distant relations who inhabit such sordid regions."

Ely looked taken aback but he continued, "What is it about them that you dislike so much?"

"Do you really know nothing?" the other mermaid cut in, astonished. "Have you no knowledge of what they have done?"

"Clearly not," her friend said angrily. "Clearly his vision is masked by blue skies and open air."

"You can continue to disparage my ignorance," Ely shot back, "or you can –"

"Ely," Ari cut him off sternly, seeing the furious

expressions on the mermaids' faces. She looked at them for a moment. "They tried to help the Zaerans, didn't they? The saltwater mermaids?"

"And still they pay," the purple-tailed mermaid hissed, though even her nastiest tone sung like notes on a fine harp.

"So you avoid contact with them because you are angry?" Ari asked, "or because you are scared?"

Both of their eyes widened at this accusation, but they did not respond with the fierce reply she braced herself to accept. For a moment, their gazes flitted to one another and then shifted back to the humans who stood so many feet higher, but remained hostage to their captivating presence.

"I see that you are a woman of great strength." The first mermaid stared at Ari, her words a low whisper. "And so perhaps you know what it is to possess such power and be unable to use it." She waved a pale hand at the bobcat, who stood haughtily behind his girl. "We all must make choices to protect our own, even if that means turning our backs on those whom we once loved."

"I ask because I want to know," Ari answered, "not because I disagree."

"I like this human," the blonde mermaid said suddenly to her companion. "She does not try to placate us like most of her kind."

"They behave most offensively," the brunette agreed, "and then pretend that we can be tamed like water dragons."

Again, Ari knew that they were prodding her for a response, but she let them have their fun and remained silent.

"Should we warn them of the dangers ahead, or let them discover it themselves?"

Giggling, the blonde zipped away from the rock and spun beneath the clear water, then burst to the surface with a jaunty shake of her long hair.

A smile curved over the other mermaid's lips, and she spoke to her friend but looked directly at Ari. "The woman may make the mistake of challenging the wrong opponent if she is not careful. I say we cut a deal."

"I'm intrigued," said the silver-tailed mermaid, as if she were the one who would have to agree to a deal.

"We are not making any kind of arrangement," Ari said firmly, before they could carry on with their plans. "And if that means you don't tell us about whatever is down this river, that is fine. It's not as if it will come as a surprise anyway."

"But you see," the second one purred mischievously, "if you don't tell us what we want to know, we could warn the forces all along the river. That would be unfortunate."

Ari was quickly growing tired of their games, but she maintained a disinterested expression. If she knew mermaids at all, she guessed that they, too, would soon become bored and let the travelers continue on their way.

"It would be even more unfortunate if they recalled your existence in these waters and decided to exploit your services as sentries to the East," she told them flatly.

"Doubtful," the brunette shot back grumpily, but she did not look so sure.

"Well," said Ari, "maybe they would not want your help, but it hardly seems worthwhile to endanger your colony for some vindictive fun."

"I liked her better when she was not spoiling my mood," the blonde huffed, and then splashed Ely in the face with her tail for good measure.

"What was that for?" he demanded, wiping water from his eyes and running a hand through his curly hair.

"You stare too much. Come here."

Ely looked at her outstretched hand with alarm, unsure of whether to trust this creature who had spent the past several minutes speaking only unfriendly, threatening words. She beckoned once again, more impatiently.

"I have a secret for you, but I won't share it if you don't hurry."

"Don't worry," the first mermaid called laughingly, "it's been years since we've drowned anyone."

Apparently deciding that it was worth the risk, Ely took a step forward and knelt by the edge of the water. Ari could not help but notice how he braced his hands against the ground, as if he could somehow keep hold of the land in case she tried to pull him in. She watched as the mermaid reached up and placed her hand on his cheek, brought his face down to hers, whispered in his ear. For a moment, they remained like that, the creature's lips a millimeter from the side of Ely's face, her blonde hair tickling his cheek. Then she turned his face to look directly into hers and smiled, something between mischief and malice, and traced her forefinger slowly across his cheek and over his lips.

"Good luck," she said coyly, as she dropped her hand back into the water and floated away from the riverbank.

The purple-tailed mermaid slid off the rock and swam to her friend's side, and then they both dove under the bright blue water and disappeared.

Ely's face was red and flushed when he stood and turned to meet Ari's eye. Almost unconsciously, he lifted a hand to touch his face and then lowered it quickly when he realized what he was doing.

"So?" Ari raised an eyebrow. "What did she say?"

He seemed to be struggling to formulate words. "There is an army massing in the forest a few miles south of here. They've been making plans for weeks but she said..." Trailing off, he ran his fingers through his wet hair and took a few steps away from her, along the edge of the river. When he turned to face her again, the color had left his cheeks and he had a worried look in his eyes.

"She said that, three days ago, the Malavi gave an order to search for a young man and a woman traveling with an anima."

"Malavi forces only, or –"

"A bounty. All paramilitary groups."

Ari let this news wash over her. She waited for a feeling of fear or anxiety, but it never came. The truth was that this was not really a surprise. She had guessed as much when they escaped from the Capital, and it had been all but confirmed by the attack on the Sonrein Plains. Now she felt the return of that most reassuring security, that calm that settled upon her during moments of danger. It was easiest to assume that everyone was an enemy.

"Is that all she told you?"

Ely hesitated, another blush spreading over his boyish face. "That's all."

"Come on, Jag." Waving at her anima, Ari began to walk down the river. "We have to move even faster now," she told Ely.

"How are we going to avoid this many hundreds of soldiers?" he asked, falling into step beside her.

She glanced at him, eyes cold. "The soldiers are not the ones to worry about."

"Who, then?"

"The paramilitary forces and rogue huntsmen, the people in the villages who have heard the news and want some extra gold." Ari moved into a jog. "The Malavi may have more power, but they're organized and that makes them predictable."

"You did not answer my first question."

"Canoes."

"Which we will find...?"

"Ideally, very soon."

"So... will we not be more vulnerable on the water than on land? We'll be even more exposed."

You think I haven't thought of that? Ari wanted to snap. He was imagining her nightmare, and though she knew that this case was an exception, it made her anxious to think of the possibilities, the dangers.

"The trees in this forest are too thin for cover – for us and for them. We have no chance on foot with an entire army camped out, and at least this way we will be able to see anyone stationed along the banks." She glanced down at her anima where he trotted by her side. "And Jagger can stay hidden beneath the walls of the canoe. That throws off their description of our party."

Ari had other reasons for wanting him to remain out of sight, but this was enough for Ely to understand. She thought of the Nyinan Forest, then of Itswild and the Belem. She was so close to freedom, if only they could hurry through these next few days of travel unscathed. It was two and a half weeks to Starling from here, but nothing they could not handle so long as they survived the length of the Aermosa River.

"I hate to discourage you," Ely said, "but we have no idea how long it will be until we happen upon some available canoes."

The only sound was a subtle growl from the bobcat on the other side of Ari. His girl quieted him with a "hush" and they fell into silence.

CHAPTER XXII.

It was no more than two hours before Ari and Ely came across a trio of canoes, turned upside down upon a set of log railings. A path led away from the site, which also included a stone fire pit and several low wooden benches. There was no other living creature anywhere to be seen, but faint footprints at the edges of the trail told Ari that someone had been here since the last rain. A few bones and an empty pouch – remnants of a hurriedly-finished meal – lay by the fire pit.

"Oars!" Ely announced triumphantly.

While Ari was inspecting the scene, the young man had wandered over to a mound of branches, most of them still heavy with fresh leaves, and uncovered a pile of nine paddles. He lifted one and swung it back and forth curiously.

"Should we take one or two?"

The canoes were long, two-person boats, somewhat roughly hewn but worn smooth and shiny by years in the water. There was no telling how easily Ari and Ely might maneuver them in the fast-moving current.

"Two."

"How adept would you say you are at paddling?" Ely asked, handing Ari a second oar and moving around to slide the boat from the rack.

"Passable." Ari lifted the opposite end and together they flipped it over and carried it across the white pebbles to the edge of the water.

"So..." Ely bit his lip in concentration.

"Jagger first," she said.

While Ari and Ely held the boat steady, the bobcat jumped over and in, landing so lightly that the canoe hardly shifted in the shallow water. Yellow eyes already narrowed anxiously, Jagger hissed and arched his back when his girl put a foot inside and rocked the boat further. Ari could see that Ely was trying not to laugh. She climbed in and said nothing, positioning herself in the back of the boat with Jagger flattened to the floor between her legs.

None of them were certain how long the Aermosa River stretched, or how far south they had already come. Everything Ari knew was based upon travelers' tales, folklore, and Dav's descriptions of the region. And even though she listened carefully and had a sharp memory, the few stories she had heard were a mere handful of the pebbles on the river bottom – miniscule and inconsequential against the overwhelming reality of the unknown landscape.

Ari did not find the water soothing like she did the mountains. When she was climbing steep trails through thick evergreens and pines, she felt small and insignificant, but still a part of the great earth. Here on the river, she simply felt paranoid. In her tranquil, focused state, that paranoia was etched into the very beat of her heart and rush of the blood in her veins. She did not sweat or gasp for breath, but her every sense was on high alert, tense energy coursing through her silent frame like the water rushing through the tunnels of the Norrte Barre Cliffs.

She had not been lying when she told Ely that she was a passable paddler. Though she felt reasonably confident in her ability to handle an oar, she knew that she was neither the fastest nor the most practiced in a boat. The Southland rivers were small and rocky, and regardless, she preferred to stay on foot or on horseback.

Ari and Jagger had never been on any kind of boat until Dav had taken them to Tyson when they were fourteen. She remembered following him to the wharf on their second day in the village, and going out in a rowboat, a tiny wooden vessel with two oars and a decaying fishing net tossed to the bottom.

Ari had been uncharacteristically nervous and so had Jagger. Dav had reassured her and she had reassured her anima and they had paddled around the little bay three times to be sure that she understood how to work the oars. She had felt rather vulnerable and powerless floating on top of the dark water and had returned to land with a lukewarm opinion of boating. Thinking back on it, she realized that Dav probably did not like boats very much either, if it had taken him that many years to introduce her to the water.

Despite her complete distaste for their current situation, Ari found Ely to be a capable partner in the bow as the current carried them quickly south. The river continued in its meandering, braided pattern, and they darted around various forks and inlets, following the path that was deepest and clearest. After a few miles, the Norrte Barre Cliffs dropped away and became a smattering of hills and mountains. The young, green forest on the left bank spread across to the other side as well, where it grew cheerfully free from the shadow of the great rocky wall.

Ari and Ely paddled the entire day without speaking or stopping. They seemed to share an understanding that this was the course necessary to make it through the region safely and swiftly. After only a few minutes on the river, they had settled into a rhythm that required nothing but the occasional "slow here" or "left fork."

Ari was grateful for the quiet, and for Ely's refraining from his usual commentary about the scenery or the colors of the sky. She could almost forget his presence and lose herself in the rush of the water, the feel of Jagger's pulse against her knee, and the sound of her own heavy heartbeat. The mermaids wished to scare her with their talk of armies assembling in the forest. What more could Malavi soldiers do that she had not already seen? *Let them come.*

Having passed so many hours in silence, Ely looked almost stricken when Ari tossed him her sword that night and told him to take another shot.

"Really?"

"No," she snapped, "I thought this would be a good joke." Ari broke a crooked limb off of a small tree branch she had picked up on the way to their campsite. "Come on, then."

Though Ely was probably wondering why she had decided to continue teaching him, and likely confused about why it was that night, in the middle of Former Military country, he did not ask any more questions. Frowning in concentration, he stepped to meet her. Ari waited. Another step. Still she stood, motionless. When Ely was close enough to reach her with the blade, she took a step back with her right foot. On cue, he slid his left foot forward to balance the space. Two more paces like this and then Ari raised her branch and attacked.

The look on Ely's face betrayed his surprise at her sudden charge, but he managed to block it in time, stepping backward with each move that she made forward. Three, four, five times he parried, but Ari's attempts became increasingly forceful and he was backing up with nowhere to go.

"Fight back!" she growled at him.

Just then, Ely stumbled on a root and, for a moment, Ari thought he was done. In a desperate save, he caught himself and swung the sword upward before she had gotten her next hit around. Now it was Ari's turn to be startled, though her stoic expression and cold grey eyes did not show it. Barely in time, she blocked the blade with her stick, which crunched tellingly with the impact. Ely came again and again, fiercer than before, focused like she had not seen him. Rewarding his intensity, Ari let him advance a few feet, allowed him to build up a feeling of pace, of force, of control of their little duel. She shifted slowly away until he had pushed her nearly back to where they had started, and she could feel that he was settling into something like a rhythm.

As soon as this pattern locked into place, Ari switched her angle and stepped forward into her next parry, an awkward cross between offense and defense that threw Ely off immediately. Taking advantage of his split-second's hesitation, Ari attacked and struck three swift blows, the first two to the sword and the third to his free shoulder, which winced but did not buckle under the whack of the branch. Though the boy stood firm, he seemed to recall his vulnerability and became suddenly timid. In two more strides, Ari had cornered him and kicked the sword from his hand.

"You gave up."

"You pummeled me." Ely massaged his shoulder and upper arm, grimacing a bit as he did so. "Was that necessary?"

Stooping to pick up her sword from where it lay a few feet away, Ari made no response to this question. "Predictability is the most dangerous flaw in any fight. Just because something works once does not mean you should ever use it again."

"How am I supposed to go on the offensive when you give me no advice and then tell me that what I did was too predictable?"

"Try it again." She thrust the weapon back into his hands. "And do something differently."

"Now?" Ely asked, looking surprised.

"Are you too tired?"

Ely raised his sword once more, and though he did try, each time he ended up on the ground, beaten with the stick, or entirely weaponless. Often the result was a combination of all three. After giving him one chance to attack, Ari was unwilling to be so kind again and did not relent even as he became increasingly weary.

Despite his cuts and bruises, Ely did not falter or complain. Instead, his determination seemed to grow, building upon his repeated failures. As instructed, he attempted all manner of different strategies, angles, and techniques – and each Ari blocked and then dismissed in so efficient a style that any less enthusiastic pupil would have given up immediately.

When at last Ari announced that they were finished for the night, Ely collapsed onto the ground, massaging a few sore spots where she had drawn blood. He let out a sigh. Ari was not sure if it was an expression of pain or content.

"Well, I've learned a lot," he announced, a hint of irony sliding into his cheery tone.

"Tomorrow we'll start working on your technique." Taking the blade from him, Ari began to sharpen it methodically against one of the white river pebbles. It made a satisfying grating noise in the darkening night.

"*Now* you're going to teach me technique?" Ely sounded flabbergasted.

"A swordsman must learn what will not work in order to understand what will," she responded, sliding her father's blade across the rock in one long motion.

"Right. Or you have some twisted idea of fun."

"Letting an incompetent magician run around, making a fool of himself with my sword?" she shot back. "Oh, yes, I do enjoy that."

He let out a laugh, pleased grin still plastered over his face. The air was warm and the rush of the braided Aermosa River sounded through the trees. A purr rumbled in Jagger's belly.

Over the next several days, they developed a routine. Every morning they rose early to watch the pale grey sky brighten to a brilliant blue, second only to the gleaming turquoise of the water. After a silent, hastened breakfast they would uncover the canoe and paddles from the night's hiding place and take to the water. Just like the first day, Ari sat in the back steering and Ely put his muscle into paddling at the bow. Though Jagger grew accustomed to the boat, he remained low and out of sight, still as a rock at the bottom of the canoe.

On occasion, they rowed by small docks or fishing huts with narrow footpaths winding away from the river. Some of these were clearly in regular use and others appeared broken or charred, long-abandoned remnants of lives once lived. Only twice had they actually seen humans by the water, and both times these fishermen had averted their eyes, as if fearing Ari or Ely's gaze.

The landscape that they passed changed little, though Ari did not find it tiresome. Sometimes the low mountains and rocks to the west flattened into stunning green fields, flecked with free-ranging livestock or horses. To their east, the river took occasional detours into the quiet forest, veering off in smaller streams and springs that bubbled through sandy beds under the sweeping fingers of the willows and the stoic presence of the tall beeches.

The only real change was the pattern of wildflowers, a shift in the colors and species that appeared upon the edges of the white, rocky beaches. The red lobelia and snowdrops had long since disappeared and been replaced by new blooms of purple and yellow and orange. Ari did not recognize any of these flowers, so different was the environment from anything she had seen.

Ely seemed to grow more relaxed in the boat, and once again began to comment on their surroundings, complimenting a peculiar rock formation as they passed, or asking if Ari knew what sort of animal might make a nest of willow branches. Mostly, they paddled on in amicable silence. When her companion did speak, Ari was patient and measured in her responses. There was something about that monotonous effort of traveling down the river that lulled her into a comfort that matched her calm. It had been many years since she had experienced this feeling, one that she could not quite name but found strangely familiar.

In the evenings, when they pulled the canoe from the

water and made camp on the edge of the wood, Ari would hand Ely her sword and they would practice dueling. She began with all of the lessons she could remember Dav teaching her as a young girl: footwork, grips, cuts and parries, disarming one's opponent. It was odd, really, trying to explain to him something that to her felt so logical, so right. She could not remember a day when sword fighting had not come naturally; she had yearned for the feel of her father's sword in her palm as soon as she had laid her six-year-old eyes upon it.

Ely was not the worst swordsman she had encountered. He caught on quickly with the footwork and the basic attacks and defenses, and when she taught him something once, he did not often need it repeated. But she found that when he learned the moves and techniques, he latched onto them in too mathematical a manner, practicing each move with a precision that was predictable, by the book. He did not have the creativity – or rather, did not embrace the creativity – that was needed to master the skill of sword fighting.

She tried to explain this, tried to beg him for more, but he did not seem to understand what it was she desired.

"It is more than following a formula. It is –"

"An art." They were five days down the river and Ely was picking himself up off the ground for what seemed like the millionth time. "So you've said."

"What else can I do to make you understand?" she asked, exasperated.

He began to trace a circle in the dirt with the tip of the sword, then stopped when he saw her look. "I do understand."

"Clearly not." She strode forward and took the weapon from his hands. "See how I hold it?"

Stretching her arm out, Ari turned the blade slowly from left to right. It was a cold, steely grey in the evening light. In that moment, as always, she felt that the leafy basket was made to fit her exactly. Ely nodded slowly.

"I *believe* that it is a part of me. An extension of my arm, my wrist, my fingers... Watch."

She twirled through their little clearing, attacking imaginary foes, carving the air with grace and precision. Stepping onto a log, she jumped across to a pile of boulders, spinning midflight to slice a pair of enemies and then bounce away to the next obstacle. The trees and rocks swirled around her, but her vision was as steady as the land itself. The earth existed as both her stage and her ally.

With a heavy breath, Ari landed a final leap and slid the blade into her belt in one motion. She turned slowly to face Ely, who was now behind her, across the clearing. His face was no longer defiant or frustrated or even amused. Instead, there was a look of quiet respect; perhaps not awe, but it was certainly something. Ari met his gaze and their eyes stayed locked for a moment, sizing each other up.

"Do you see?" she asked him again, quietly.

A thoughtful smile cracked his lips, though his eyes remained serious. He nodded but did not speak, and so Ari knew that he did see.

"Right." Walking to Jagger, Ari gave her anima a stroke and sat by his side. "Well, we can continue tomorrow."

They were both quiet for a minute as the girl combed through her anima's fur, searching for tangles or burrs or anything out of the ordinary. He purred softly, a deep rumble in his belly that warmed her hands and her heart.

"It's beautiful." Ely's voice broke the silence and Ari looked up from Jagger's coat to see him still watching her. "The way you fight. How long have you been able to do that?"

Going back to her task, Ari shrugged off this compliment. "There is not much else to do when one grows up in Nyin."

"Name one other swordsman from that village half as accomplished as you."

"There's a man south of Irlanda with a decent ability."

"Exactly."

Ari pursed her lips.

"You did not make it this far on boredom," Ely told her. "That's all I'm saying."

"There is a point when such passions become necessary for survival," Ari replied. "If we are lucky, that change occurs before we are old enough to understand what we have become."

"Do you regret what you are?" The question hung in the air for a moment. Ari could feel how it shook, how Ely let it slip out without thinking of his boldness.

"I was always going to become some version of this," she said at last. Her words floated quietly to join his in the space between them, and she waited. The thought crossed her mind that, if Icario was still living in Fraling, he was not all that far away from them. This realization filled her with an unwarranted sense of anxiety.

Ely shook his head. "I don't believe that."

Jagger's purring had stopped, and even without looking Ari knew that her anima had his ears pinned to his head.

"I did not ask you what you believed." Her voice was cold.

"I don't think there's anything wrong with –"

"What gives you the idea that you have any right to share your opinion?"

"Why do you always do this?" He came right back. "You always stop me before I can say anything of consequence."

"When I believe that might actually happen, I will be sure to listen."

"How is it that you manage to be the same silent thief no matter who you are talking to or what you are doing?"

"Is this supposed to be criticism?" She frowned at him, more confused than anything.

"No, I'm – just... don't you ever get tired?"

"I have no idea what you mean," Ari snapped.

"It isn't always a bad thing to open up. To have friends."

"If I wanted to make friends," she responded evenly, "I would have changed my name and moved to a new city."

"Changed your name?"

Too late, Ari realized her mistake. "One can never be too cautious," she told him.

If Ely thought this was suspicious, he did not press on. It seemed that he was finally growing tired of barraging her with questions and unwanted opinions. Stretching out onto his back, the young man folded his arms behind his head and sighed contentedly.

"Thank you for teaching me," he said after a minute. "Really."

"It won't do much good until you find yourself a sword." Ari settled down so that she was lying back-to-back with her anima.

"You don't want to give me yours and keep that stick?"

The smile in his voice almost made her grin back.

Chapter XXIII.

The scenery on either side of the river was slowly changing. Even though Ari had never been to this part of the country, she sensed that they were very near to reaching their destination. There was a buzz in the air, a tension that grew as they traveled farther and farther downstream.

Someone must know...

Though the water continued its braided pattern through the pale, pebbled basin, the land beyond became nearly flat, a succession of gently rolling hills which were adorned with rough, green rushes that waved like sea grass.

The grass rustled under a stiff breeze that made everything move, and yet it seemed stiller and quieter than the windless days had been. There had been frequent signs of mermaids over the past several days – a glint of colorful tail or an errant giggle rising above the water to brush their ears with sweet tones – and Ari had half expected them to cause more trouble. But now that the mountains and forest had disappeared, they were gone entirely, stopped by whatever invisible border they had chosen to protect themselves from their wayward sisters to the south.

Now and then, the canoe would startle a heron out of the rushes and it would beat its pale wings and hurry into the sky. When this happened, Jagger would lift his head and his ears would turn circles, tracking the bird in its steady flight away, away, away. Then, satisfied that it was a bird and nothing more, he would lower his chin to his paws and sigh. Ari knew that he was bored and tired of days in the boat. She found it hard to disagree. Her arms ached with the endless exertion and her knees were raw and bruised from kneeling on the hard wood. At least she was doing something; Jagger had no job but to lie quietly out of sight.

More troubling than the physical discomfort was the knowledge that they were now truly out in the open. Though Ari still believed that they were no more disadvantaged then those who tracked them from the land, it was not quite so comforting knowing that they would not be able to find shelter at night, or cover, should they face an attack.

"Do you think we should go on foot?"

"The water will get us out of here faster," Ely answered, tone betraying his surprise at being asked his opinion for the second time in a week. He did not miss a beat. "Are you worried about the lack of cover?"

"No." She paused. "But I was thinking about it."

"If speed will cut down the risk enough, I suggest sticking with the canoe."

Ari considered this for a minute and then nodded before realizing he could not see her from where he sat in the boat. "When we get closer to the sea we will leave the canoe and go on foot."

Almost mechanically, Ely leaned into his next stroke, driving them forward at a greater speed. For a short moment, she watched him paddle, watched his lean muscles work under his tunic, stretching out and then drawing back against the rushing water. Then she doubled her own efforts to match his as best she could, and they rushed on over the quiet water.

They made very good time that day, and Ari knew it because she began to smell the saltwater in the air, the heavy humidity that drifted off the ocean to coat the miles of coastline with its unmistakable scent. Still, they probably had at least half of a day to go, and there was no telling what kind of dangers might await them as they grew closer to Konchot and the territories by the sea.

The Malavi presence was no less powerful in these southeastern coastal villages, but from what Ari had heard over the past several years, it was much less well organized. The uprising led by the mermaids, and joined by a handful of smaller towns, had shaken the Malavi forces and brought brutal retaliation. Unlike the rest of the country, however, this crackdown had only inspired further rebellion, even in the areas that had previously remained silent. It was a wild, unpredictable response, one of sporadic revolts and undermanned attacks that never managed to thwart the Malavi, but the people of the sea did not give up.

Long ago forsaken by the Zaera army, the villages were under constant surveillance, dominated by paranoid Malavi troops that had infiltrated every aspect of life. They would go six months – maybe a year, or even two – without event and then everything would explode. News of the clashes reached the ears of the entire country and the story was always the same.

Another uprising crushed in Konchot.
Fifty villagers murdered in Aguela.
Maroun fishermen have attacked the resident forces.
Malavi battalions killed them.
Every last one.

Each time Ari heard this sort of news she had to wonder what inspired these people to be so foolish time after time. Didn't they understand that they were all going to die? Didn't they know that the soldiers would find their families and make them suffer? Whatever the reason, these vain attempts at resistance had birthed a mighty but unstable Malavi power in the territory towards which Ari and Ely now paddled.

The wind picked up even more as they neared the sea and big grey clouds rolled in over their heads. It did not look like rain – not yet – but the clouds gave the whole landscape an ominous appearance and darkened the bright turquoise water to a shady blue. The scruffy fields and gentle hills seemed to almost touch the sky, or rather, the sky hung so low that it almost touched the earth.

Ely paused his paddling for a moment and turned to look at her. There were words in his eyes and on his lips, but before he could share them aloud, Ari held up a finger. There was a woman standing on the shore.

She was small and thin, with mousy brown hair that seemed to be greying, though it might have only been the pale light playing across her face. Her long, grey dress billowed around her skinny frame in the wind, like sails on a tired ship. As they passed, she stared out at them, eyes fixed, mournful. Then she raised one hand in a silent salutation.

"Don't respond," Ari told Ely quickly, when she saw that he was about to wave back.

"She looks lonely," was all he said.

"Something is not right," Ari whispered, to herself as much as anything.

"Where is she going?" Ely asked suddenly.

Ari turned around quickly to see the woman retreating rapidly eastward, across the open plain. As she ran, she hiked up her dress and hurried along with the extra fabric swinging back and forth, in time with her uneven gait. Soon, she had disappeared, ghostlike, over the crest of a small hill. The bank seemed so eerily empty that Ari half-believed she had imagined her.

"We need to get off this boat," she said.

"Now?"

"Now," she repeated, more vehemently.

"I'm sure it was nothing," Ely countered, but Ari gave a sharp pry with her oar and turned the boat towards the opposite shore.

Jagger was beginning to stand, growing nervous as he heard the change in his girl's voice. Ari did not bother to correct him because they were so close to land.

"Oi!" A cry careened across the open riverbed and she immediately regretted this decision.

"Go, go, go!" she urged Ely, digging into her own paddle with renewed enthusiasm.

They reached the western bank and leapt out of the canoe before it had even touched bottom. As soon as Ari had dropped her oar onto the rocks, she heard a whistling and automatically threw herself to the ground. An arrow shot through the space where she had stood only moments before.

"Ely!" she screamed at her companion, who was a few paces ahead and making himself an easy target.

He turned to find her voice and a second arrow flew by his left shoulder, missing by inches. Eyes widening, Ely followed her lead and fell to the earth, rolling to take cover behind a single boulder that lay between them.

"Did you get a look at them?"

"The archers?" Ari shook her head. "No. They came out of nowhere."

"That woman. She was the signal."

They were pressed together, bodies side-by-side in the three feet of space afforded them by the rock. Ari could feel his heart racing; its quickened pulse joined hers to create a hectic pattern.

"We need to get off the shore and into the grass," she told him quietly. "At least we'll have some protection there."

Together, they rolled out and crawled on elbows and knees away from the water, moving as quickly as possible to the shelter of the wind-blown sea grass. Ari's anima was already crouched among the stiff green stalks, peering anxiously out at his girl as she made her way to him. The cat let out an audible sigh when she arrived. Ari lifted a hand to brush the top of his head.

"Shhhh," she murmured softly. Reassured, he darted forward to clear the way.

Now up onto her hands and knees, Ari moved faster. A few more arrows whizzed above them but none found its mark in the grass. They were going to get away. Where they would run, Ari did not know, but they were going to get away.

And then she felt something jump in her heart just as Jagger let out a yowl and a woman screamed in pain.

"Jag, no!"

Without thinking, Ari sprung forward onto her feet. A few yards ahead stood a group of men and women with weapons drawn. The woman at the front was grasping at her leg, which was quickly becoming covered with bright red blood. All of the soldiers raised their swords and bows to point at Ari.

"Here, Jagger," she ordered before they could say anything.

The bobcat had frozen at her first cry and now he slunk back to her side, positioning himself just in front of her so that she could not take a step without tripping over his bristling back. The group seemed to eye her up and down for a moment. Briefly, Ari wondered if they were surprised by what they saw. Mostly she wondered how she and Ely were going to escape.

"Drop all your weapons," the bleeding woman said, though not very convincingly.

A second woman stepped forward and motioned at them with a long broadsword. "Drop them," she repeated.

Ely had stood and moved to Ari's side, and now she could feel him looking at her expectantly. Perhaps he thought that they could fight their way out of this. But even she, who so hated to surrender any battle, knew that this was not their fight to win. The squadron in front of them was multiplying as more and more soldiers appeared from their positions where they had lain crouched beneath the grass. It was a clever ambush; the archers across the river had driven them right into waiting arms.

Ari did not take the time to count the soldiers, but she knew there were near forty. She squeezed the sword hilt in her right hand. "Let us keep our arms," she said. "We promise not to resist."

The woman who had taken charge smiled at this. "We have orders. And we are not so unwise as to accept the word of someone with your reputation."

"It is not a dishonorable one," Ari retorted coldly, bristling at this accusation.

"That does not make it any more trustworthy." She nodded at the men behind her. "Take their blades and bind their hands."

Ari handed over her silver dagger and sword and Ely passed them his knife. Before they could say another word or move to tie her hands, she knelt down and pressed her forehead to Jagger's, closed her eyes, and let her heart reach his.

"Step away from the animal," the woman told her forcefully.

Obeying these orders, Ari stood tall and turned to face her captors. The silvery brown cat shot away through the grass. A shout went up and several soldiers raised their bows before realizing that the bobcat was too far out of sight to shoot.

Wham. The woman's hand moved like lightning to collide with the side of Ari's face and she gasped in pained surprise.

"I did not give you permission to send the cat away."

In the back of her mind, Ari saw her anima running free, a shadow across the waving hills. She straightened and set her jaw.

"You said nothing at all about it."

Whack. A second blow bludgeoned the other side of her face.

"Captain!" one of the men reprimanded just as Ely shouted, "Ari!"

Water sprung into her eyes as she felt her cheek sting with the impact. It was all she could do to keep her hands off the knives hidden in her hunting boots. Vision blurred, she felt Ely move closer to her but she waved him away.

"Captain," the man's voice said again, "we need to move."

"Then hurry and bind them," the woman snapped. "And let Behn deal with the thief. I don't want to hear from her."

Rough hands grabbed at her, forcing her arms behind her back and wrapping her wrists tight with a thick band of rope. Someone had yanked her pack from her shoulder. The tears were clearing from her eyes and the world was beginning to settle once more; she could see that Ely was being bound in front of her, a man and a woman standing guard on either side. He began to turn, looking to meet her eye, but she shook her head quickly.

The soldiers began to walk them southwest across the sea grass plain and Ari saw that Behn, her assigned guard, was not much older than she, a strong but boyish young man with wide eyes and short red hair. Watching her was probably punishment for his inexperience. Feeling her gaze, he looked at her and she gave him a fierce glare. He averted his eyes immediately.

The rest of the troop was a variety of ages and appearances, though most, like the captain and the bleeding woman, seemed to be middle aged and hardened from years of physical labor. Their haphazard dress made Ari almost certain that they were not Malavi, but rather a local group who had pledged their allegiance – for money, or for survival – at some point during the war.

She thought of the woman on the shore and wondered how she had been convinced to serve as lookout. Despite her swelling face, Ari felt little animosity towards the mousy-haired ghost, or even most of the paramilitary force that now dragged her and Ely southward. She could not blame them for the choices they had made. In this war, it was every woman for herself.

At least two hours passed as they walked south, and the

river was soon forgotten behind them, a distant memory of rushing water, of something other than endless miles of sea rushes. Their captors seemed restless and Ari began to understand that their injured comrade was the only reason they were not moving faster. She took a certain small pleasure in knowing that Jagger had ruined at least one part of their plan. This satisfaction was short-lived, however, as they approached a small town nestled between two slightly-taller-than-usual grassy hills.

Ari did not recognize the village. She had spent little time in this region, and of those long-ago visits she remembered nothing but the smell of the sea in the air and the feeling of loneliness before that great expanse of water. The human settlements had been inconsequential to her then. Now, she wished that she had paid closer attention.

With no other choice and desperate for any information that might improve their circumstances, Ari strained to hear the anxious banter of the motley crew. Muttered conversation drifted in and out, intermixed with whispers of tired feet and worries of a coming storm.

After a long several minutes, Ari concluded that they were at least a day's journey from Konchot, which, as she had predicted, lay to the east. The town where they were to be held had a long name that she could not quite make out, but most of the soldiers called it Carseile. It was home to a few poor farmers and a large population of fishermen and sea merchants.

"His wrist is bleeding," the man on Ely's left told his companion about an hour and a half into their trek. "We should loosen the ties."

"Marla might not like that," she answered. "Maybe we should ask her."

"If we ask anyone it should be Dilan. She's in charge."

"Not if Marla has anything to say about it." Both of their voices had dropped to a whisper. "And Dilan's hurt anyway."

"I say we just loosen them. They won't know the difference." He paused. "Damned bobcat."

The man glanced over his shoulder to see if Ari had heard this and she looked away. She saw Jagger and he was still free, a pale ghost before an endless sea.

Chapter XXIV.

Carseile turned out to be a quiet, quaint town, a typical fisherman's village with slick stone streets and rows of cottages that were once painted various shades of red, blue, and yellow, but now faded by the incessant drive of wind and water. Tired donkeys towed carts laden with fish freshly pulled from the sea and children ran about with baskets ready to fill at that day's market.

The hum of laughter and chatter died down as the soldiers trooped through with their prisoners in tow. Ari felt the eyes upon her, nervous, expectant. She held her head high and glared around the street, daring them to meet her gaze. Only the children did. The adults looked away and, startled by her bruised face or embarrassed by her fierceness, continued about their business.

It was only a few minutes before the paramilitary group came to a halt before a row of well-dressed soldiers who blocked their path. They wore clean, blue uniforms and carried shiny silver sabers on their hips.

"Good work." The man at the front stopped them with a hand raised, palm out. "We'll take them from here."

Though the paramilitary men and women were greater in number, they looked nervous. Some of the men in the back glanced at each other apprehensively, but most looked to the leaders at the front for direction.

"We can take them to headquarters," said Dilan, the wounded woman.

The man looked her up and down, eyes lingering over her mangled leg. He gave a derisive smile. "I think you've gone far enough."

"No one else has come close to capturing them," she protested hotly. "We deserve to finish the job."

"Then consider your job finished," he spat. There was a pause as he considered the mass of people before him. "On second thought, we could use some assistance." He pointed at the three soldiers holding Ari and Ely. "You three and... Marla. You can supervise."

The glee on Marla's face at having been chosen over her rival was obvious. Dilan's subdued reaction indicated that this was not the first time the Former Military leadership had used them in this game. Ari glanced at Ely, who was watching the exchange with a pained expression. She looked away again and returned to studying their new captors. This arrangement would alter their chances of escape, though it was not yet clear exactly how much.

The Malavi squadron, a group of about twenty, began to move on and the three paramilitary soldiers shoved Ari and Ely forward once more. They followed directly behind a beaming Marla, who cast her gaze about the empty avenue with triumphant abandon.

Distracted by the brief confrontation, Ari had not noticed the villagers scattering upon sight of the Malavi troops. The once-busy little street had fallen absolutely silent except for the sound of stiff riding boots marching across the cobblestones. Behn's grip on her arm had become sweaty and uncomfortably strong. Ari flexed her bicep, hoping he would loosen up, but instead he gave her a frantic look and held on even more tightly.

She took a slow breath and resigned herself to ignoring Behn's forced company. For the first time since the mermaid's message, she considered the item sitting in its pouch on her belt. She had been so concerned about their safety that she had not thought enough about why they had been captured in the first place. Why hadn't the soldiers simply killed them and taken the dragith? Had the Former Military kept its real goal a secret from its allies?

"Through here," one of the men ordered. They all turned through a low archway into a secluded alley.

On either side were several doors, each monitored by a uniformed Malavi officer. The woman by the first door on the right nodded and stepped aside, allowing the whole group to pass through. There was not much to see once they entered, nothing more than some grim off-white walls and a long, low-ceilinged hall. Again, they turned off at the first door on the right and descended immediately down a flight of very steep stairs.

In his harried eagerness to lead her down, Behn pushed Ari a bit too hard and she stumbled off the first step, unable to catch herself with her hands tied behind her back. Before he could grab her, she had bumped into the soldiers in front of them, and a train of grunting and cursing flew down the stairs as everyone in the narrow stairwell grasped for nonexistent bannisters.

Barely righting herself, Ari took the opportunity that she saw. She braced herself against the wall and kicked out at the man in front of her, sending him flying forward into half a dozen others. As they began tumbling down the steps, she turned to locate Behn, who was frozen in befuddlement, and backed straight into him, slicing her bindings apart on his drawn sword. With hands free, she ducked his first attack and punched him in the stomach, then wrenched the blade from his grasp as he paused to regroup.

She was heading back up the stairs, casting around for her knife and sword, when she heard a call.

"Another step and he's dead."

Ari knew Ely had been behind her. She knew she had entered the stairwell first. But somehow there he was, eight steps down in the grip of that malicious Marla, the captain smiling again like she had just been named Queen.

Ari met her gaze with icy grey eyes. "You are going to kill us anyway, aren't you? Why should it matter that it happens now?"

The grin was still plastered on Marla's face, but her eyes hardened. "Just as coldhearted as they made you out to be."

"How does it feel to be in the presence of equals?"

Ari knew that she was only making it worse by taunting the captain, but something about the woman's self-satisfied spite made her skin crawl. The stair seemed to have frozen in time, all sound and movement sucked away into a vacuum as the soldiers around them waited for whatever was to come. For a moment, all Ari could see was Marla, the tip of her sword pressed into Ely's stomach.

And then there came the sound of heels clicking across the passage above. A figure blocked the light from the doorway so that the entire stairwell plunged into darkness.

"Marla," snapped an irritated male voice, "lower your weapon immediately. And someone grab the girl."

Unable to see, Ari tried to raise Behn's sword to protect herself, but hands grasped at her from behind before she could turn to face them. Someone kicked her in the back of the knees and she buckled to the ground, her face slamming against the stone step on the way down. The ropes were reapplied, this time much more tightly. She felt warm blood trickling down her cheek.

"On your feet," an angry voice hissed, yanking her upwards so quickly she thought her shoulder might pop out of its socket.

These were not Behn's hands that now steered her down the stair. The person at the top had moved and light flooded back inside, though it grew increasingly dim and grimy as they progressed downwards. Ely and Marla had turned the corner at the bottom of the steps and disappeared from sight. Ari had the vague, frantic thought that they were taking him away to kill him in punishment for her attempted escape.

The adrenaline was quickly ebbing away and pain was shooting through her knees, her head, and her arms. The blow she had received on the way down made her head spin and with each step she saw lights pop before her throbbing eyes. When they reached the bottom of the stairs, her new captor shoved her forward so quickly that she almost fell once more and was yet again jerked back with exaggerated force.

"Unless you wish to carry me," she told him icily, "I think it's best you let me walk of my own accord."

For this unsolicited comment she received a knock to the back of the head. "Speak again and it'll be my sword."

"Empty threats are very unbecoming."

Another cuff but no weapon. If her head were not splitting with pain, Ari might have smiled. The guard suddenly released his grip and pushed her down to the ground. A door clanged shut and she found herself in a prison cell, alone. Her surroundings, dark and vague, seemed to swim before her and she felt a strange sense of misunderstanding, like this was a dream, something that could not truly be happening.

Ari did not get caught. She most definitely did not get caught by malfunctioning paramilitary troops and thrown into Former Military dungeons in nameless seaside villages. She wished that her head would stop spinning and throbbing and she wished that she had her sword and most of all she wished that Jagger were there. This last desire, however, she pushed immediately out of her head. Years of experience had prepared her for situations like this. She would figure it out. She always did.

But there were so many unknowns, so many questions raging through her muddled brain. Why hadn't they been questioned at all? Why hadn't their captors searched them for the dragith immediately? Where were her belongings, her sword and dagger? Where was Ely?

She should not have accepted this job in the first place. If she had just ignored Daerecles' threats, she would not be here, with Jagger so far away and the clumsy city boy in another cell awaiting her help. Threats to her life were nothing. As long as Jagger was safe, she would be fine. Other people made everything more complicated. She'd always known that, and yet here she was, trapped. Why hadn't she just abandoned Ely weeks ago?

"Oh, a thousand dead stars," Ari cursed under her breath. She never would have left him. She couldn't. Maybe this meant she was weak. Either way, she had to get free.

Her little prison, a tiny, windowless room with a dirt floor, seemed to be one of several along a cell block, though Ari could only make out so much through the bars and down the dim passage. The unit across from her was empty, as was the one to its immediate right. The rest she could not see well enough, but assumed that Ely must be in one of them. For a moment, she considered calling his name, and then thought better of it. The whole dungeon was so silent, so still. Nothing moved and nothing echoed and, somehow, she felt more underground than she had in the center of the Norrte Barre Cliffs.

The man had not removed the ropes around her wrists and, in a strange way, Ari was glad because it gave her something to do while her mind worked to unravel the dilemma before her. She squirmed around on the ground until she could reach her hands to her feet. Gritting her teeth, she stretched her fingers into her right boot and removed the bronze-handled dagger, which she flipped around so that the blade faced upward. With a quick motion, she sliced through the rope and felt herself come free.

She slid her knife back into her shoe and rubbed her wrists. They felt raw and sore from hours bent under the pressure of the tight ropes, and her fingers came away with traces of blood. If she were alone, there was no doubt that she could fight her way out with her two knives. Whenever someone next came to open her cell she would be able to make a break for it. But Ely created a whole other problem. She would have to rescue him. And probably protect him on their way out.

"Ari." She heard a whisper. "Ari." It came again.

Unwilling to reply, she moved to the door of her prison and looked out. There was Ely, only a few feet away and completely free from his bindings and his cell.

"You look awful," he said, approaching her door. "How did you get the ropes off?"

Ari just stared at him for a moment. "Knife. How did you get out of your cell?"

Ely grinned and wiggled his fingers. "Melted the lock."

She started to smile and winced in pain. "Do you want to get me out of here?"

"No, I really thought I'd –"

"Ely."

He grimaced under her withering glare. "I've got it, hold on."

Stepping back from the cell bars, Ari watched as he held his hands before the lock. They hovered only a centimeter away, seeming to vibrate with power. The small metal piece glowed a hot, fiery red and then it began to warp, like ripples running out across a disturbed pond. It melted, dripping down the metal bars and onto the floor, where it congealed once more into a solid, grey puddle.

For a few seconds, Ari gazed at the place where the lock had been, now a strange, empty hole in the vertical pattern of the metal door. She was not sure whether she could touch it.

"It's not hot," Ely said, reading her mind. "Come on."

He opened the door and she stepped out. "You are somewhat useful after all."

"You are welcome," he said, and fell into step beside her. "Where to?"

"Get our weapons and get out of here. I am *not* leaving

without my sword," she added fiercely when he opened his mouth to reply.

Holding up a hand in defense, Ely shook his head. "I was only going to ask where you think they are holding them."

Ari put a finger to her lips and pointed ahead, where they had arrived at the stone stairway. Remembering that Ely was not armed, she handed him her hunting knife and motioned at him to follow behind her. Wonderfully – *stupidly*, Ari thought – there were no soldiers posted at the entrance to the dungeon; in seconds, they had emerged into the daylight of the little hall above.

"Wow," Ely said. "You look *really* awful."

"So you've said," Ari whispered, irritated. "Quiet."

"I mean, your face –"

She clamped a hand over his mouth. There were footsteps coming down the passage. Thinking quickly, Ari opened the door across the hall and pulled Ely inside. It was dark and small, only a few yards deep and half that across.

"Ow!" Ely hissed; he had stepped on her foot and she had retaliated with a jab to the ribs.

"Move," Ari ordered, pushing him aside and shifting around to put her ear to the door.

"Is this a closet?" He seemed more concerned about her choice of hiding place than he was about the immediate danger before them.

Quieting her breathing, Ari ignored him and closed her eyes. The wood panel shivered with each heavy step that passed through the hall outside. She strained to hear through the jumble of voices.

"... spotted the man past Konchot."

"Where?"

"Don't remember, do I? Or I would've said."

"Cut the arguing, men."

More steps and scuffling.

"And she said we were to transport the locals home..."

"Ask Jaan."

"What time is the..."

"Did you sleep through the meeting?"

It was incessant chatter and repartee, nothing useful except for the fact that all the soldiers seemed to be emptying from the building, a detail that Ari found very promising. She was about to turn away and tell Ely that they were almost in the clear when she heard it.

"Lieutenant!" The man was very nearly screaming.

"Quiet down, officer."

"Where's the general?!"

"He has important –"

"They've escaped!" the officer shouted desperately. "I don't know how, but they've escaped!"

The entire building descended into chaos. Even through the closed door, Ari could feel the energy escalating into a frantic roar. There did not seem to be any sense of order; the soldiers ran back and forth without really knowing what to do.

"Men!" A commanding voice bellowed out and all of the noise stopped, a raging fire snuffed out with one swift breath.

There came a chorus of "yes, sir!" and then terrified silence.

"Well?" the general roared. "Organize yourselves and *find them*! I want six men in the dungeon, eighty in the streets and the rest here with me. No word gets out until they're back in their cells, ten men per prisoner. Go!"

The passage jumped to life once more, but now the feet hurried along in time with one another and the shouts that filled the air were to rally the troops and give orders.

"Commander Filin's squadron to the eastern border!"

"Twenty men after me, grab your bows."

"Send word to the barracks to saddle thirty-five horses."

Ari no longer needed to press her ear to the door to know what was going on. The look on Ely's face told her that he fully comprehended the situation.

"This is good," she whispered.

"Good?"

"Three-quarters of them are leaving," she said. "And they'll leave the headquarters minimally guarded."

"So?"

"So, we can get our packs and weapons and get out of the building largely unseen."

"Largely," he repeated skeptically.

"There may be a few casualties."

"Ari, this is insane."

Pursing her lips, she gave him an angry look that was lost in the blackness of the little closet. "This is what I do for a living, Ely. Trust me."

"Even if we get out of here, we still have to –" He stopped when he realized what she had just said. "You never ask me to trust you."

"Because frankly, I don't care whether you do. You still have to do as I say. And I'm not asking."

"Of course you aren't."

"In twelve seconds, I am going to open the door and we will go straight down the hall to the headquarters. In that room, I will hold off any opposition while you locate our weapons, which are stored either in a closet in the back corner, or inside a central desk or cabinet." She put her hand on the door handle. "Understood?"

"How do you know –"

"Creativity is not their strong suit," she whispered quickly. "We have to go before they get any more organized."

Before Ely could affirm or protest, she opened the door, taking care to push it just far enough for them to exit without making a noise. By this point, there were only four soldiers in the hall and they were all heading purposefully towards the exit. Ari took off in the opposite direction at a swift walk, stepping silently along the dingy corridor. Footsteps slightly more audible, Ely followed in her wake. She thought of Jagger and, as she often did when attempting such covert tasks, imagined how he would make himself invisible in this situation, a nonexistent shadow gliding past the tangible world.

They made it by several more open doors without notice. The doorway at the end of the hall was so close that Ari was beginning to think they would get lucky and arrive without incident. Then, just as they passed the last room on the left, two men entered the hall behind them and let up a cry.

"Prisoners in the hallway!"

Both Ari and Ely began to run. There was no need for stealth now, only speed. In seconds, they had reached the final door; Ari threw it open without slowing down.

"Grab them!" ordered the general, recognizable by his loud, commanding voice.

There were only five soldiers in the room but more would be coming soon, now that their location had been announced. Three went for Ari but she was too fast and too determined, ducking their misguided swings with ease and dealing a few of her own blows without even pulling the bronze dagger. Ely knocked out one man with a well-aimed punch and leapt away from outstretched arms, flying towards the back of the room where he saw a big, multi-shelved desk.

When four more soldiers arrived, Ari drew her knife. It did not matter that the women attacking her had swords or that the men coming down the hall were twice as strong. They could not match her skill and they fell before her like mosquitos swatted out of the summer air. But each time that she shoved one aside, two more seemed to appear, and the room, which she had hardly had time to assess, was growing smaller by the second.

"Ely!" she implored, "hurry!"

"I'm – trying!" he grunted, sliding under a long table to avoid one soldier's sword.

"Don't let them get their weapons!" The general was

caught behind a swarm of his own soldiers, unable to stop Ely as the young man pulled open a large drawer and grasped Ari's sword.

In a swift motion, he had thrown their packs over his shoulder and tossed the silver dagger into the air. "Catch!"

For a moment, Ely and Ari both watched it spin, a sparkling blur across the crowded room, and then she caught the curved handle, the blade that fit so well into her fingers, and she was doubly armed. The men and women pushing in around her stood no chance. They could hardly operate when they were on top of each other like this, but Ari had no problem dancing in and out of the swirling bodies and weapons, because it was a dance to which she had memorized every step and every movement, to which she could move with her eyes shut. If the clink of steel and the fall of boots were music, she could leap and spin to the rhythm better than the rest, certainly better than anyone else in that room.

And if perhaps Ely lacked experience or the same passion for Ari's dance, he had her sword, and he knew what he had to do. The three soldiers converging upon him were surprised by the welcome that they received, just as four of the seven around Ari fell, wounded by the silver dagger. Then Ely went on the offensive and leapt onto the table, catching one woman in the thigh and disarming a short man who tried to block his path. From his perch, he could see their exit ahead.

"Let's go!" he told Ari. "I've got this."

As he spoke, he jumped down to land on a soldier who was heading for Ari. The man crumpled to the ground with a grunt and Ely wrestled his sword from his grip. Ducking an enemy's blade, Ari slid the bronze-handled dagger into her boot and, standing again, held out her hand. Ely was by her side and her sword was in her fingers. Now that they were both fully armed, there was no question of escape, only of how long it would take. Ari's confidence, never lacking before, swelled with her sword in her hand.

They were out the door in a few seconds, sprinting down the dingy corridor with the general's words flying at their heels: "All soldiers after them! Alert the streets!"

There was a parade of footsteps behind them and no way they could make it out of the village in a footrace, but when Ari glanced at Ely, he was smiling.

"You're starting to enjoy this too much," she told him as they burst outside and pushed through a pair of guards in the alley.

"We just escaped a Malavi military prison!" he crowed, jumping out of the way as Ari hurled her dagger at an oncoming soldier.

She yanked the knife out of his fallen body and broke into a sprint once more. "Not a very good one."

"Where do we go now?"

A trio of arrows very nearly missed their heads as they turned onto the main street. They needed horses, or a way to get out of the town without being seen. A fourth arrow whizzed so close to Ari's left arm that it ripped through her tunic.

"We can't make it like this," she said. "Look for a fishery."

"What?"

"Look for signs, anything."

Just then a horn blasted three long notes. Somewhere in the distance, a second one replied with the same pattern. The streets, already full of pounding feet and the shouts of soldiers, began to sound with the rapid clip of hooves on the cobblestones.

"This way!"

Sliding the silver dagger into her belt, Ari pulled Ely down a lane to the left. Set into the paneled wall of a tiny green cottage was a double-hung door, the top of which was open. Without pausing, Ari leapt the bottom door and slid inside, Ely right behind her.

"Stop where you are!"

A man stood before them, dressed in tired fishing clothes and holding an old, dull broadsword with the tip pointed straight at Ari's chest. He wore no shoes, and the room, which seemed to serve as a shop, a kitchen, and a sitting area, was in great disarray.

"Please," Ari said, lowering her own weapon to her side, "we only wish to stay here for a few minutes."

"And risk our lives?" He shook his head darkly. "I think not."

Two heads poked out from behind a sagging armchair, dark curls spiraling away from little round faces that stared, wide-eyed, at the strange man and woman who had leapt unceremoniously into their home.

"The Malavi army is after us," Ely said, waving Ari off when she turned to silence him. "We have done nothing to harm them or this village yet we were thrown into their prison and only just managed to escape. The people of the sea are known all over the country for their independent will." He looked the man in the eye, searching for a sign of recognition, of empathy. "This is a chance to save someone else from the pain you have experienced."

"You know nothing of our pain," the fisherman told him harshly, but his voice seemed to break a bit and his eyes were no longer so cold.

"Where is their mother?" Ari asked quietly.

The little girl and boy had come out from behind the chair and were hiding a few feet behind their father. Ari could see that their clothes were tattered and poorly mended, stained with dirt and grease, but their faces shone clean as if they had just been bathed. The boy, a few inches shorter than his sister, smiled curiously up at Ari.

The man suddenly noticed that his children had entered the room and seemed startled to learn that they were in the presence of these strangers. He motioned at them to go away but they did not budge. Waddling forward, the girl clung to her father's leg and the boy took a few steps closer to Ari.

Sheathing his sword and reaching out to pull his son back to him, the fisherman glared at Ari. "That is none of your business."

"The Malavi military killed both of my parents," Ari said bluntly. "These days it is easier to assume pain than it is peace."

There was a pause, a heavy silence. "Who are you?"

Ari felt something flip in her stomach and took a deep breath, looking the fisherman straight in the eye.

"This is Elyrah Novian. And my name is Ariana Debouryne."

Her heart was pounding out of her chest. She did not know why she had done it, but somehow, she knew it was right. "Debouryne?" the man repeated slowly, stunned. "But... You cannot be...?"

Ely was staring at her, at last truly shocked. Ari nodded. "I am the Princess of Organa."

Acknowledgments

I would like to thank Atmosphere Press for seeing in this story and these characters what I saw in them. In particular, my gratitude to Kyle McCord and Nick Courtright for their guidance and dedication.

Thank you, from the bottom of my heart, to all the people who read the many pieces and versions of this book and provided invaluable edits and encouragement along the way: Karl Barkley, Grace Cassino, Claire Flynn, Jenny Hausler, Claire Weintraub, Theresa Jones, Mae Dodd, Juliette Sweeney, Catherine Valentine, Rachel Allore, Angela Li, Hannah Epstein, Emily Haston, Erin Heald, Maddy Howell, Andrew Carter, Julia Hartman, Scott Barkley, John Barkley, and my parents, Carolyn and James Barkley.

Most of all, thanks to Jorge Santoyo, who probably knows more about Ari and Ely than he ever bargained for and who never once complained when "Can I read you this sentence?" turned into a two-hour discussion. My eternal gratitude for the hours you spent reading, debating plot lines, and telling me I could do this.

About Atmosphere Press

Atmosphere Press is an independent, full-service publisher for excellent books in all genres and for all audiences. Learn more about what we do at atmospherepress.com.

We encourage you to check out some of Atmosphere's latest releases, which are available at Amazon.com and via order from your local bookstore:

Relatively Painless, short stories by Dylan Brody
Nate's New Age, a novel by Michael Hanson
The Size of the Moon, a novel by E.J. Michaels
The Red Castle, a novel by Noah Verhoeff
American Genes, a novel by Kirby Nielsen
Newer Testaments, a novel by Philip Brunetti
All Things in Time, a novel by Sue Buyer
Hobson's Mischief, a novel by Caitlin Decatur
The Black-Marketer's Daughter, a novel by Suman Mallick
The Farthing Quest, a novel by Casey Bruce
This Side of Babylon, a novel by James Stoia
Within the Gray, a novel by Jenna Ashlyn
Where No Man Pursueth, a novel by Micheal E. Jimerson
Here's Waldo, a novel by Nick Olson
Tales of Little Egypt, a historical novel by James Gilbert
For a Better Life, a novel by Julia Reid Galosy
Big Man Small Europe, poetry by Tristan Niskanen
The Hidden Life, a novel by Robert Castle
Big Beasts, a novel by Patrick Scott
Alvarado, a novel by John W. Horton III
Nothing to Get Nostalgic About, a novel by Eddie Brophy
Whose Mary Kate, a novel by Jane Leclere Doyle
Vanity: Murder in the Name of Sin, a novel by Rhiannon Garrard

ABOUT THE AUTHOR

Allyson S. Barkley is the author of *A Memory of Light*, the first book in the *Until the Stars Are Dead* fantasy series.

Born and raised in Charlottesville, Virginia, Allyson grew up an avid reader, writer, and horseback rider. She finds herself particularly inspired by hikes in far-off places, strangers in coffee shops, and clever music lyrics.

Allyson earned a bachelor's degree from the University of North Carolina at Chapel Hill. She lives in Raleigh, North Carolina with her partner and their two cats.

9 781637 529638